KATY

Model … One

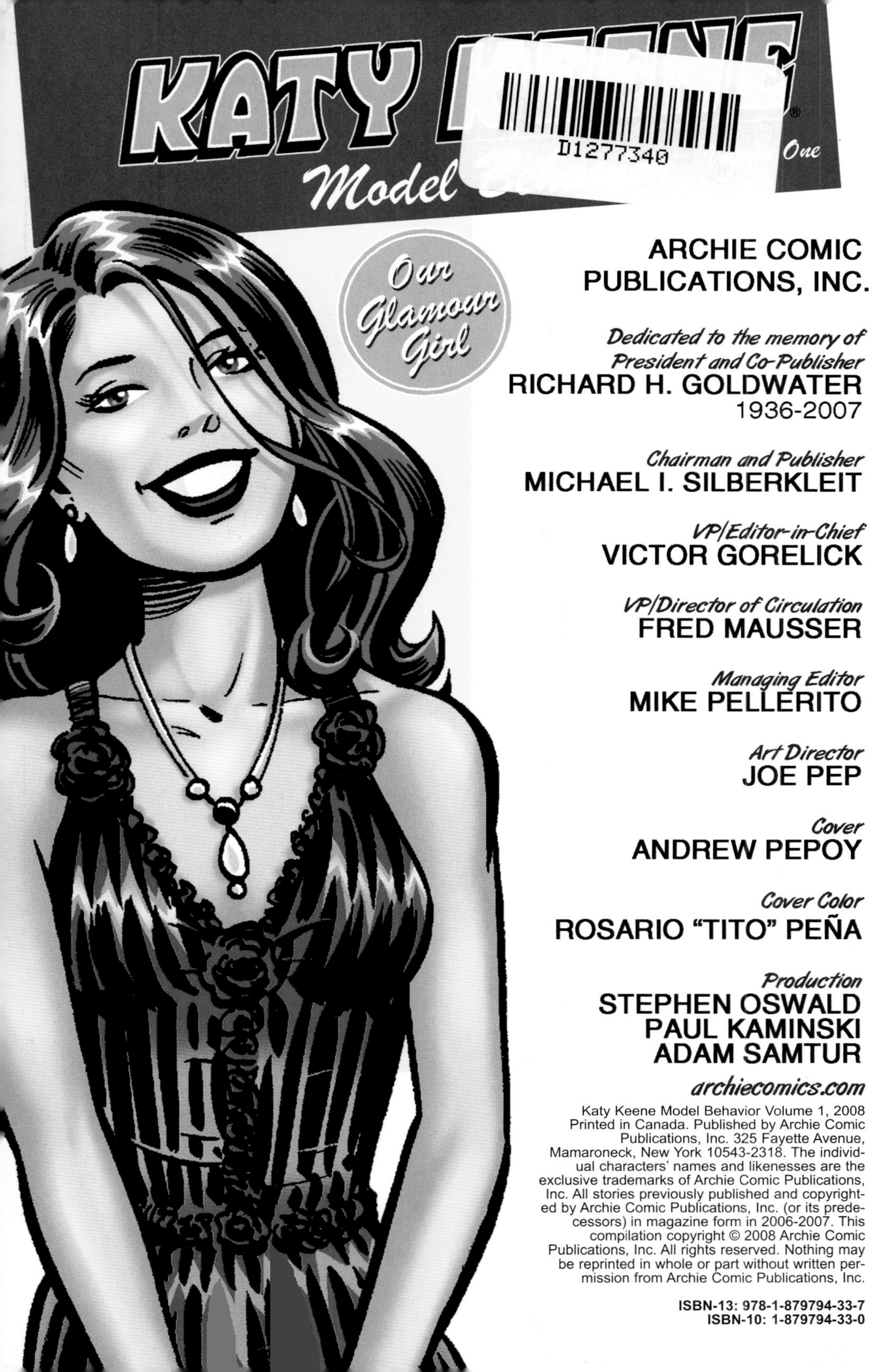
Our Glamour Girl

ARCHIE COMIC
PUBLICATIONS, INC.

Dedicated to the memory of
President and Co-Publisher
RICHARD H. GOLDWATER
1936-2007

Chairman and Publisher
MICHAEL I. SILBERKLEIT

VP/Editor-in-Chief
VICTOR GORELICK

VP/Director of Circulation
FRED MAUSSER

Managing Editor
MIKE PELLERITO

Art Director
JOE PEP

Cover
ANDREW PEPOY

Cover Color
ROSARIO "TITO" PEÑA

Production
STEPHEN OSWALD
PAUL KAMINSKI
ADAM SAMTUR

archiecomics.com

Katy Keene Model Behavior Volume 1, 2008 Printed in Canada. Published by Archie Comic Publications, Inc. 325 Fayette Avenue, Mamaroneck, New York 10543-2318.

ISBN-13: 978-1-879794-33-7
ISBN-10: 1-879794-33-0

contents

Katy Keene
Model Behavior

All New Exclusive

4

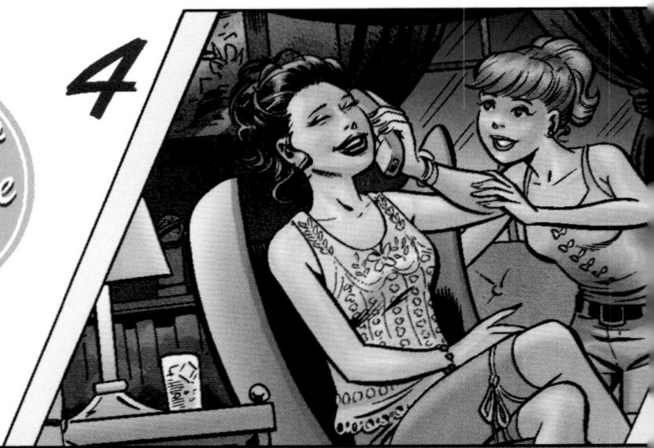

37

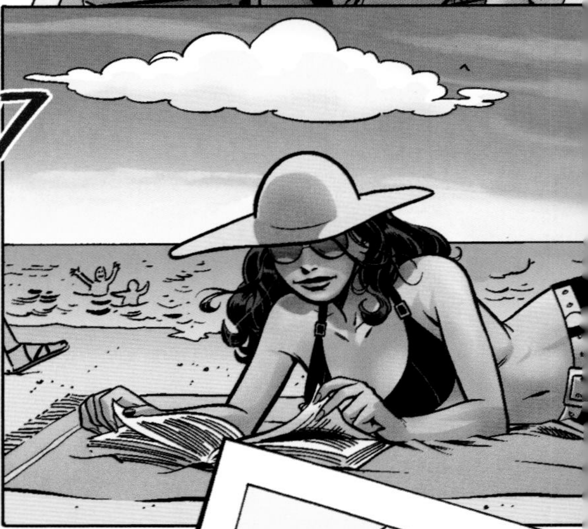

55

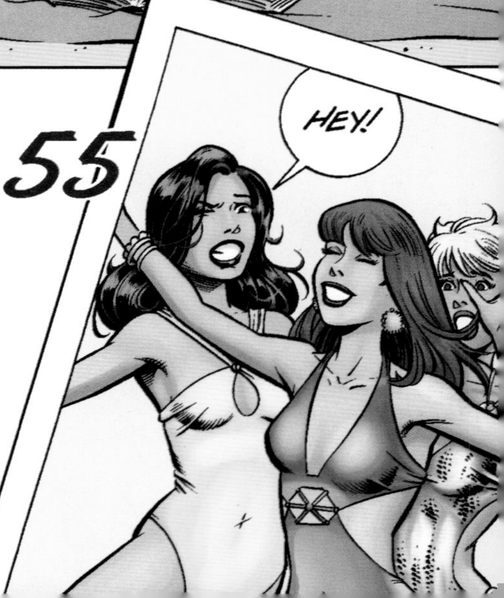
HEY!

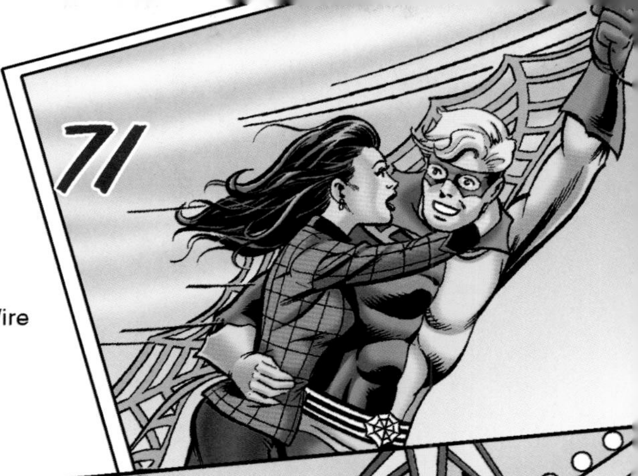
71

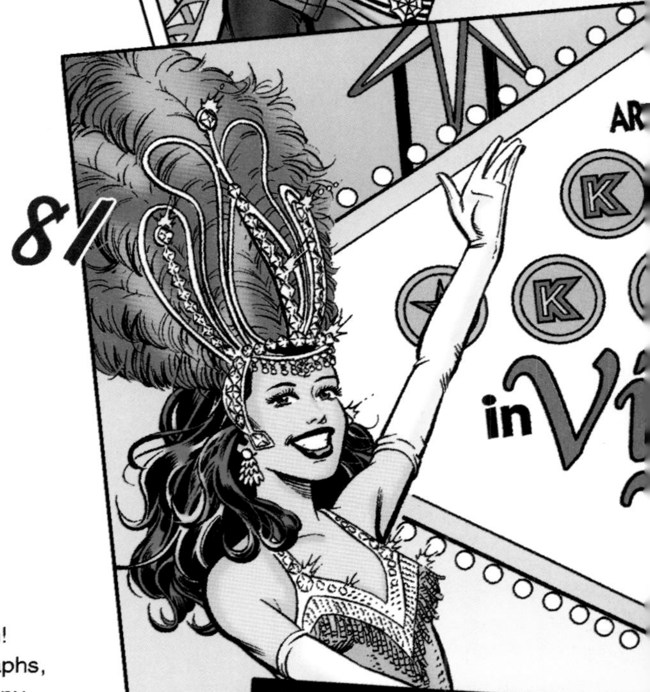
81

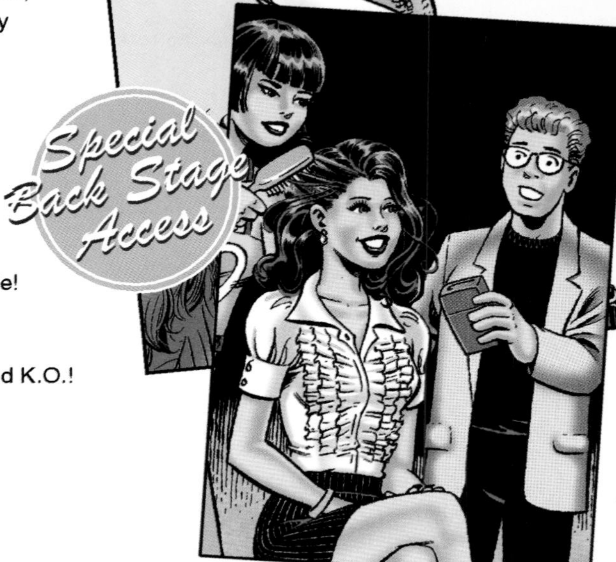
Special Back Stage Access

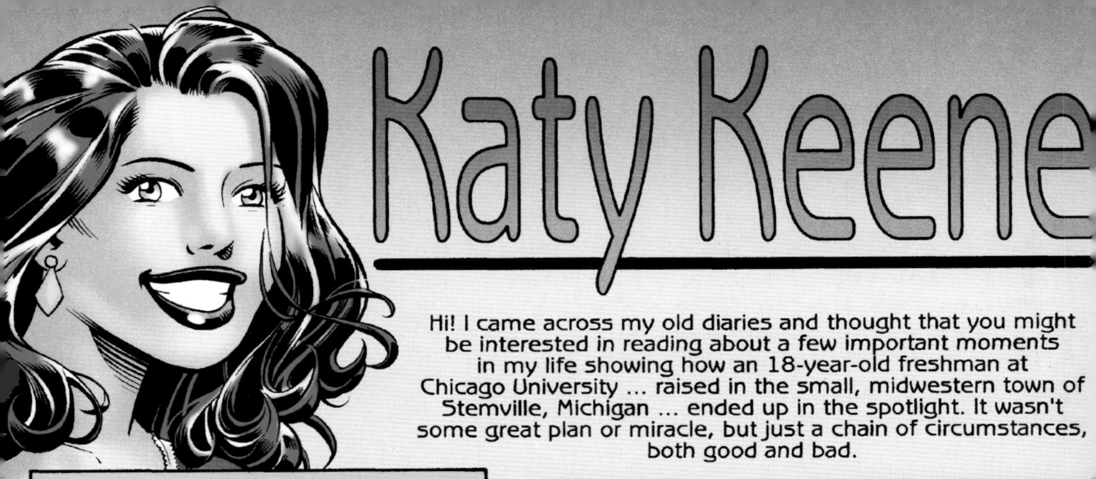

Katy Keene

Hi! I came across my old diaries and thought that you might be interested in reading about a few important moments in my life showing how an 18-year-old freshman at Chicago University ... raised in the small, midwestern town of Stemville, Michigan ... ended up in the spotlight. It wasn't some great plan or miracle, but just a chain of circumstances, both good and bad.

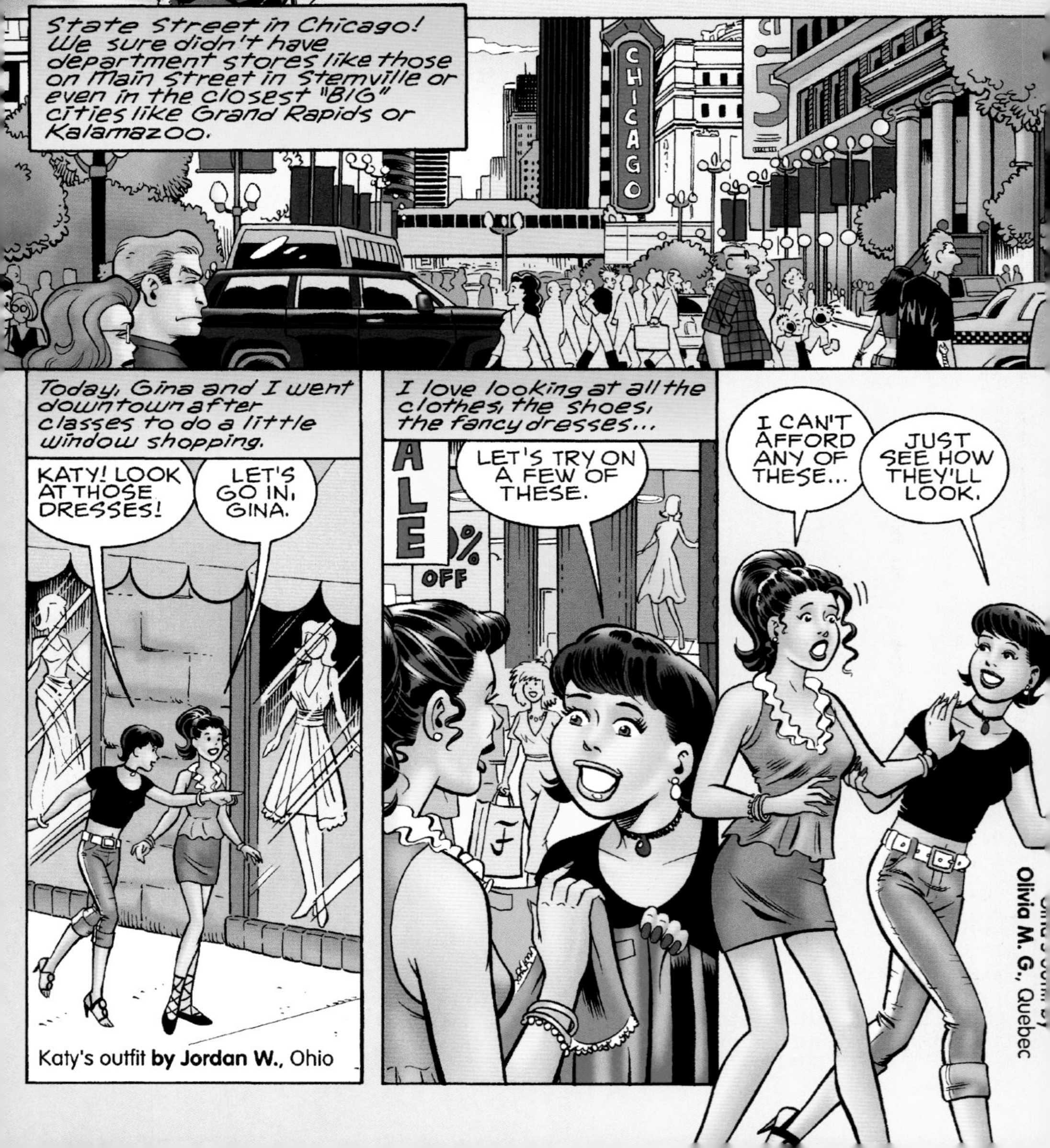

State Street in Chicago! We sure didn't have department stores like those on Main Street in Stemville or even in the closest "BIG" cities like Grand Rapids or Kalamazoo.
CHICAGO
Today, Gina and I went downtown after classes to do a little window shopping.
KATY! LOOK AT THOSE DRESSES!
LET'S GO IN, GINA.
Katy's outfit by Jordan W., Ohio
I love looking at all the clothes, the shoes, the fancy dresses...
LET'S TRY ON A FEW OF THESE.
I CAN'T AFFORD ANY OF THESE...
JUST SEE HOW THEY'LL LOOK.
Olivia M. G., Quebec

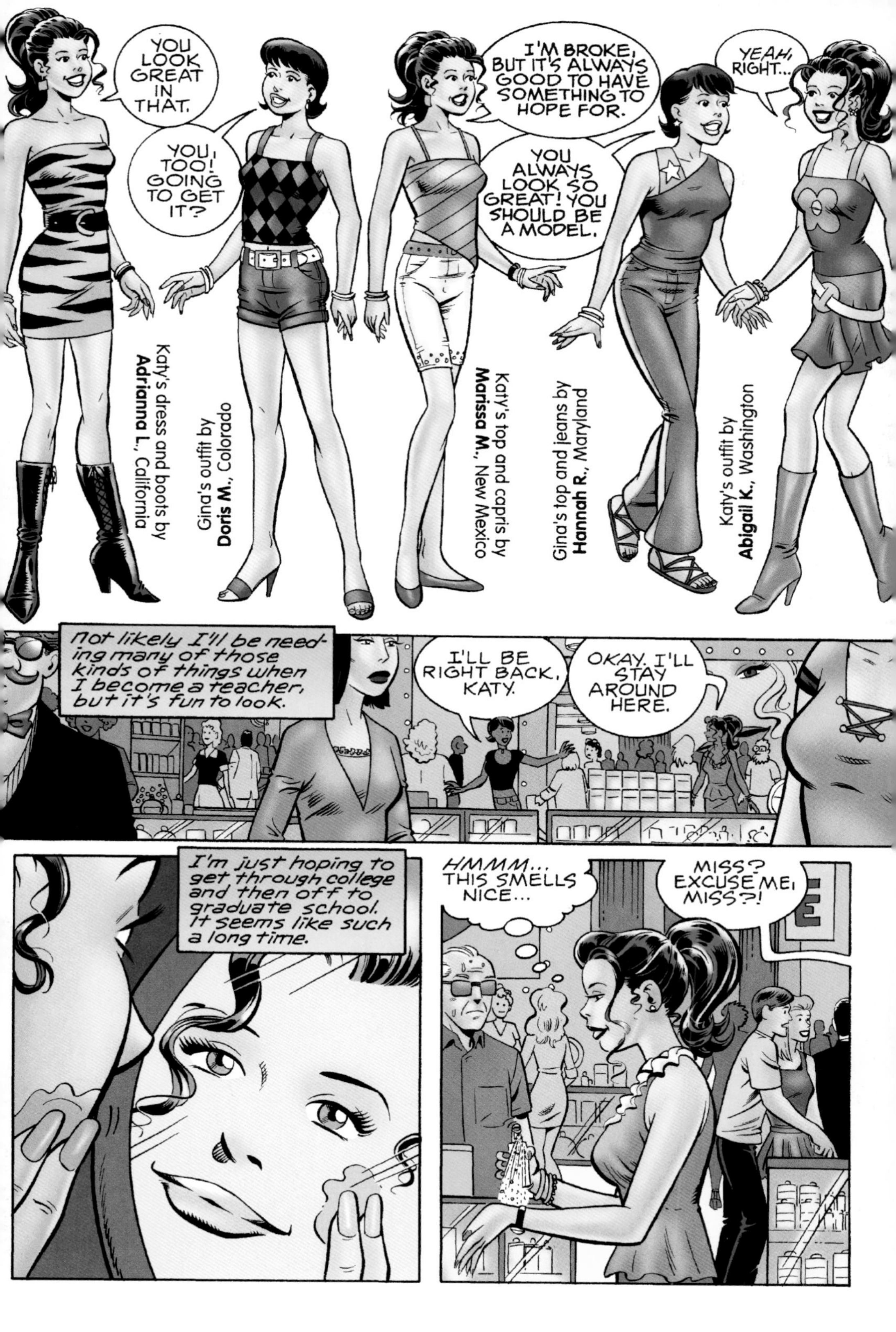

YOU LOOK GREAT IN THAT.
YOU, TOO! GOING TO GET IT?
I'M BROKE, BUT IT'S ALWAYS GOOD TO HAVE SOMETHING TO HOPE FOR.
YOU ALWAYS LOOK SO GREAT! YOU SHOULD BE A MODEL.
YEAH, RIGHT...
Katy's dress and boots by **Adrianna L.**, California
Gina's outfit by **Doris M.**, Colorado
Katy's top and capris by **Marissa M.**, New Mexico
Gina's top and jeans by **Hannah R.**, Maryland
Katy's outfit by **Abigail K.**, Washington
Not likely I'll be needing many of those kinds of things when I become a teacher, but it's fun to look.
I'LL BE RIGHT BACK, KATY.
OKAY. I'LL STAY AROUND HERE.
I'm just hoping to get through college and then off to graduate school. It seems like such a long time.
HMMM... THIS SMELLS NICE...
MISS? EXCUSE ME, MISS?!

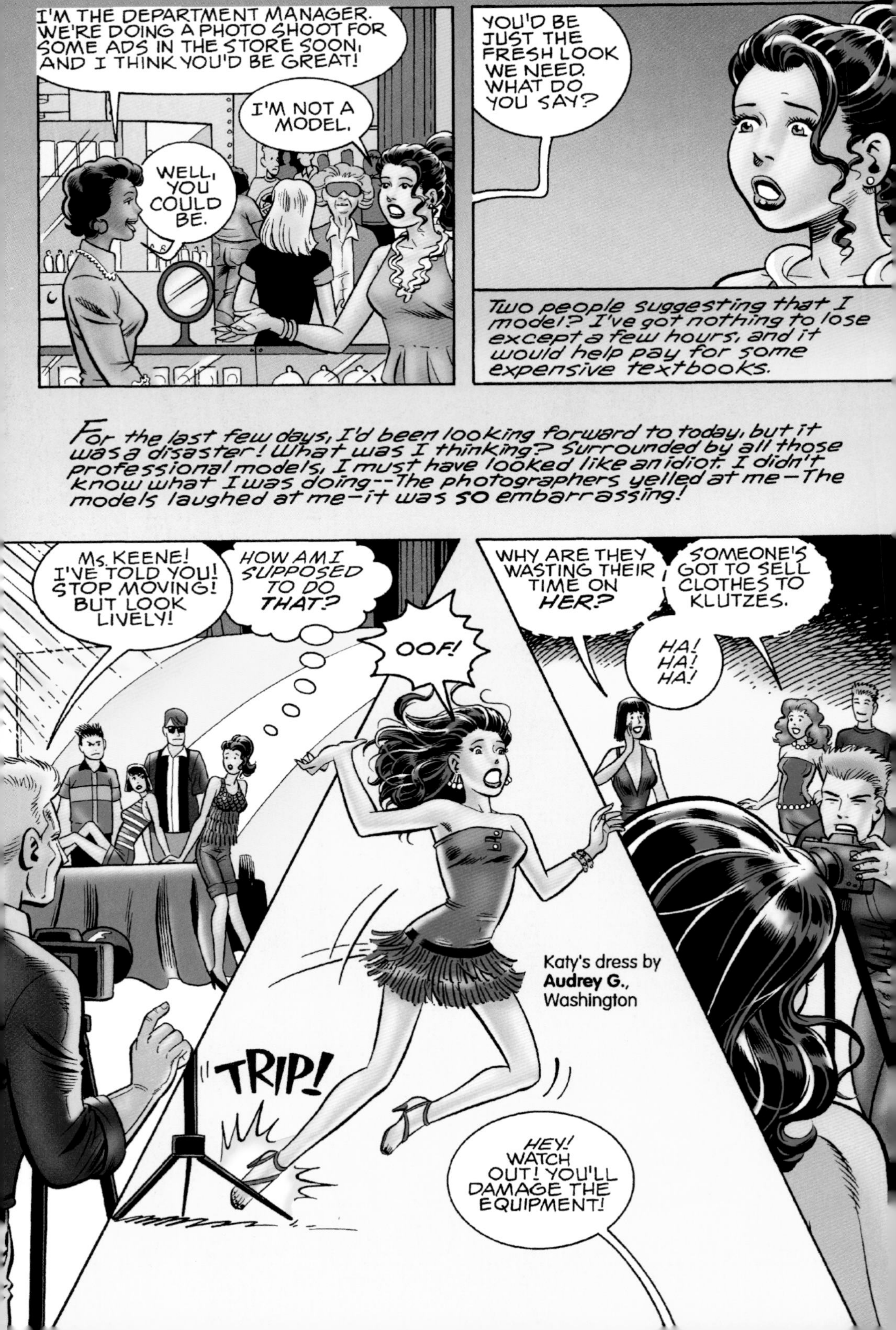
I'M THE DEPARTMENT MANAGER. WE'RE DOING A PHOTO SHOOT FOR SOME ADS IN THE STORE SOON, AND I THINK YOU'D BE GREAT!
I'M NOT A MODEL.
WELL, YOU COULD BE.
YOU'D BE JUST THE FRESH LOOK WE NEED. WHAT DO YOU SAY?
Two people suggesting that I model? I've got nothing to lose except a few hours, and it would help pay for some expensive textbooks.
For the last few days, I'd been looking forward to today, but it was a disaster! What was I thinking? Surrounded by all those professional models, I must have looked like an idiot. I didn't know what I was doing--The photographers yelled at me—The models laughed at me—it was so embarrassing!
Ms. KEENE! I'VE TOLD YOU! STOP MOVING! BUT LOOK LIVELY!
HOW AM I SUPPOSED TO DO THAT?
OOF!
WHY ARE THEY WASTING THEIR TIME ON HER?
SOMEONE'S GOT TO SELL CLOTHES TO KLUTZES.
HA! HA! HA!
Katy's dress by Audrey G., Washington
TRIP!
HEY! WATCH OUT! YOU'LL DAMAGE THE EQUIPMENT!

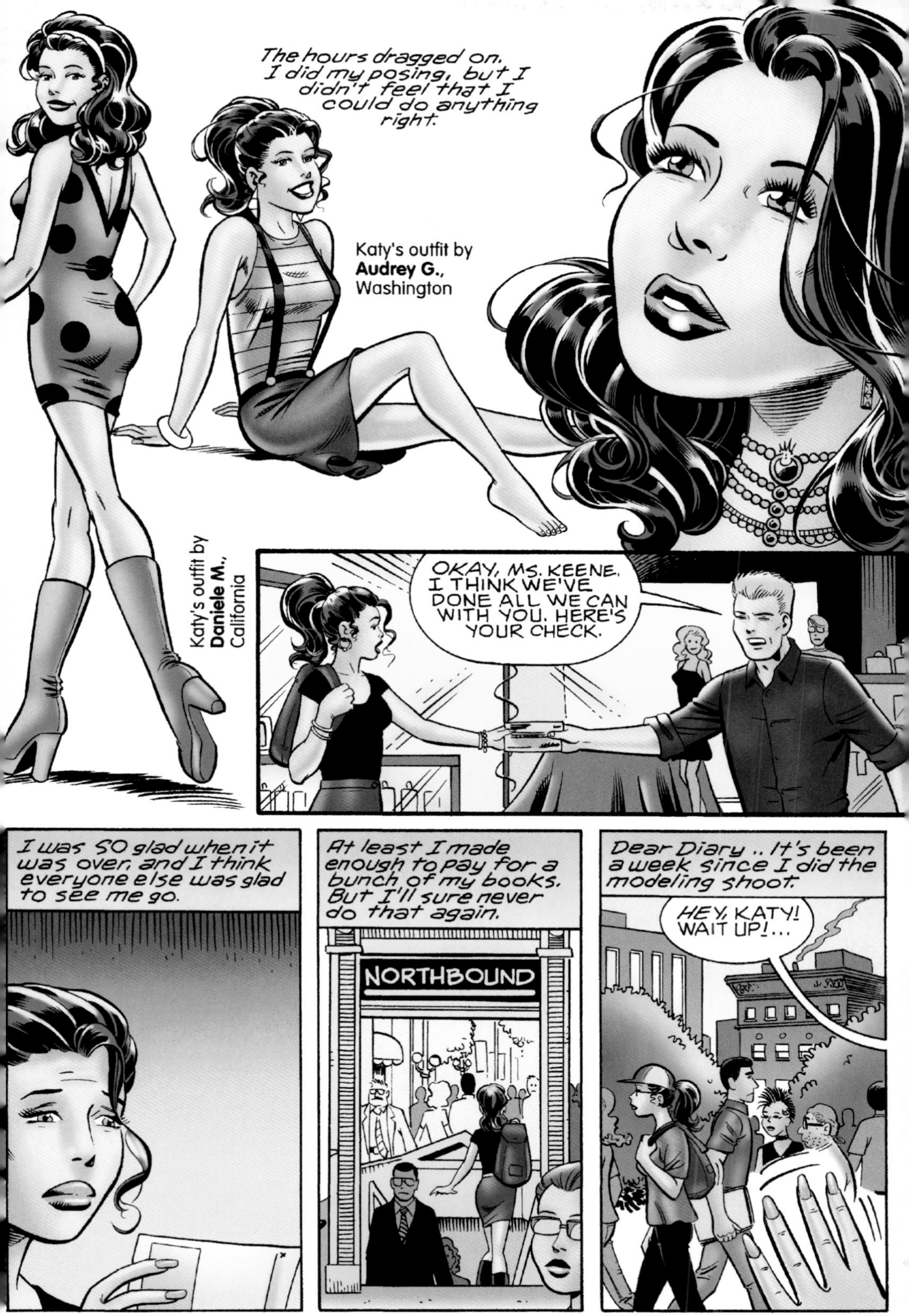

The hours dragged on. I did my posing, but I didn't feel that I could do anything right.
Katy's outfit by Audrey G., Washington
Katy's outfit by Daniele M., California
OKAY, MS. KEENE. I THINK WE'VE DONE ALL WE CAN WITH YOU. HERE'S YOUR CHECK.
I was SO glad when it was over, and I think everyone else was glad to see me go.
At least I made enough to pay for a bunch of my books. But I'll sure never do that again.
NORTHBOUND
Dear Diary .. It's been a week since I did the modeling shoot.
HEY, KATY! WAIT UP!...

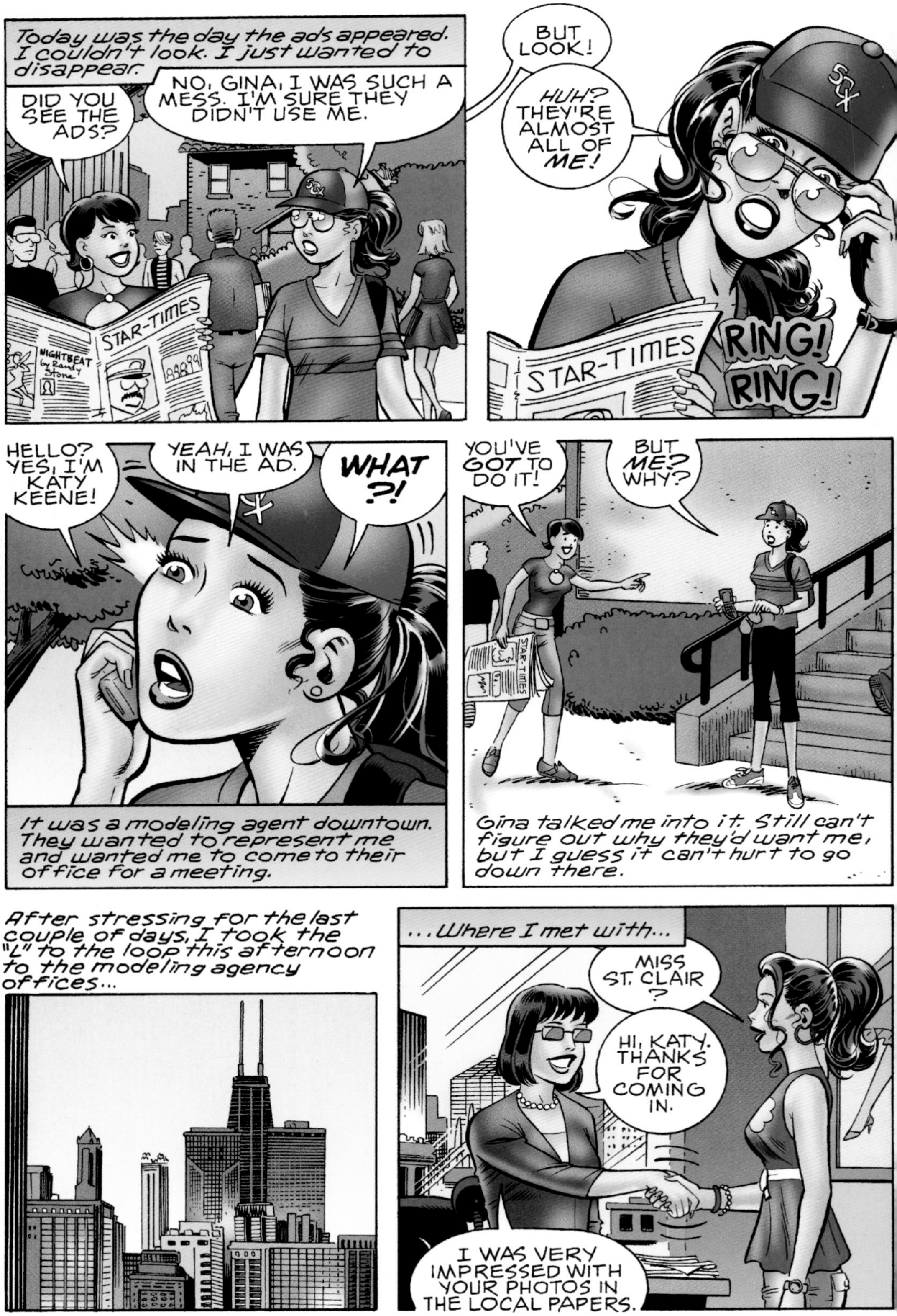
Today was the day the ads appeared. I couldn't look. I just wanted to disappear.
DID YOU SEE THE ADS?
NO, GINA, I WAS SUCH A MESS. I'M SURE THEY DIDN'T USE ME.
STAR-TIMES
NIGHTBEAT by Randy Stone
BUT LOOK!
HUH? THEY'RE ALMOST ALL OF ME!
STAR-TIMES
RING! RING!
HELLO? YES, I'M KATY KEENE!
YEAH, I WAS IN THE AD.
WHAT ?!
It was a modeling agent downtown. They wanted to represent me and wanted me to come to their office for a meeting.
YOU'VE GOT TO DO IT!
BUT ME? WHY?
STAR-TIMES
Gina talked me into it. Still can't figure out why they'd want me, but I guess it can't hurt to go down there.
After stressing for the last couple of days, I took the "L" to the loop this afternoon to the modeling agency offices...
...Where I met with...
MISS ST. CLAIR ?
HI, KATY. THANKS FOR COMING IN.
I WAS VERY IMPRESSED WITH YOUR PHOTOS IN THE LOCAL PAPERS.

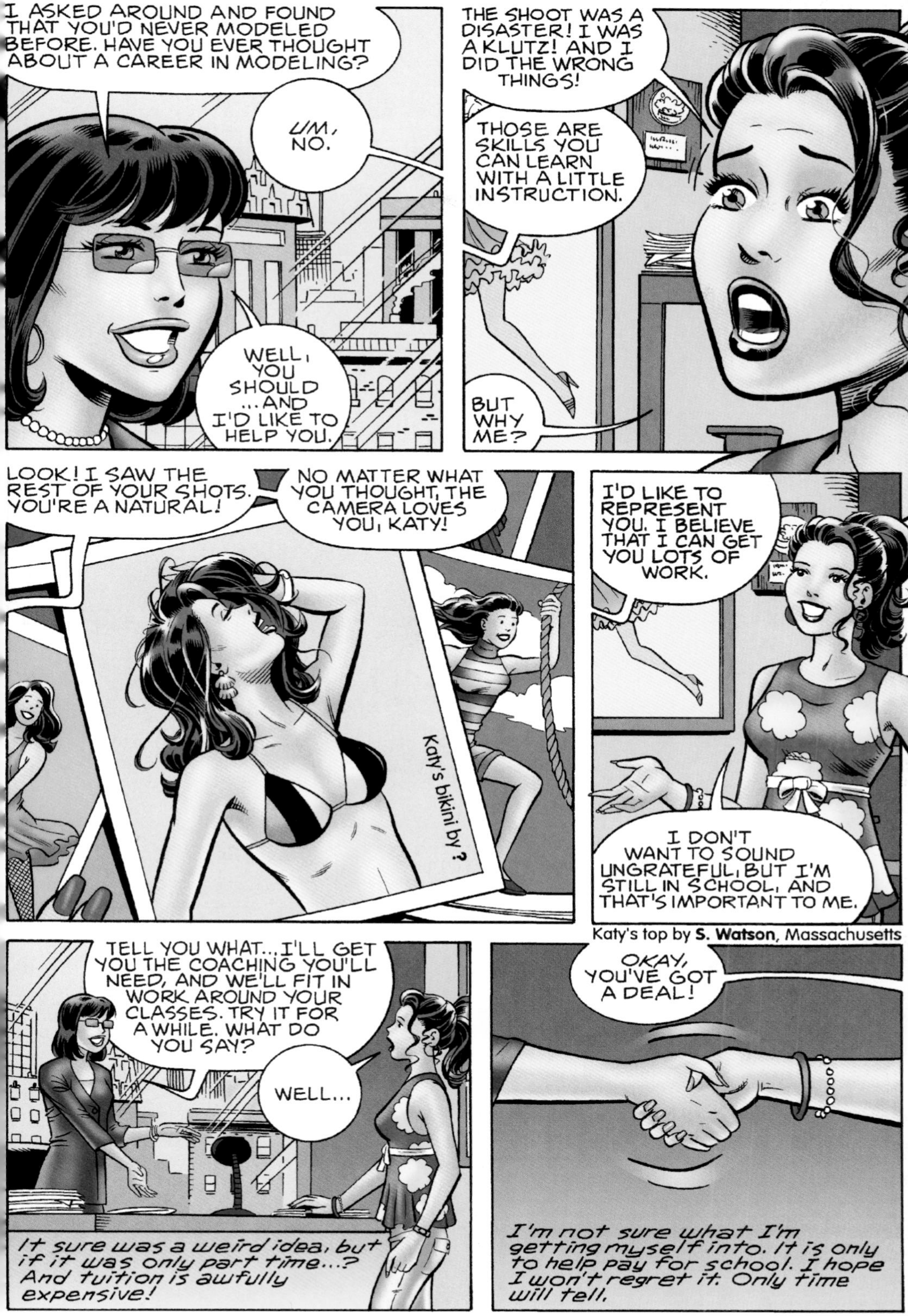
I ASKED AROUND AND FOUND THAT YOU'D NEVER MODELED BEFORE. HAVE YOU EVER THOUGHT ABOUT A CAREER IN MODELING?
UM, NO.
WELL, YOU SHOULD ...AND I'D LIKE TO HELP YOU.
THE SHOOT WAS A DISASTER! I WAS A KLUTZ! AND I DID THE WRONG THINGS!
THOSE ARE SKILLS YOU CAN LEARN WITH A LITTLE INSTRUCTION.
BUT WHY ME?
LOOK! I SAW THE REST OF YOUR SHOTS. YOU'RE A NATURAL!
NO MATTER WHAT YOU THOUGHT, THE CAMERA LOVES YOU, KATY!
Katy's bikini by ?
I'D LIKE TO REPRESENT YOU. I BELIEVE THAT I CAN GET YOU LOTS OF WORK.
I DON'T WANT TO SOUND UNGRATEFUL, BUT I'M STILL IN SCHOOL, AND THAT'S IMPORTANT TO ME.
Katy's top by S. Watson, Massachusetts
TELL YOU WHAT... I'LL GET YOU THE COACHING YOU'LL NEED, AND WE'LL FIT IN WORK AROUND YOUR CLASSES. TRY IT FOR A WHILE. WHAT DO YOU SAY?
WELL...
It sure was a weird idea, but if it was only part time...? And tuition is awfully expensive!
OKAY, YOU'VE GOT A DEAL!
I'm not sure what I'm getting myself into. It is only to help pay for school. I hope I won't regret it. Only time will tell.

KATY KEENE

It was nearing the end of my sophomore year and, despite my misgivings and doubts, my modeling work was taking off...

At the grocery store today...at the checkout... were two magazines with ME on their covers! I still can't get used to it, but BOY!...are things crazy busy. It's getting harder and harder to keep up with my schoolwork, especially when I sometimes spend the weekends in...

mary claire

Spring Fashion Finds!

Your Hair and what not to do with it

own body

nails on fire!

Look Like a Movie Star!

200 Shoes!

OPOLITAN

Escaping the No-Date Zone Tonight!

Hair Se of the and Fa

Keep thos eye ow yo

Katy's dress by **Lauren D., ?**

...New York...

Katy's dress by **Margaret S.**, Arizona

...or California.

Katy's bikini by **Elly S.**, Florida

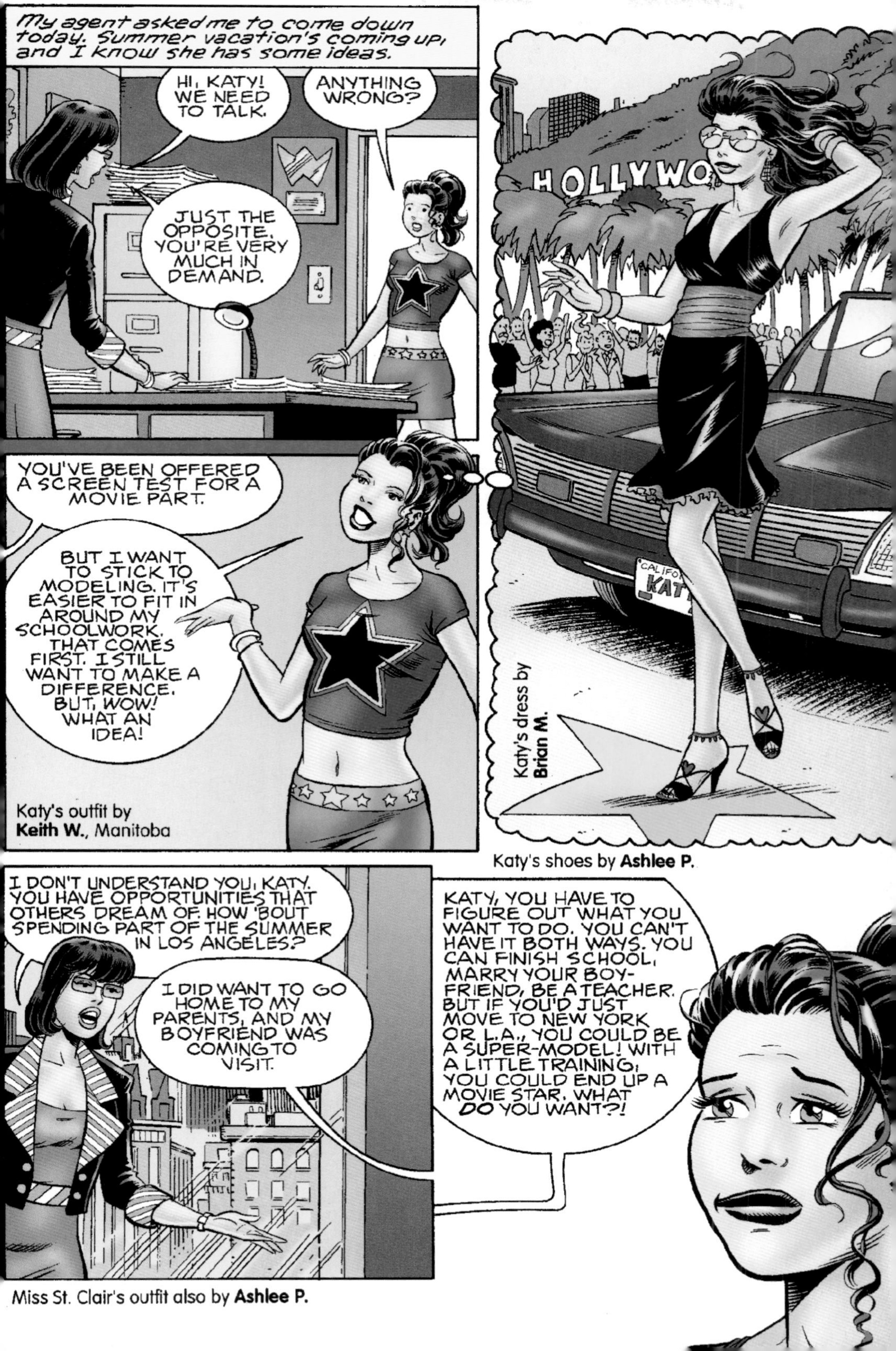
My agent asked me to come down today. Summer vacation's coming up, and I know she has some ideas.
HI, KATY! WE NEED TO TALK.
ANYTHING WRONG?
JUST THE OPPOSITE. YOU'RE VERY MUCH IN DEMAND.
YOU'VE BEEN OFFERED A SCREEN TEST FOR A MOVIE PART.
BUT I WANT TO STICK TO MODELING. IT'S EASIER TO FIT IN AROUND MY SCHOOLWORK. THAT COMES FIRST. I STILL WANT TO MAKE A DIFFERENCE. BUT, WOW! WHAT AN IDEA!
Katy's outfit by Keith W., Manitoba
HOLLYWO
CALIFO
KAT
Katy's dress by Brian M.
Katy's shoes by Ashlee P.
I DON'T UNDERSTAND YOU, KATY. YOU HAVE OPPORTUNITIES THAT OTHERS DREAM OF. HOW 'BOUT SPENDING PART OF THE SUMMER IN LOS ANGELES?
I DID WANT TO GO HOME TO MY PARENTS, AND MY BOYFRIEND WAS COMING TO VISIT.
KATY, YOU HAVE TO FIGURE OUT WHAT YOU WANT TO DO. YOU CAN'T HAVE IT BOTH WAYS. YOU CAN FINISH SCHOOL, MARRY YOUR BOYFRIEND, BE A TEACHER. BUT IF YOU'D JUST MOVE TO NEW YORK OR L.A., YOU COULD BE A SUPER-MODEL! WITH A LITTLE TRAINING, YOU COULD END UP A MOVIE STAR. WHAT *DO* YOU WANT?!
Miss St. Clair's outfit also by Ashlee P.

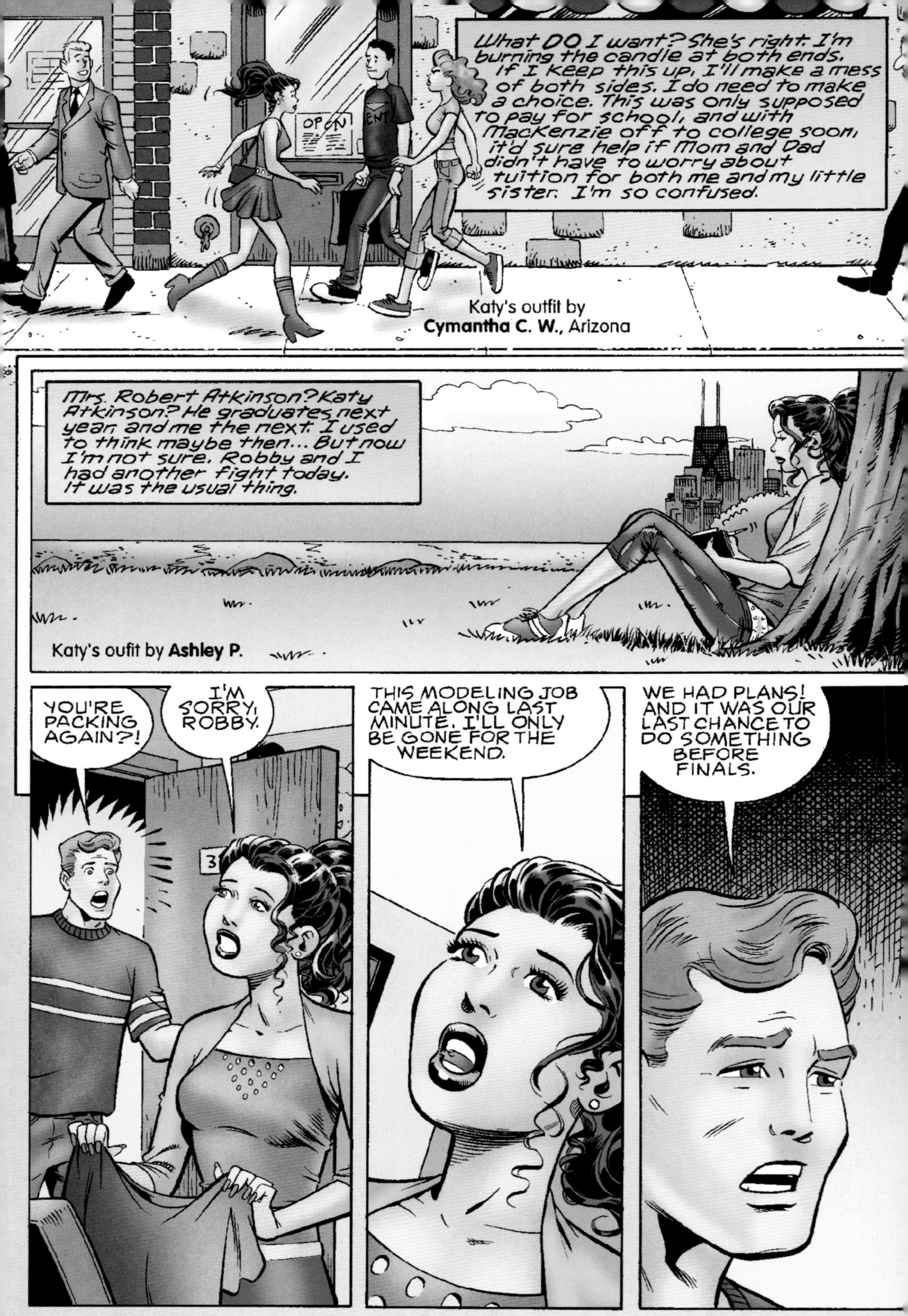
What DO I want? She's right. I'm burning the candle at both ends. If I keep this up, I'll make a mess of both sides. I do need to make a choice. This was only supposed to pay for school, and with Mackenzie off to college soon, it'd sure help if Mom and Dad didn't have to worry about tuition for both me and my little sister. I'm so confused.
OPEN
Mrs. Robert Atkinson? Katy Atkinson? He graduates next year, and me the next. I used to think maybe then... But now I'm not sure. Robby and I had another fight today. It was the usual thing.
YOU'RE PACKING AGAIN?!
I'M SORRY, ROBBY.
THIS MODELING JOB CAME ALONG LAST MINUTE. I'LL ONLY BE GONE FOR THE WEEKEND.
WE HAD PLANS! AND IT WAS OUR LAST CHANCE TO DO SOMETHING BEFORE FINALS.

Katy's outfit by **Cymantha C. W.**, Arizona

Katy's oufit by **Ashley P.**

Katy's outfit by **Molly,** Tennessee

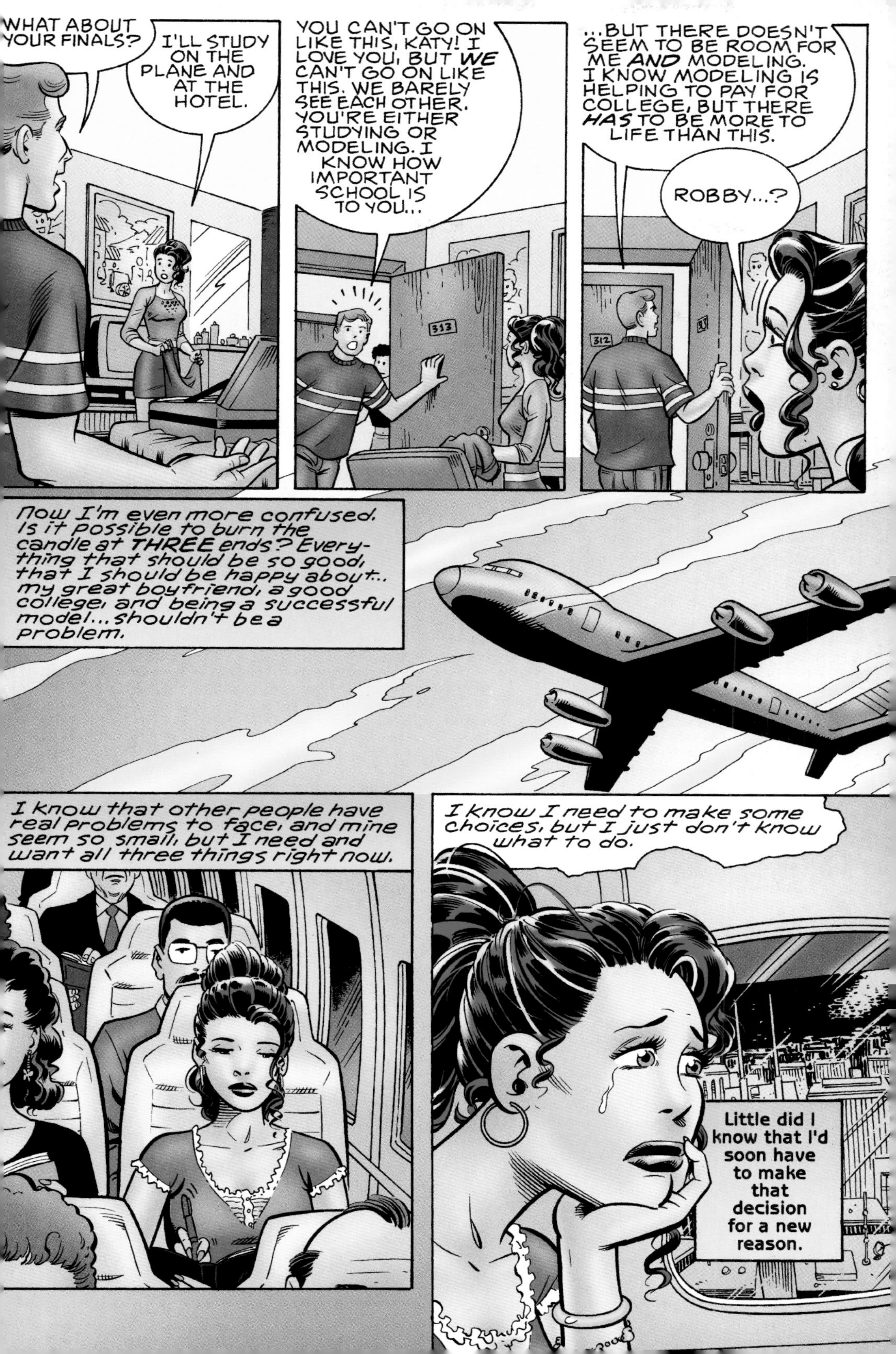
WHAT ABOUT YOUR FINALS?
I'LL STUDY ON THE PLANE AND AT THE HOTEL.
YOU CAN'T GO ON LIKE THIS, KATY! I LOVE YOU, BUT WE CAN'T GO ON LIKE THIS. WE BARELY SEE EACH OTHER. YOU'RE EITHER STUDYING OR MODELING. I KNOW HOW IMPORTANT SCHOOL IS TO YOU...
313
...BUT THERE DOESN'T SEEM TO BE ROOM FOR ME AND MODELING. I KNOW MODELING IS HELPING TO PAY FOR COLLEGE, BUT THERE HAS TO BE MORE TO LIFE THAN THIS.
ROBBY...?
312
Now I'm even more confused. Is it possible to burn the candle at THREE ends? Everything that should be so good, that I should be happy about... my great boyfriend, a good college, and being a successful model... shouldn't be a problem.
I know that other people have real problems to face, and mine seem so small, but I need and want all three things right now.
I know I need to make some choices, but I just don't know what to do.
Little did I know that I'd soon have to make that decision for a new reason.

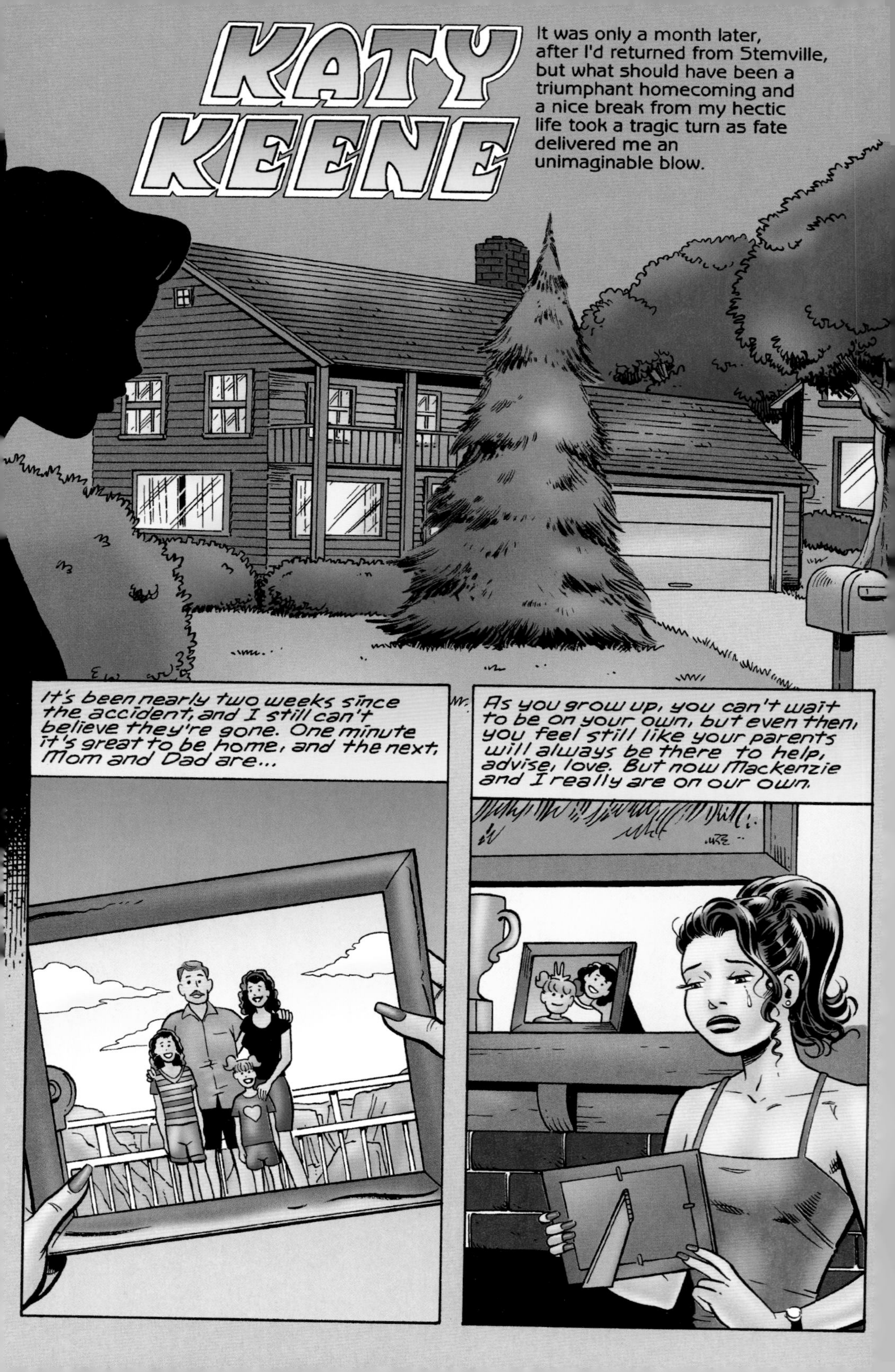
KATY KEENE
It was only a month later, after I'd returned from Stemville, but what should have been a triumphant homecoming and a nice break from my hectic life took a tragic turn as fate delivered me an unimaginable blow.
It's been nearly two weeks since the accident, and I still can't believe they're gone. One minute it's great to be home, and the next, Mom and Dad are...
As you grow up, you can't wait to be on your own, but even then, you feel still like your parents will always be there to help, advise, love. But now Mackenzie and I really are on our own.

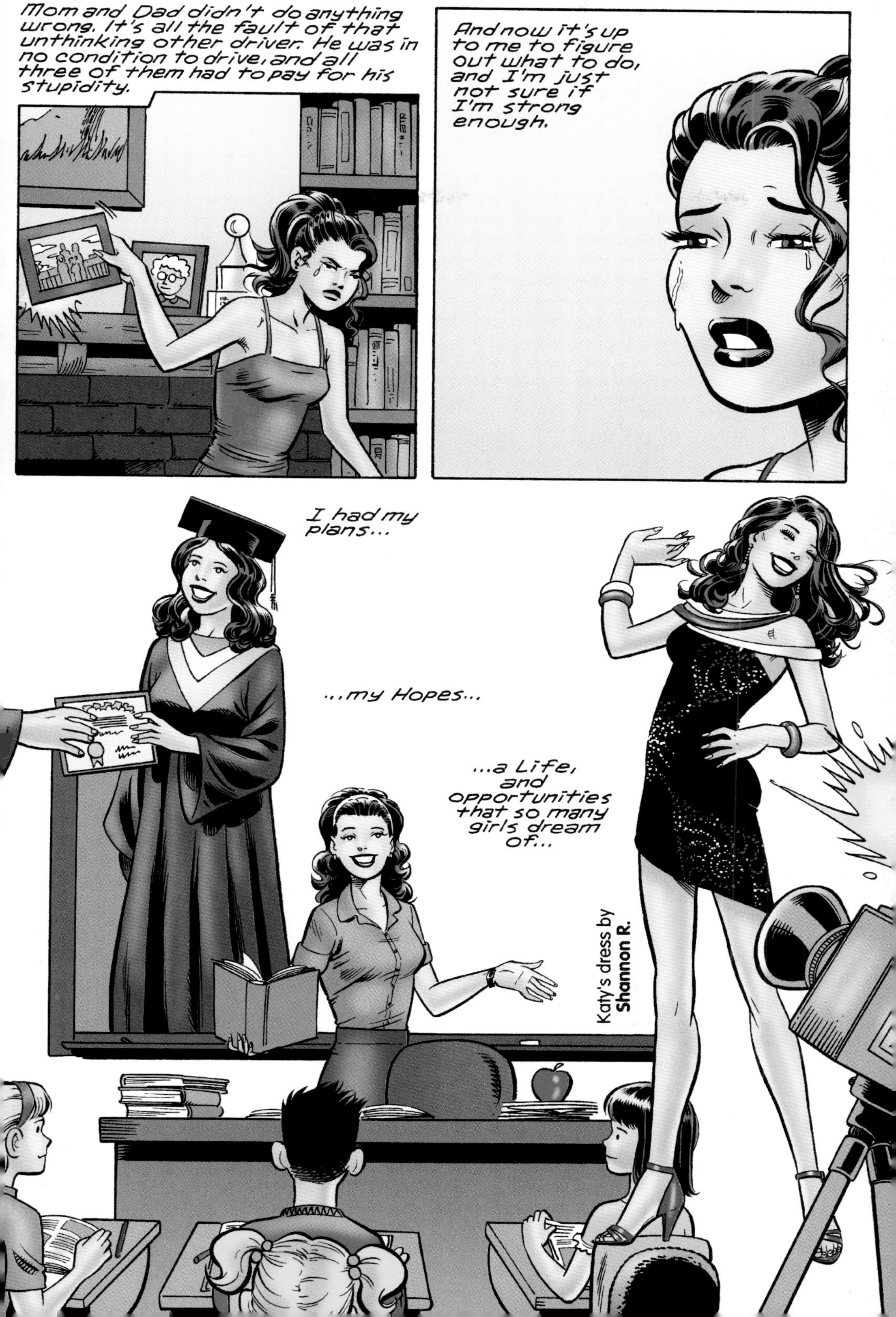
Mom and Dad didn't do anything wrong. It's all the fault of that unthinking other driver. He was in no condition to drive, and all three of them had to pay for his stupidity.
And now it's up to me to figure out what to do, and I'm just not sure if I'm strong enough.
I had my plans...
...my Hopes...
...a Life, and opportunities that so many girls dream of...
Katy's dress by Shannon R.

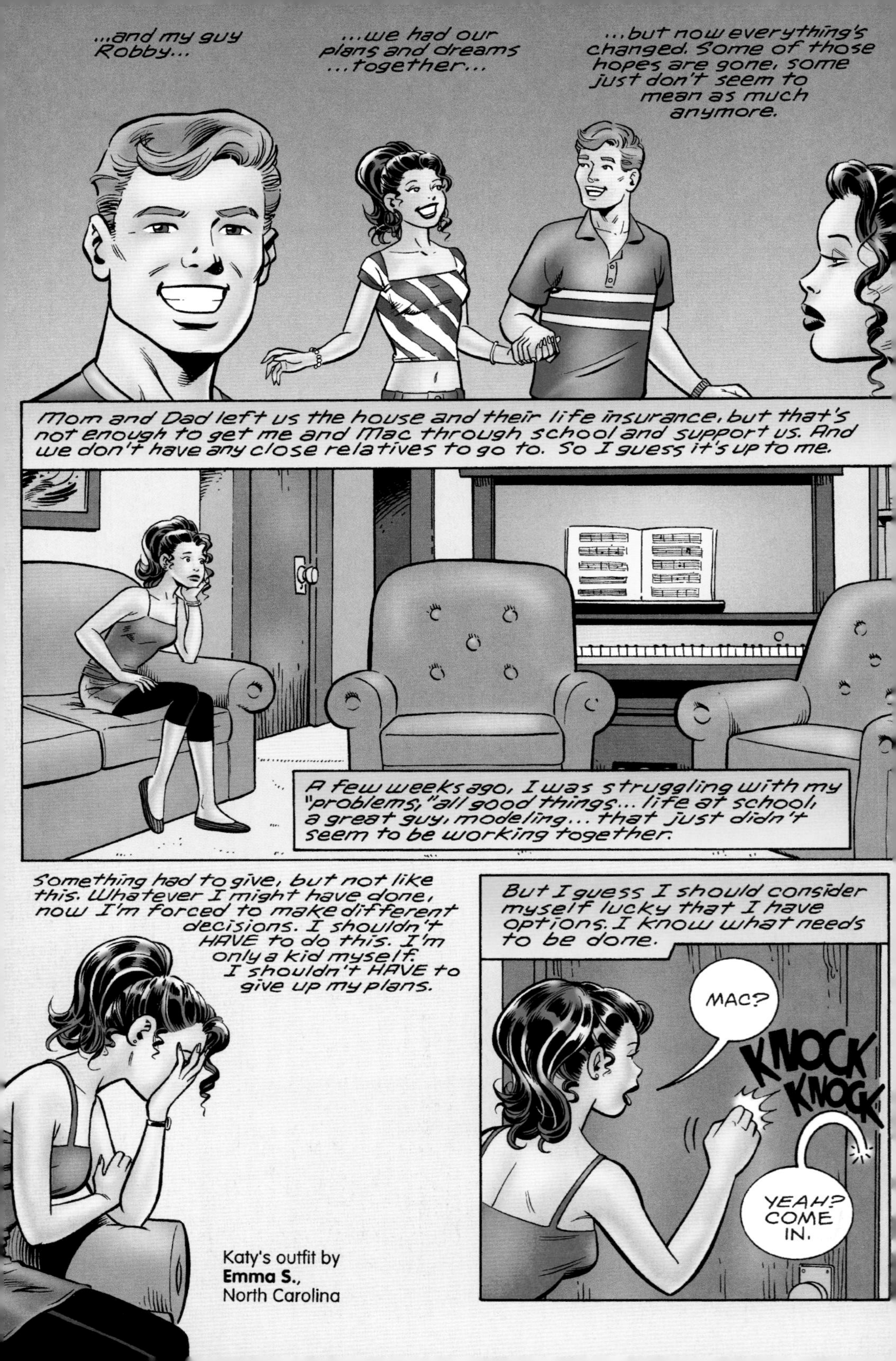
...and my guy Robby...
...we had our plans and dreams ...together...
...but now everything's changed. Some of those hopes are gone, some just don't seem to mean as much anymore.
Mom and Dad left us the house and their life insurance, but that's not enough to get me and Mac through school and support us. And we don't have any close relatives to go to. So I guess it's up to me.
A few weeks ago, I was struggling with my "problems," all good things... life at school, a great guy, modeling... that just didn't seem to be working together.
Something had to give, but not like this. Whatever I might have done, now I'm forced to make different decisions. I shouldn't HAVE to do this. I'm only a kid myself. I shouldn't HAVE to give up my plans.
But I guess I should consider myself lucky that I have options. I know what needs to be done.
MAC?
KNOCK KNOCK
YEAH? COME IN.

Katy's outfit by **Emma S.**, North Carolina

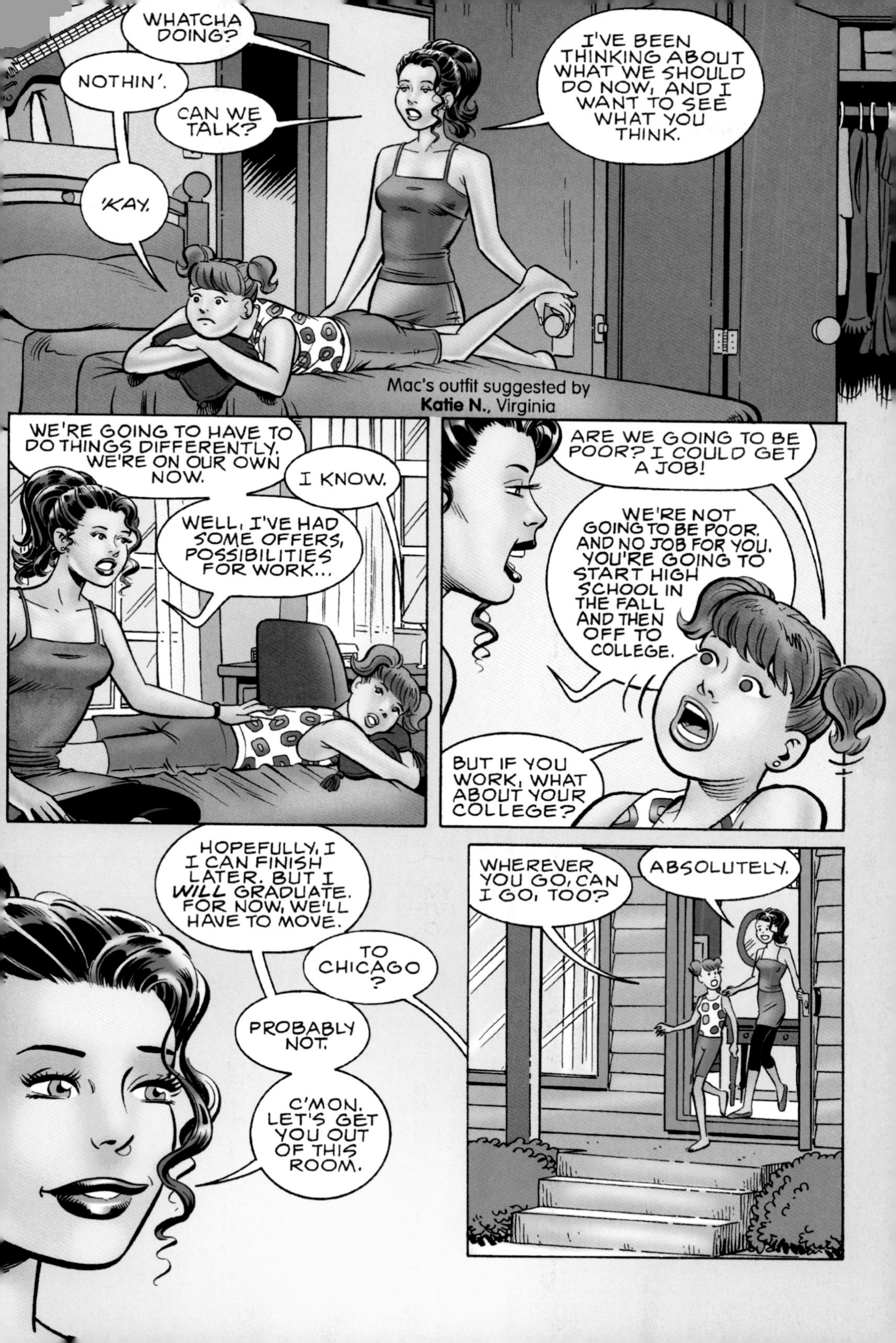
WHATCHA DOING?
NOTHIN'.
CAN WE TALK?
'KAY.
I'VE BEEN THINKING ABOUT WHAT WE SHOULD DO NOW, AND I WANT TO SEE WHAT YOU THINK.
Mac's outfit suggested by **Katie N.**, Virginia
WE'RE GOING TO HAVE TO DO THINGS DIFFERENTLY. WE'RE ON OUR OWN NOW.
I KNOW.
WELL, I'VE HAD SOME OFFERS, POSSIBILITIES FOR WORK...
ARE WE GOING TO BE POOR? I COULD GET A JOB!
WE'RE NOT GOING TO BE POOR. AND NO JOB FOR YOU. YOU'RE GOING TO START HIGH SCHOOL IN THE FALL AND THEN OFF TO COLLEGE.
BUT IF YOU WORK, WHAT ABOUT YOUR COLLEGE?
HOPEFULLY, I CAN FINISH LATER. BUT I *WILL* GRADUATE. FOR NOW, WE'LL HAVE TO MOVE.
TO CHICAGO?
PROBABLY NOT.
C'MON. LET'S GET YOU OUT OF THIS ROOM.
WHEREVER YOU GO, CAN I GO, TOO?
ABSOLUTELY.

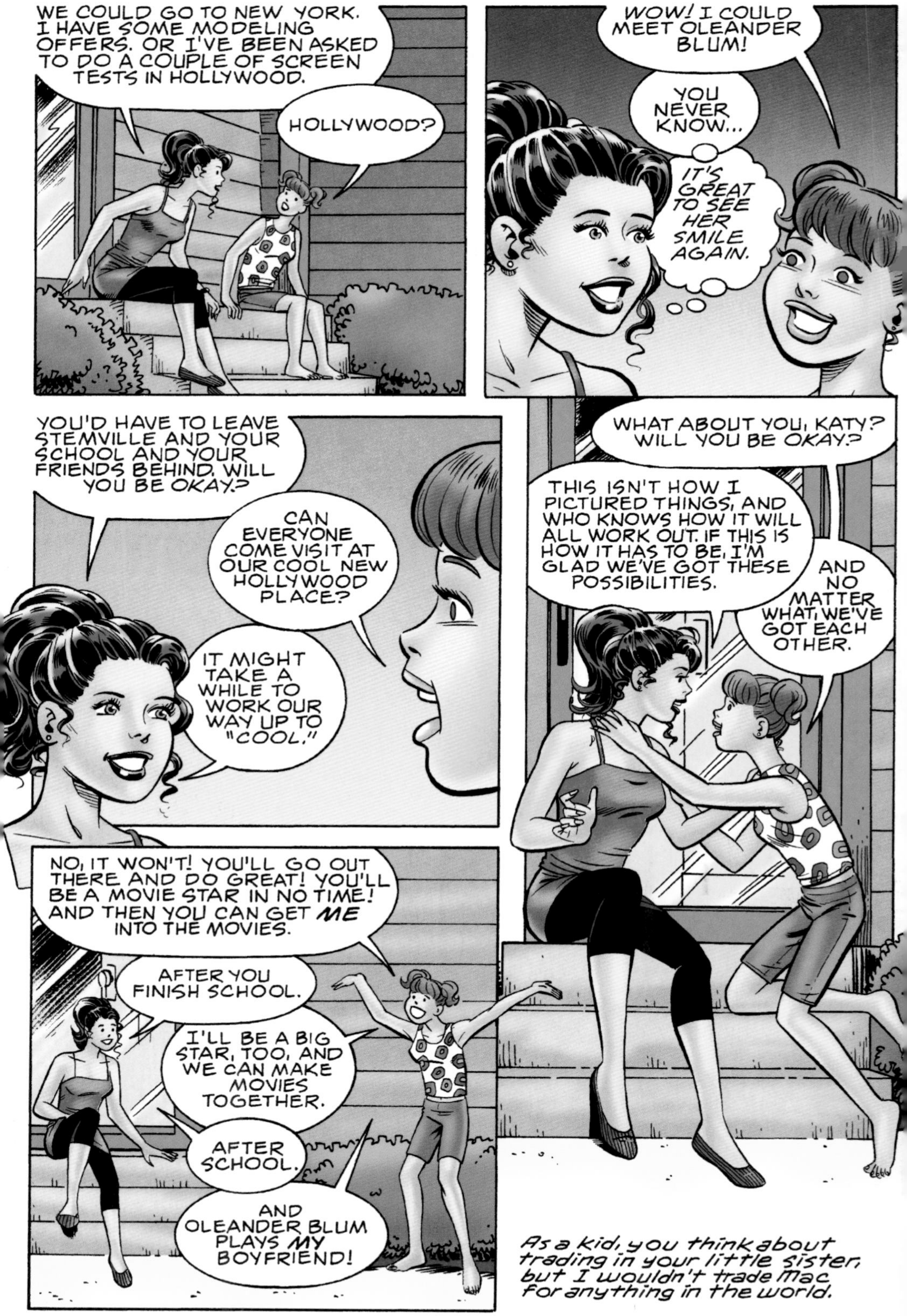

WE COULD GO TO NEW YORK. I HAVE SOME MODELING OFFERS. OR I'VE BEEN ASKED TO DO A COUPLE OF SCREEN TESTS IN HOLLYWOOD.
HOLLYWOOD?
WOW! I COULD MEET OLEANDER BLUM!
YOU NEVER KNOW...
IT'S GREAT TO SEE HER SMILE AGAIN.
YOU'D HAVE TO LEAVE STEMVILLE AND YOUR SCHOOL AND YOUR FRIENDS BEHIND. WILL YOU BE OKAY?
CAN EVERYONE COME VISIT AT OUR COOL NEW HOLLYWOOD PLACE?
IT MIGHT TAKE A WHILE TO WORK OUR WAY UP TO "COOL."
NO, IT WON'T! YOU'LL GO OUT THERE AND DO GREAT! YOU'LL BE A MOVIE STAR IN NO TIME! AND THEN YOU CAN GET ME INTO THE MOVIES.
AFTER YOU FINISH SCHOOL.
I'LL BE A BIG STAR, TOO, AND WE CAN MAKE MOVIES TOGETHER.
AFTER SCHOOL.
AND OLEANDER BLUM PLAYS MY BOYFRIEND!
WHAT ABOUT YOU, KATY? WILL YOU BE OKAY?
THIS ISN'T HOW I PICTURED THINGS, AND WHO KNOWS HOW IT WILL ALL WORK OUT. IF THIS IS HOW IT HAS TO BE, I'M GLAD WE'VE GOT THESE POSSIBILITIES.
AND NO MATTER WHAT, WE'VE GOT EACH OTHER.
As a kid, you think about trading in your little sister, but I wouldn't trade Mac for anything in the world.

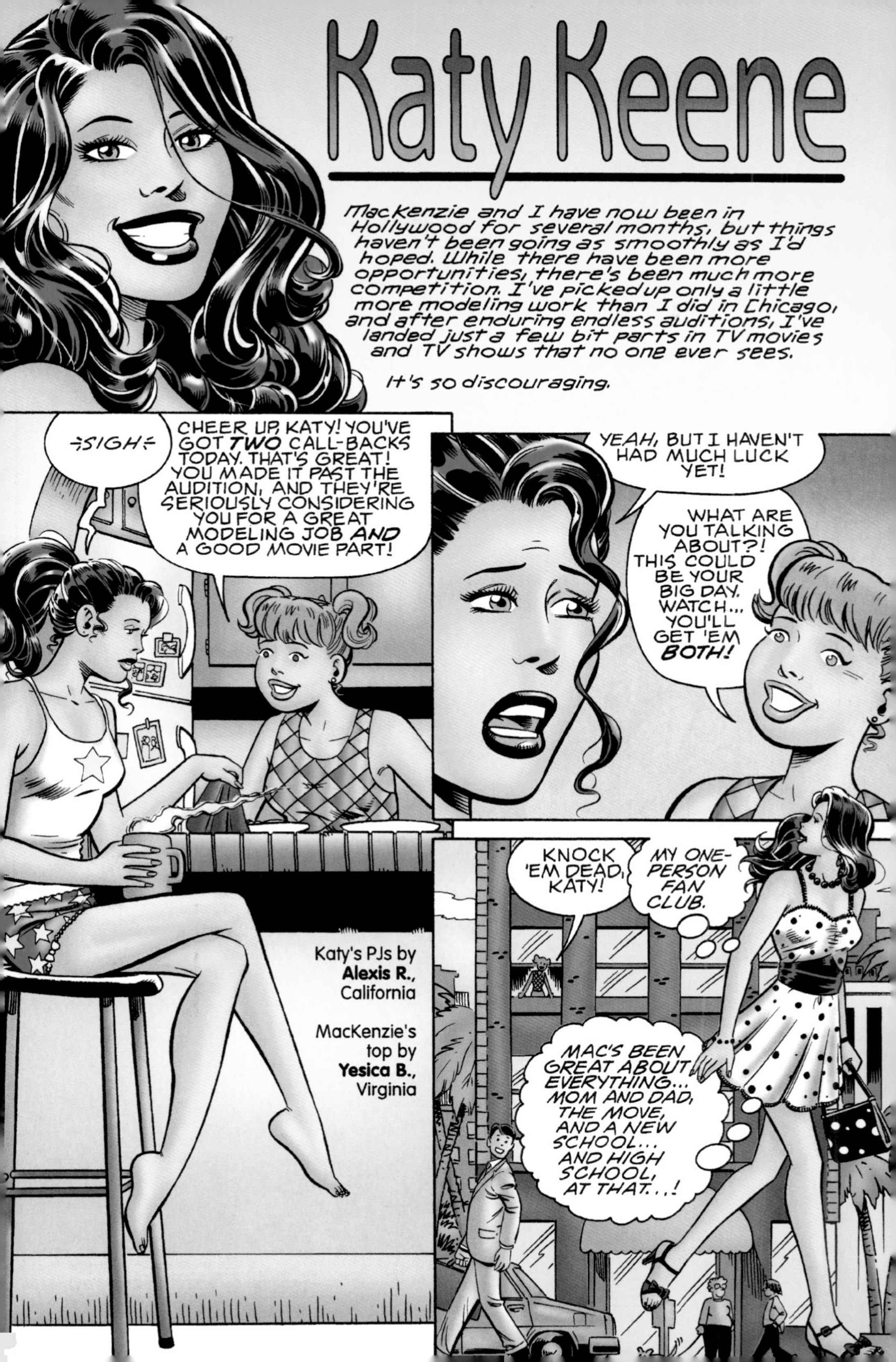
Katy Keene
Mackenzie and I have now been in Hollywood for several months, but things haven't been going as smoothly as I'd hoped. While there have been more opportunities, there's been much more competition. I've picked up only a little more modeling work than I did in Chicago, and after enduring endless auditions, I've landed just a few bit parts in TV movies and TV shows that no one ever sees.
It's so discouraging.
SIGH
CHEER UP, KATY! YOU'VE GOT TWO CALL-BACKS TODAY. THAT'S GREAT! YOU MADE IT PAST THE AUDITION, AND THEY'RE SERIOUSLY CONSIDERING YOU FOR A GREAT MODELING JOB AND A GOOD MOVIE PART!
YEAH, BUT I HAVEN'T HAD MUCH LUCK YET!
WHAT ARE YOU TALKING ABOUT?! THIS COULD BE YOUR BIG DAY. WATCH... YOU'LL GET 'EM BOTH!
KNOCK 'EM DEAD, KATY!
MY ONE-PERSON FAN CLUB.
MAC'S BEEN GREAT ABOUT EVERYTHING... MOM AND DAD, THE MOVE, AND A NEW SCHOOL... AND HIGH SCHOOL, AT THAT...!
Katy's PJs by Alexis R., California
MacKenzie's top by Yesica B., Virginia

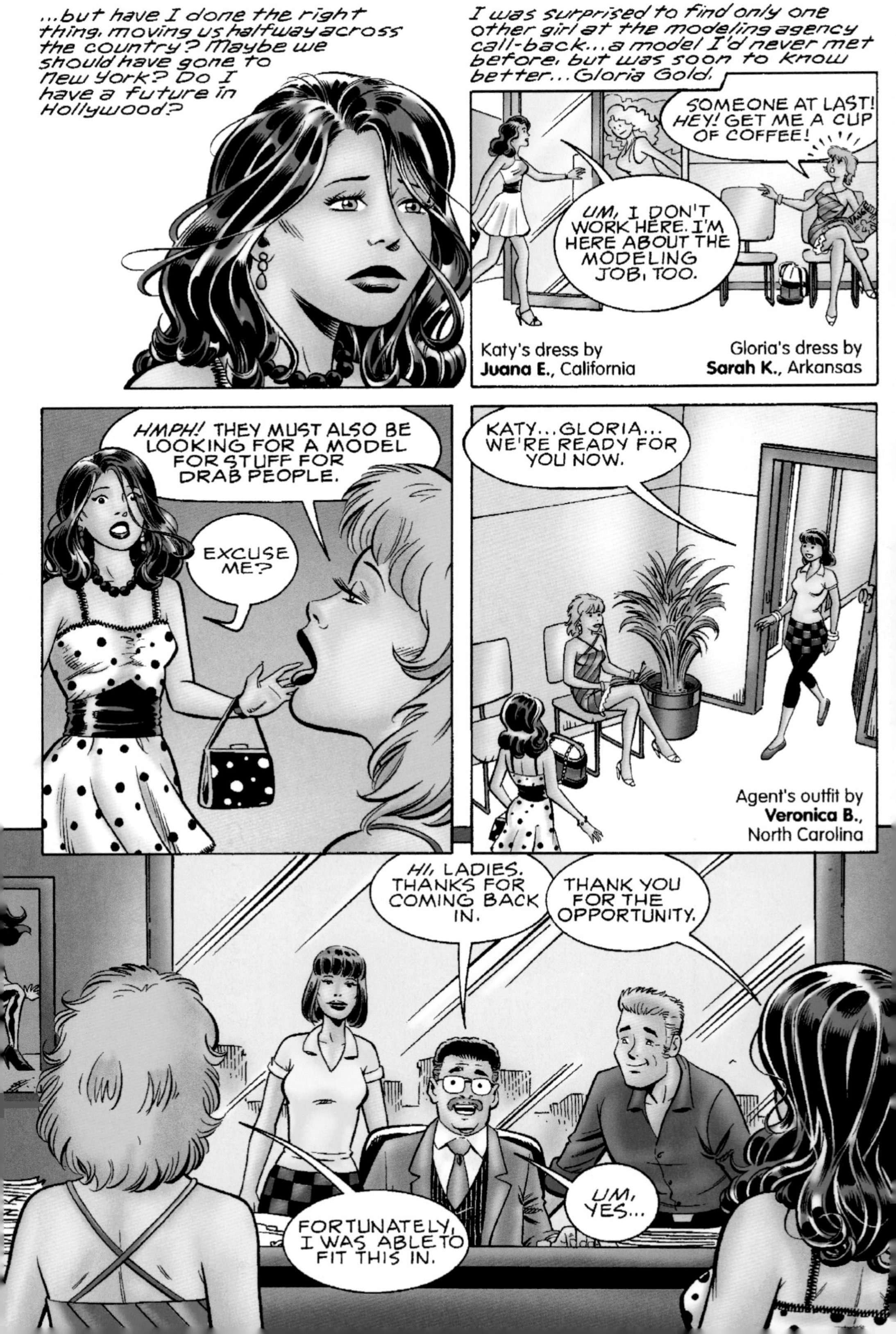
...but have I done the right thing, moving us halfway across the country? Maybe we should have gone to New York? Do I have a future in Hollywood?
I was surprised to find only one other girl at the modeling agency call-back...a model I'd never met before, but was soon to know better...Gloria Gold.
SOMEONE AT LAST! HEY! GET ME A CUP OF COFFEE!
UM, I DON'T WORK HERE. I'M HERE ABOUT THE MODELING JOB, TOO.
Katy's dress by Juana E., California
Gloria's dress by Sarah K., Arkansas
HMPH! THEY MUST ALSO BE LOOKING FOR A MODEL FOR STUFF FOR DRAB PEOPLE.
EXCUSE ME?
KATY...GLORIA... WE'RE READY FOR YOU NOW.
Agent's outfit by Veronica B., North Carolina
HI, LADIES. THANKS FOR COMING BACK IN.
THANK YOU FOR THE OPPORTUNITY.
FORTUNATELY, I WAS ABLE TO FIT THIS IN.
UM, YES...

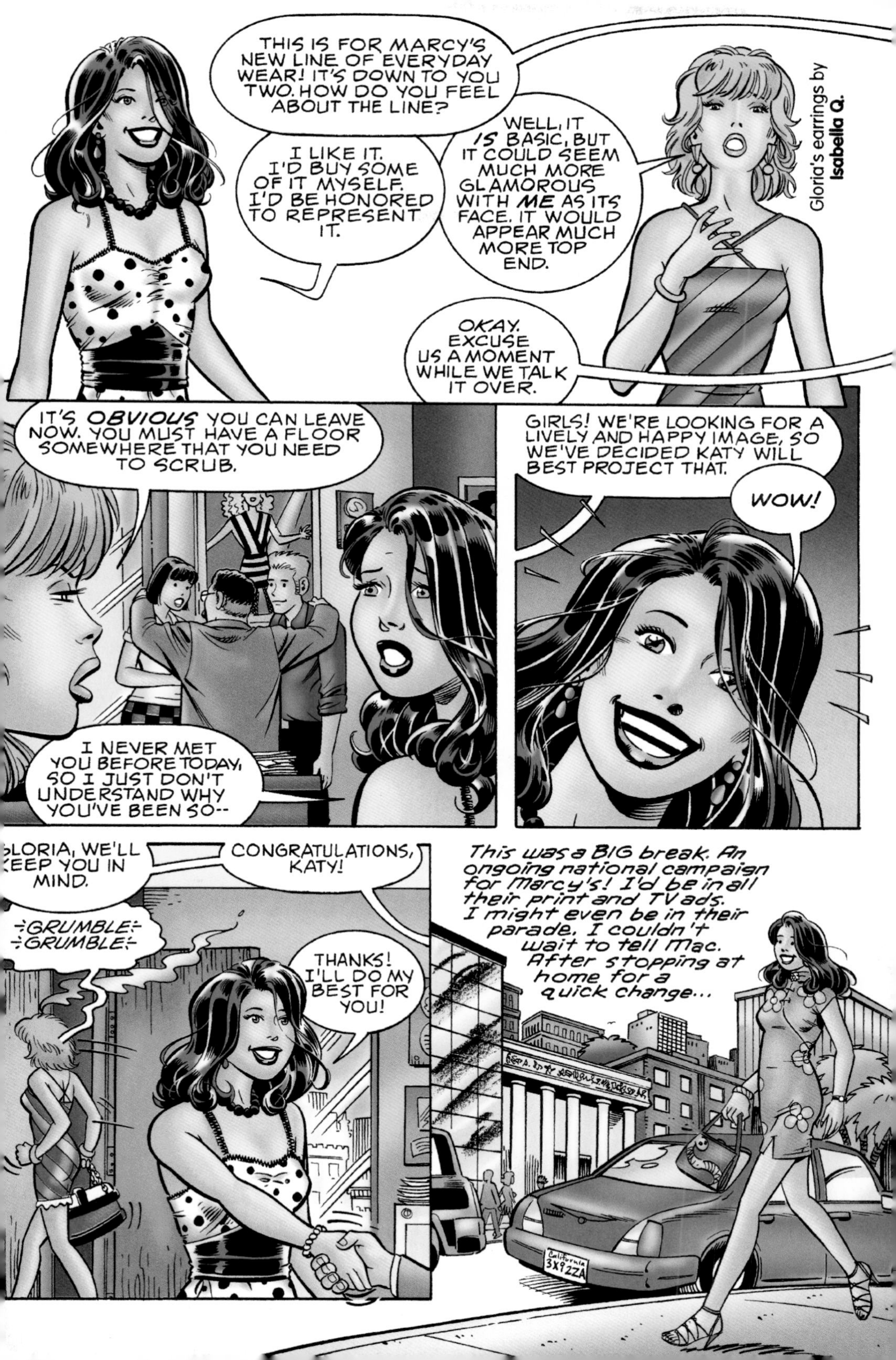
THIS IS FOR MARCY'S NEW LINE OF EVERYDAY WEAR! IT'S DOWN TO YOU TWO. HOW DO YOU FEEL ABOUT THE LINE?
I LIKE IT. I'D BUY SOME OF IT MYSELF. I'D BE HONORED TO REPRESENT IT.
WELL, IT *IS* BASIC, BUT IT COULD SEEM MUCH MORE GLAMOROUS WITH *ME* AS ITS FACE. IT WOULD APPEAR MUCH MORE TOP END.
Gloria's earrings by **Isabella Q.**
OKAY. EXCUSE US A MOMENT WHILE WE TALK IT OVER.
IT'S *OBVIOUS* YOU CAN LEAVE NOW. YOU MUST HAVE A FLOOR SOMEWHERE THAT YOU NEED TO SCRUB.
I NEVER MET YOU BEFORE TODAY, SO I JUST DON'T UNDERSTAND WHY YOU'VE BEEN SO--
GIRLS! WE'RE LOOKING FOR A LIVELY AND HAPPY IMAGE, SO WE'VE DECIDED KATY WILL BEST PROJECT THAT.
WOW!
GLORIA, WE'LL KEEP YOU IN MIND.
CONGRATULATIONS, KATY!
÷GRUMBLE÷ ÷GRUMBLE÷
THANKS! I'LL DO MY BEST FOR YOU!
This was a BIG break. An ongoing national campaign for Marcy's! I'd be in all their print and TV ads. I might even be in their parade. I couldn't wait to tell Mac. After stopping at home for a quick change...
California 3X92ZA

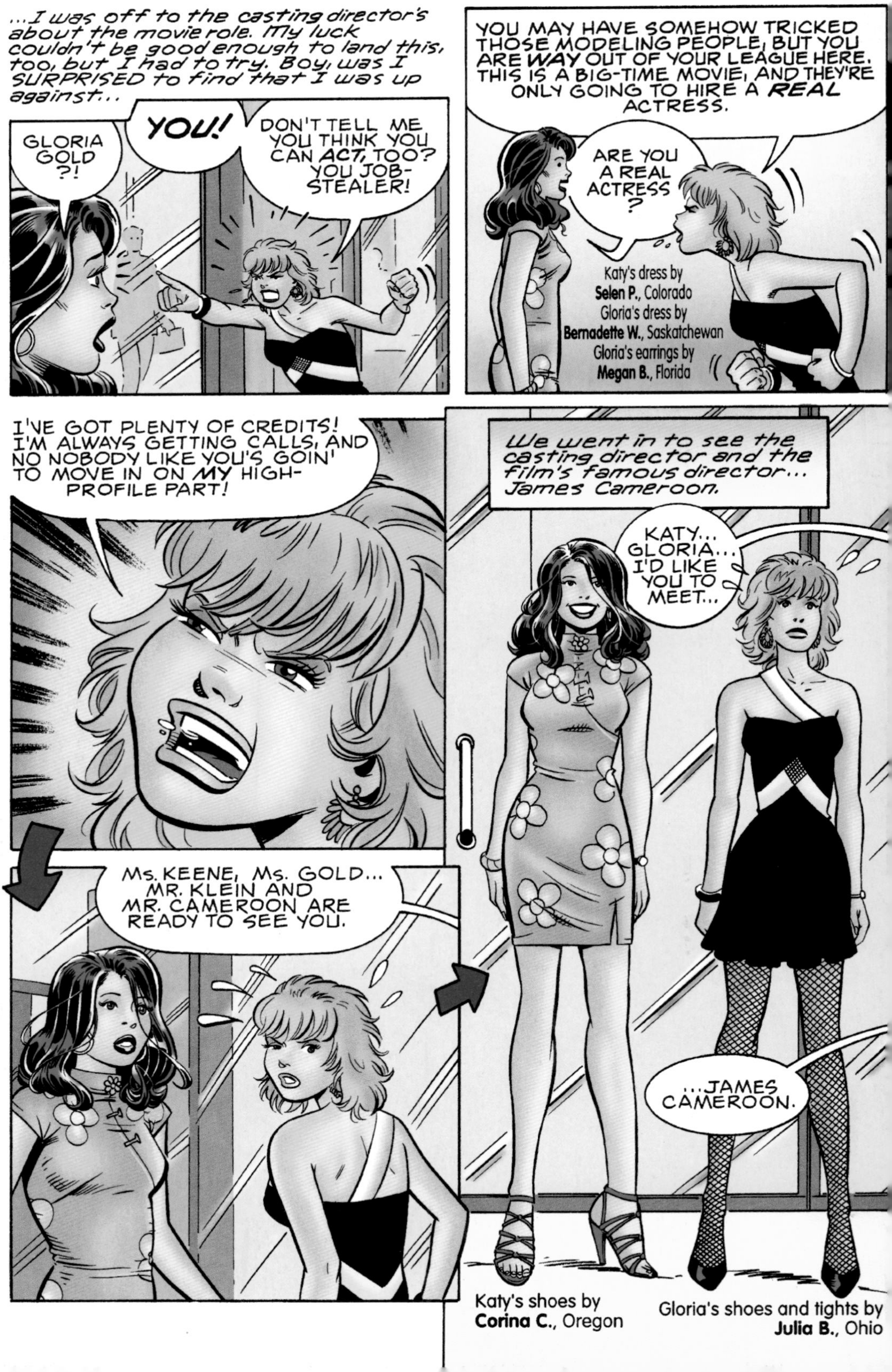

...I was off to the casting director's about the movie role. My luck couldn't be good enough to land this, too, but I had to try. Boy, was I SURPRISED to find that I was up against...
GLORIA GOLD ?!
YOU!
DON'T TELL ME YOU THINK YOU CAN ACT, TOO? YOU JOB-STEALER!
YOU MAY HAVE SOMEHOW TRICKED THOSE MODELING PEOPLE, BUT YOU ARE WAY OUT OF YOUR LEAGUE HERE. THIS IS A BIG-TIME MOVIE, AND THEY'RE ONLY GOING TO HIRE A REAL ACTRESS.
ARE YOU A REAL ACTRESS ?
Katy's dress by Selen P., Colorado
Gloria's dress by Bernadette W., Saskatchewan
Gloria's earrings by Megan B., Florida
I'VE GOT PLENTY OF CREDITS! I'M ALWAYS GETTING CALLS, AND NO NOBODY LIKE YOU'S GOIN' TO MOVE IN ON MY HIGH-PROFILE PART!
Ms. KEENE, Ms. GOLD... MR. KLEIN AND MR. CAMEROON ARE READY TO SEE YOU.
We went in to see the casting director and the film's famous director... James Cameroon.
KATY... GLORIA... I'D LIKE YOU TO MEET...
...JAMES CAMEROON.
Katy's shoes by Corina C., Oregon
Gloria's shoes and tights by Julia B., Ohio

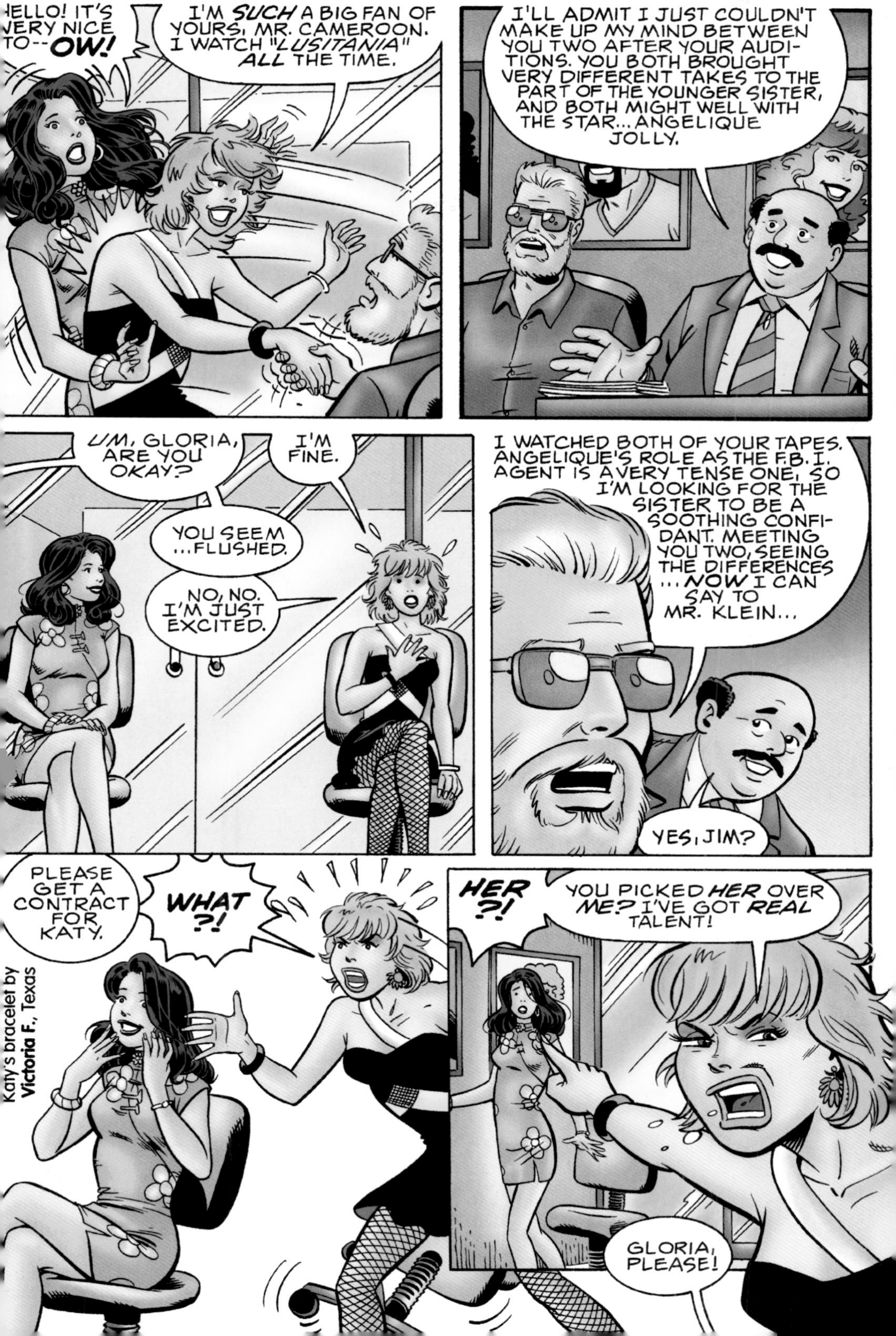
HELLO! IT'S VERY NICE TO--OW!
I'M SUCH A BIG FAN OF YOURS, MR. CAMEROON. I WATCH "LUSITANIA" ALL THE TIME.
I'LL ADMIT I JUST COULDN'T MAKE UP MY MIND BETWEEN YOU TWO AFTER YOUR AUDITIONS. YOU BOTH BROUGHT VERY DIFFERENT TAKES TO THE PART OF THE YOUNGER SISTER, AND BOTH MIGHT WELL WITH THE STAR... ANGELIQUE JOLLY.
UM, GLORIA, ARE YOU OKAY?
I'M FINE.
YOU SEEM ...FLUSHED.
NO, NO. I'M JUST EXCITED.
I WATCHED BOTH OF YOUR TAPES. ANGELIQUE'S ROLE AS THE F.B.I. AGENT IS A VERY TENSE ONE, SO I'M LOOKING FOR THE SISTER TO BE A SOOTHING CONFIDANT. MEETING YOU TWO, SEEING THE DIFFERENCES ...NOW I CAN SAY TO MR. KLEIN...
YES, JIM?
PLEASE GET A CONTRACT FOR KATY.
WHAT ?!
HER ?!
YOU PICKED HER OVER ME? I'VE GOT REAL TALENT!
GLORIA, PLEASE!
Katy's bracelet by Victoria F., Texas

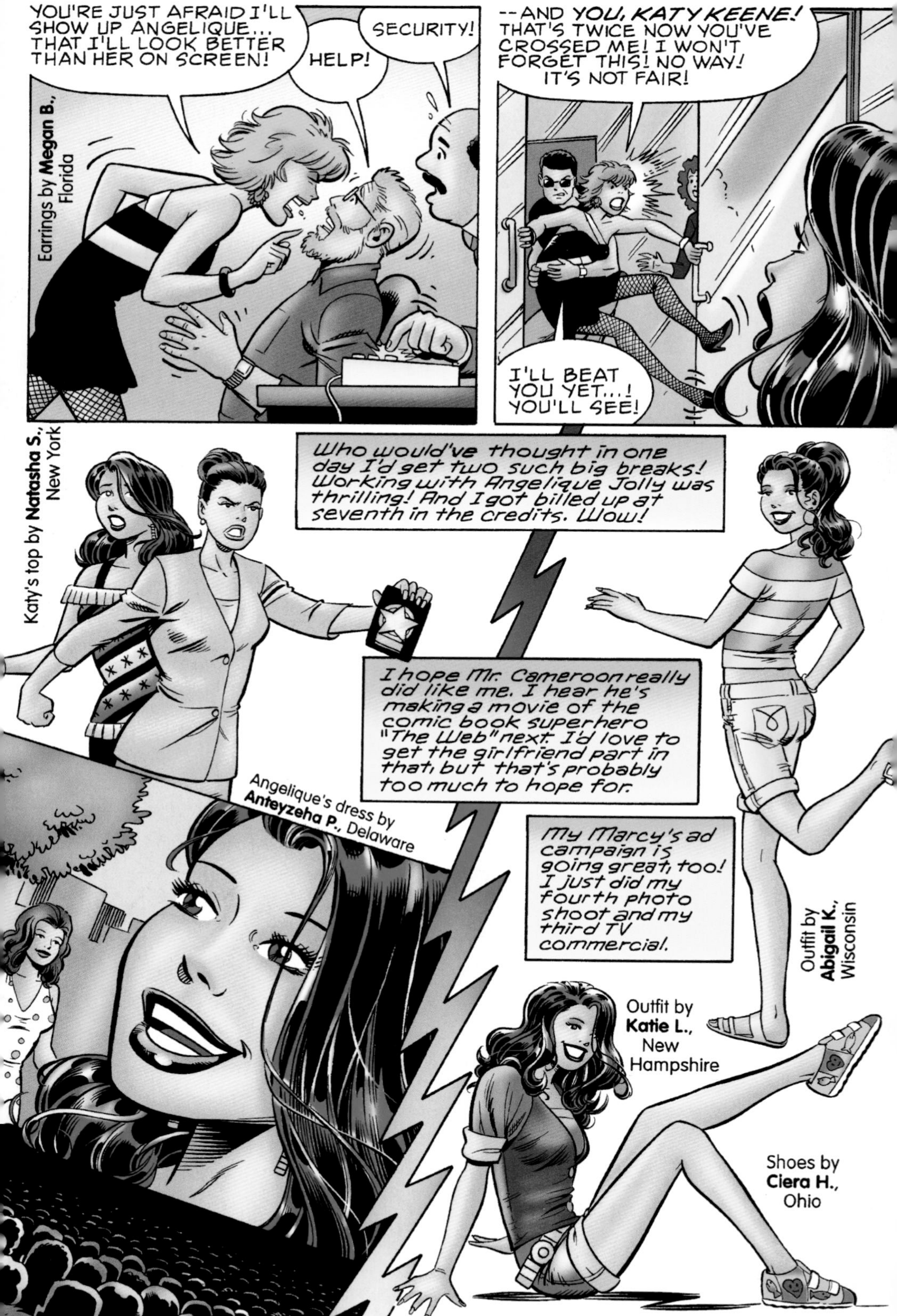
YOU'RE JUST AFRAID I'LL SHOW UP ANGELIQUE... THAT I'LL LOOK BETTER THAN HER ON SCREEN!
HELP!
SECURITY!
Earrings by Megan B., Florida
--AND YOU, KATY KEENE! THAT'S TWICE NOW YOU'VE CROSSED ME! I WON'T FORGET THIS! NO WAY! IT'S NOT FAIR!
I'LL BEAT YOU YET...! YOU'LL SEE!
Katy's top by Natasha S., New York
Who would've thought in one day I'd get two such big breaks! Working with Angelique Jolly was thrilling! And I got billed up at seventh in the credits. Wow!
I hope Mr. Cameroon really did like me. I hear he's making a movie of the comic book superhero "The Web" next. I'd love to get the girlfriend part in that, but that's probably too much to hope for.
Angelique's dress by Anteyzeha P., Delaware
My Marcy's ad campaign is going great, too! I just did my fourth photo shoot and my third TV commercial.
Outfit by Abigail K., Wisconsin
Outfit by Katie L., New Hampshire
Shoes by Ciera H., Ohio

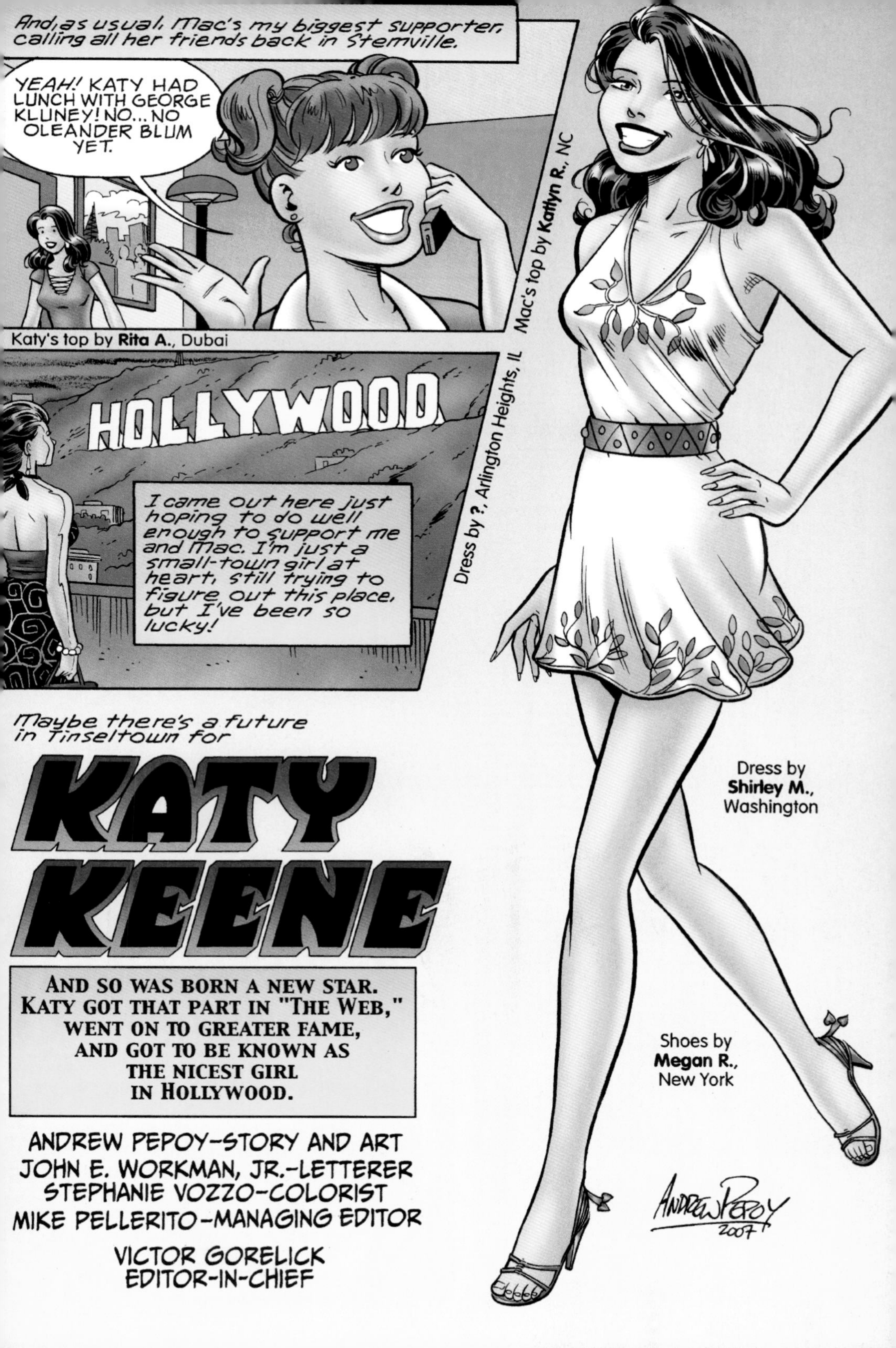

And, as usual, Mac's my biggest supporter, calling all her friends back in Stemville.
YEAH! KATY HAD LUNCH WITH GEORGE KLUNEY! NO... NO OLEANDER BLUM YET.
Katy's top by Rita A., Dubai
Mac's top by Katlyn R., NC
HOLLYWOOD
I came out here just hoping to do well enough to support me and Mac. I'm just a small-town girl at heart, still trying to figure out this place, but I've been so lucky!
Dress by ?, Arlington Heights, IL
Maybe there's a future in Tinseltown for
KATY KEENE
AND SO WAS BORN A NEW STAR. KATY GOT THAT PART IN "THE WEB," WENT ON TO GREATER FAME, AND GOT TO BE KNOWN AS THE NICEST GIRL IN HOLLYWOOD.
Dress by Shirley M., Washington
Shoes by Megan R., New York
ANDREW PEPOY–STORY AND ART
JOHN E. WORKMAN, JR.–LETTERER
STEPHANIE VOZZO–COLORIST
MIKE PELLERITO–MANAGING EDITOR
VICTOR GORELICK EDITOR-IN-CHIEF
ANDREW PEPOY 2007

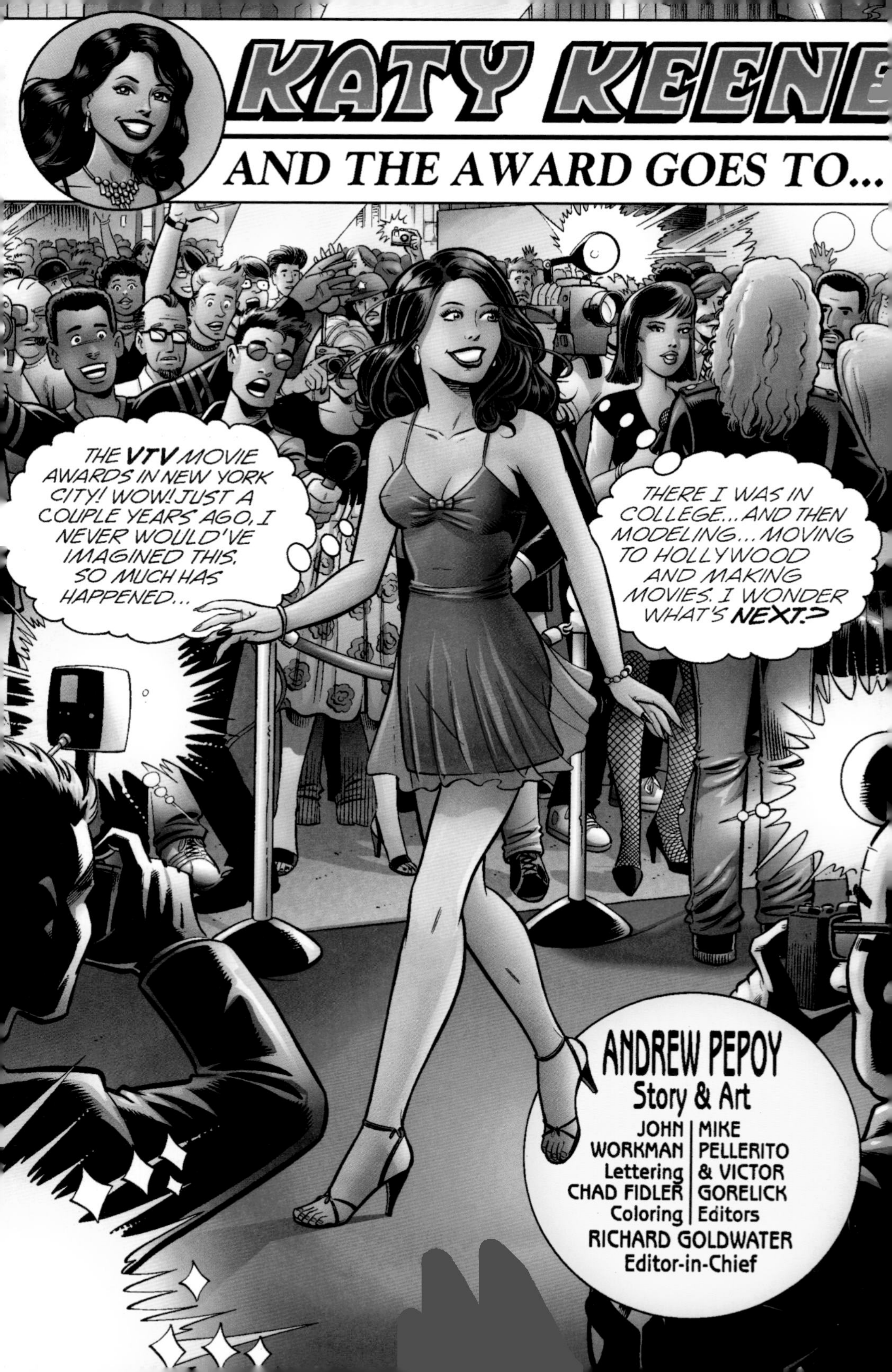

KATY KEENE
AND THE AWARD GOES TO...
THE VTV MOVIE AWARDS IN NEW YORK CITY! WOW! JUST A COUPLE YEARS AGO, I NEVER WOULD'VE IMAGINED THIS. SO MUCH HAS HAPPENED...
THERE I WAS IN COLLEGE... AND THEN MODELING... MOVING TO HOLLYWOOD AND MAKING MOVIES. I WONDER WHAT'S NEXT?
ANDREW PEPOY Story & Art
JOHN WORKMAN Lettering
CHAD FIDLER Coloring
MIKE PELLERITO & VICTOR GORELICK Editors
RICHARD GOLDWATER Editor-in-Chief

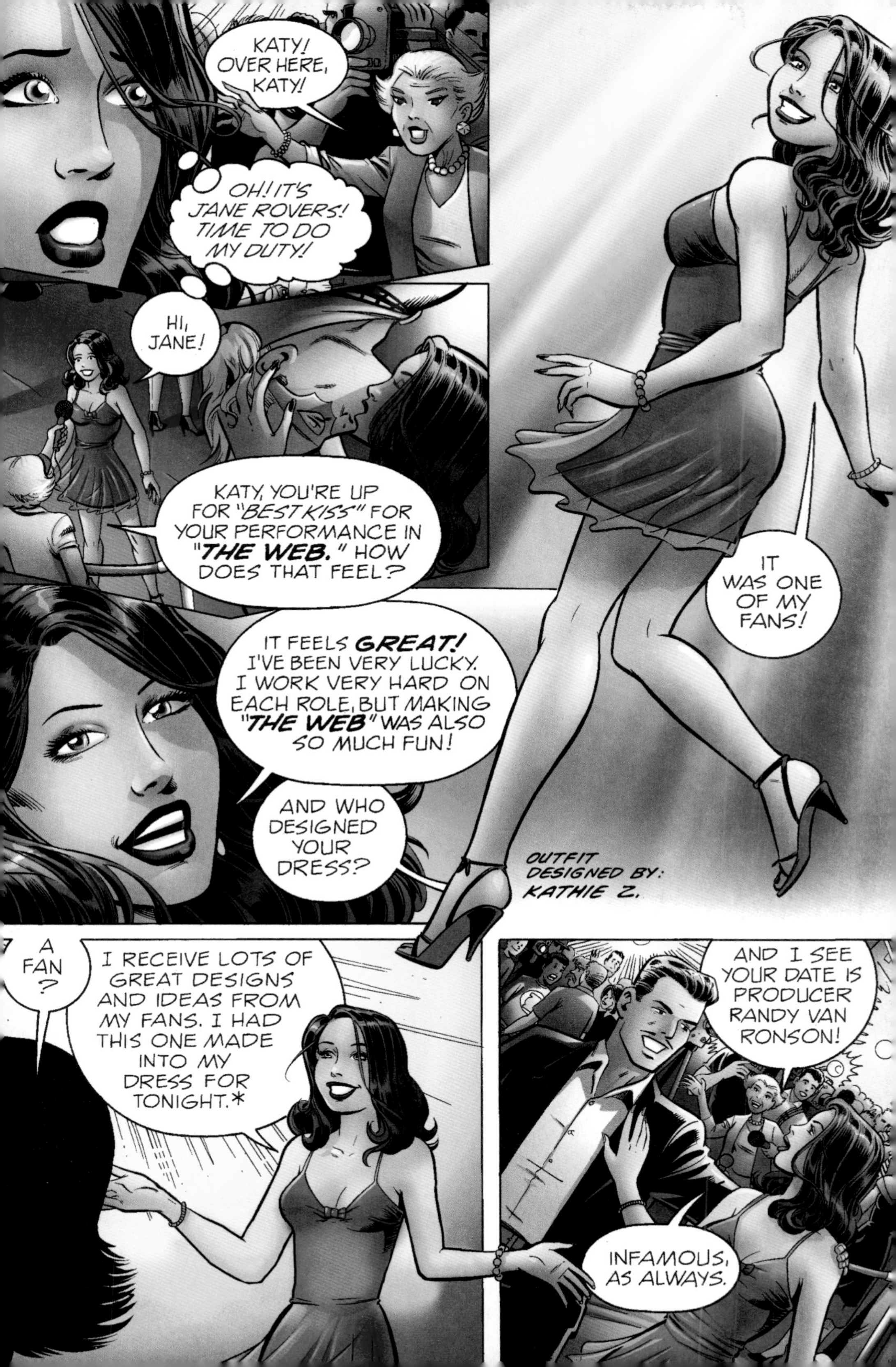
KATY! OVER HERE, KATY!
OH! IT'S JANE ROVERS! TIME TO DO MY DUTY!
HI, JANE!
KATY, YOU'RE UP FOR "BEST KISS" FOR YOUR PERFORMANCE IN "THE WEB." HOW DOES THAT FEEL?
IT FEELS GREAT! I'VE BEEN VERY LUCKY. I WORK VERY HARD ON EACH ROLE, BUT MAKING "THE WEB" WAS ALSO SO MUCH FUN!
AND WHO DESIGNED YOUR DRESS?
IT WAS ONE OF MY FANS!
OUTFIT DESIGNED BY: KATHIE Z.
A FAN?
I RECEIVE LOTS OF GREAT DESIGNS AND IDEAS FROM MY FANS. I HAD THIS ONE MADE INTO MY DRESS FOR TONIGHT.*
AND I SEE YOUR DATE IS PRODUCER RANDY VAN RONSON!
INFAMOUS, AS ALWAYS.

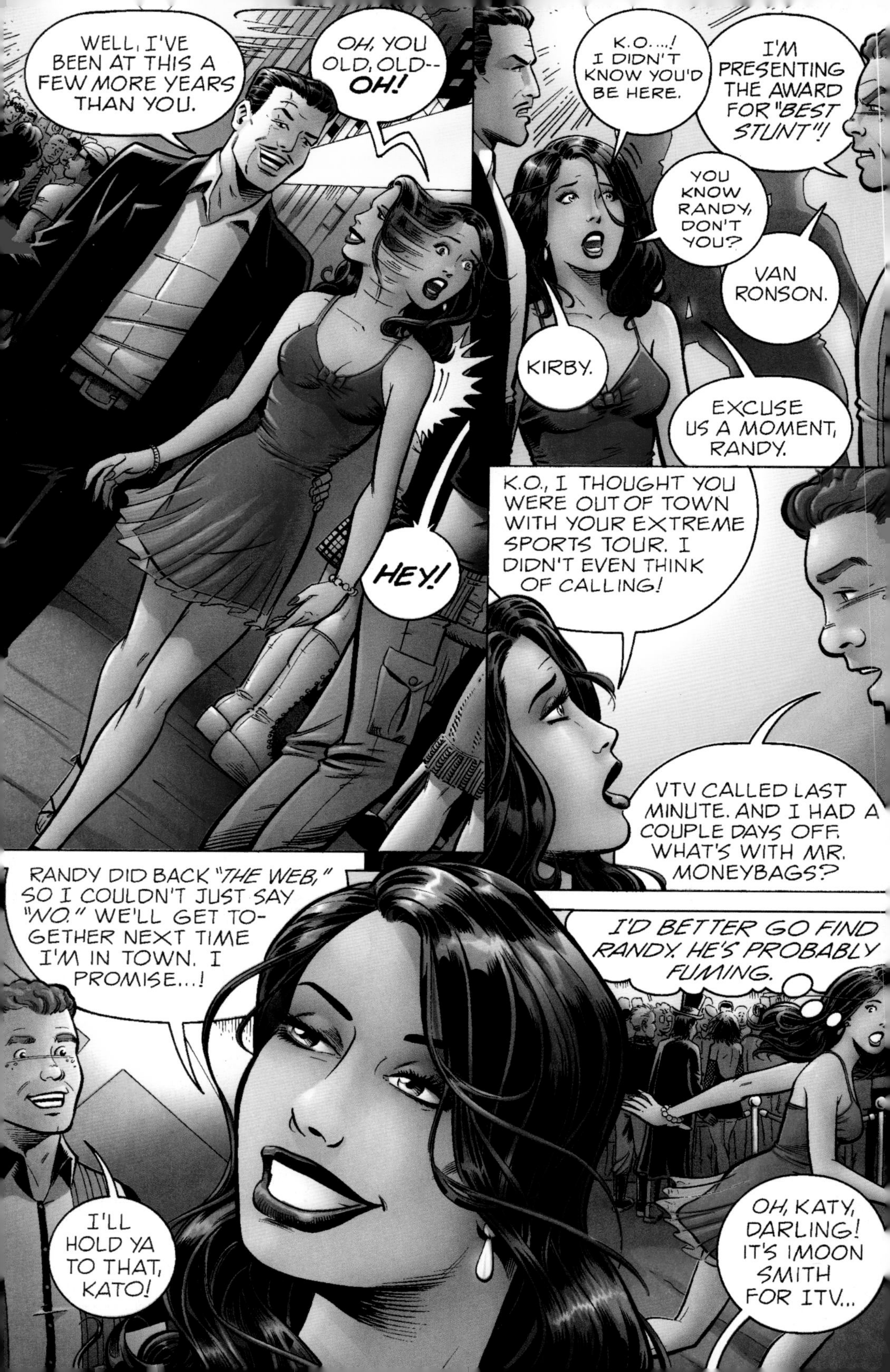
WELL, I'VE BEEN AT THIS A FEW MORE YEARS THAN YOU.
OH, YOU OLD, OLD-- OH!
HEY!
K.O....! I DIDN'T KNOW YOU'D BE HERE.
I'M PRESENTING THE AWARD FOR "BEST STUNT"!
YOU KNOW RANDY, DON'T YOU?
VAN RONSON.
KIRBY.
EXCUSE US A MOMENT, RANDY.
K.O., I THOUGHT YOU WERE OUT OF TOWN WITH YOUR EXTREME SPORTS TOUR. I DIDN'T EVEN THINK OF CALLING!
VTV CALLED LAST MINUTE. AND I HAD A COUPLE DAYS OFF. WHAT'S WITH MR. MONEYBAGS?
RANDY DID BACK "THE WEB," SO I COULDN'T JUST SAY "NO." WE'LL GET TO-GETHER NEXT TIME I'M IN TOWN. I PROMISE...!
I'LL HOLD YA TO THAT, KATO!
I'D BETTER GO FIND RANDY. HE'S PROBABLY FUMING.
OH, KATY, DARLING! IT'S IMOON SMITH FOR ITV...

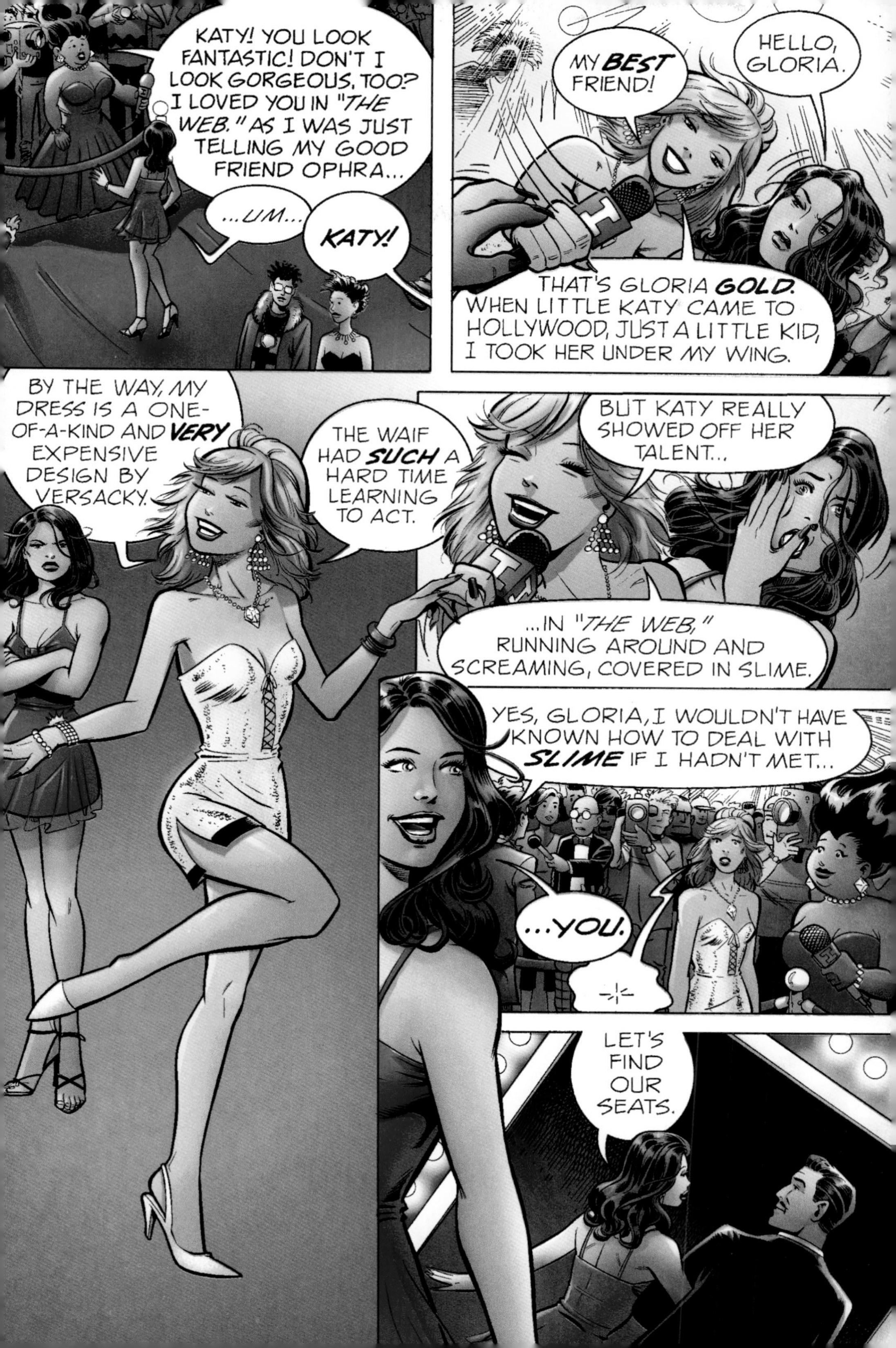
KATY! YOU LOOK FANTASTIC! DON'T I LOOK GORGEOUS, TOO? I LOVED YOU IN "THE WEB." AS I WAS JUST TELLING MY GOOD FRIEND OPHRA...
...UM...
KATY!
MY BEST FRIEND!
HELLO, GLORIA.
THAT'S GLORIA GOLD. WHEN LITTLE KATY CAME TO HOLLYWOOD, JUST A LITTLE KID, I TOOK HER UNDER MY WING.
BY THE WAY, MY DRESS IS A ONE-OF-A-KIND AND VERY EXPENSIVE DESIGN BY VERSACKY.
THE WAIF HAD SUCH A HARD TIME LEARNING TO ACT.
BUT KATY REALLY SHOWED OFF HER TALENT...
...IN "THE WEB," RUNNING AROUND AND SCREAMING, COVERED IN SLIME.
YES, GLORIA, I WOULDN'T HAVE KNOWN HOW TO DEAL WITH SLIME IF I HADN'T MET...
...YOU.
LET'S FIND OUR SEATS.

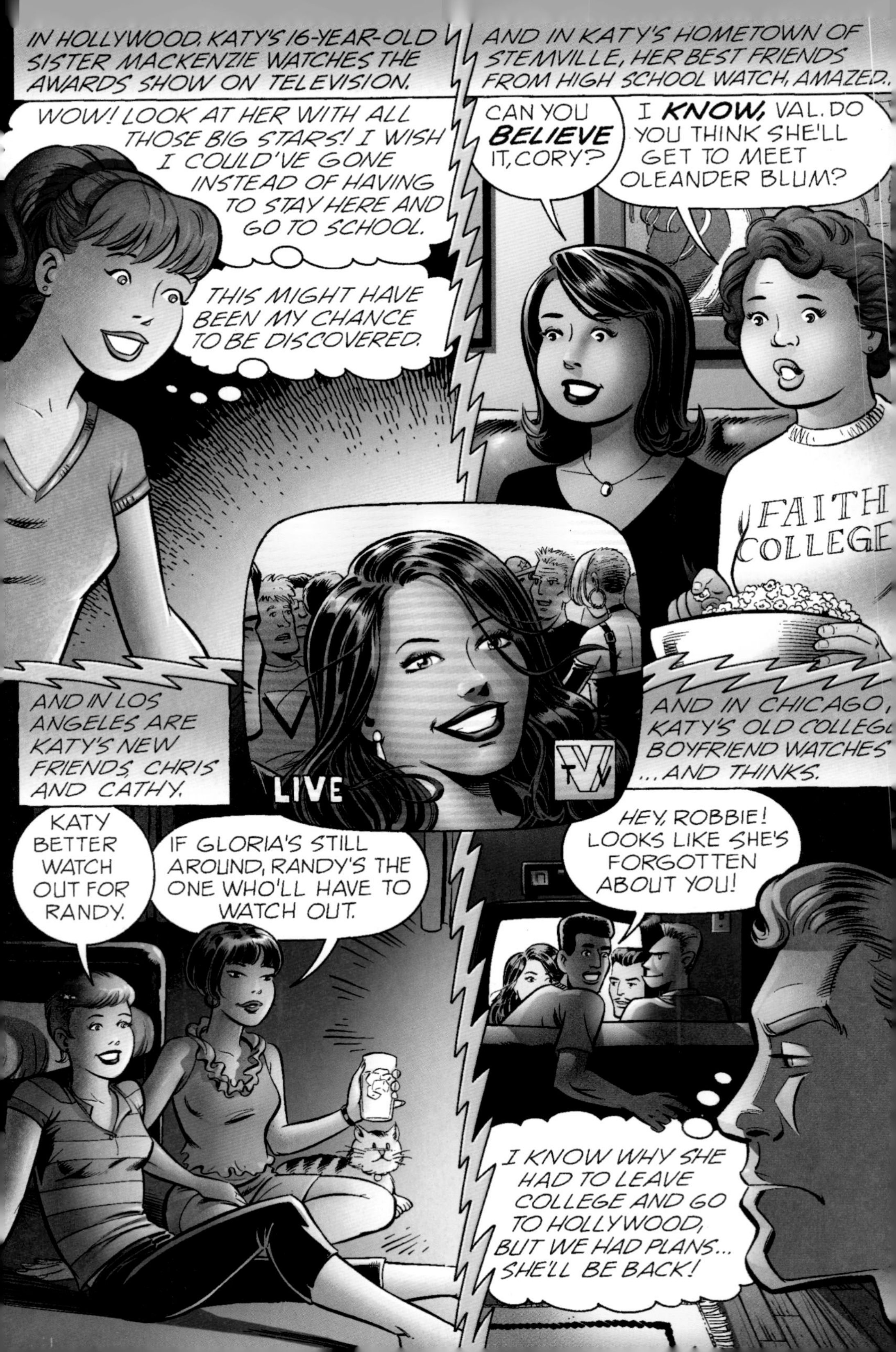
IN HOLLYWOOD, KATY'S 16-YEAR-OLD SISTER MACKENZIE WATCHES THE AWARDS SHOW ON TELEVISION.
WOW! LOOK AT HER WITH ALL THOSE BIG STARS! I WISH I COULD'VE GONE INSTEAD OF HAVING TO STAY HERE AND GO TO SCHOOL.
THIS MIGHT HAVE BEEN MY CHANCE TO BE DISCOVERED.
AND IN KATY'S HOMETOWN OF STEMVILLE, HER BEST FRIENDS FROM HIGH SCHOOL WATCH, AMAZED.
CAN YOU BELIEVE IT, CORY?
I KNOW, VAL. DO YOU THINK SHE'LL GET TO MEET OLEANDER BLUM?
FAITH COLLEGE
LIVE
AND IN LOS ANGELES ARE KATY'S NEW FRIENDS, CHRIS AND CATHY.
KATY BETTER WATCH OUT FOR RANDY.
IF GLORIA'S STILL AROUND, RANDY'S THE ONE WHO'LL HAVE TO WATCH OUT.
AND IN CHICAGO, KATY'S OLD COLLEGE BOYFRIEND WATCHES ...AND THINKS.
HEY, ROBBIE! LOOKS LIKE SHE'S FORGOTTEN ABOUT YOU!
I KNOW WHY SHE HAD TO LEAVE COLLEGE AND GO TO HOLLYWOOD, BUT WE HAD PLANS... SHE'LL BE BACK!

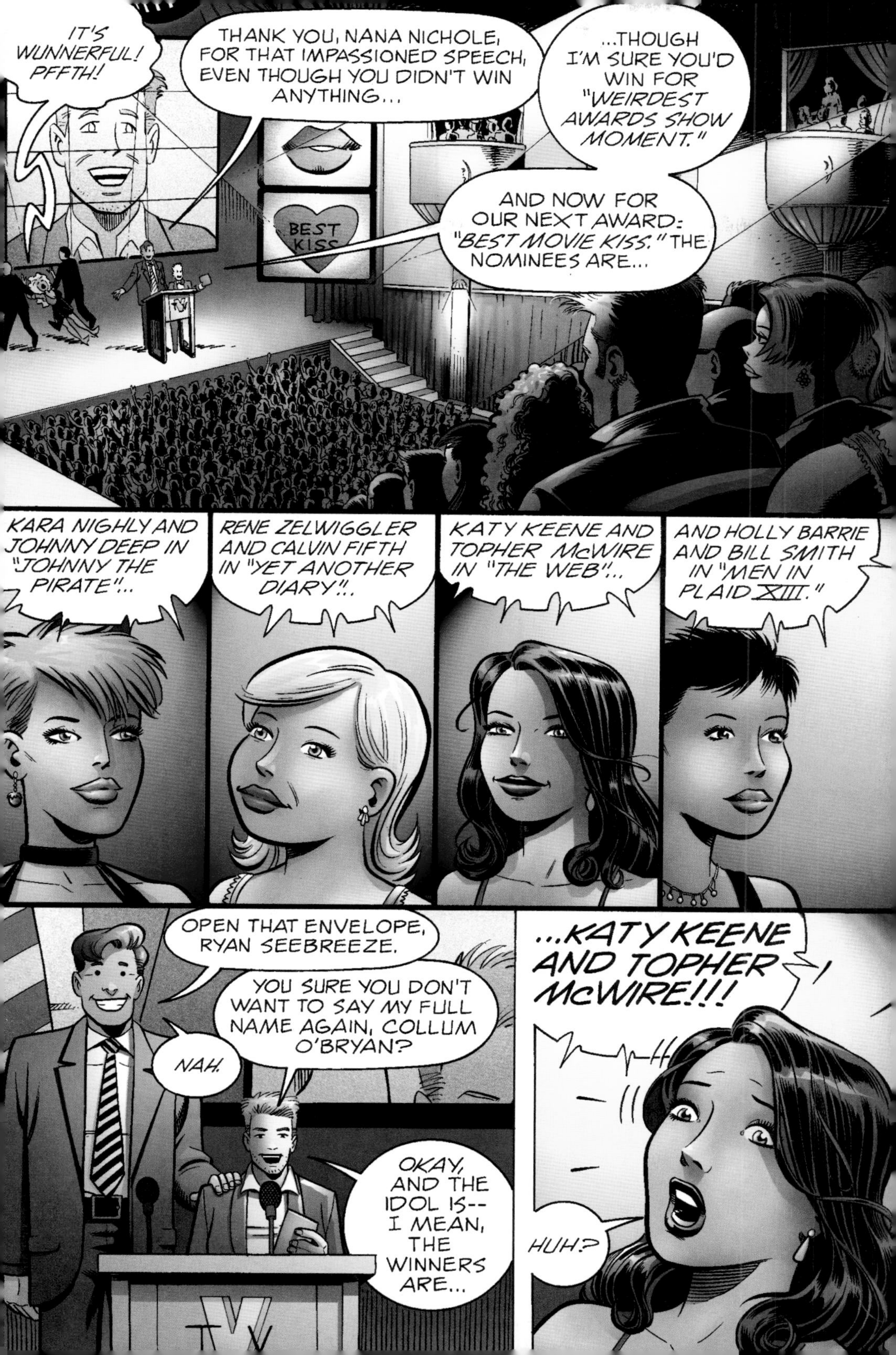
IT'S WUNNERFUL! PFFTH!
THANK YOU, NANA NICHOLE, FOR THAT IMPASSIONED SPEECH, EVEN THOUGH YOU DIDN'T WIN ANYTHING...
...THOUGH I'M SURE YOU'D WIN FOR "WEIRDEST AWARDS SHOW MOMENT."
BEST KISS
AND NOW FOR OUR NEXT AWARD: "BEST MOVIE KISS." THE NOMINEES ARE...
KARA NIGHLY AND JOHNNY DEEP IN "JOHNNY THE PIRATE"...
RENE ZELWIGGLER AND CALVIN FIFTH IN "YET ANOTHER DIARY"...
KATY KEENE AND TOPHER McWIRE IN "THE WEB"...
AND HOLLY BARRIE AND BILL SMITH IN "MEN IN PLAID XIII."
OPEN THAT ENVELOPE, RYAN SEEBREEZE.
YOU SURE YOU DON'T WANT TO SAY MY FULL NAME AGAIN, COLLUM O'BRYAN?
NAH.
OKAY, AND THE IDOL IS-- I MEAN, THE WINNERS ARE...
...KATY KEENE AND TOPHER McWIRE!!!
HUH?

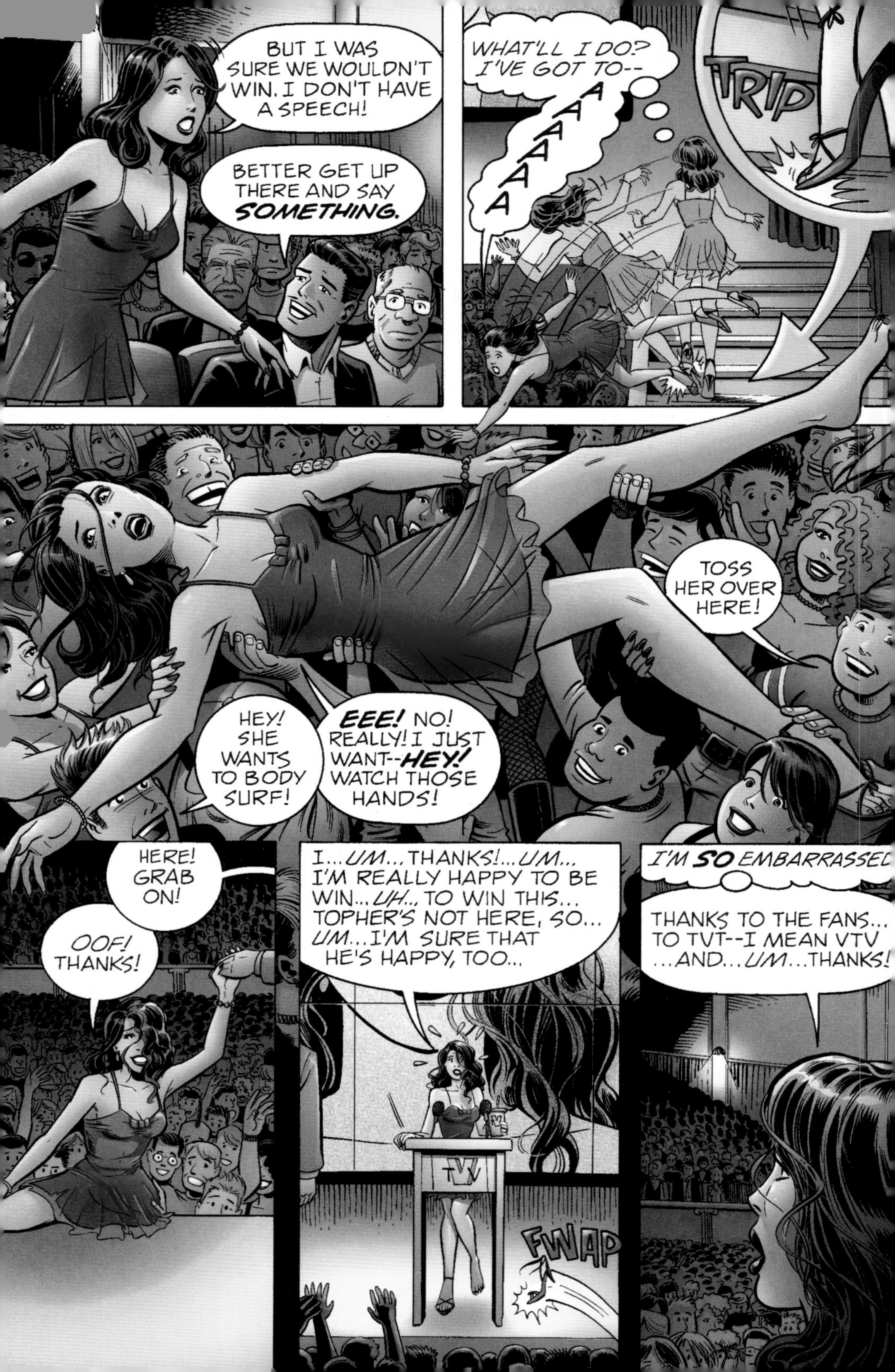

BUT I WAS SURE WE WOULDN'T WIN. I DON'T HAVE A SPEECH!
BETTER GET UP THERE AND SAY SOMETHING.
WHAT'LL I DO? I'VE GOT TO--
AAAAAA
TRIP
TOSS HER OVER HERE!
HEY! SHE WANTS TO BODY SURF!
EEE! NO! REALLY! I JUST WANT--HEY! WATCH THOSE HANDS!
HERE! GRAB ON!
OOF! THANKS!
I...UM..., THANKS!...UM... I'M REALLY HAPPY TO BE WIN...UH..., TO WIN THIS... TOPHER'S NOT HERE, SO... UM...I'M SURE THAT HE'S HAPPY, TOO...
FWAP
I'M SO EMBARRASSED
THANKS TO THE FANS... TO TVT--I MEAN VTV ...AND...UM...THANKS!

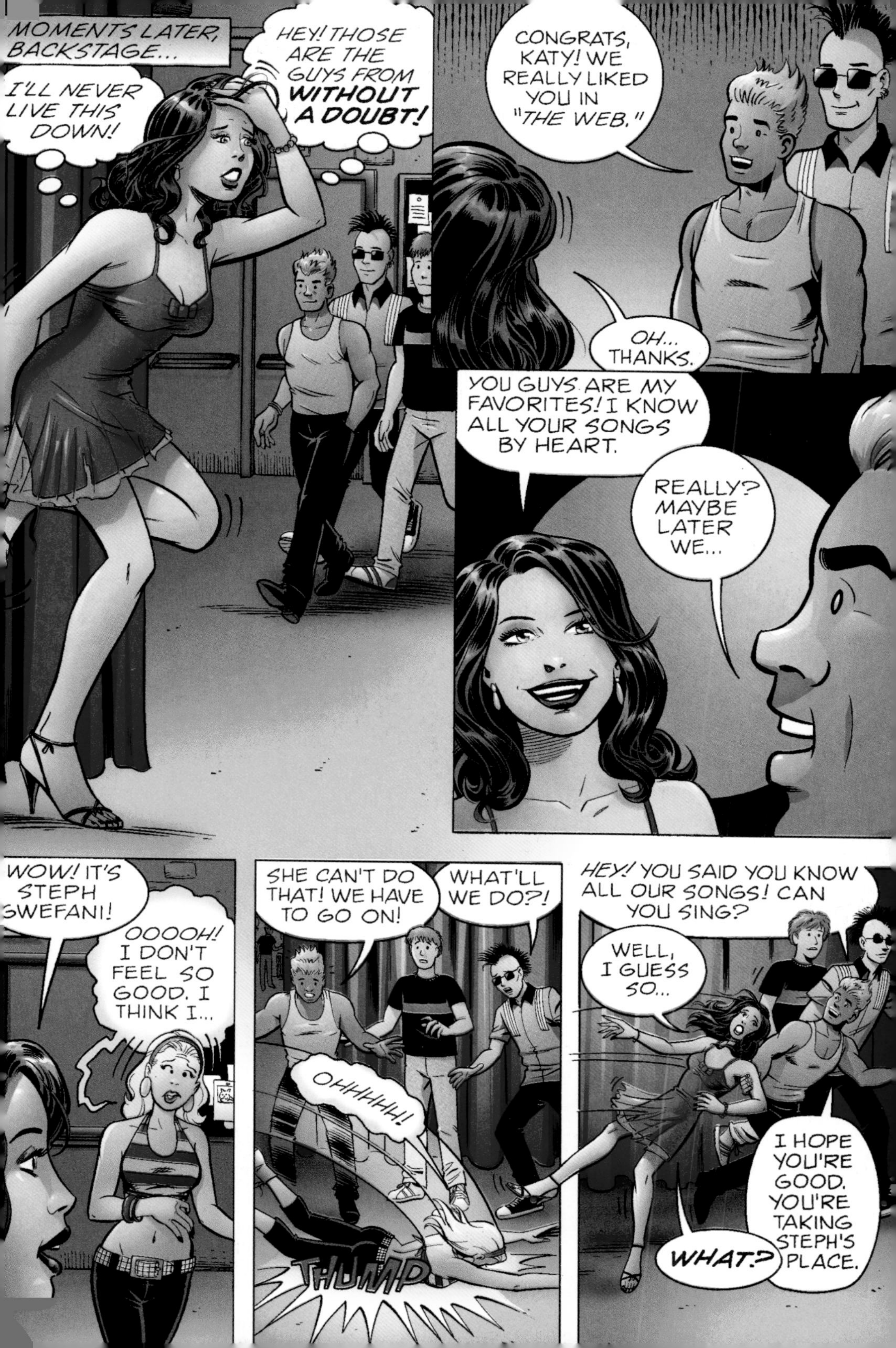

MOMENTS LATER, BACKSTAGE...
I'LL NEVER LIVE THIS DOWN!
HEY! THOSE ARE THE GUYS FROM **WITHOUT A DOUBT!**
CONGRATS, KATY! WE REALLY LIKED YOU IN "THE WEB."
OH... THANKS.
YOU GUYS ARE MY FAVORITES! I KNOW ALL YOUR SONGS BY HEART.
REALLY? MAYBE LATER WE...
WOW! IT'S STEPH SWEFANI!
OOOOH! I DON'T FEEL SO GOOD. I THINK I...
SHE CAN'T DO THAT! WE HAVE TO GO ON!
WHAT'LL WE DO?!
OHHHHH!
THUMP
HEY! YOU SAID YOU KNOW ALL OUR SONGS! CAN YOU SING?
WELL, I GUESS SO...
I HOPE YOU'RE GOOD. YOU'RE TAKING STEPH'S PLACE.
WHAT?

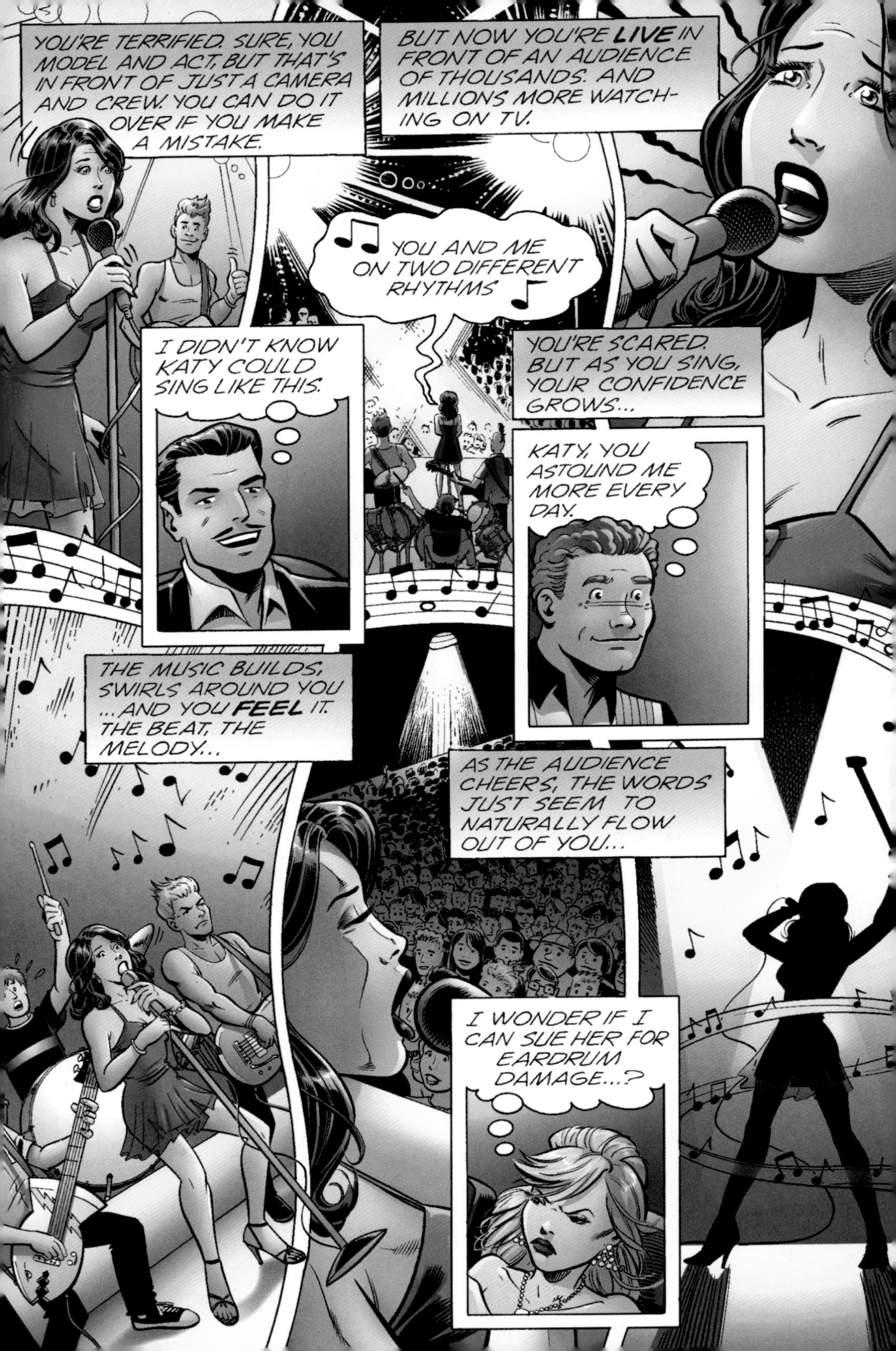
YOU'RE TERRIFIED. SURE, YOU MODEL AND ACT, BUT THAT'S IN FRONT OF JUST A CAMERA AND CREW. YOU CAN DO IT OVER IF YOU MAKE A MISTAKE.
BUT NOW YOU'RE **LIVE** IN FRONT OF AN AUDIENCE OF THOUSANDS. AND MILLIONS MORE WATCHING ON TV.
YOU AND ME ON TWO DIFFERENT RHYTHMS
I DIDN'T KNOW KATY COULD SING LIKE THIS.
YOU'RE SCARED. BUT AS YOU SING, YOUR CONFIDENCE GROWS...
KATY, YOU ASTOUND ME MORE EVERY DAY.
THE MUSIC BUILDS, SWIRLS AROUND YOU ...AND YOU **FEEL** IT. THE BEAT, THE MELODY...
AS THE AUDIENCE CHEERS, THE WORDS JUST SEEM TO NATURALLY FLOW OUT OF YOU...
I WONDER IF I CAN SUE HER FOR EARDRUM DAMAGE...?

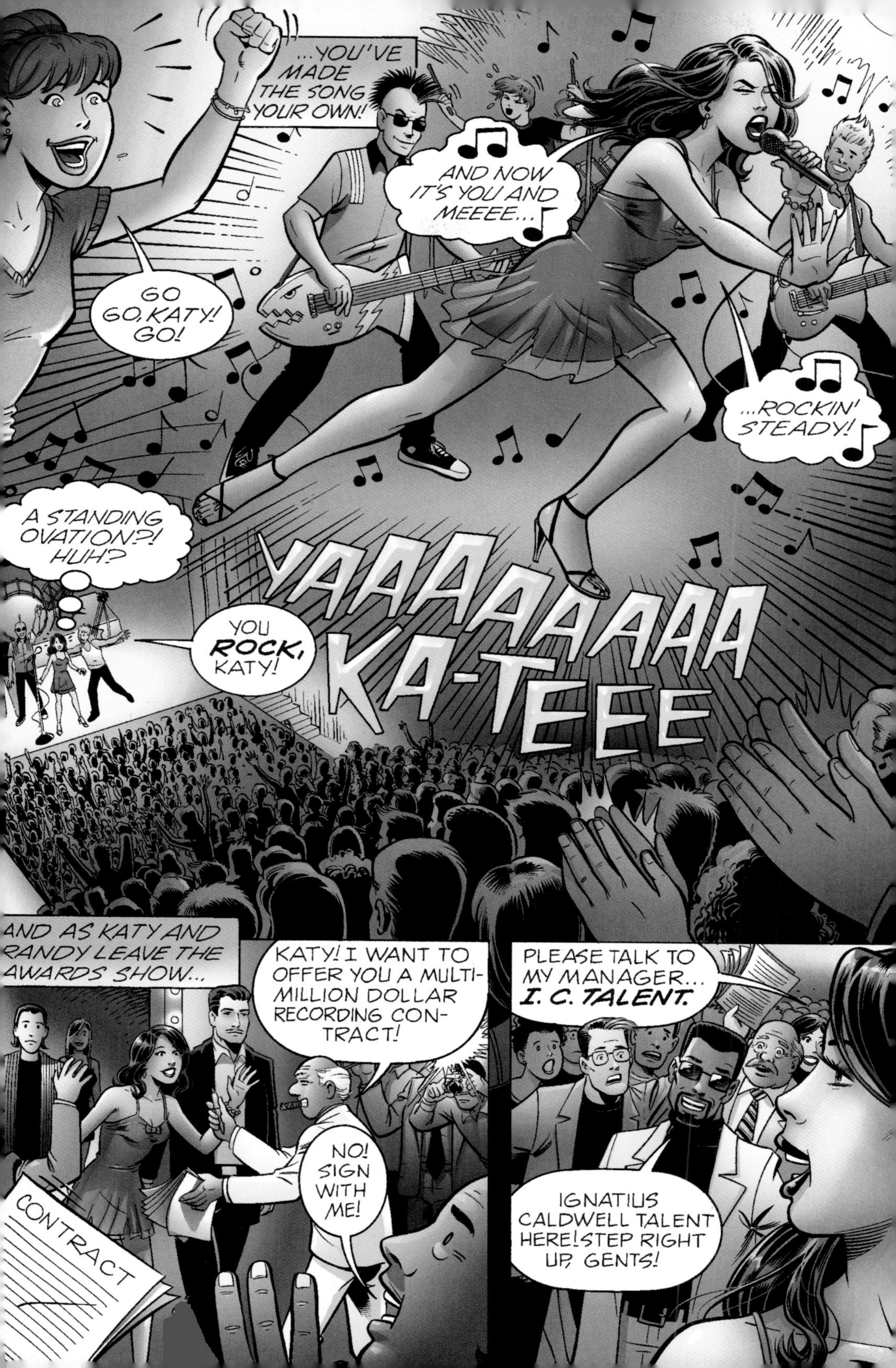
...YOU'VE MADE THE SONG YOUR OWN!
AND NOW IT'S YOU AND MEEEE...
GO GO, KATY! GO!
...ROCKIN' STEADY!
A STANDING OVATION?! HUH?
YOU ROCK, KATY!
YAAAAAAAAA KA-TEEE
AND AS KATY AND RANDY LEAVE THE AWARDS SHOW...
KATY! I WANT TO OFFER YOU A MULTI-MILLION DOLLAR RECORDING CONTRACT!
NO! SIGN WITH ME!
CONTRACT
PLEASE TALK TO MY MANAGER... I. C. TALENT.
IGNATIUS CALDWELL TALENT HERE! STEP RIGHT UP, GENTS!

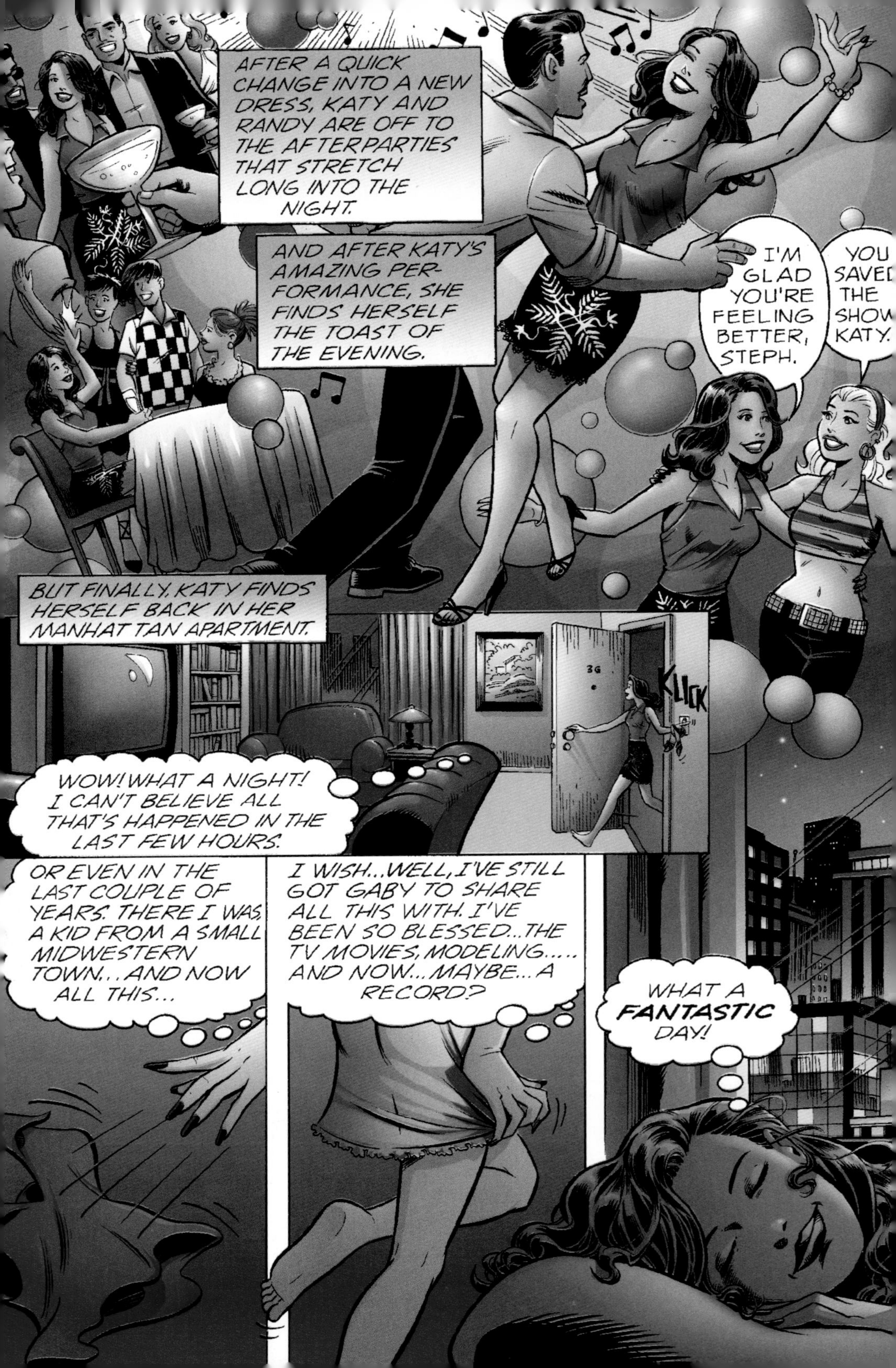
AFTER A QUICK CHANGE INTO A NEW DRESS, KATY AND RANDY ARE OFF TO THE AFTERPARTIES THAT STRETCH LONG INTO THE NIGHT.
AND AFTER KATY'S AMAZING PER-FORMANCE, SHE FINDS HERSELF THE TOAST OF THE EVENING.
I'M GLAD YOU'RE FEELING BETTER, STEPH.
YOU SAVED THE SHOW KATY.
BUT FINALLY, KATY FINDS HERSELF BACK IN HER MANHATTAN APARTMENT.
3G
KLICK
WOW! WHAT A NIGHT! I CAN'T BELIEVE ALL THAT'S HAPPENED IN THE LAST FEW HOURS.
OR EVEN IN THE LAST COUPLE OF YEARS. THERE I WAS, A KID FROM A SMALL MIDWESTERN TOWN... AND NOW ALL THIS...
I WISH...WELL, I'VE STILL GOT GABY TO SHARE ALL THIS WITH. I'VE BEEN SO BLESSED...THE TV MOVIES, MODELING..... AND NOW... MAYBE... A RECORD?
WHAT A **FANTASTIC** DAY!

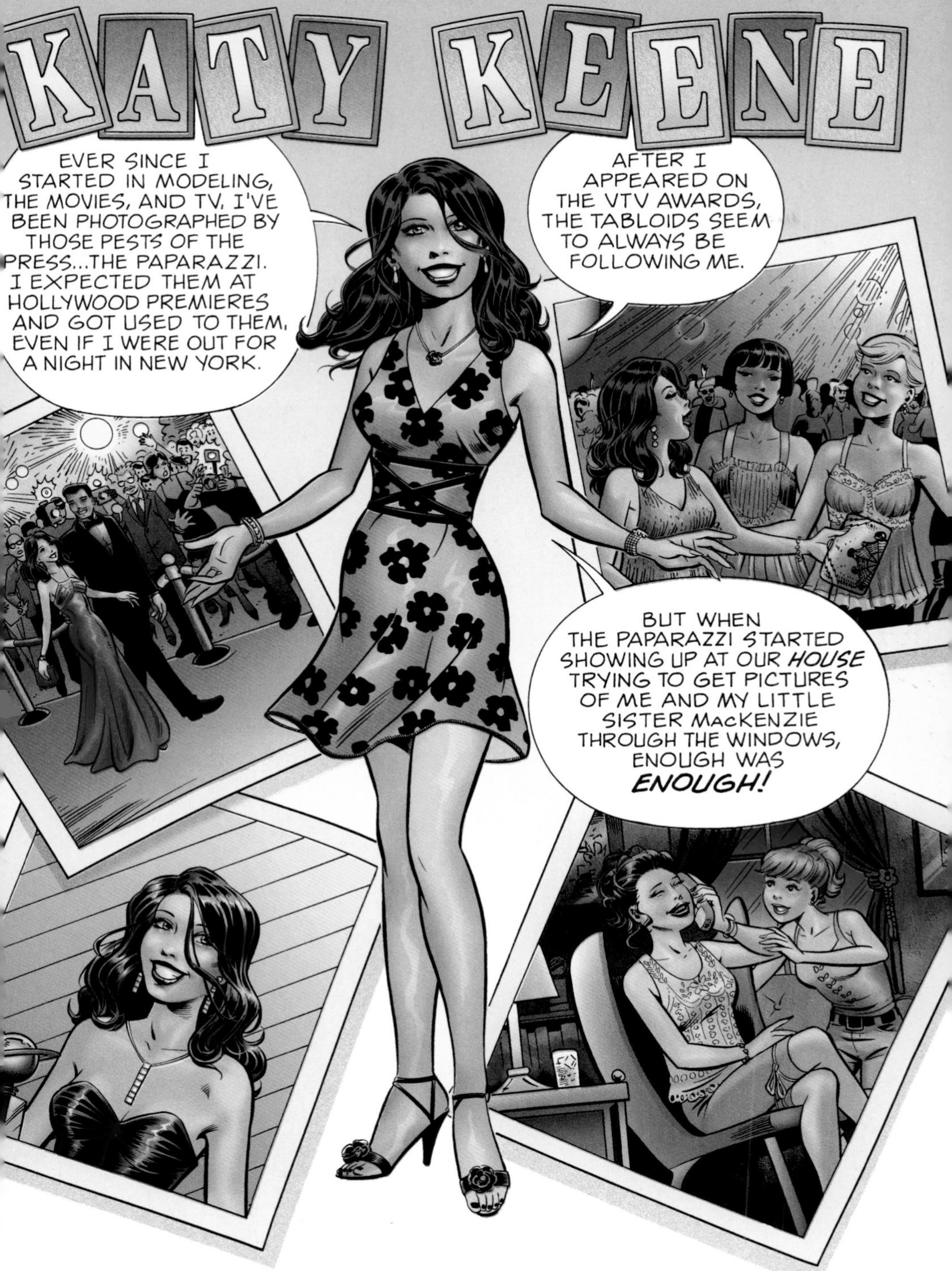
KATY KEENE
EVER SINCE I STARTED IN MODELING, THE MOVIES, AND TV, I'VE BEEN PHOTOGRAPHED BY THOSE PESTS OF THE PRESS...THE PAPARAZZI. I EXPECTED THEM AT HOLLYWOOD PREMIERES AND GOT USED TO THEM, EVEN IF I WERE OUT FOR A NIGHT IN NEW YORK.
AFTER I APPEARED ON THE VTV AWARDS, THE TABLOIDS SEEM TO ALWAYS BE FOLLOWING ME.
BUT WHEN THE PAPARAZZI STARTED SHOWING UP AT OUR *HOUSE* TRYING TO GET PICTURES OF ME AND MY LITTLE SISTER MacKENZIE THROUGH THE WINDOWS, ENOUGH WAS *ENOUGH!*

ANDREW PEPOY Story & Art | **JOHN WORKMAN** Lettering | **GEORGE FREEMAN** Colorist | **MIKE PELLERITO & VICTOR GORELICK** Editors | **RICHARD GOLDWATER** Editor-in-Chief

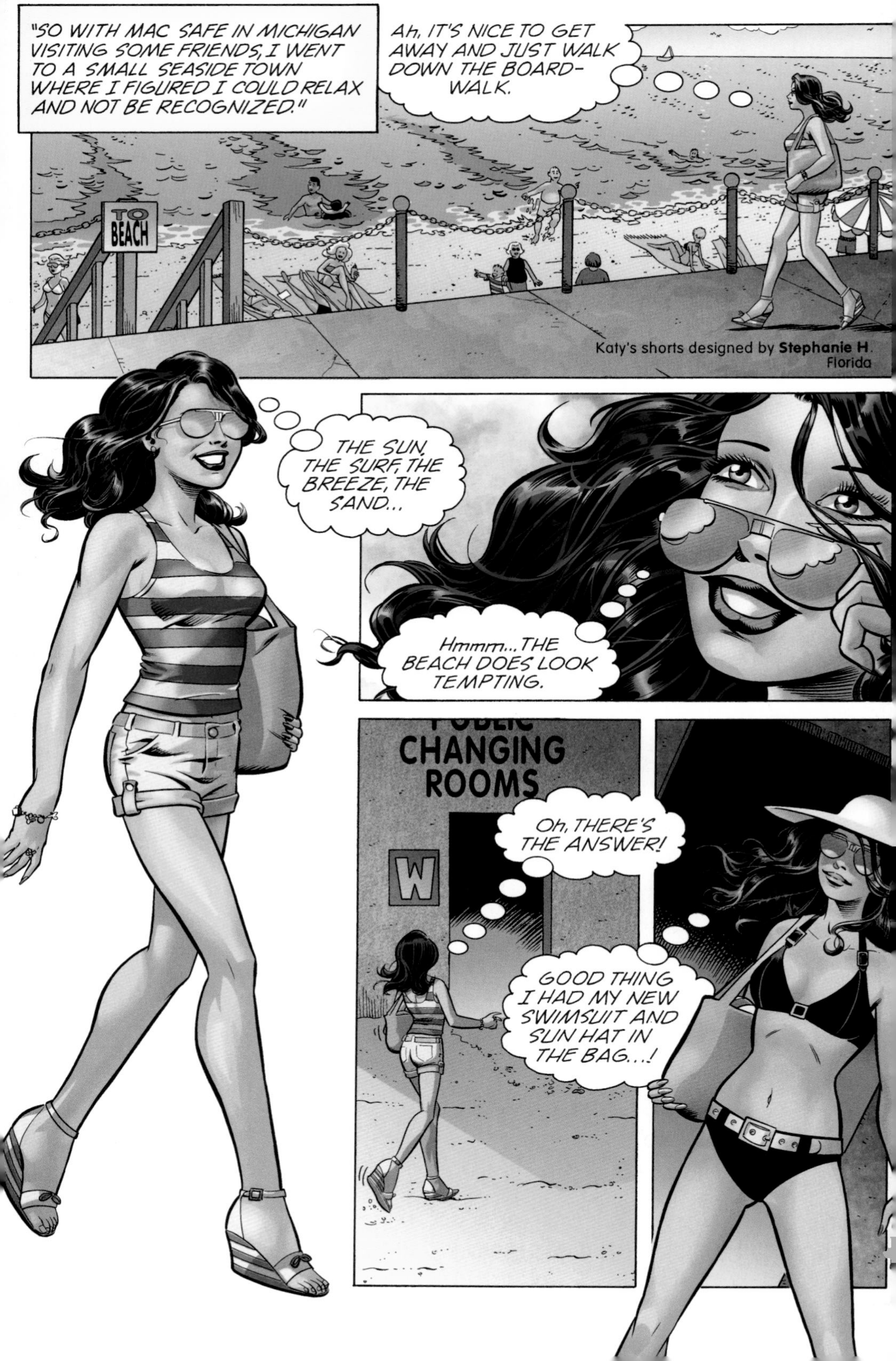
"SO WITH MAC SAFE IN MICHIGAN VISITING SOME FRIENDS, I WENT TO A SMALL SEASIDE TOWN WHERE I FIGURED I COULD RELAX AND NOT BE RECOGNIZED."
Ah, IT'S NICE TO GET AWAY AND JUST WALK DOWN THE BOARD-WALK.
TO BEACH
Katy's shorts designed by **Stephanie H**.
Florida
THE SUN, THE SURF, THE BREEZE, THE SAND...
Hmmm... THE BEACH DOES LOOK TEMPTING.
CHANGING ROOMS
W
Oh, THERE'S THE ANSWER!
GOOD THING I HAD MY NEW SWIMSUIT AND SUN HAT IN THE BAG...!

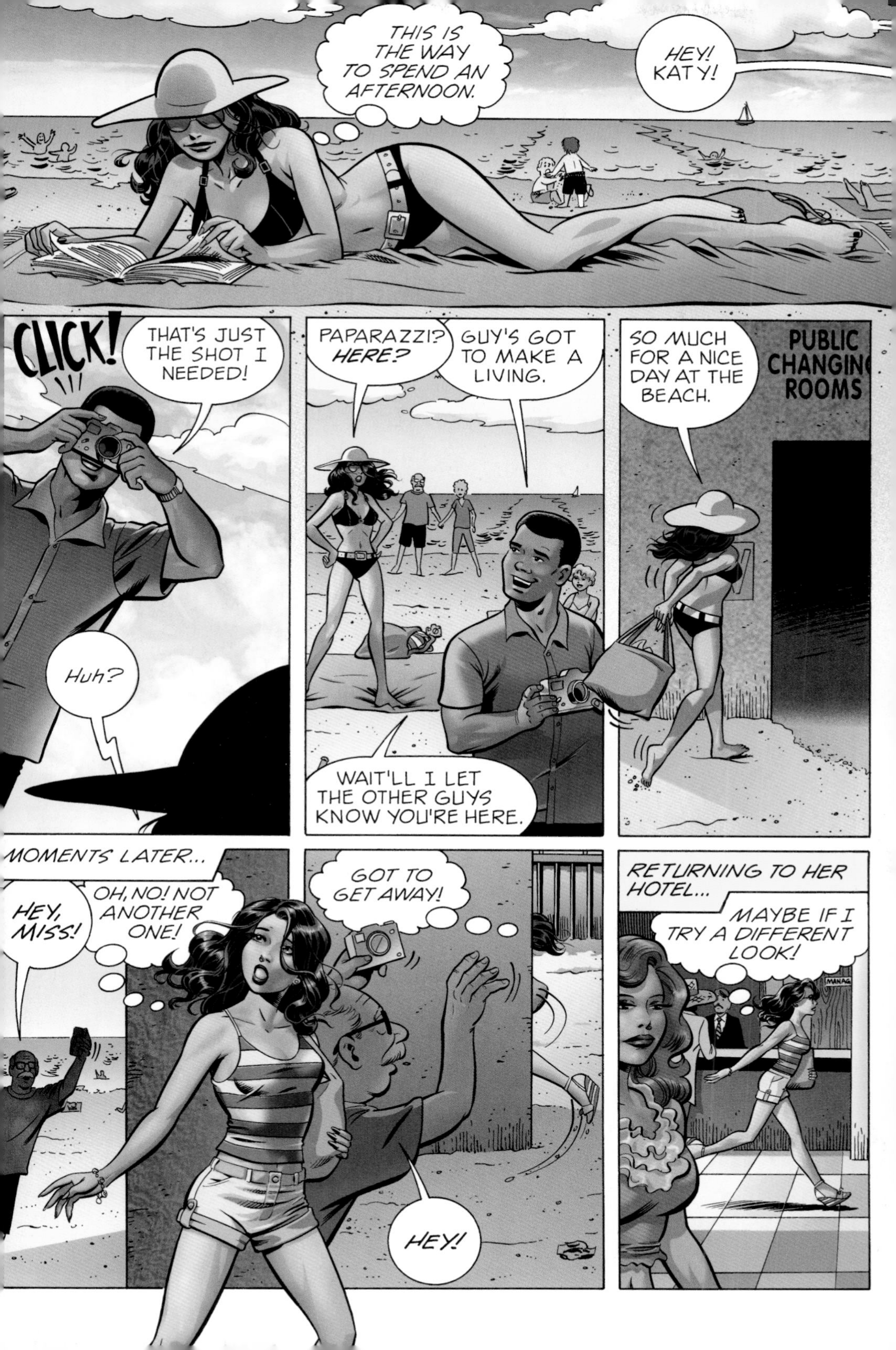
THIS IS THE WAY TO SPEND AN AFTERNOON.
HEY! KATY!
CLICK!
THAT'S JUST THE SHOT I NEEDED!
Huh?
PAPARAZZI? HERE?
GUY'S GOT TO MAKE A LIVING.
WAIT'LL I LET THE OTHER GUYS KNOW YOU'RE HERE.
SO MUCH FOR A NICE DAY AT THE BEACH.
PUBLIC CHANGING ROOMS
MOMENTS LATER...
HEY, MISS!
OH, NO! NOT ANOTHER ONE!
GOT TO GET AWAY!
HEY!
RETURNING TO HER HOTEL...
MAYBE IF I TRY A DIFFERENT LOOK!

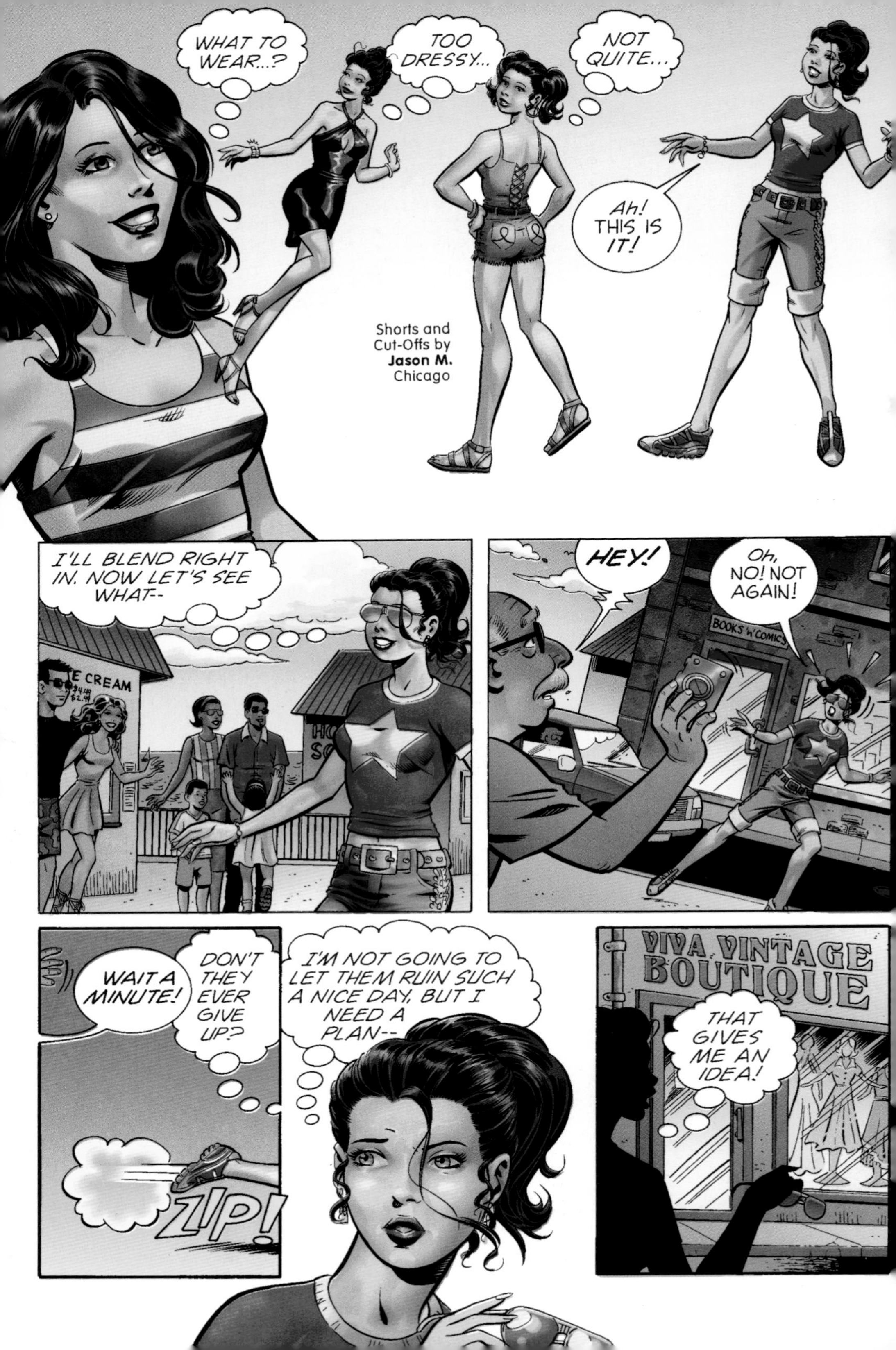
WHAT TO WEAR...?
TOO DRESSY...
NOT QUITE...
Ah! THIS IS IT!
Shorts and Cut-Offs by **Jason M.** Chicago
I'LL BLEND RIGHT IN. NOW LET'S SEE WHAT--
E CREAM
HEY!
Oh, NO! NOT AGAIN!
BOOKS 'N' COMICS
WAIT A MINUTE!
DON'T THEY EVER GIVE UP?
ZIP!
I'M NOT GOING TO LET THEM RUIN SUCH A NICE DAY, BUT I NEED A PLAN--
VIVA VINTAGE BOUTIQUE
THAT GIVES ME AN IDEA!

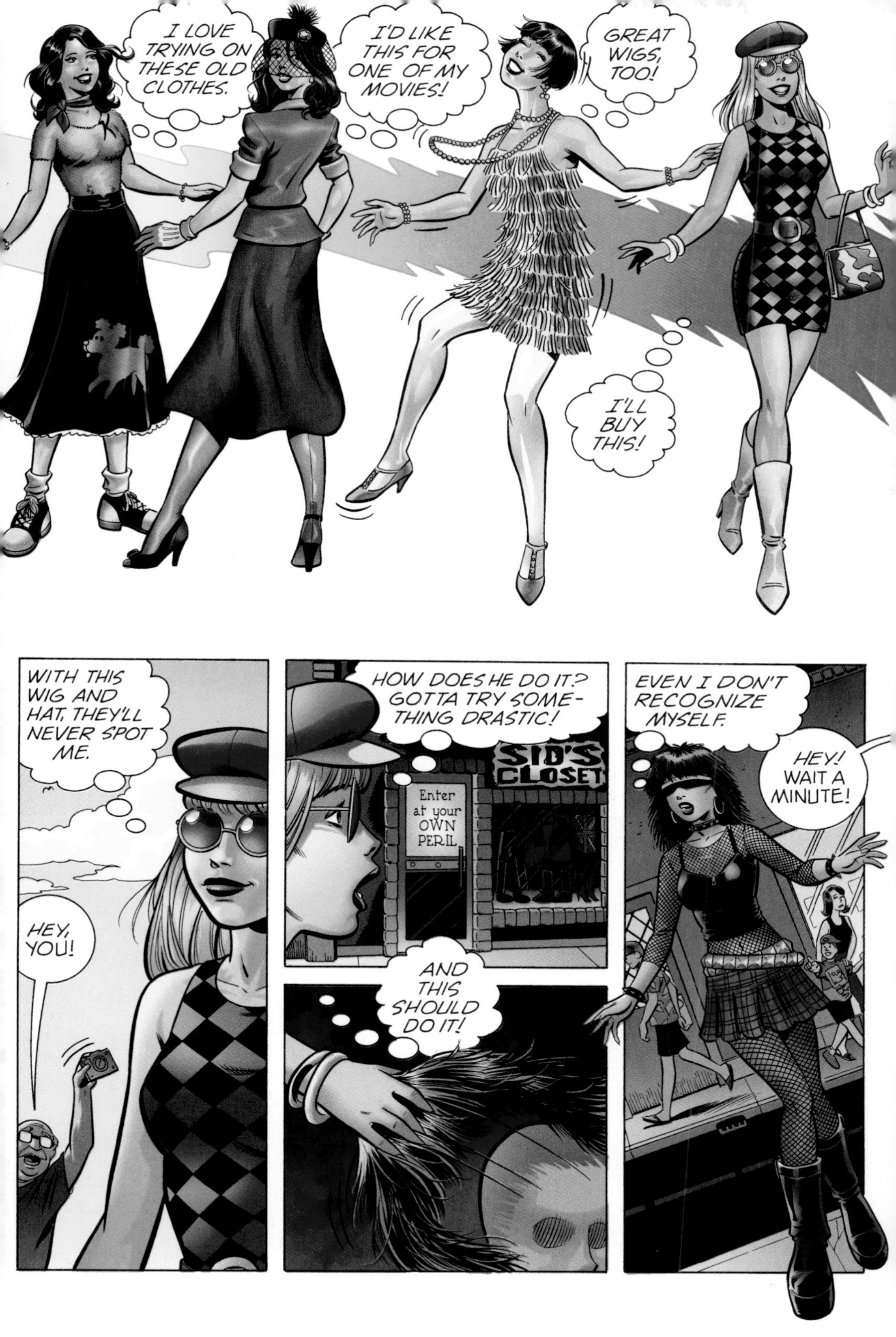
I LOVE TRYING ON THESE OLD CLOTHES.
I'D LIKE THIS FOR ONE OF MY MOVIES!
GREAT WIGS, TOO!
I'LL BUY THIS!
WITH THIS WIG AND HAT, THEY'LL NEVER SPOT ME.
HEY, YOU!
HOW DOES HE DO IT? GOTTA TRY SOME-THING DRASTIC!
SID'S CLOSET
Enter at your OWN PERIL
AND THIS SHOULD DO IT!
EVEN I DON'T RECOGNIZE MYSELF.
HEY! WAIT A MINUTE!

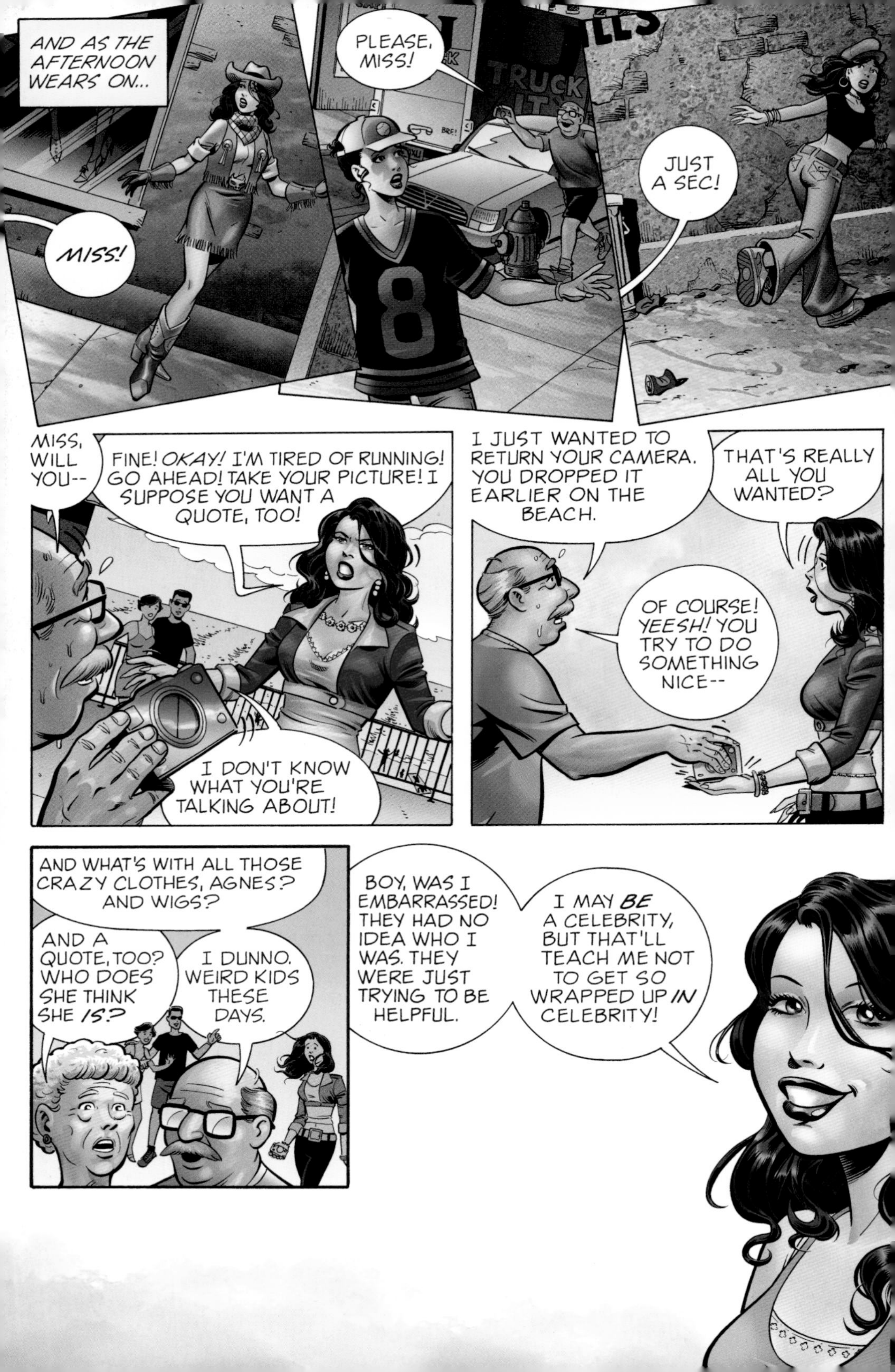

AND AS THE AFTERNOON WEARS ON...
MISS!
PLEASE, MISS!
JUST A SEC!
MISS, WILL YOU--
FINE! *OKAY!* I'M TIRED OF RUNNING! GO AHEAD! TAKE YOUR PICTURE! I SUPPOSE YOU WANT A QUOTE, TOO!
I DON'T KNOW WHAT YOU'RE TALKING ABOUT!
I JUST WANTED TO RETURN YOUR CAMERA. YOU DROPPED IT EARLIER ON THE BEACH.
THAT'S REALLY ALL YOU WANTED?
OF COURSE! *YEESH!* YOU TRY TO DO SOMETHING NICE--
AND WHAT'S WITH ALL THOSE CRAZY CLOTHES, AGNES? AND WIGS?
AND A QUOTE, TOO? WHO DOES SHE THINK SHE *IS?*
I DUNNO. WEIRD KIDS THESE DAYS.
BOY, WAS I EMBARRASSED! THEY HAD NO IDEA WHO I WAS. THEY WERE JUST TRYING TO BE HELPFUL.
I MAY *BE* A CELEBRITY, BUT THAT'LL TEACH ME NOT TO GET SO WRAPPED UP *IN* CELEBRITY!

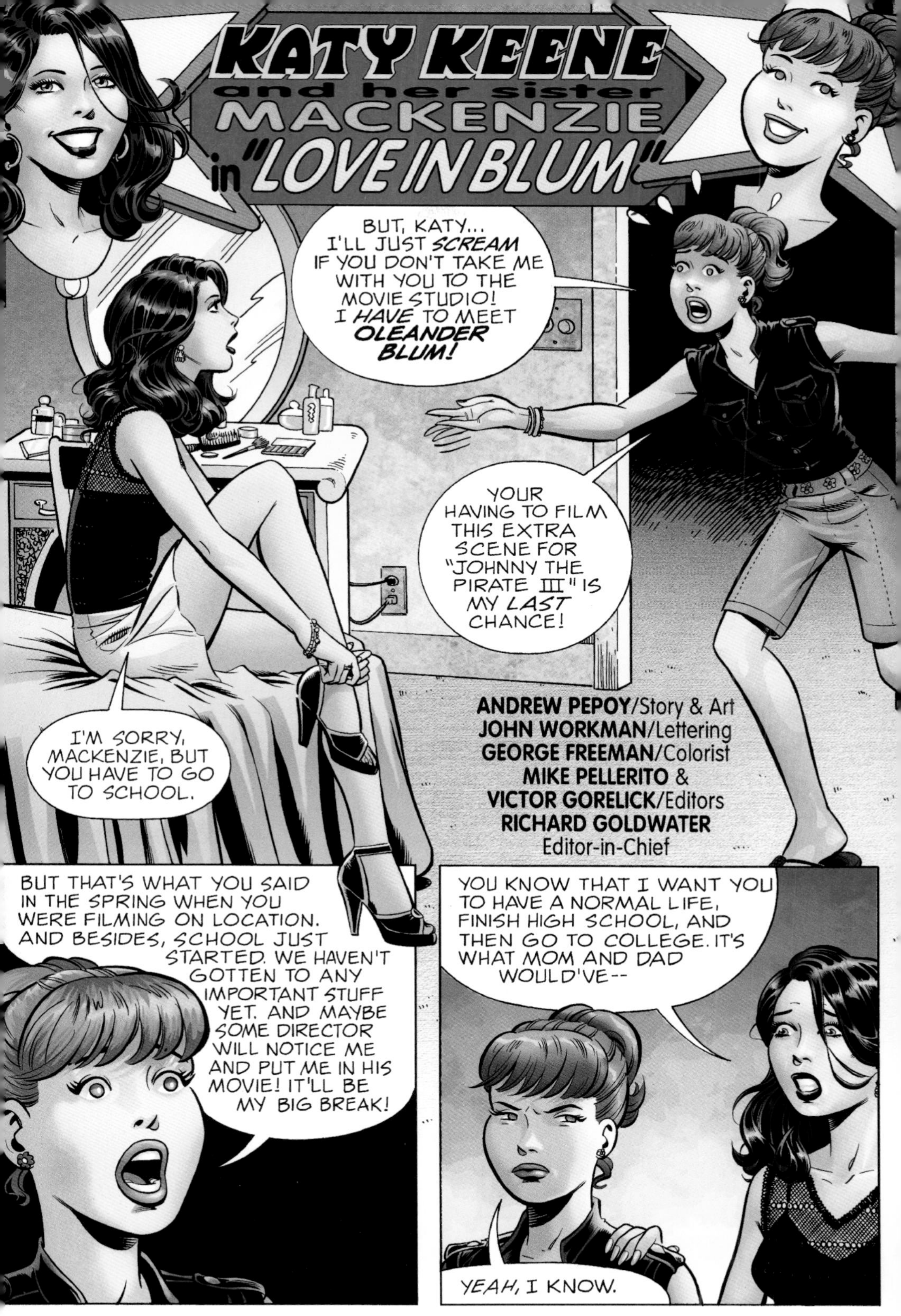
KATY KEENE and her sister MACKENZIE in "LOVE IN BLUM"
BUT, KATY... I'LL JUST SCREAM IF YOU DON'T TAKE ME WITH YOU TO THE MOVIE STUDIO! I HAVE TO MEET OLEANDER BLUM!
YOUR HAVING TO FILM THIS EXTRA SCENE FOR "JOHNNY THE PIRATE III" IS MY LAST CHANCE!
I'M SORRY, MACKENZIE, BUT YOU HAVE TO GO TO SCHOOL.
ANDREW PEPOY/Story & Art
JOHN WORKMAN/Lettering
GEORGE FREEMAN/Colorist
MIKE PELLERITO & VICTOR GORELICK/Editors
RICHARD GOLDWATER Editor-in-Chief
BUT THAT'S WHAT YOU SAID IN THE SPRING WHEN YOU WERE FILMING ON LOCATION. AND BESIDES, SCHOOL JUST STARTED. WE HAVEN'T GOTTEN TO ANY IMPORTANT STUFF YET. AND MAYBE SOME DIRECTOR WILL NOTICE ME AND PUT ME IN HIS MOVIE! IT'LL BE MY BIG BREAK!
YOU KNOW THAT I WANT YOU TO HAVE A NORMAL LIFE, FINISH HIGH SCHOOL, AND THEN GO TO COLLEGE. IT'S WHAT MOM AND DAD WOULD'VE--
YEAH, I KNOW.

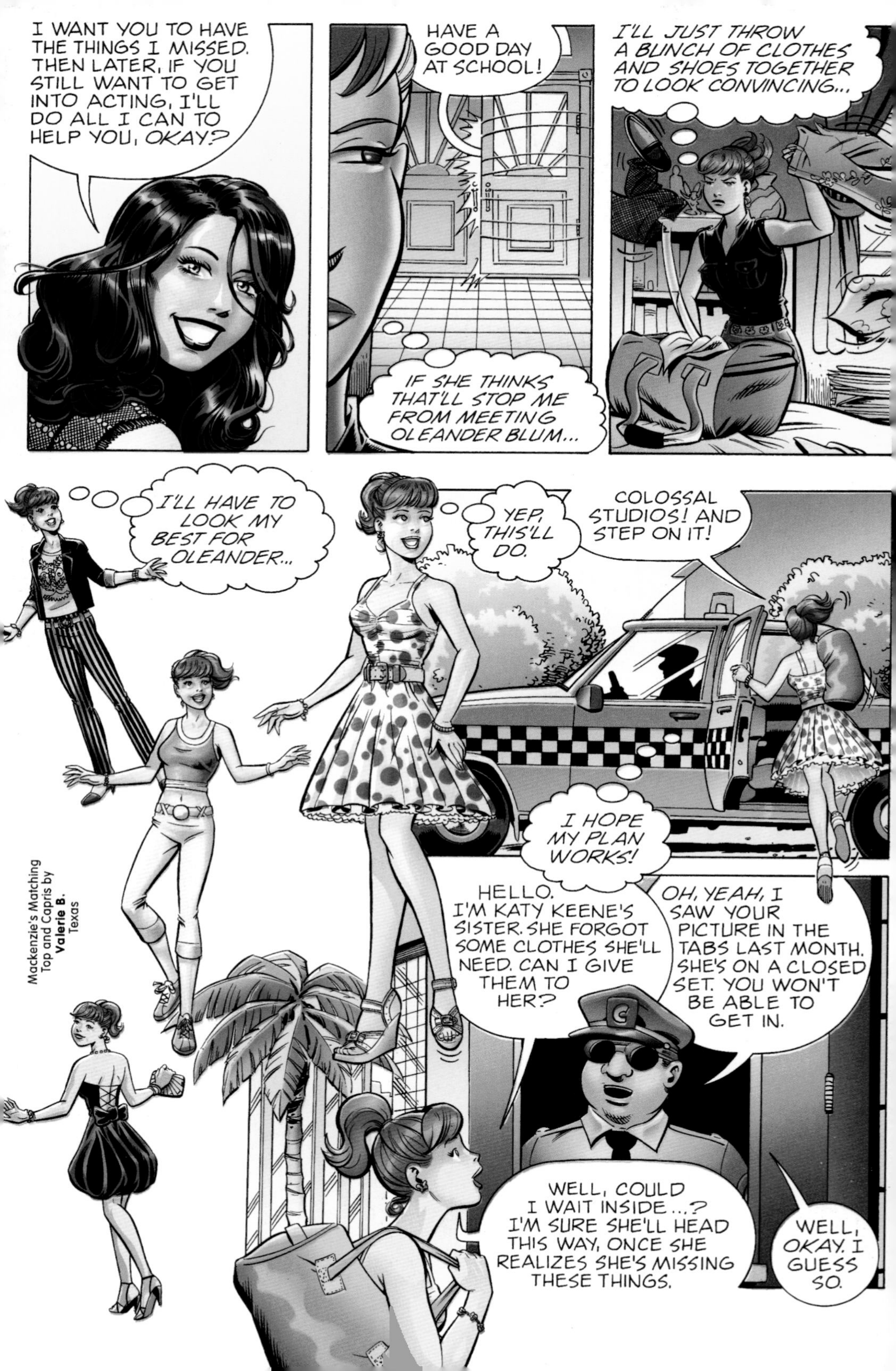
I WANT YOU TO HAVE THE THINGS I MISSED. THEN LATER, IF YOU STILL WANT TO GET INTO ACTING, I'LL DO ALL I CAN TO HELP YOU, OKAY?
HAVE A GOOD DAY AT SCHOOL!
IF SHE THINKS THAT'LL STOP ME FROM MEETING OLEANDER BLUM...
I'LL JUST THROW A BUNCH OF CLOTHES AND SHOES TOGETHER TO LOOK CONVINCING...
I'LL HAVE TO LOOK MY BEST FOR OLEANDER...
YEP, THIS'LL DO.
COLOSSAL STUDIOS! AND STEP ON IT!
I HOPE MY PLAN WORKS!
Mackenzie's Matching Top and Capris by Valerie B. Texas
HELLO. I'M KATY KEENE'S SISTER. SHE FORGOT SOME CLOTHES SHE'LL NEED. CAN I GIVE THEM TO HER?
OH, YEAH, I SAW YOUR PICTURE IN THE TABS LAST MONTH. SHE'S ON A CLOSED SET. YOU WON'T BE ABLE TO GET IN.
WELL, COULD I WAIT INSIDE...? I'M SURE SHE'LL HEAD THIS WAY, ONCE SHE REALIZES SHE'S MISSING THESE THINGS.
WELL, OKAY. I GUESS SO.

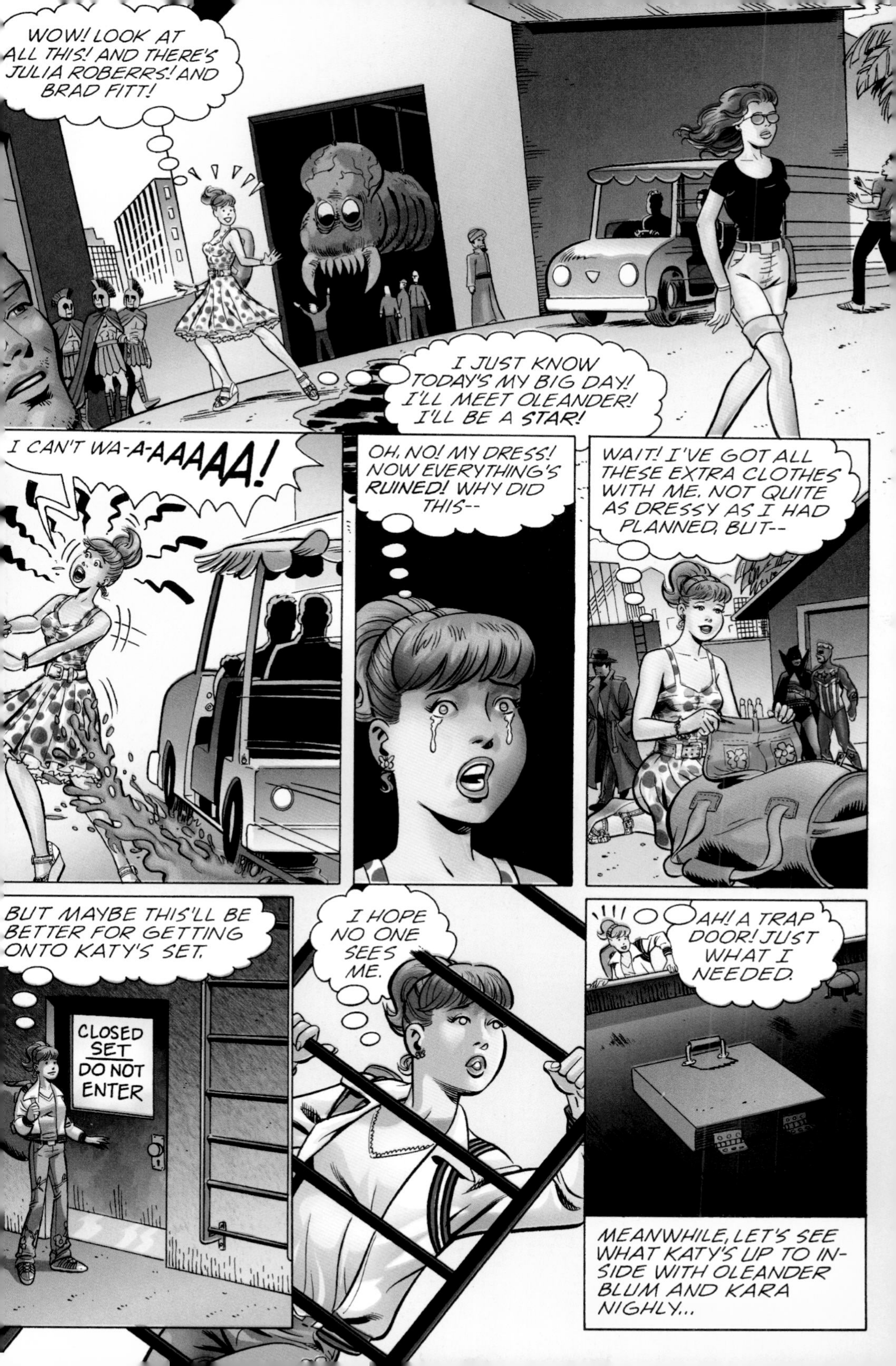
WOW! LOOK AT ALL THIS! AND THERE'S JULIA ROBERRS! AND BRAD FITT!
I JUST KNOW TODAY'S MY BIG DAY! I'LL MEET OLEANDER! I'LL BE A STAR!
I CAN'T WA-A-AAAAA!
OH, NO! MY DRESS! NOW EVERYTHING'S RUINED! WHY DID THIS--
WAIT! I'VE GOT ALL THESE EXTRA CLOTHES WITH ME. NOT QUITE AS DRESSY AS I HAD PLANNED, BUT--
BUT MAYBE THIS'LL BE BETTER FOR GETTING ONTO KATY'S SET.
CLOSED SET DO NOT ENTER
I HOPE NO ONE SEES ME.
AH! A TRAP DOOR! JUST WHAT I NEEDED.
MEANWHILE, LET'S SEE WHAT KATY'S UP TO IN-SIDE WITH OLEANDER BLUM AND KARA NIGHLY...

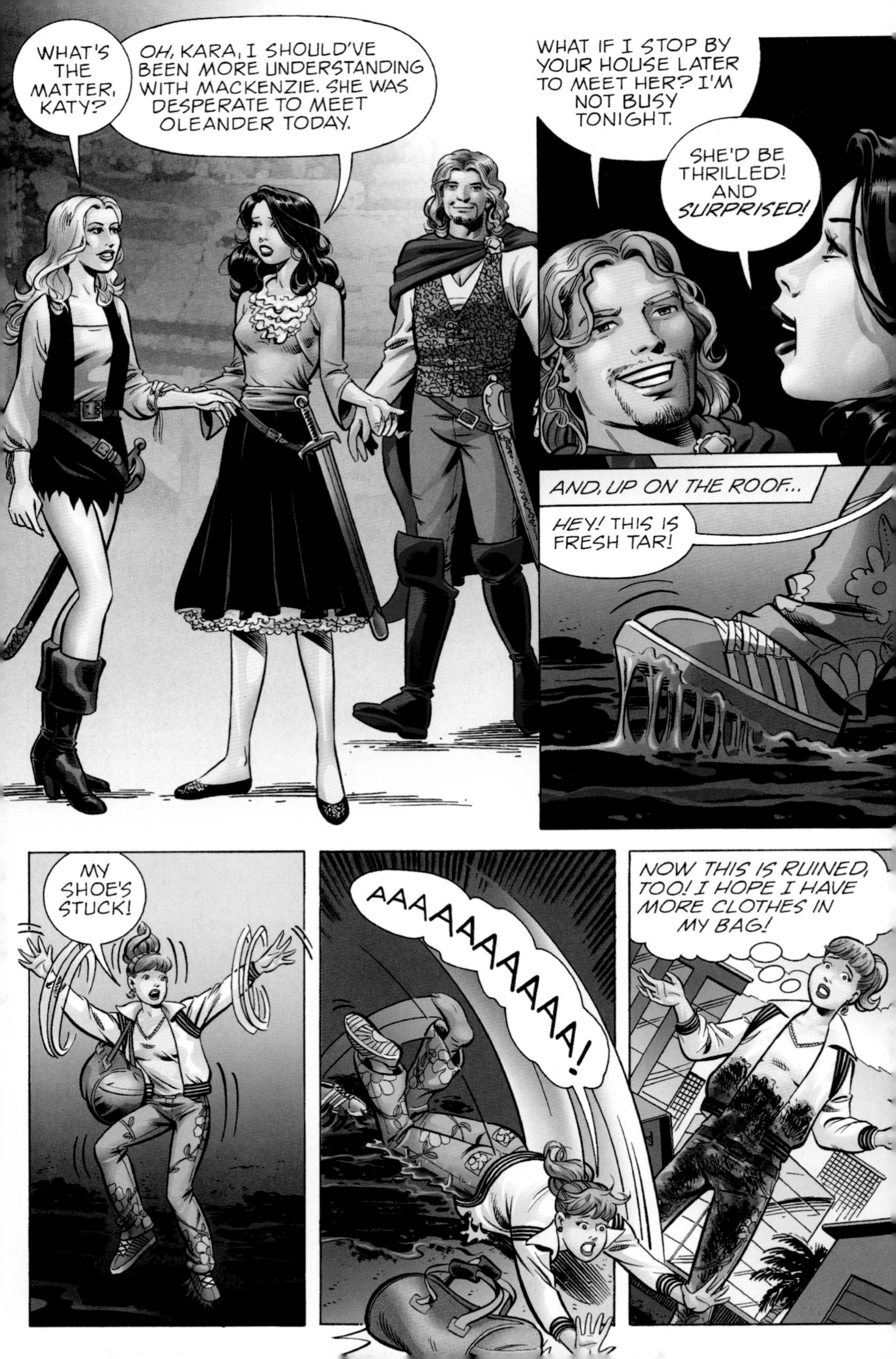
WHAT'S THE MATTER, KATY?
OH, KARA, I SHOULD'VE BEEN MORE UNDERSTANDING WITH MACKENZIE. SHE WAS DESPERATE TO MEET OLEANDER TODAY.
WHAT IF I STOP BY YOUR HOUSE LATER TO MEET HER? I'M NOT BUSY TONIGHT.
SHE'D BE THRILLED! AND SURPRISED!
AND, UP ON THE ROOF...
HEY! THIS IS FRESH TAR!
MY SHOE'S STUCK!
AAAAAAAAAAAA!
NOW THIS IS RUINED, TOO! I HOPE I HAVE MORE CLOTHES IN MY BAG!

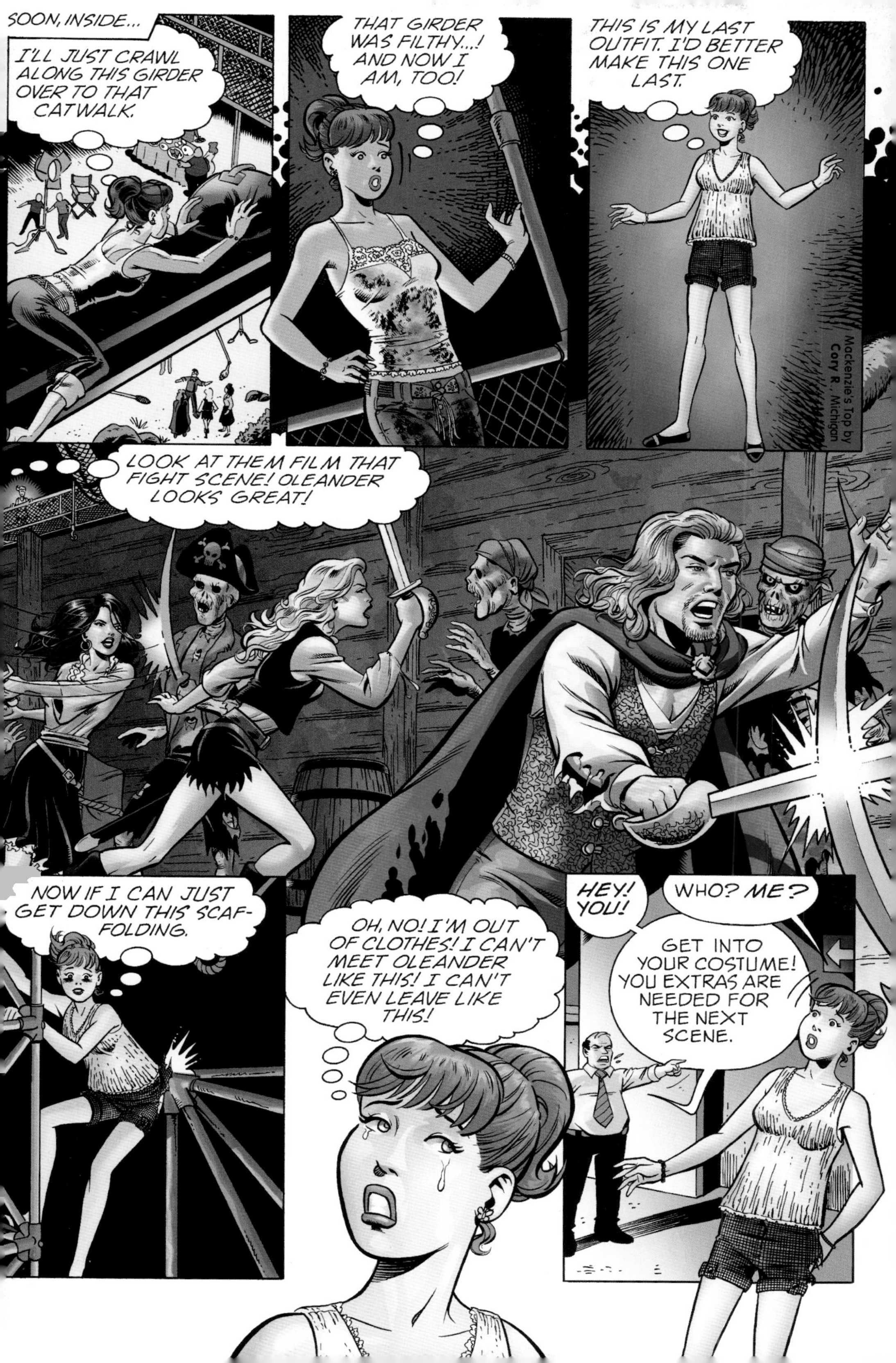
SOON, INSIDE...
I'LL JUST CRAWL ALONG THIS GIRDER OVER TO THAT CATWALK.
THAT GIRDER WAS FILTHY...! AND NOW I AM, TOO!
THIS IS MY LAST OUTFIT. I'D BETTER MAKE THIS ONE LAST.
Mackenzie's Top by Cory R., Michigan
LOOK AT THEM FILM THAT FIGHT SCENE! OLEANDER LOOKS GREAT!
NOW IF I CAN JUST GET DOWN THIS SCAF-FOLDING.
OH, NO! I'M OUT OF CLOTHES! I CAN'T MEET OLEANDER LIKE THIS! I CAN'T EVEN LEAVE LIKE THIS!
HEY! YOU!
WHO? ME?
GET INTO YOUR COSTUME! YOU EXTRAS ARE NEEDED FOR THE NEXT SCENE.

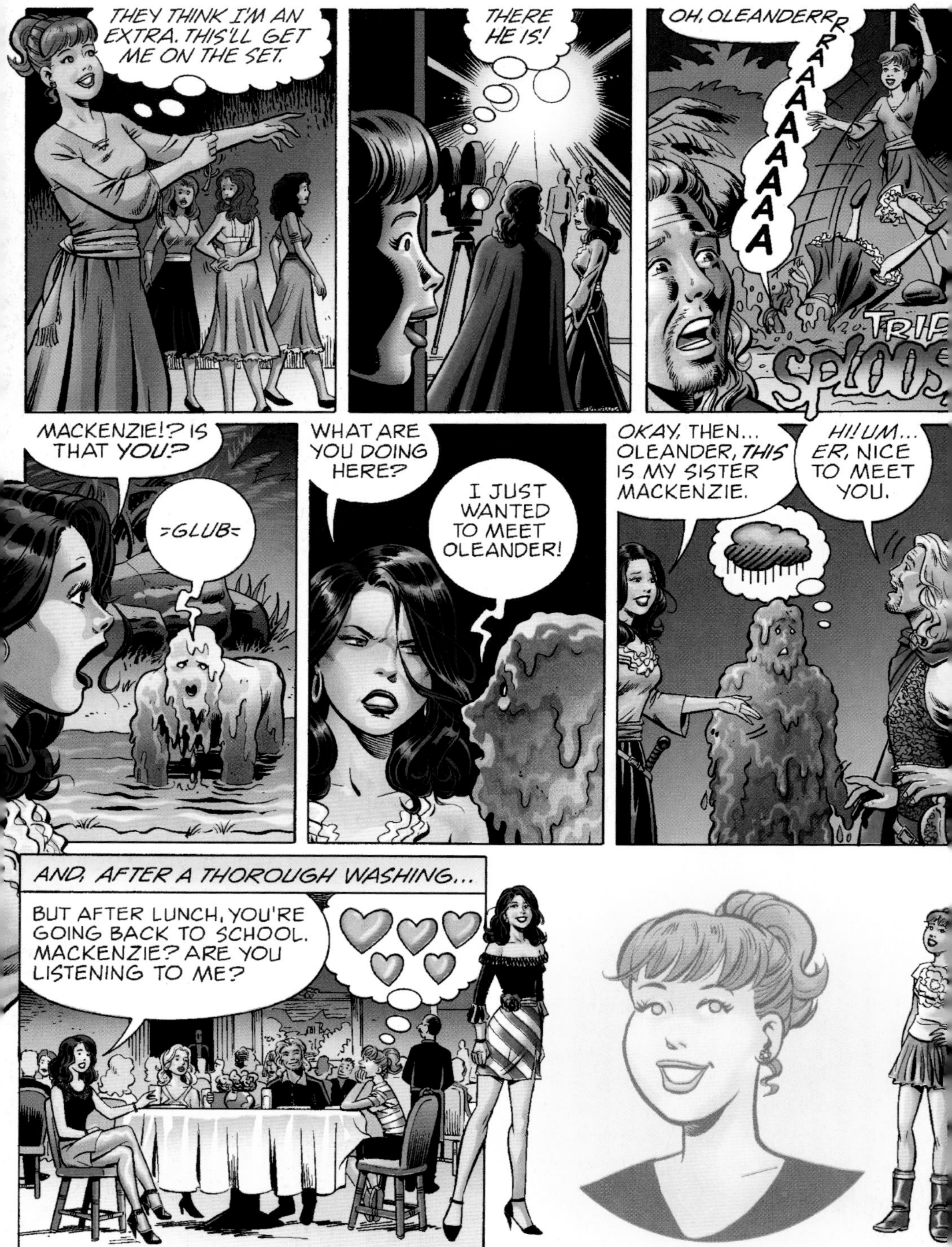
THEY THINK I'M AN EXTRA. THIS'LL GET ME ON THE SET.
THERE HE IS!
OH, OLEANDERRRRAAAAAAAAA
TRIP
SPLOOS
MACKENZIE!? IS THAT YOU?
=GLUB=
WHAT ARE YOU DOING HERE?
I JUST WANTED TO MEET OLEANDER!
OKAY, THEN... OLEANDER, THIS IS MY SISTER MACKENZIE.
HI! UM... ER, NICE TO MEET YOU.
AND, AFTER A THOROUGH WASHING...
BUT AFTER LUNCH, YOU'RE GOING BACK TO SCHOOL. MACKENZIE? ARE YOU LISTENING TO ME?

KATY KEENE

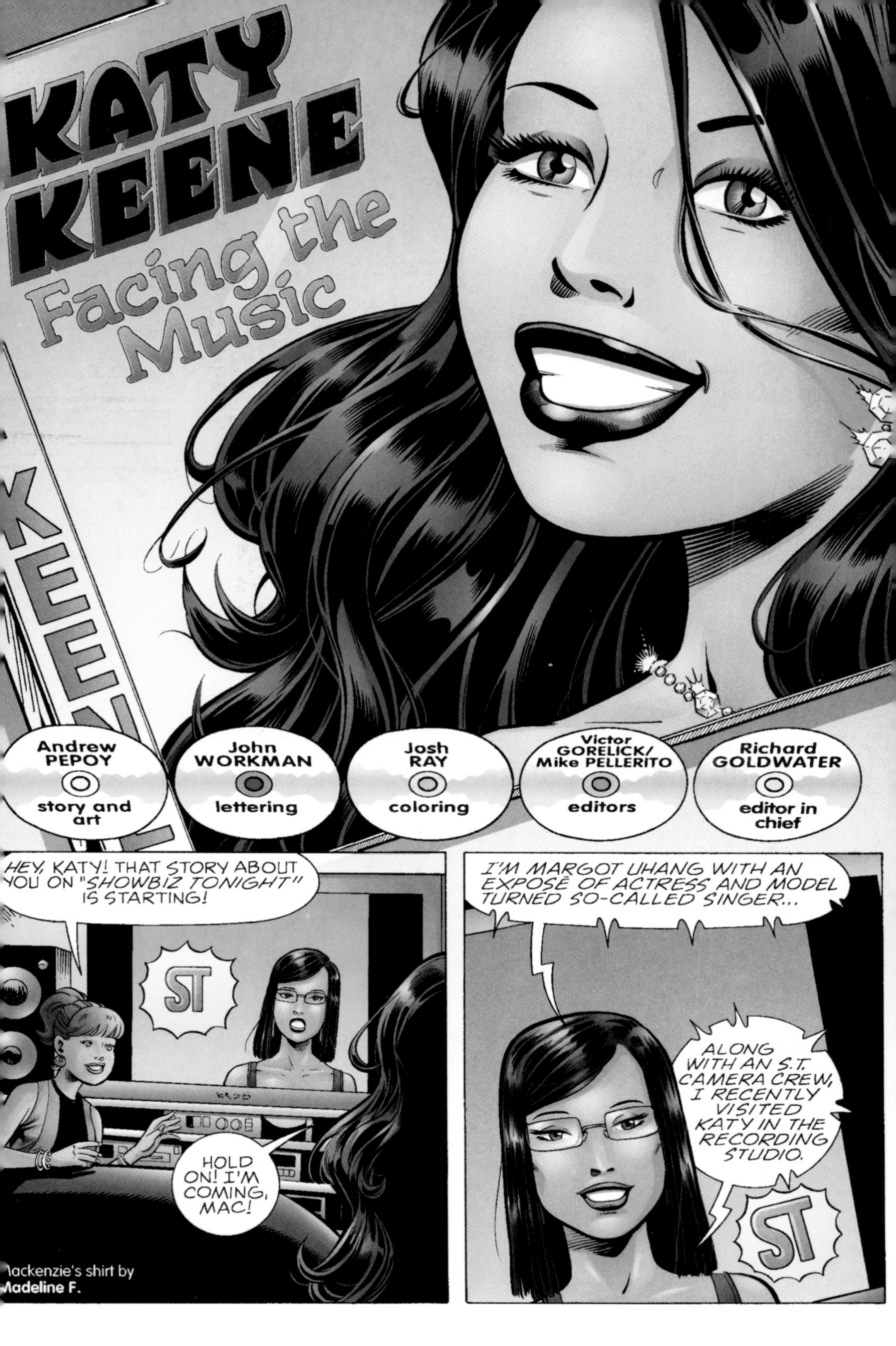
KATY KEENE
Facing the Music
Andrew PEPOY story and art
John WORKMAN lettering
Josh RAY coloring
Victor GORELICK/ Mike PELLERITO editors
Richard GOLDWATER editor in chief
HEY, KATY! THAT STORY ABOUT YOU ON "SHOWBIZ TONIGHT" IS STARTING!
HOLD ON! I'M COMING, MAC!
I'M MARGOT UHANG WITH AN EXPOSÉ OF ACTRESS AND MODEL TURNED SO-CALLED SINGER...
ALONG WITH AN S.T. CAMERA CREW, I RECENTLY VISITED KATY IN THE RECORDING STUDIO.
ackenzie's shirt by
adeline F.

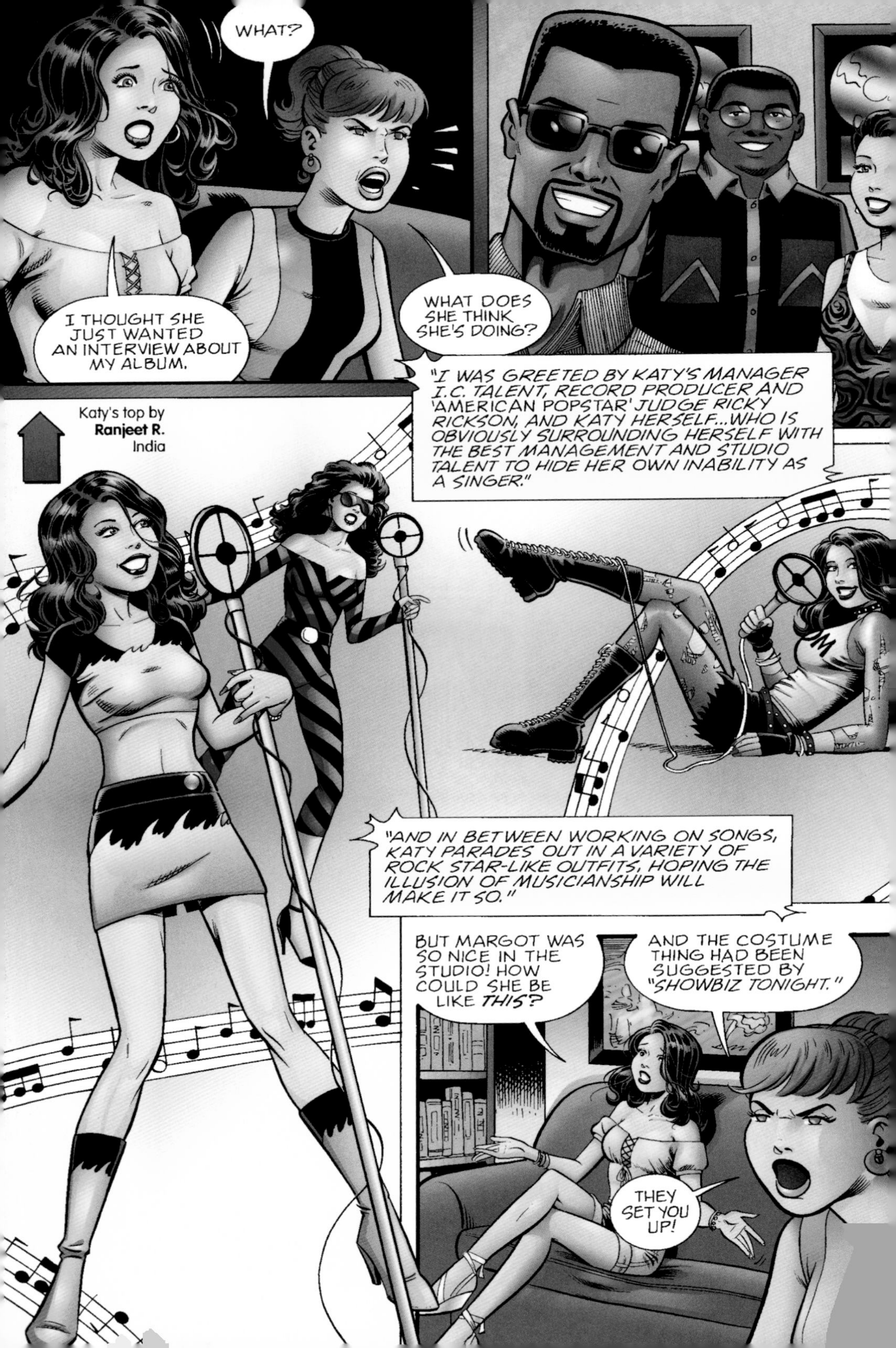
WHAT?
I THOUGHT SHE JUST WANTED AN INTERVIEW ABOUT MY ALBUM.
WHAT DOES SHE THINK SHE'S DOING?
"I WAS GREETED BY KATY'S MANAGER I.C. TALENT, RECORD PRODUCER AND 'AMERICAN POPSTAR' JUDGE RICKY RICKSON, AND KATY HERSELF...WHO IS OBVIOUSLY SURROUNDING HERSELF WITH THE BEST MANAGEMENT AND STUDIO TALENT TO HIDE HER OWN INABILITY AS A SINGER."
Katy's top by Ranjeet R. India
"AND IN BETWEEN WORKING ON SONGS, KATY PARADES OUT IN A VARIETY OF ROCK STAR-LIKE OUTFITS, HOPING THE ILLUSION OF MUSICIANSHIP WILL MAKE IT SO."
BUT MARGOT WAS SO NICE IN THE STUDIO! HOW COULD SHE BE LIKE THIS?
AND THE COSTUME THING HAD BEEN SUGGESTED BY "SHOWBIZ TONIGHT."
THEY SET YOU UP!

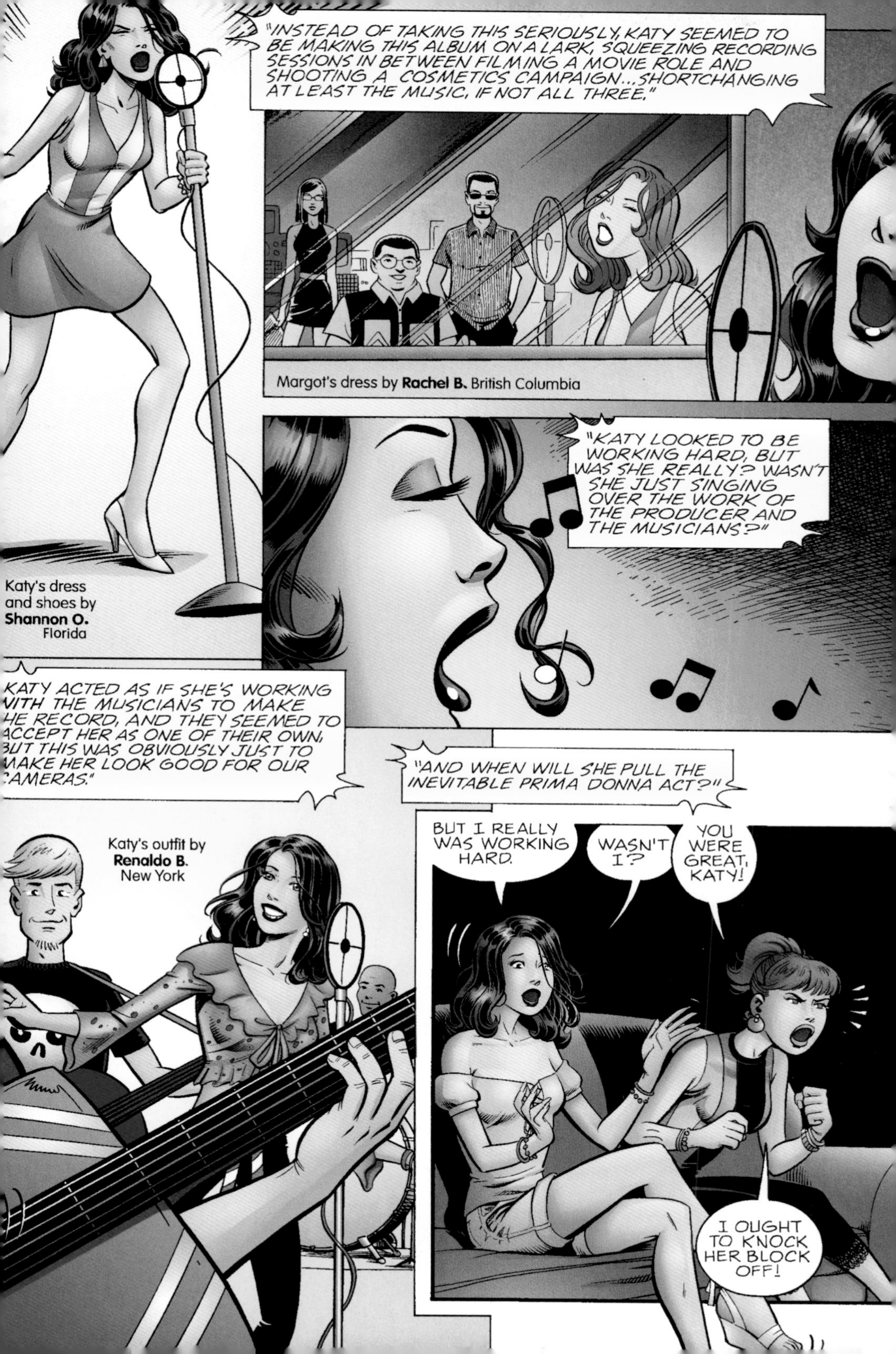
"INSTEAD OF TAKING THIS SERIOUSLY, KATY SEEMED TO BE MAKING THIS ALBUM ON A LARK, SQUEEZING RECORDING SESSIONS IN BETWEEN FILMING A MOVIE ROLE AND SHOOTING A COSMETICS CAMPAIGN... SHORTCHANGING AT LEAST THE MUSIC, IF NOT ALL THREE."
Margot's dress by **Rachel B.** British Columbia
Katy's dress and shoes by **Shannon O.** Florida
"KATY LOOKED TO BE WORKING HARD, BUT WAS SHE REALLY? WASN'T SHE JUST SINGING OVER THE WORK OF THE PRODUCER AND THE MUSICIANS?"
KATY ACTED AS IF SHE'S WORKING WITH THE MUSICIANS TO MAKE HE RECORD, AND THEY SEEMED TO ACCEPT HER AS ONE OF THEIR OWN, BUT THIS WAS OBVIOUSLY JUST TO MAKE HER LOOK GOOD FOR OUR CAMERAS."
Katy's outfit by **Renaldo B.** New York
"AND WHEN WILL SHE PULL THE INEVITABLE PRIMA DONNA ACT?"
BUT I REALLY WAS WORKING HARD.
WASN'T I?
YOU WERE GREAT, KATY!
I OUGHT TO KNOCK HER BLOCK OFF!

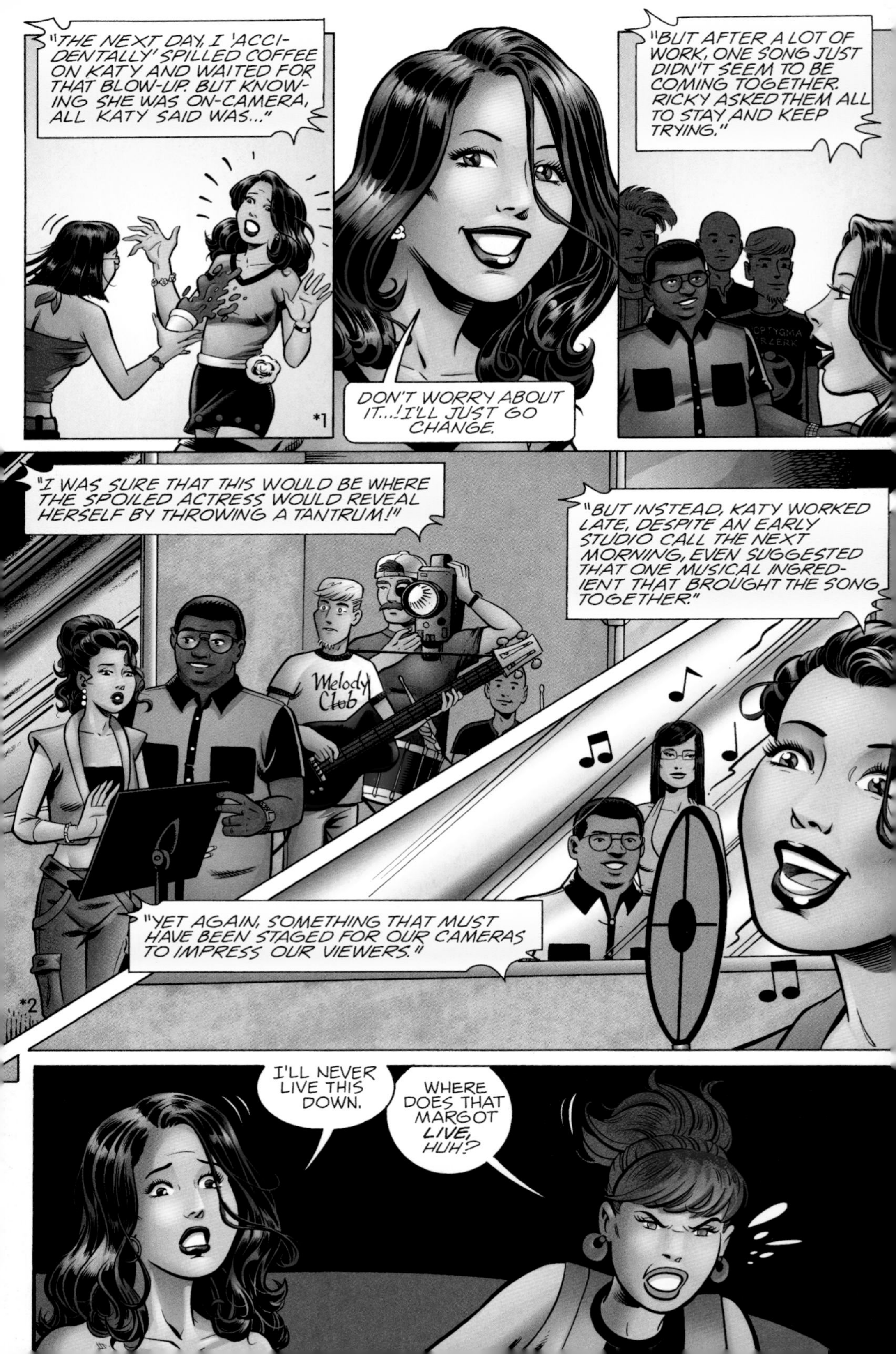
"THE NEXT DAY, I 'ACCIDENTALLY' SPILLED COFFEE ON KATY AND WAITED FOR THAT BLOW-UP. BUT KNOWING SHE WAS ON-CAMERA, ALL KATY SAID WAS..."
*1
DON'T WORRY ABOUT IT...! I'LL JUST GO CHANGE.
"BUT AFTER A LOT OF WORK, ONE SONG JUST DIDN'T SEEM TO BE COMING TOGETHER. RICKY ASKED THEM ALL TO STAY AND KEEP TRYING."
"I WAS SURE THAT THIS WOULD BE WHERE THE SPOILED ACTRESS WOULD REVEAL HERSELF BY THROWING A TANTRUM!"
Melody Club
"BUT INSTEAD, KATY WORKED LATE, DESPITE AN EARLY STUDIO CALL THE NEXT MORNING, EVEN SUGGESTED THAT ONE MUSICAL INGREDIENT THAT BROUGHT THE SONG TOGETHER."
"YET AGAIN, SOMETHING THAT MUST HAVE BEEN STAGED FOR OUR CAMERAS TO IMPRESS OUR VIEWERS."
*2
I'LL NEVER LIVE THIS DOWN.
WHERE DOES THAT MARGOT LIVE, HUH?

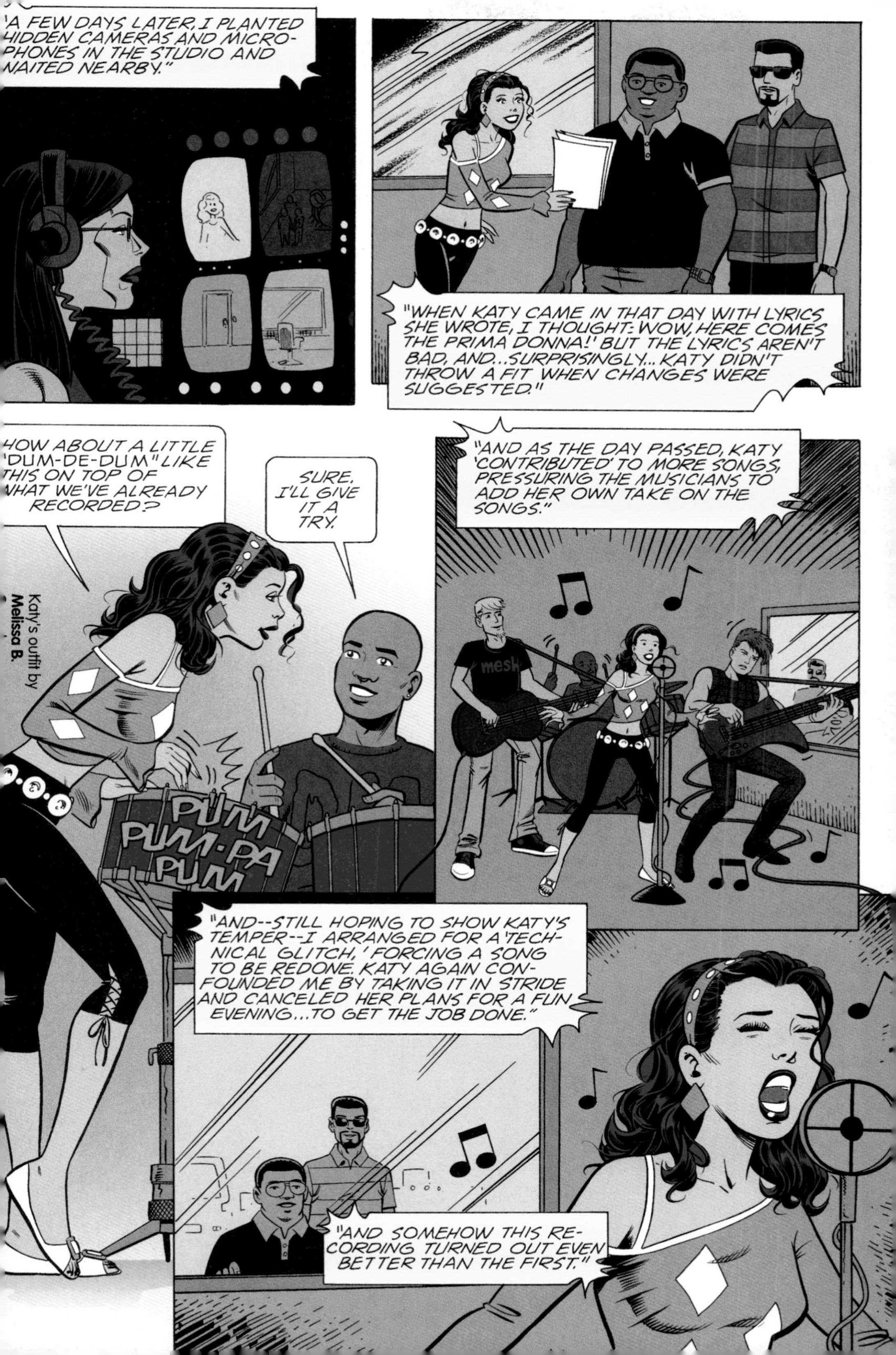
"A FEW DAYS LATER, I PLANTED HIDDEN CAMERAS AND MICROPHONES IN THE STUDIO AND WAITED NEARBY."
"WHEN KATY CAME IN THAT DAY WITH LYRICS SHE WROTE, I THOUGHT: 'WOW, HERE COMES THE PRIMA DONNA!' BUT THE LYRICS AREN'T BAD, AND...SURPRISINGLY... KATY DIDN'T THROW A FIT WHEN CHANGES WERE SUGGESTED."
HOW ABOUT A LITTLE "DUM-DE-DUM" LIKE THIS ON TOP OF WHAT WE'VE ALREADY RECORDED?
SURE. I'LL GIVE IT A TRY.
PUM PUM-PA PUM
"AND AS THE DAY PASSED, KATY 'CONTRIBUTED' TO MORE SONGS, PRESSURING THE MUSICIANS TO ADD HER OWN TAKE ON THE SONGS."
mesh
"AND--STILL HOPING TO SHOW KATY'S TEMPER--I ARRANGED FOR A 'TECHNICAL GLITCH,' FORCING A SONG TO BE REDONE. KATY AGAIN CONFOUNDED ME BY TAKING IT IN STRIDE AND CANCELED HER PLANS FOR A FUN EVENING...TO GET THE JOB DONE."
"AND SOMEHOW THIS RECORDING TURNED OUT EVEN BETTER THAN THE FIRST."
Katy's outfit by Melissa B.

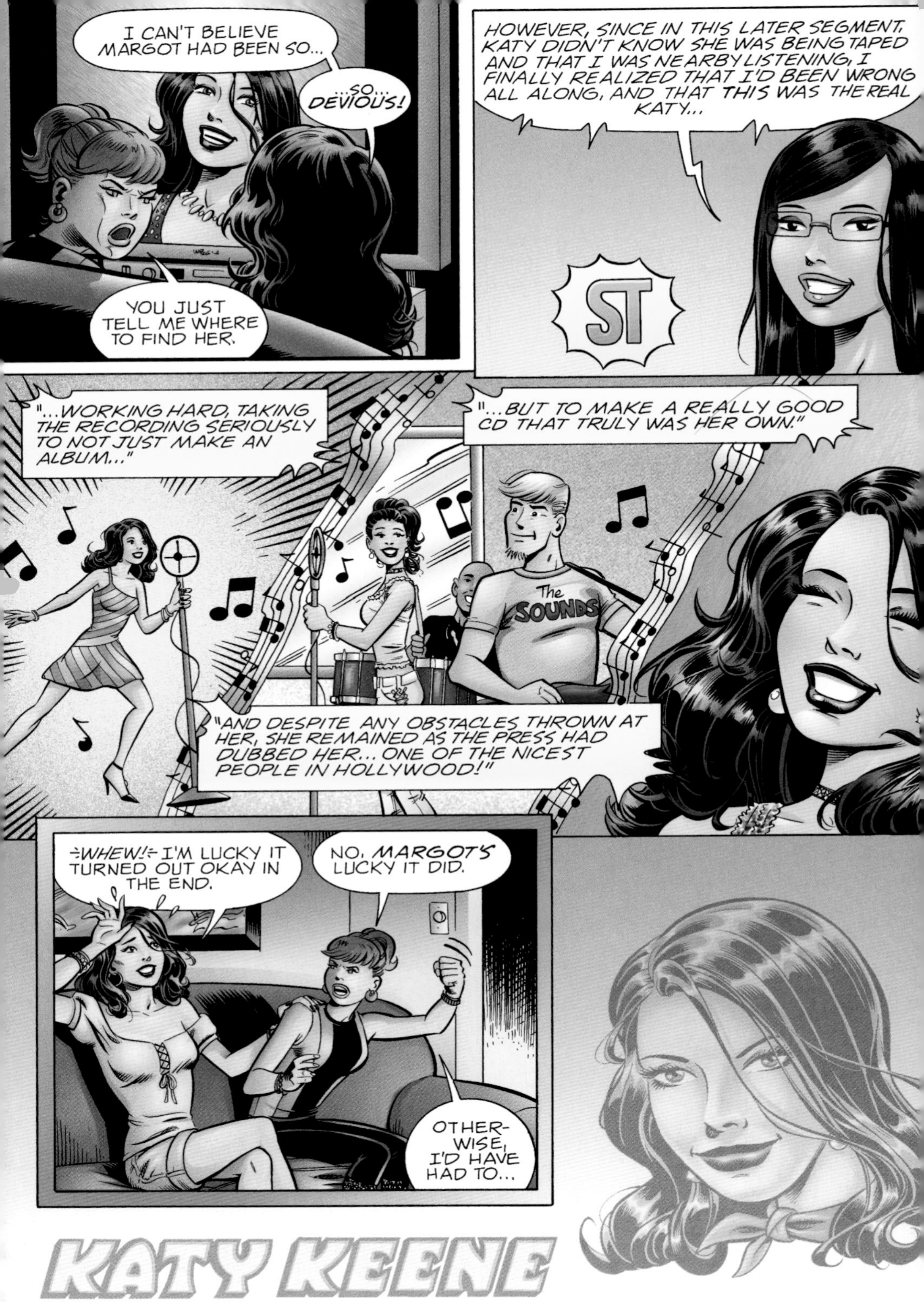
I CAN'T BELIEVE MARGOT HAD BEEN SO...
...SO... DEVIOUS!
YOU JUST TELL ME WHERE TO FIND HER.
HOWEVER, SINCE IN THIS LATER SEGMENT, KATY DIDN'T KNOW SHE WAS BEING TAPED AND THAT I WAS NEARBY LISTENING, I FINALLY REALIZED THAT I'D BEEN WRONG ALL ALONG, AND THAT THIS WAS THE REAL KATY...
ST
"...WORKING HARD, TAKING THE RECORDING SERIOUSLY TO NOT JUST MAKE AN ALBUM..."
"...BUT TO MAKE A REALLY GOOD CD THAT TRULY WAS HER OWN."
The SOUNDS
"AND DESPITE ANY OBSTACLES THROWN AT HER, SHE REMAINED AS THE PRESS HAD DUBBED HER... ONE OF THE NICEST PEOPLE IN HOLLYWOOD!"
=WHEW!= I'M LUCKY IT TURNED OUT OKAY IN THE END.
NO, MARGOT'S LUCKY IT DID.
OTHER-WISE, I'D HAVE HAD TO...
KATY KEENE

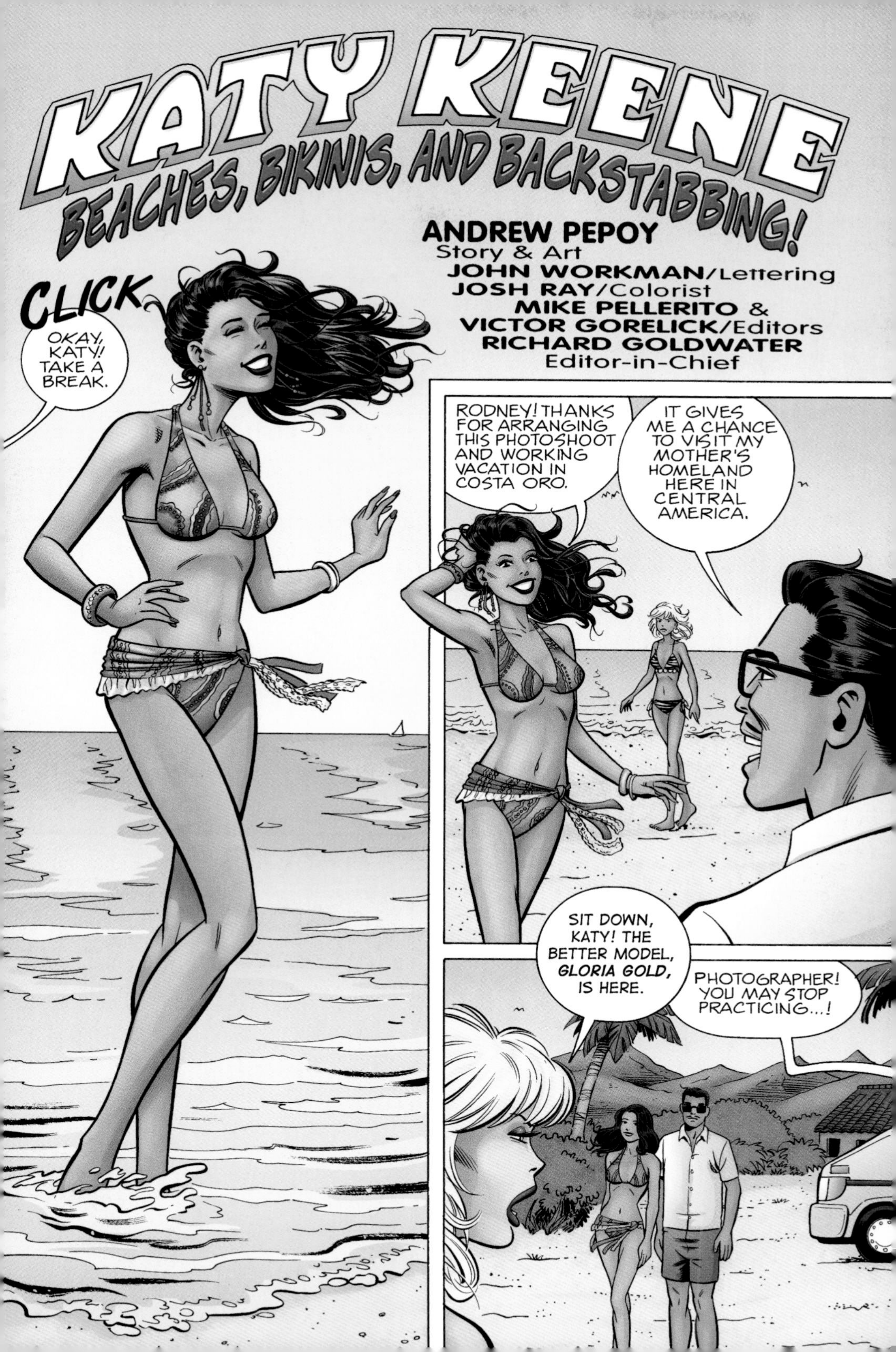
KATY KEENE
BEACHES, BIKINIS, AND BACKSTABBING!
ANDREW PEPOY
Story & Art
JOHN WORKMAN/Lettering
JOSH RAY/Colorist
MIKE PELLERITO &
VICTOR GORELICK/Editors
RICHARD GOLDWATER
Editor-in-Chief
CLICK
OKAY, KATY! TAKE A BREAK.
RODNEY! THANKS FOR ARRANGING THIS PHOTOSHOOT AND WORKING VACATION IN COSTA ORO.
IT GIVES ME A CHANCE TO VISIT MY MOTHER'S HOMELAND HERE IN CENTRAL AMERICA.
SIT DOWN, KATY! THE BETTER MODEL, GLORIA GOLD, IS HERE.
PHOTOGRAPHER! YOU MAY STOP PRACTICING...!

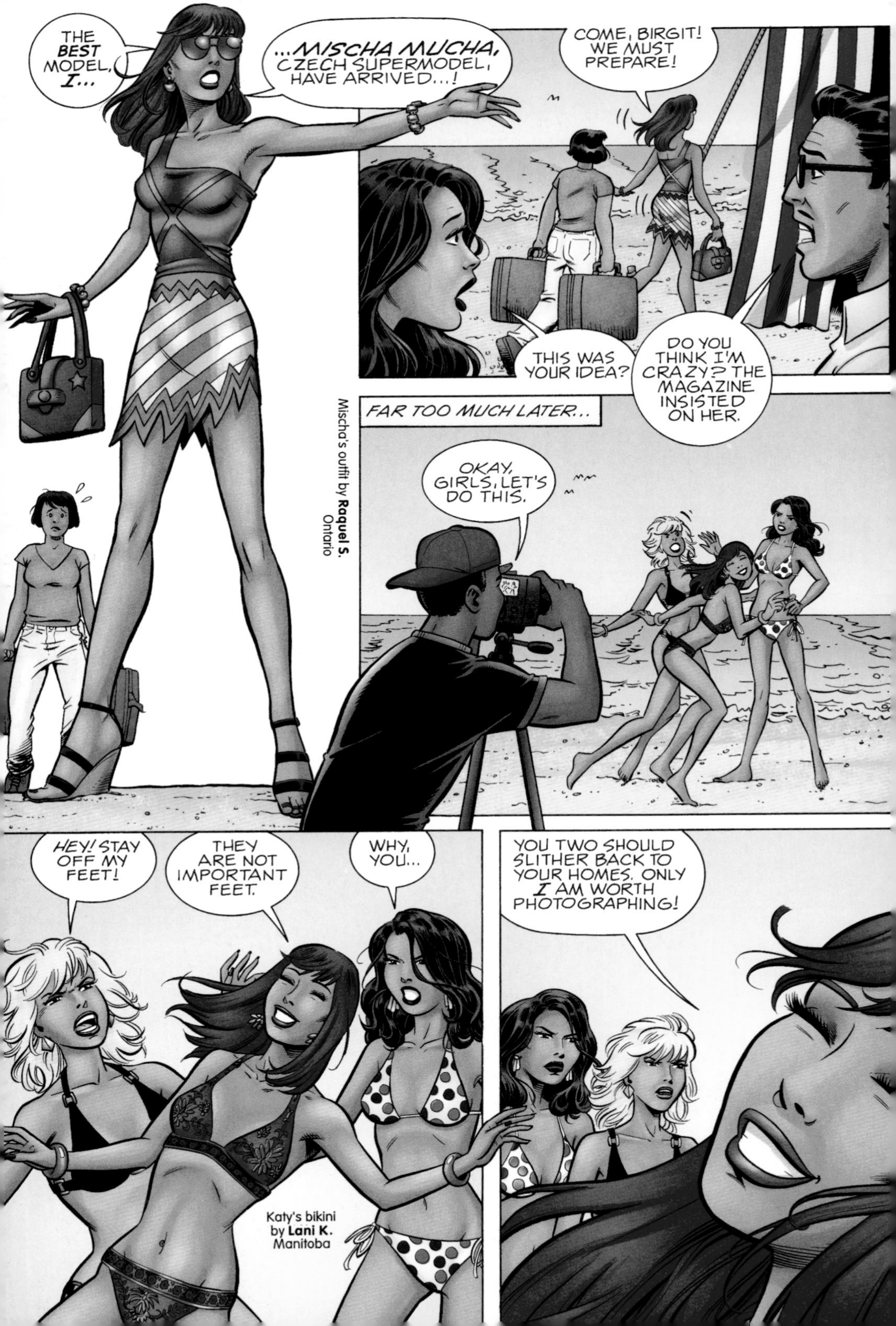
THE BEST MODEL, I...
...MISCHA MUCHA, CZECH SUPERMODEL, HAVE ARRIVED...!
COME, BIRGIT! WE MUST PREPARE!
THIS WAS YOUR IDEA?
DO YOU THINK I'M CRAZY? THE MAGAZINE INSISTED ON HER.
Mischa's outfit by Raquel S. Ontario
FAR TOO MUCH LATER...
OKAY, GIRLS, LET'S DO THIS.
HEY! STAY OFF MY FEET!
THEY ARE NOT IMPORTANT FEET.
WHY, YOU...
Katy's bikini by Lani K. Manitoba
YOU TWO SHOULD SLITHER BACK TO YOUR HOMES. ONLY I AM WORTH PHOTOGRAPHING!

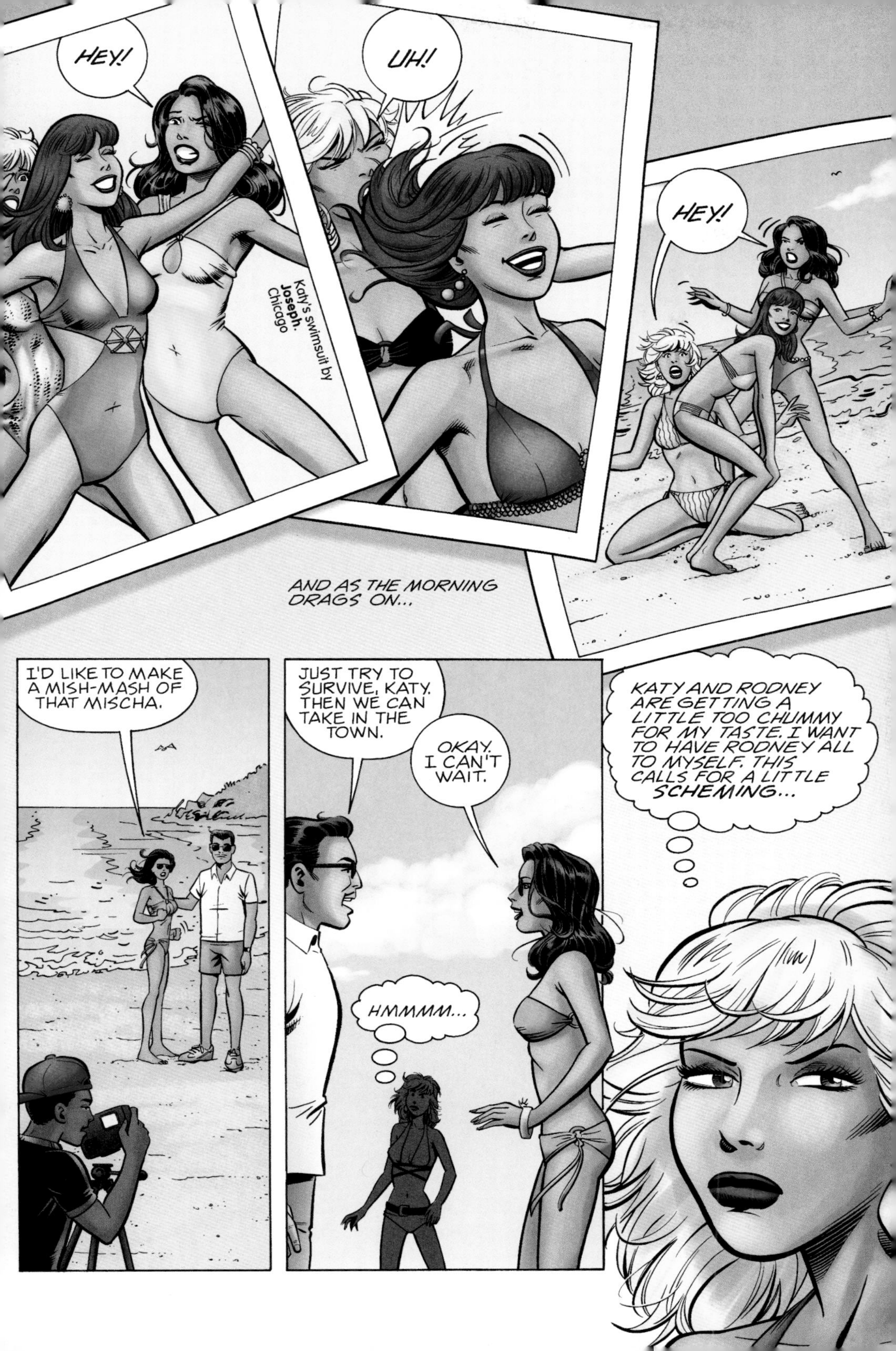
HEY!
Katy's swimsuit by Joseph. Chicago
UH!
HEY!
AND AS THE MORNING DRAGS ON...
I'D LIKE TO MAKE A MISH-MASH OF THAT MISCHA.
JUST TRY TO SURVIVE, KATY. THEN WE CAN TAKE IN THE TOWN.
OKAY. I CAN'T WAIT.
HMMMM...
KATY AND RODNEY ARE GETTING A LITTLE TOO CHUMMY FOR MY TASTE. I WANT TO HAVE RODNEY ALL TO MYSELF. THIS CALLS FOR A LITTLE SCHEMING...

THOSE TWO PEASANTS ARE GETTINK IN THE VAY UF MY BEAUTY...

...UND MY VAY TO THE AMERICAN MILLIONAIRE.

I MUST SCHEME...

LATER, AS THE PHOTO-GRAPHER SORTS THE DAY'S PHOTOS ON HIS COMPUTER IN HIS VAN...

WHAT A DAY! THAT MISCHA IS MORE TROUBLE--

CLICK

Mischa's bikini by **Karen H.** Illinois

RING! RING!

HELLO?

I VILL NOT BE TREATED THIS VAY!

I'LL BE RIGHT OVER.

CLICK CLICK

SOUNDS LIKE SHE'S AT IT AGAIN!

UH-OH! THE PHOTO-GRAPHER DOESN'T NOTICE THAT IN HIS HURRY, HE'S DROPPED THE PHOTOS INTO THE WRONG FOLDERS.

MISCHA   68-412

GLORIA   X-9

KATY

GROUP

HE'S GONE! NOW'S MY CHANCE!

IF I CAN DELETE ALL OF KATY'S PICS, SHE'LL HAVE TO RESHOOT THEM-- LEAVING RODNEY TO *ME!*

CLICK CLICK

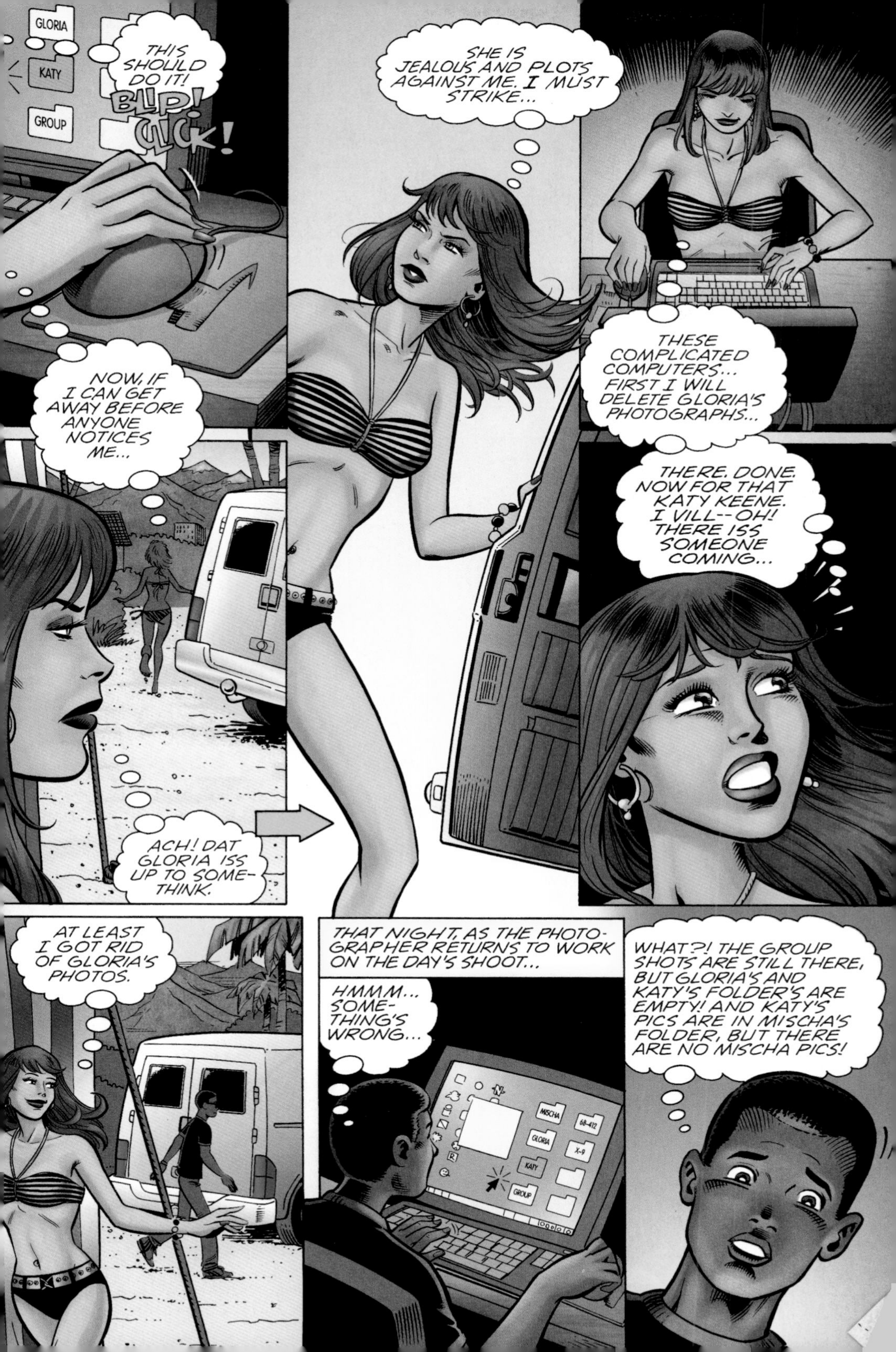
GLORIA
KATY
GROUP
THIS SHOULD DO IT!
BLIP! CLICK!
NOW, IF I CAN GET AWAY BEFORE ANYONE NOTICES ME...
SHE IS JEALOUS AND PLOTS AGAINST ME. I MUST STRIKE...
ACH! DAT GLORIA ISS UP TO SOME-THINK.
THESE COMPLICATED COMPUTERS... FIRST I WILL DELETE GLORIA'S PHOTOGRAPHS...
THERE. DONE. NOW FOR THAT KATY KEENE. I VILL--OH! THERE ISS SOMEONE COMING...
AT LEAST I GOT RID OF GLORIA'S PHOTOS.
THAT NIGHT, AS THE PHOTOGRAPHER RETURNS TO WORK ON THE DAY'S SHOOT...
HMMM... SOME-THING'S WRONG...
MISCHA
68-412
GLORIA
X-9
KATY
GROUP
WHAT?! THE GROUP SHOTS ARE STILL THERE, BUT GLORIA'S AND KATY'S FOLDER'S ARE EMPTY! AND KATY'S PICS ARE IN MISCHA'S FOLDER, BUT THERE ARE NO MISCHA PICS!

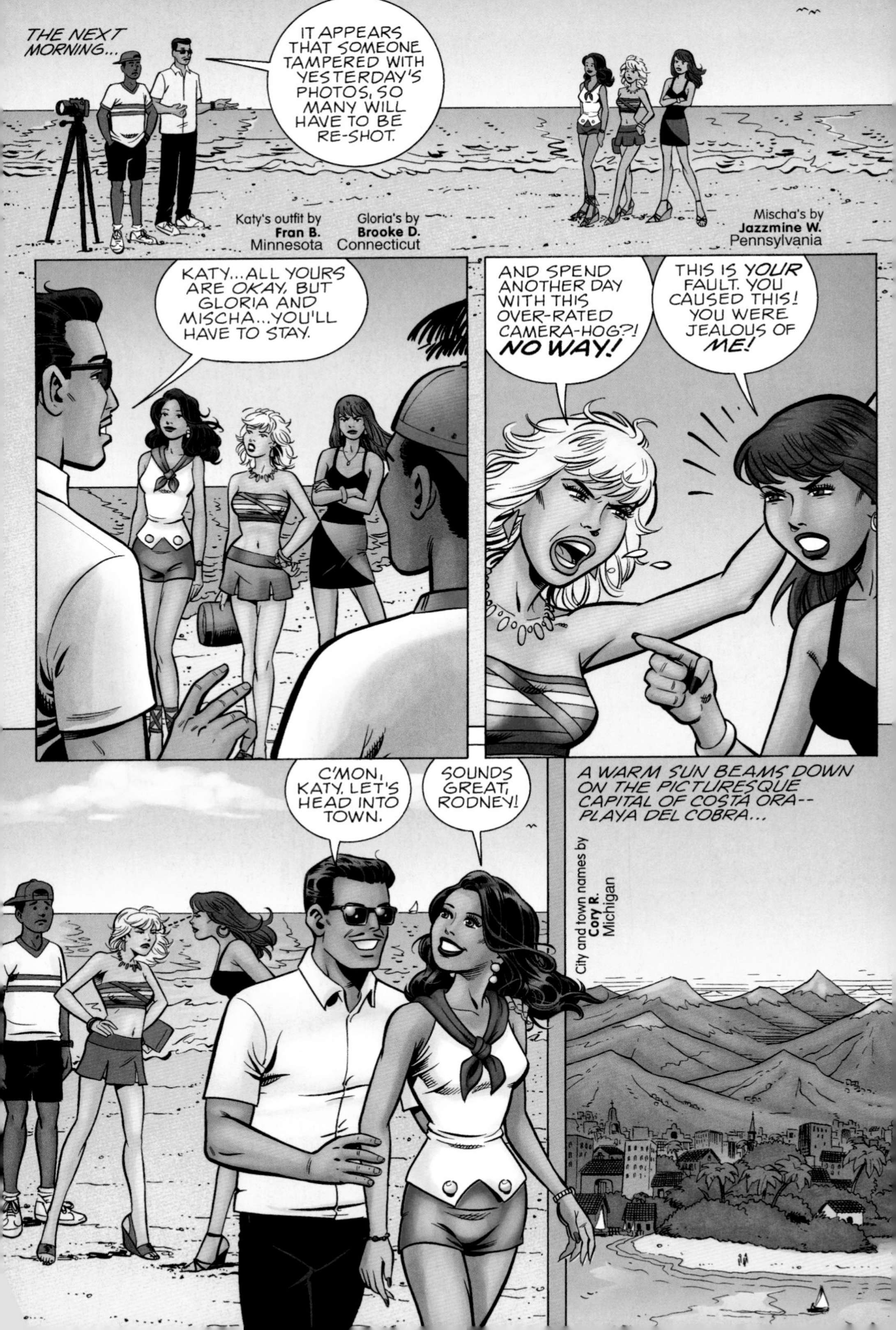
THE NEXT MORNING...
IT APPEARS THAT SOMEONE TAMPERED WITH YESTERDAY'S PHOTOS, SO MANY WILL HAVE TO BE RE-SHOT.
Katy's outfit by Fran B. Minnesota
Gloria's by Brooke D. Connecticut
Mischa's by Jazzmine W. Pennsylvania
KATY...ALL YOURS ARE OKAY, BUT GLORIA AND MISCHA...YOU'LL HAVE TO STAY.
AND SPEND ANOTHER DAY WITH THIS OVER-RATED CAMERA-HOG?! NO WAY!
THIS IS YOUR FAULT. YOU CAUSED THIS! YOU WERE JEALOUS OF ME!
C'MON, KATY. LET'S HEAD INTO TOWN.
SOUNDS GREAT, RODNEY!
A WARM SUN BEAMS DOWN ON THE PICTURESQUE CAPITAL OF COSTA ORA-- PLAYA DEL COBRA...
City and town names by Cory R. Michigan

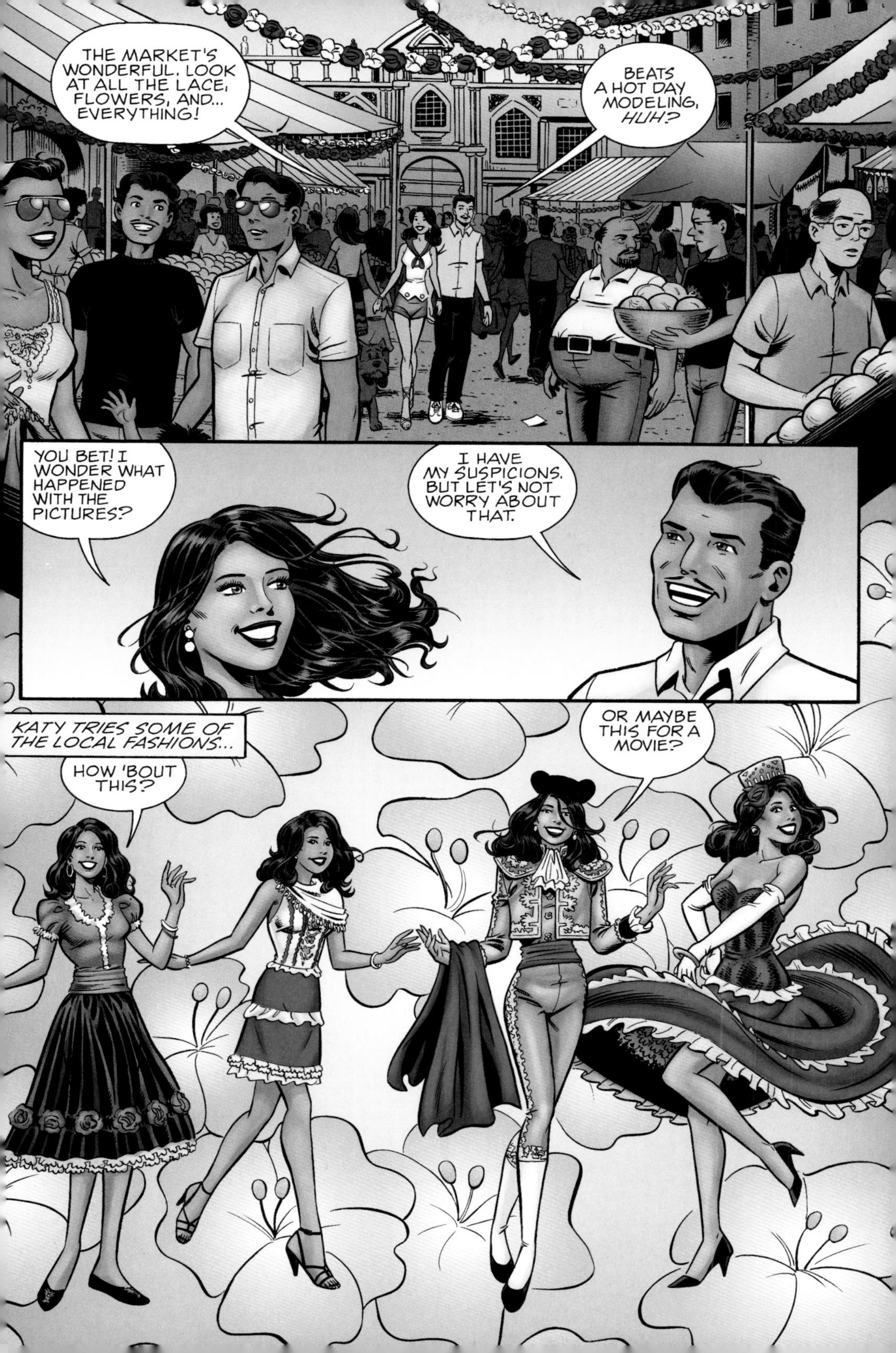
THE MARKET'S WONDERFUL. LOOK AT ALL THE LACE, FLOWERS, AND... EVERYTHING!
BEATS A HOT DAY MODELING, HUH?
YOU BET! I WONDER WHAT HAPPENED WITH THE PICTURES?
I HAVE MY SUSPICIONS. BUT LET'S NOT WORRY ABOUT THAT.
KATY TRIES SOME OF THE LOCAL FASHIONS...
HOW 'BOUT THIS?
OR MAYBE THIS FOR A MOVIE?

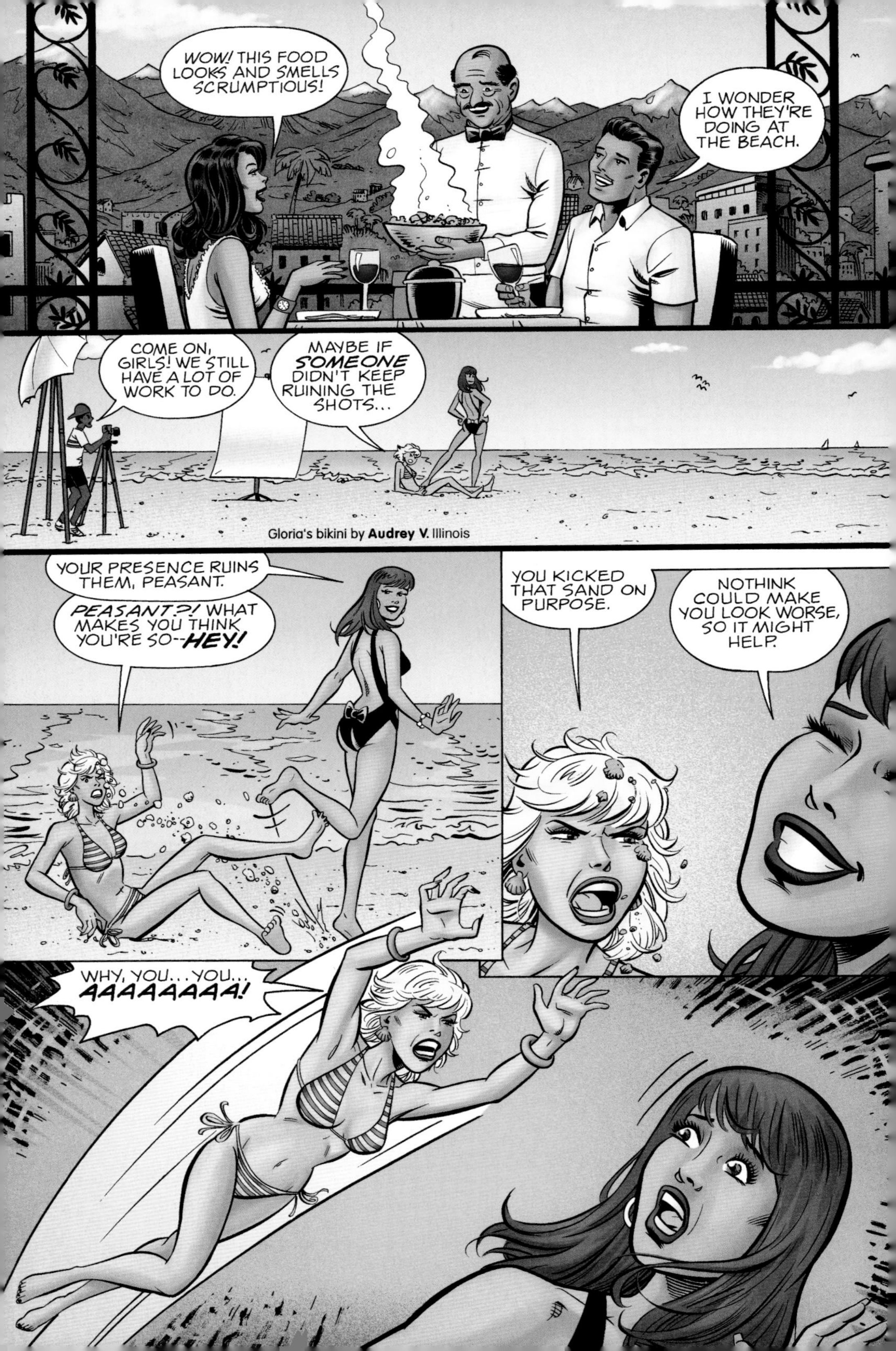
WOW! THIS FOOD LOOKS AND SMELLS SCRUMPTIOUS!
I WONDER HOW THEY'RE DOING AT THE BEACH.
COME ON, GIRLS! WE STILL HAVE A LOT OF WORK TO DO.
MAYBE IF SOMEONE DIDN'T KEEP RUINING THE SHOTS...
YOUR PRESENCE RUINS THEM, PEASANT.
PEASANT?! WHAT MAKES YOU THINK YOU'RE SO--HEY!
YOU KICKED THAT SAND ON PURPOSE.
NOTHINK COULD MAKE YOU LOOK WORSE, SO IT MIGHT HELP.
WHY, YOU... YOU... AAAAAAAA!

Gloria's bikini by **Audrey V.** Illinois

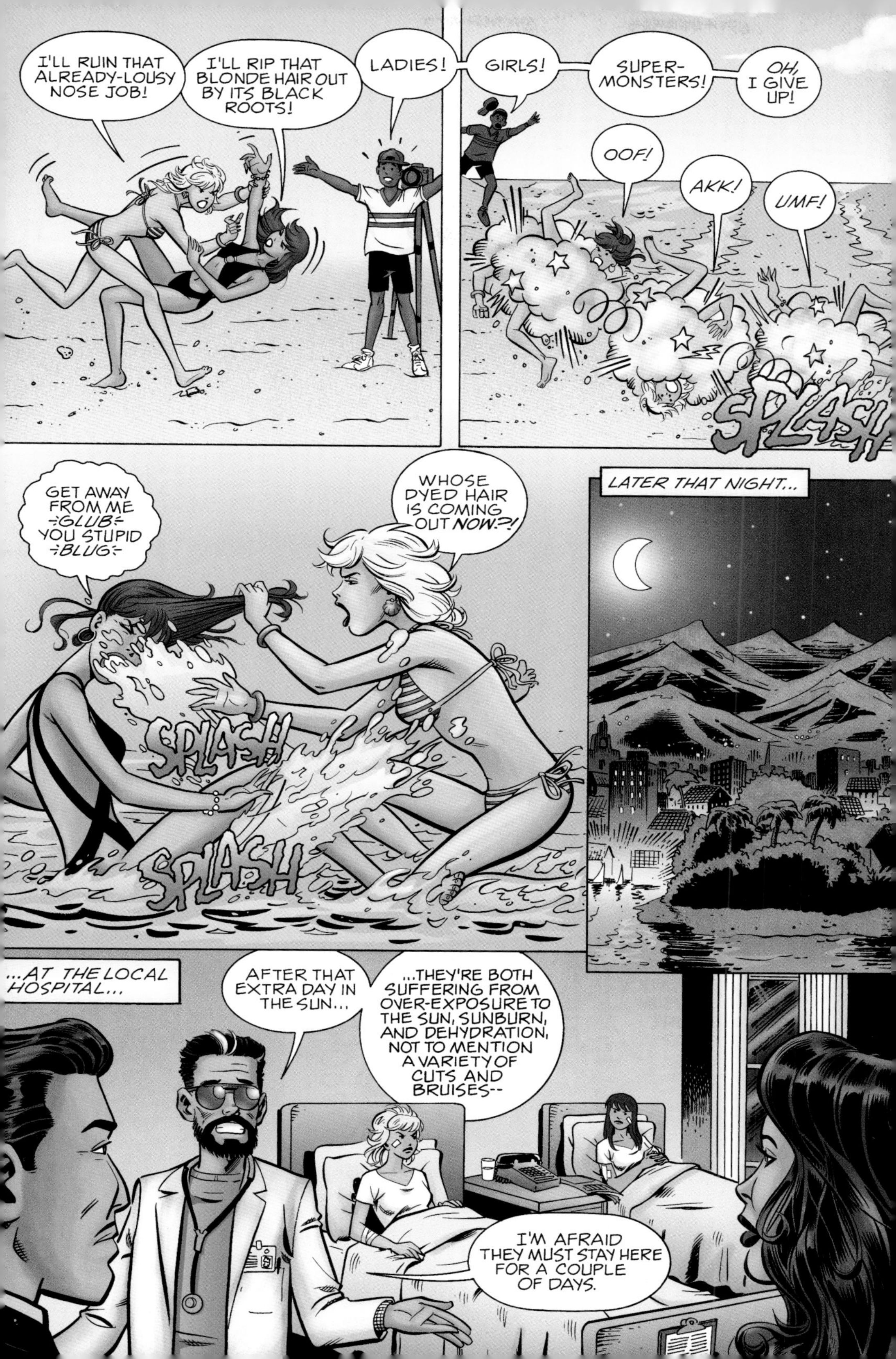

I'LL RUIN THAT ALREADY-LOUSY NOSE JOB!
I'LL RIP THAT BLONDE HAIR OUT BY ITS BLACK ROOTS!
LADIES!
GIRLS!
SUPER-MONSTERS!
OH, I GIVE UP!
OOF!
AKK!
UMF!
SPLASH
GET AWAY FROM ME -GLUB- YOU STUPID -BLUG-
WHOSE DYED HAIR IS COMING OUT NOW?!
SPLASH
SPLASH
LATER THAT NIGHT...
...AT THE LOCAL HOSPITAL...
AFTER THAT EXTRA DAY IN THE SUN...
...THEY'RE BOTH SUFFERING FROM OVER-EXPOSURE TO THE SUN, SUNBURN, AND DEHYDRATION, NOT TO MENTION A VARIETY OF CUTS AND BRUISES--
I'M AFRAID THEY MUST STAY HERE FOR A COUPLE OF DAYS.

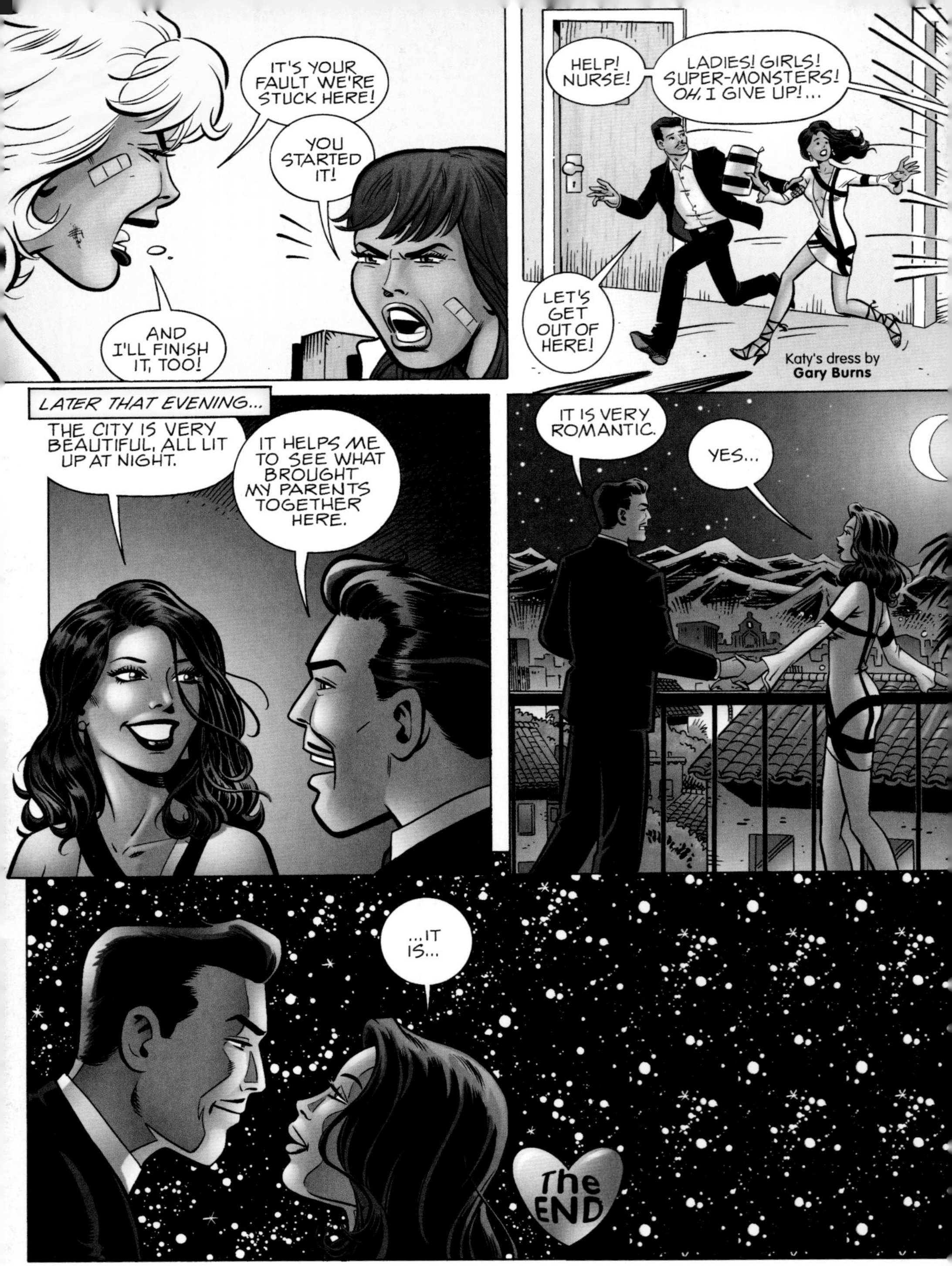
IT'S YOUR FAULT WE'RE STUCK HERE!
YOU STARTED IT!
AND I'LL FINISH IT, TOO!
HELP! NURSE!
LADIES! GIRLS! SUPER-MONSTERS! OH, I GIVE UP!...
LET'S GET OUT OF HERE!
Katy's dress by Gary Burns
LATER THAT EVENING...
THE CITY IS VERY BEAUTIFUL, ALL LIT UP AT NIGHT.
IT HELPS ME TO SEE WHAT BROUGHT MY PARENTS TOGETHER HERE.
IT IS VERY ROMANTIC.
YES...
...IT IS...
The END

KATY KEENE

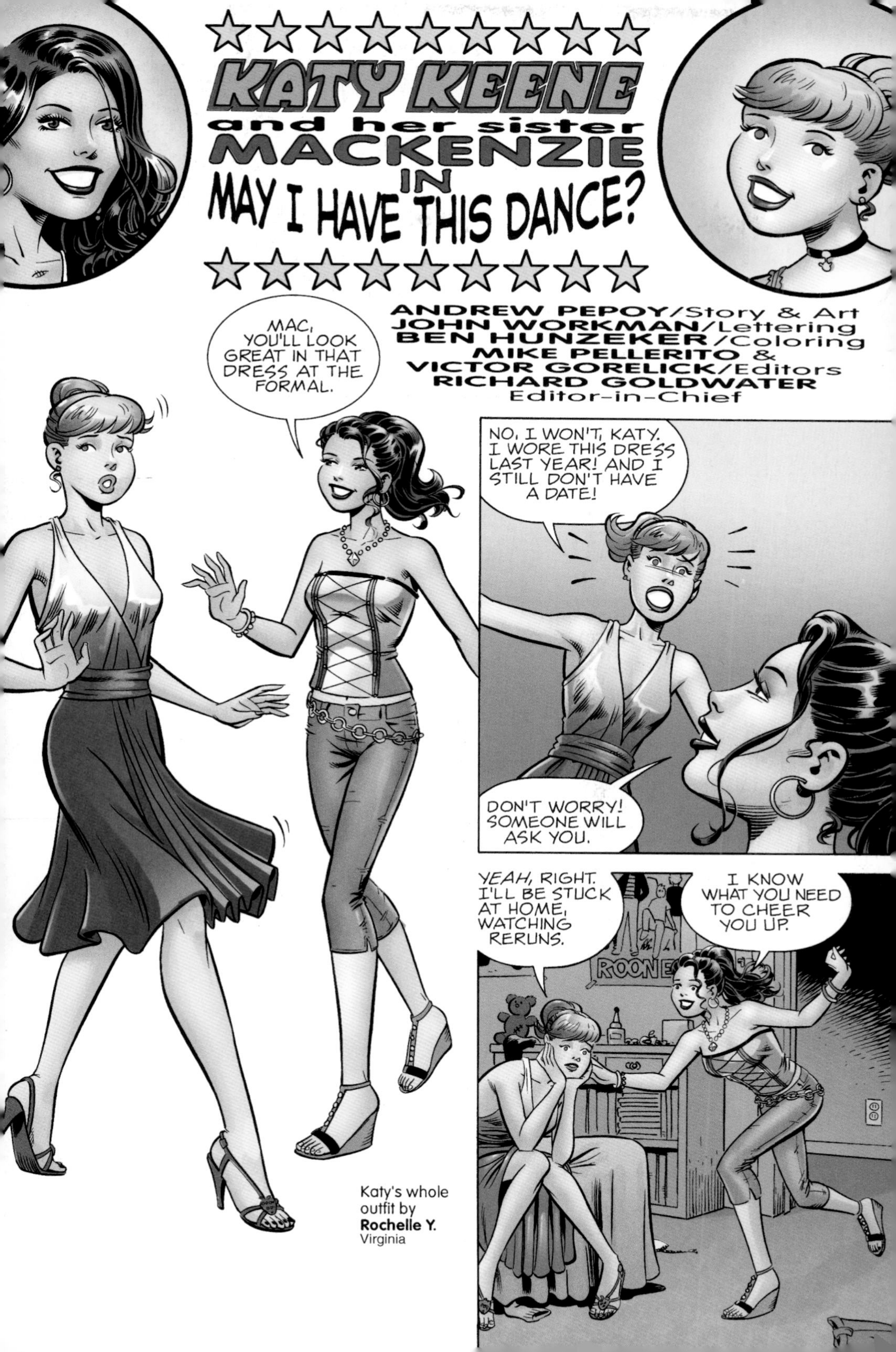

KATY KEENE
and her sister
MACKENZIE
IN
MAY I HAVE THIS DANCE?
ANDREW PEPOY/Story & Art
JOHN WORKMAN/Lettering
BEN HUNZEKER/Coloring
MIKE PELLERITO &
VICTOR GORELICK/Editors
RICHARD GOLDWATER
Editor-in-Chief
MAC, YOU'LL LOOK GREAT IN THAT DRESS AT THE FORMAL.
Katy's whole outfit by Rochelle Y. Virginia
NO, I WON'T, KATY. I WORE THIS DRESS LAST YEAR! AND I STILL DON'T HAVE A DATE!
DON'T WORRY! SOMEONE WILL ASK YOU.
YEAH, RIGHT. I'LL BE STUCK AT HOME, WATCHING RERUNS.
I KNOW WHAT YOU NEED TO CHEER YOU UP.

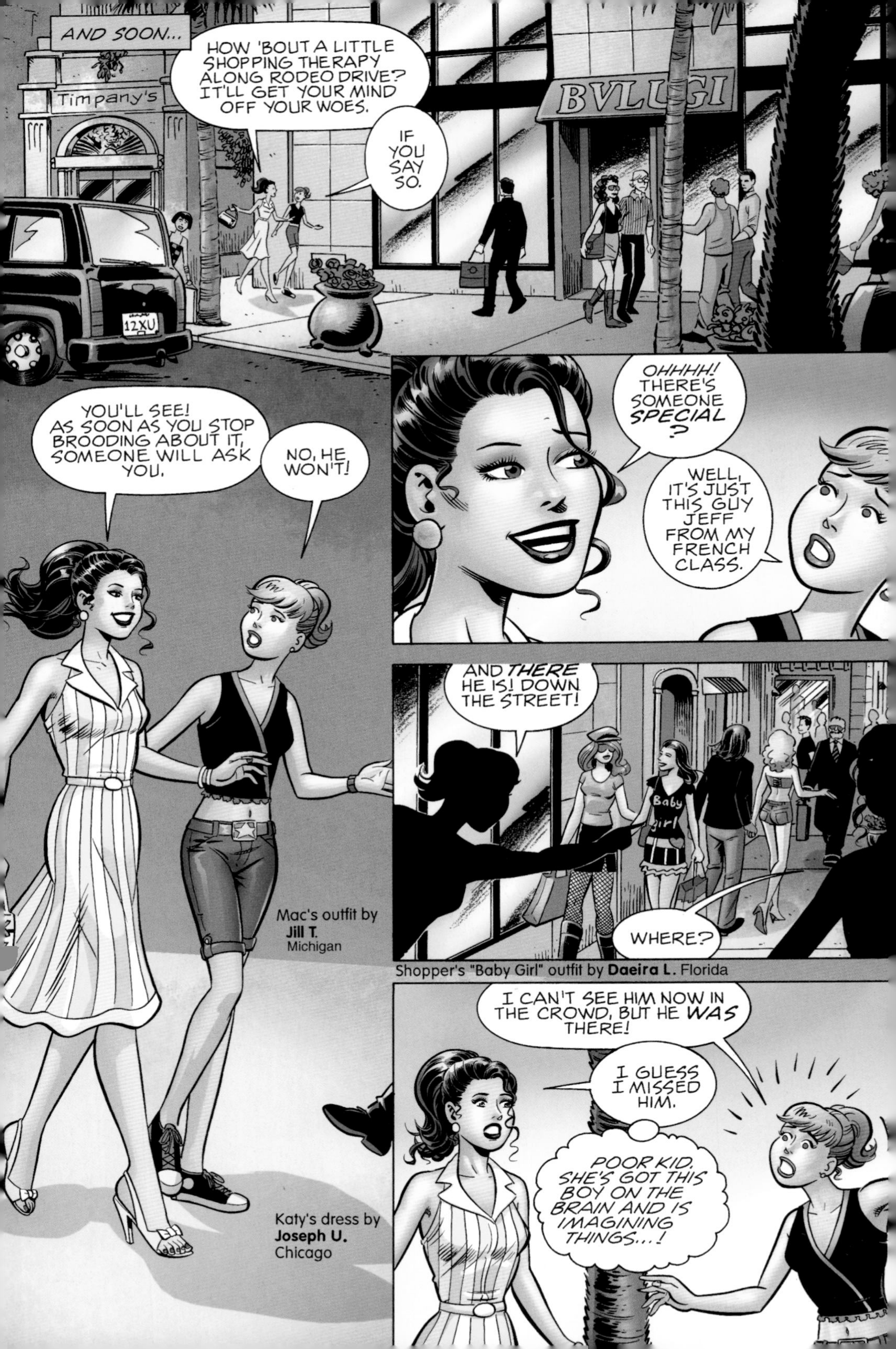
AND SOON...
Timpany's
HOW 'BOUT A LITTLE SHOPPING THERAPY ALONG RODEO DRIVE? IT'LL GET YOUR MIND OFF YOUR WOES.
IF YOU SAY SO.
BVLUGI
12XU
YOU'LL SEE! AS SOON AS YOU STOP BROODING ABOUT IT, SOMEONE WILL ASK YOU.
NO, HE WON'T!
OHHHH! THERE'S SOMEONE SPECIAL?
WELL, IT'S JUST THIS GUY JEFF FROM MY FRENCH CLASS.
AND THERE HE IS! DOWN THE STREET!
Baby girl
WHERE?
I CAN'T SEE HIM NOW IN THE CROWD, BUT HE WAS THERE!
I GUESS I MISSED HIM.
POOR KID. SHE'S GOT THIS BOY ON THE BRAIN AND IS IMAGINING THINGS...!

Mac's outfit by **Jill T.** Michigan

Katy's dress by **Joseph U.** Chicago

Shopper's "Baby Girl" outfit by **Daeira L.** Florida

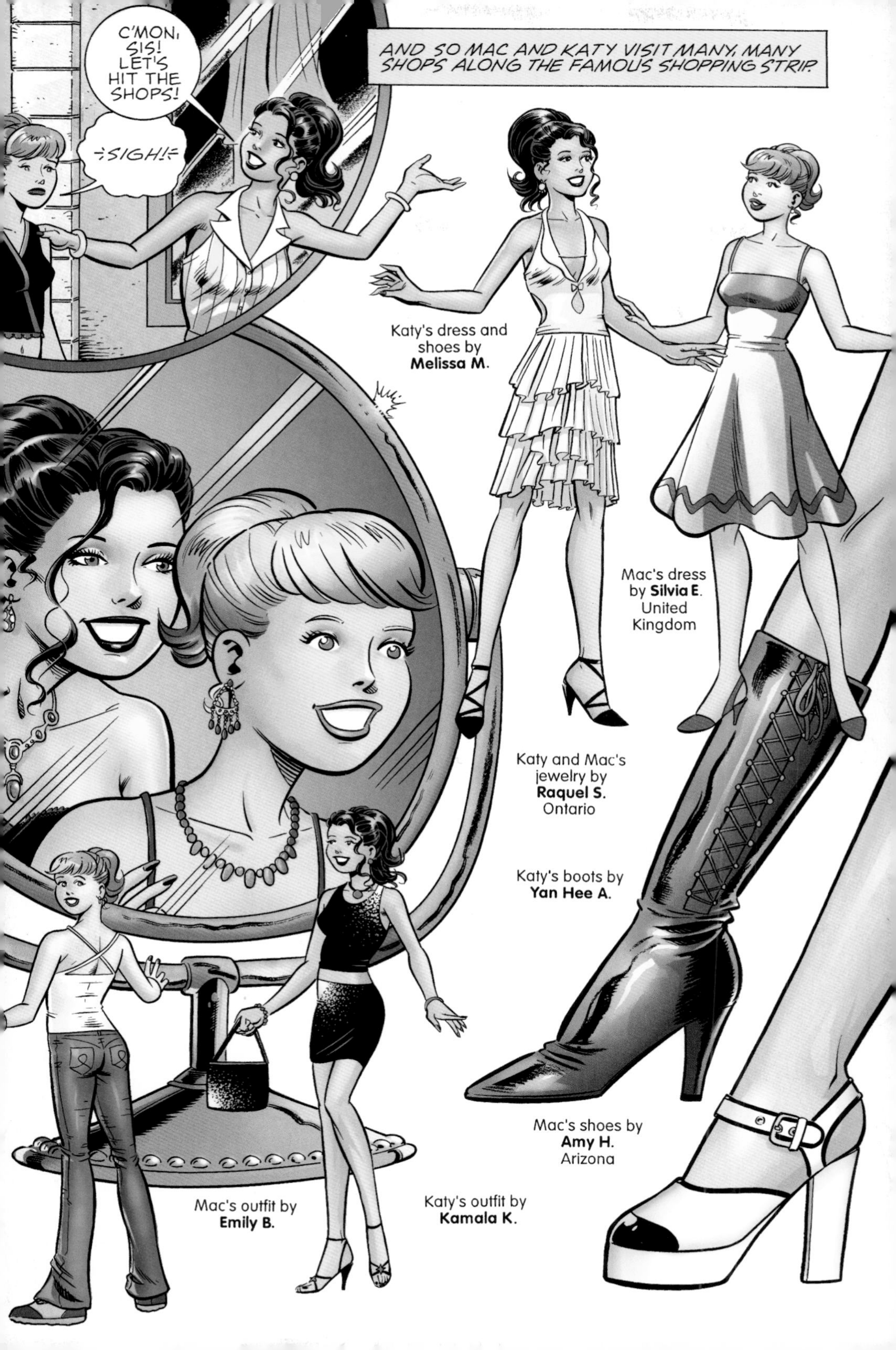
C'MON, SIS! LET'S HIT THE SHOPS!
÷SIGH!÷
AND SO MAC AND KATY VISIT MANY, MANY SHOPS ALONG THE FAMOUS SHOPPING STRIP.
Katy's dress and shoes by **Melissa M.**
Mac's dress by **Silvia E.** United Kingdom
Katy and Mac's jewelry by **Raquel S.** Ontario
Katy's boots by **Yan Hee A.**
Mac's shoes by **Amy H.** Arizona
Mac's outfit by **Emily B.**
Katy's outfit by **Kamala K.**

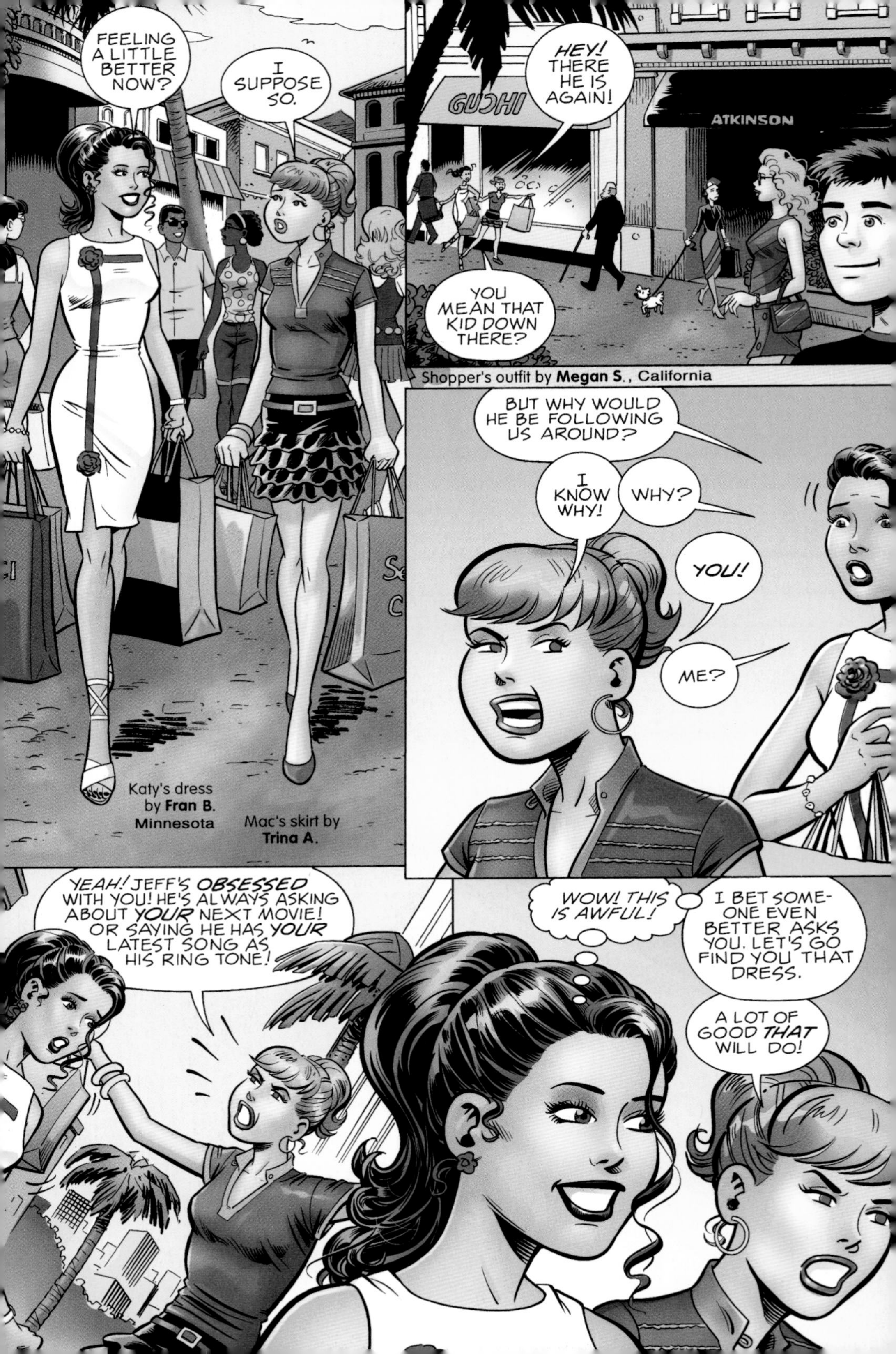
FEELING A LITTLE BETTER NOW?
I SUPPOSE SO.
Katy's dress by Fran B. Minnesota
Mac's skirt by Trina A.
GUCHI
ATKINSON
HEY! THERE HE IS AGAIN!
YOU MEAN THAT KID DOWN THERE?
Shopper's outfit by Megan S., California
BUT WHY WOULD HE BE FOLLOWING US AROUND?
I KNOW WHY!
WHY?
YOU!
ME?
YEAH! JEFF'S OBSESSED WITH YOU! HE'S ALWAYS ASKING ABOUT YOUR NEXT MOVIE! OR SAYING HE HAS YOUR LATEST SONG AS HIS RING TONE!
WOW! THIS IS AWFUL!
I BET SOME-ONE EVEN BETTER ASKS YOU. LET'S GO FIND YOU THAT DRESS.
A LOT OF GOOD THAT WILL DO!

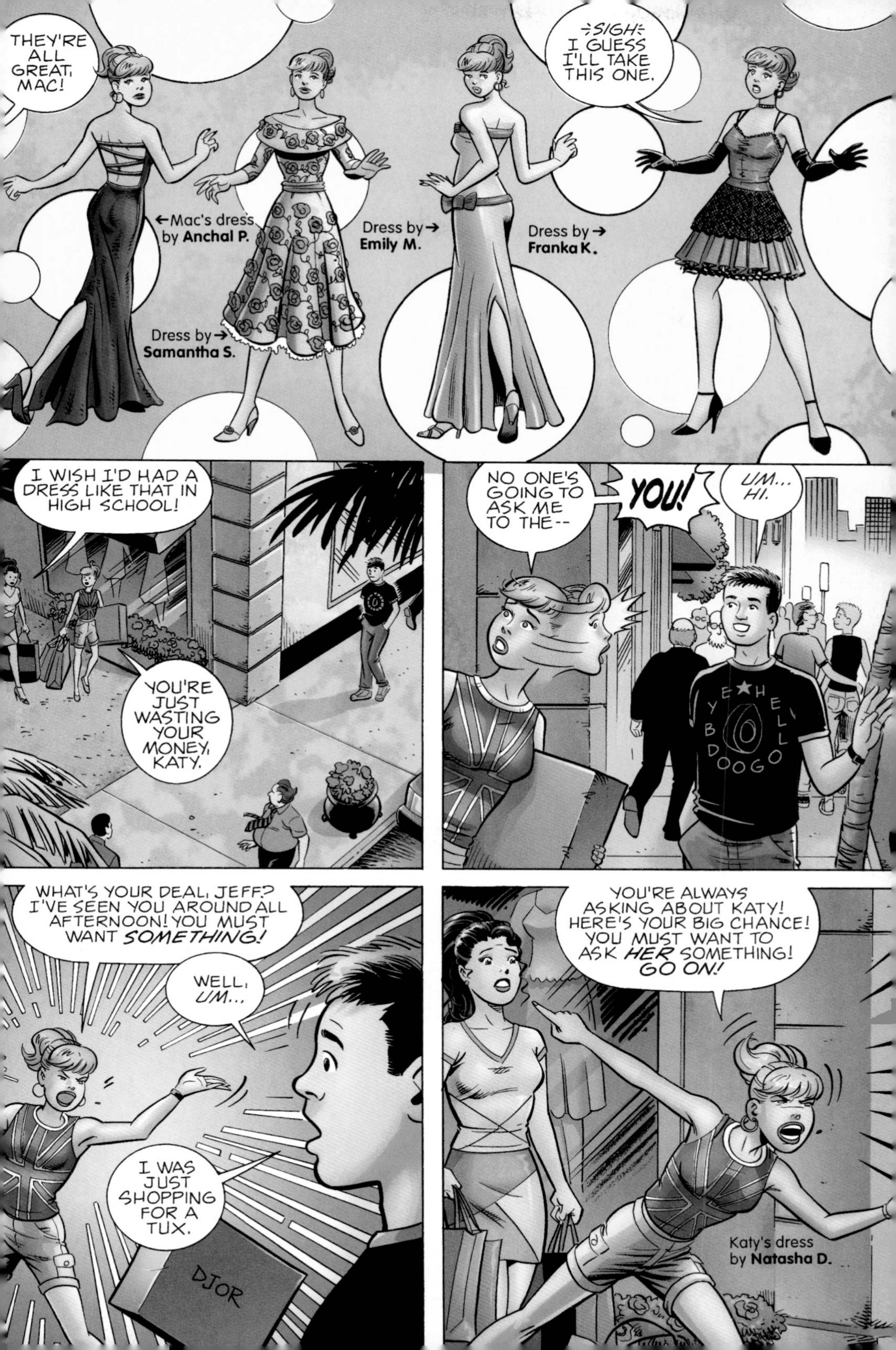
THEY'RE ALL GREAT, MAC!
←Mac's dress by Anchal P.
Dress by→ Samantha S.
Dress by→ Emily M.
Dress by→ Franka K.
∹SIGH∹ I GUESS I'LL TAKE THIS ONE.
I WISH I'D HAD A DRESS LIKE THAT IN HIGH SCHOOL!
YOU'RE JUST WASTING YOUR MONEY, KATY.
NO ONE'S GOING TO ASK ME TO THE--
YOU!
UM... HI.
WHAT'S YOUR DEAL, JEFF? I'VE SEEN YOU AROUND ALL AFTERNOON! YOU MUST WANT SOMETHING!
WELL, UM...
I WAS JUST SHOPPING FOR A TUX.
DJOR
YOU'RE ALWAYS ASKING ABOUT KATY! HERE'S YOUR BIG CHANCE! YOU MUST WANT TO ASK HER SOMETHING! GO ON!
Katy's dress by Natasha D.

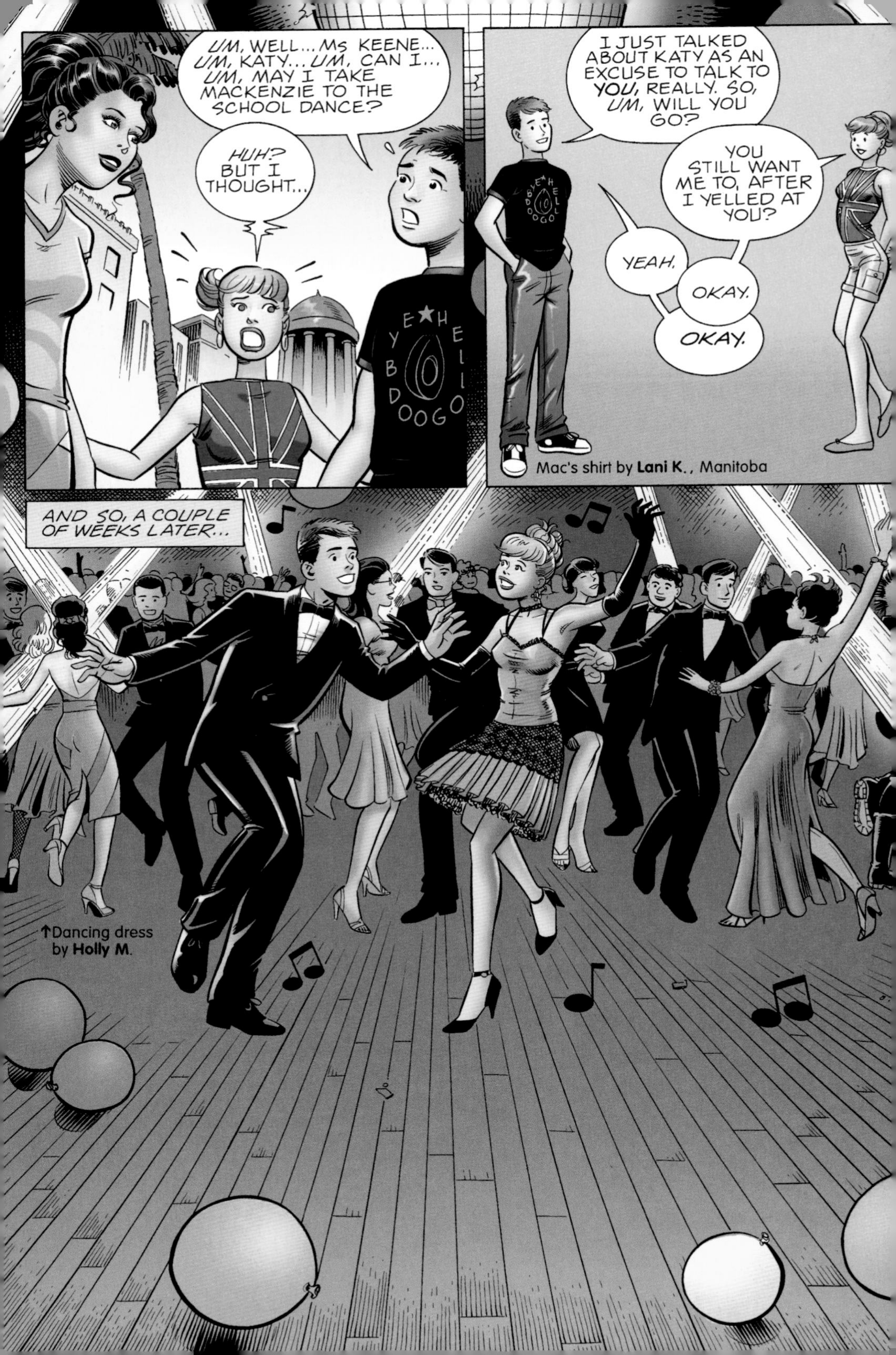
UM, WELL... Ms KEENE... UM, KATY... UM, CAN I... UM, MAY I TAKE MACKENZIE TO THE SCHOOL DANCE?
HUH? BUT I THOUGHT...
I JUST TALKED ABOUT KATY AS AN EXCUSE TO TALK TO YOU, REALLY. SO, UM, WILL YOU GO?
YOU STILL WANT ME TO, AFTER I YELLED AT YOU?
YEAH.
OKAY.
OKAY.
Mac's shirt by Lani K., Manitoba
AND SO, A COUPLE OF WEEKS LATER...
↑Dancing dress by Holly M.

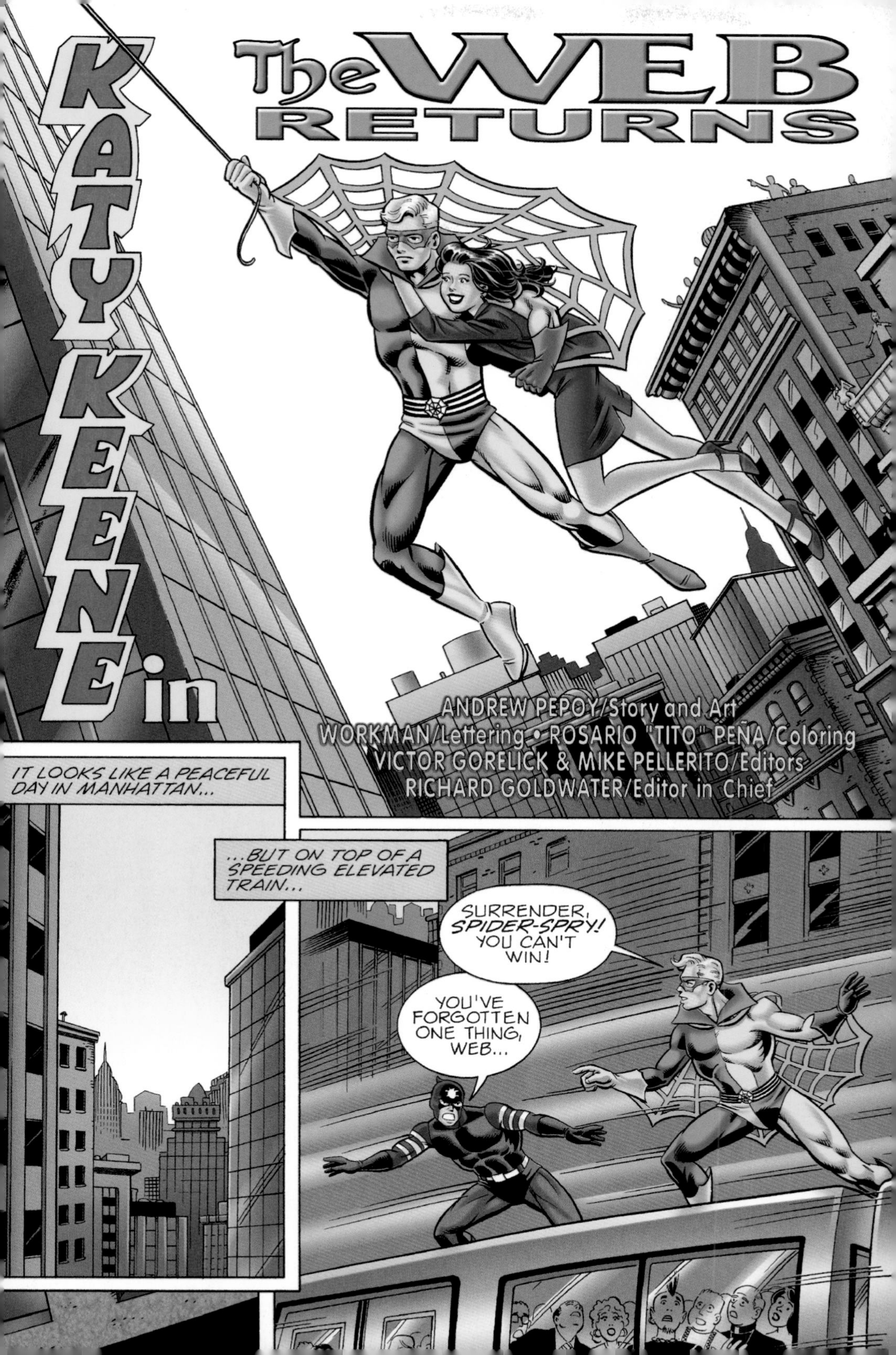
KATY KEENE in
The WEB RETURNS
ANDREW PEPOY/Story and Art
WORKMAN/Lettering • ROSARIO "TITO" PEÑA/Coloring
VICTOR GORELICK & MIKE PELLERITO/Editors
RICHARD GOLDWATER/Editor in Chief
IT LOOKS LIKE A PEACEFUL DAY IN MANHATTAN...
...BUT ON TOP OF A SPEEDING ELEVATED TRAIN...
SURRENDER, SPIDER-SPRY! YOU CAN'T WIN!
YOU'VE FORGOTTEN ONE THING, WEB...

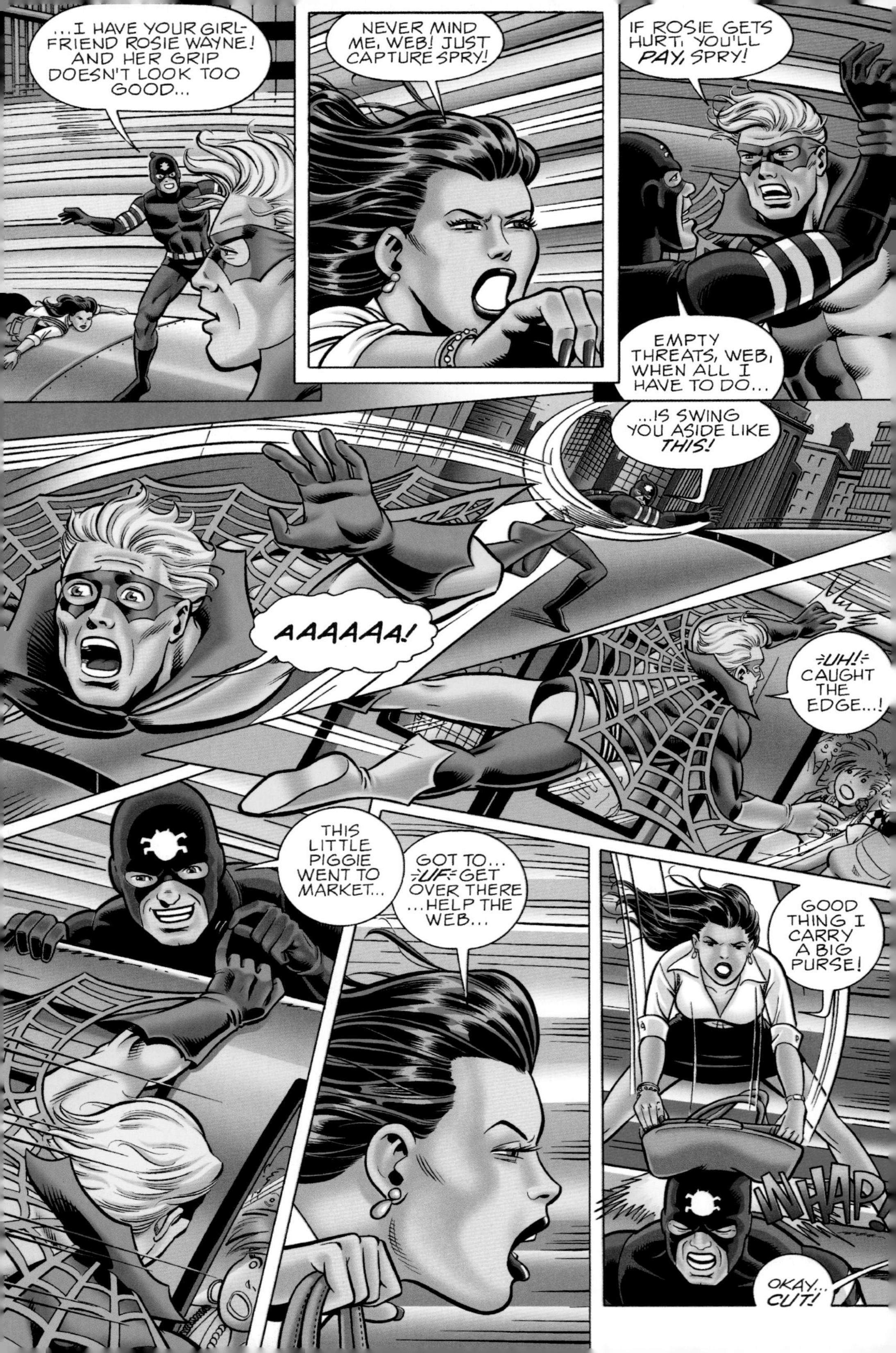
...I HAVE YOUR GIRL-FRIEND ROSIE WAYNE! AND HER GRIP DOESN'T LOOK TOO GOOD...
NEVER MIND ME, WEB! JUST CAPTURE SPRY!
IF ROSIE GETS HURT, YOU'LL PAY, SPRY!
EMPTY THREATS, WEB, WHEN ALL I HAVE TO DO...
...IS SWING YOU ASIDE LIKE THIS!
AAAAAA!
UH! CAUGHT THE EDGE...!
THIS LITTLE PIGGIE WENT TO MARKET...
GOT TO... UF GET OVER THERE ...HELP THE WEB...
GOOD THING I CARRY A BIG PURSE!
WHAP!
OKAY... CUT!

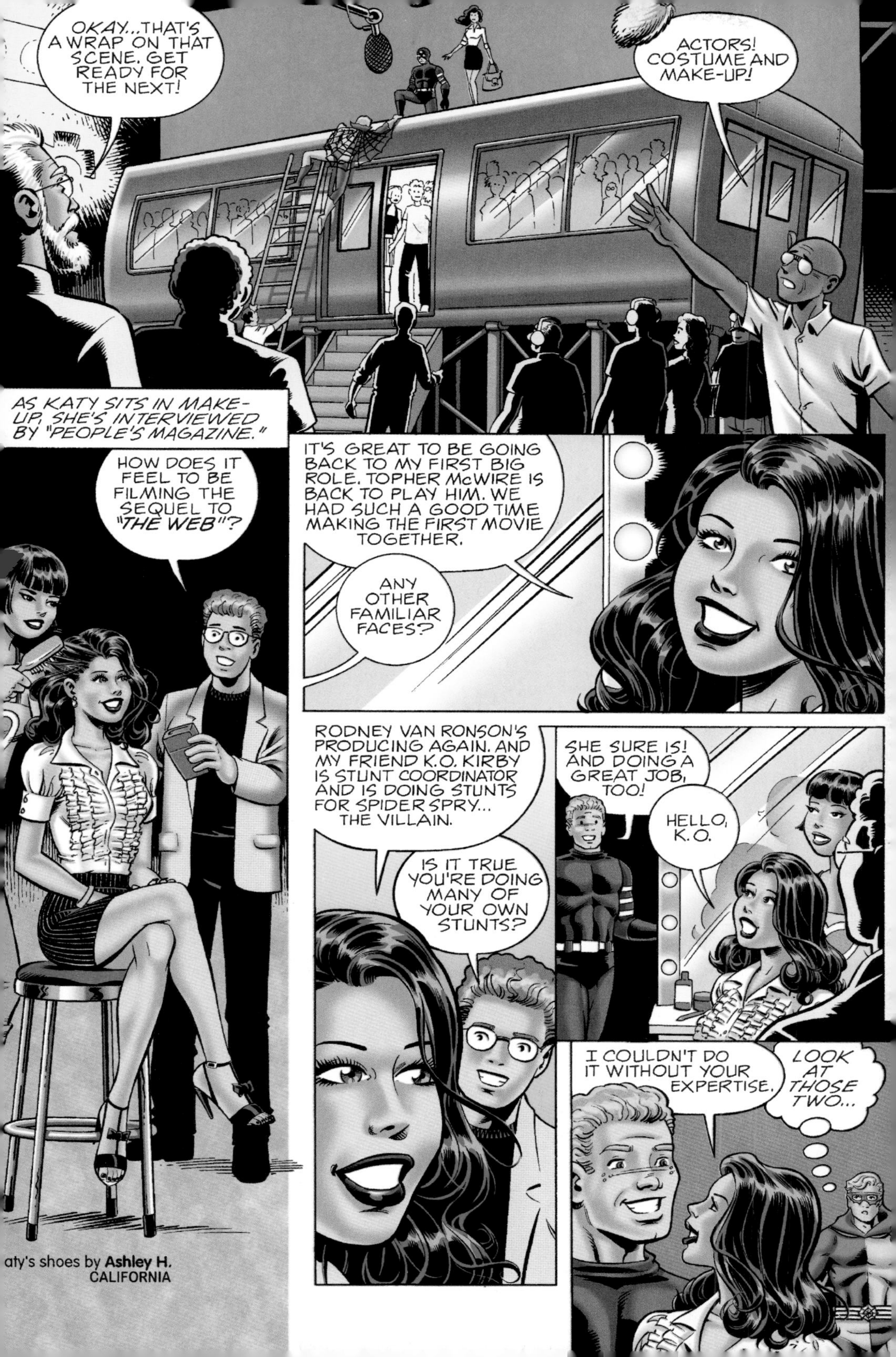
OKAY...THAT'S A WRAP ON THAT SCENE. GET READY FOR THE NEXT!
ACTORS! COSTUME AND MAKE-UP!
AS KATY SITS IN MAKE-UP, SHE'S INTERVIEWED BY "PEOPLE'S MAGAZINE."
HOW DOES IT FEEL TO BE FILMING THE SEQUEL TO "THE WEB"?
IT'S GREAT TO BE GOING BACK TO MY FIRST BIG ROLE. TOPHER McWIRE IS BACK TO PLAY HIM. WE HAD SUCH A GOOD TIME MAKING THE FIRST MOVIE TOGETHER.
ANY OTHER FAMILIAR FACES?
RODNEY VAN RONSON'S PRODUCING AGAIN. AND MY FRIEND K.O. KIRBY IS STUNT COORDINATOR AND IS DOING STUNTS FOR SPIDER SPRY... THE VILLAIN.
IS IT TRUE YOU'RE DOING MANY OF YOUR OWN STUNTS?
SHE SURE IS! AND DOING A GREAT JOB, TOO!
HELLO, K.O.
I COULDN'T DO IT WITHOUT YOUR EXPERTISE.
LOOK AT THOSE TWO...
aty's shoes by Ashley H. CALIFORNIA

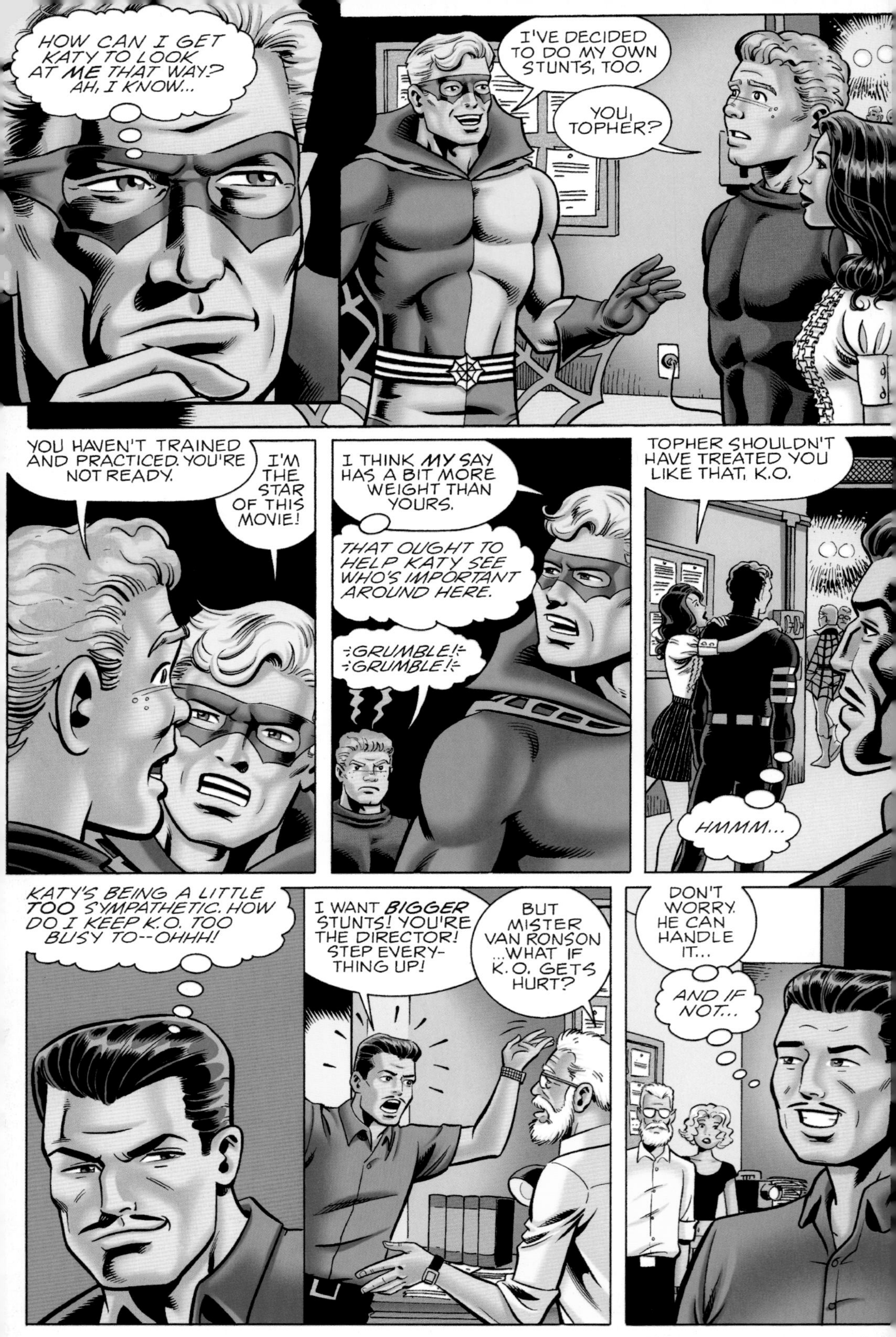
HOW CAN I GET KATY TO LOOK AT ME THAT WAY? AH, I KNOW...
I'VE DECIDED TO DO MY OWN STUNTS, TOO.
YOU, TOPHER?
YOU HAVEN'T TRAINED AND PRACTICED. YOU'RE NOT READY.
I'M THE STAR OF THIS MOVIE!
I THINK MY SAY HAS A BIT MORE WEIGHT THAN YOURS.
THAT OUGHT TO HELP KATY SEE WHO'S IMPORTANT AROUND HERE.
GRUMBLE! GRUMBLE!
TOPHER SHOULDN'T HAVE TREATED YOU LIKE THAT, K.O.
HMMM...
KATY'S BEING A LITTLE TOO SYMPATHETIC. HOW DO I KEEP K.O. TOO BUSY TO--OHHH!
I WANT BIGGER STUNTS! YOU'RE THE DIRECTOR! STEP EVERY-THING UP!
BUT MISTER VAN RONSON ...WHAT IF K.O. GETS HURT?
DON'T WORRY. HE CAN HANDLE IT...
AND IF NOT...

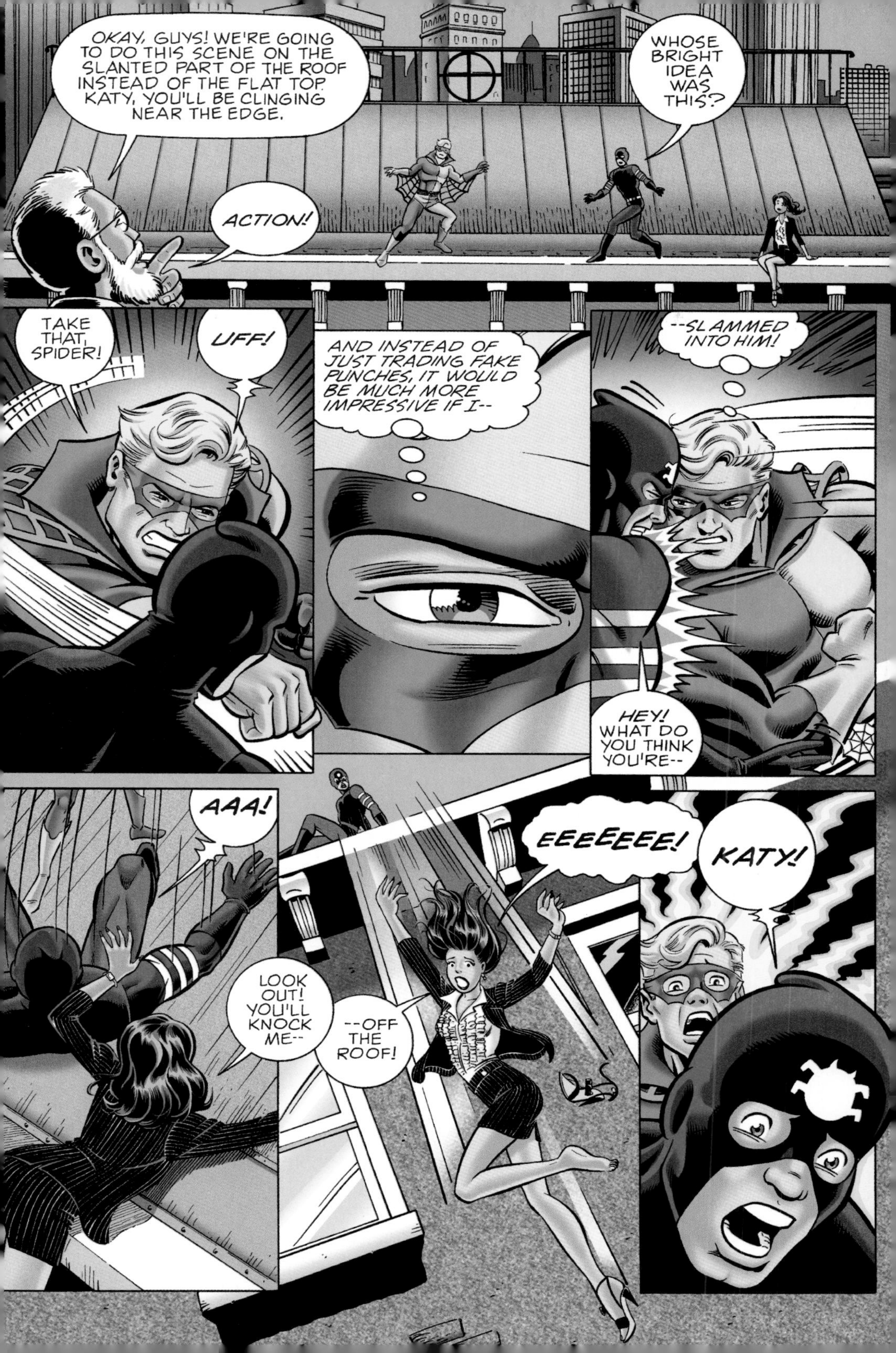
OKAY, GUYS! WE'RE GOING TO DO THIS SCENE ON THE SLANTED PART OF THE ROOF INSTEAD OF THE FLAT TOP. KATY, YOU'LL BE CLINGING NEAR THE EDGE.
WHOSE BRIGHT IDEA WAS THIS?
ACTION!
TAKE THAT, SPIDER!
UFF!
AND INSTEAD OF JUST TRADING FAKE PUNCHES, IT WOULD BE MUCH MORE IMPRESSIVE IF I--
--SLAMMED INTO HIM!
HEY! WHAT DO YOU THINK YOU'RE--
AAA!
LOOK OUT! YOU'LL KNOCK ME--
--OFF THE ROOF!
EEEEEEE!
KATY!

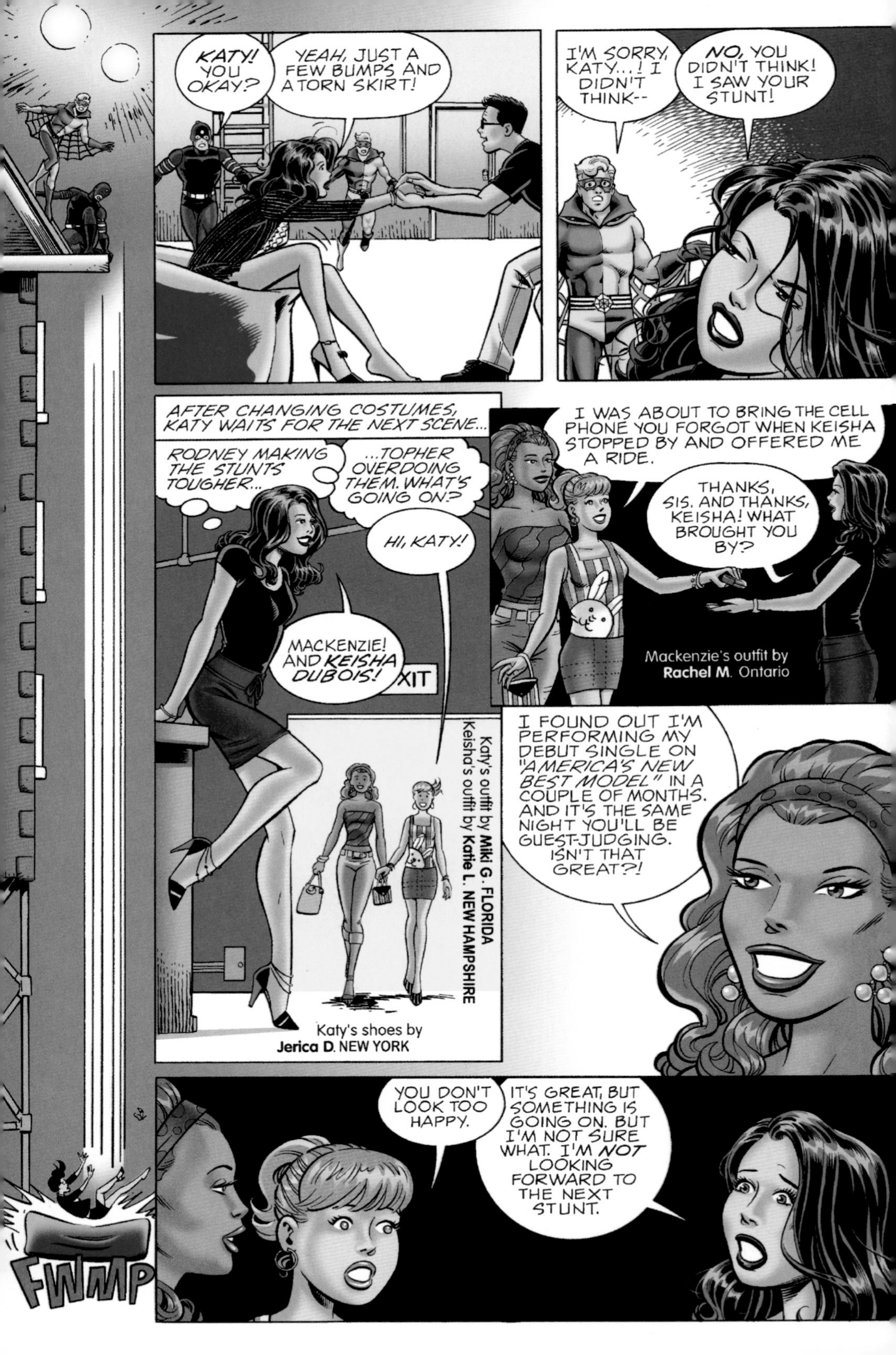
KATY! YOU OKAY?
YEAH, JUST A FEW BUMPS AND A TORN SKIRT!
I'M SORRY, KATY...! I DIDN'T THINK--
NO, YOU DIDN'T THINK! I SAW YOUR STUNT!
FWMP
AFTER CHANGING COSTUMES, KATY WAITS FOR THE NEXT SCENE...
RODNEY MAKING THE STUNTS TOUGHER...
...TOPHER OVERDOING THEM. WHAT'S GOING ON?
HI, KATY!
MACKENZIE! AND KEISHA DUBOIS!
XIT
Katy's outfit by Miki G. FLORIDA
Keisha's outfit by Katie L. NEW HAMPSHIRE
Katy's shoes by Jerica D. NEW YORK
I WAS ABOUT TO BRING THE CELL PHONE YOU FORGOT WHEN KEISHA STOPPED BY AND OFFERED ME A RIDE.
THANKS, SIS. AND THANKS, KEISHA! WHAT BROUGHT YOU BY?
Mackenzie's outfit by Rachel M. Ontario
I FOUND OUT I'M PERFORMING MY DEBUT SINGLE ON "AMERICA'S NEW BEST MODEL" IN A COUPLE OF MONTHS. AND IT'S THE SAME NIGHT YOU'LL BE GUEST-JUDGING. ISN'T THAT GREAT?!
YOU DON'T LOOK TOO HAPPY.
IT'S GREAT, BUT SOMETHING IS GOING ON. BUT I'M NOT SURE WHAT. I'M NOT LOOKING FORWARD TO THE NEXT STUNT.

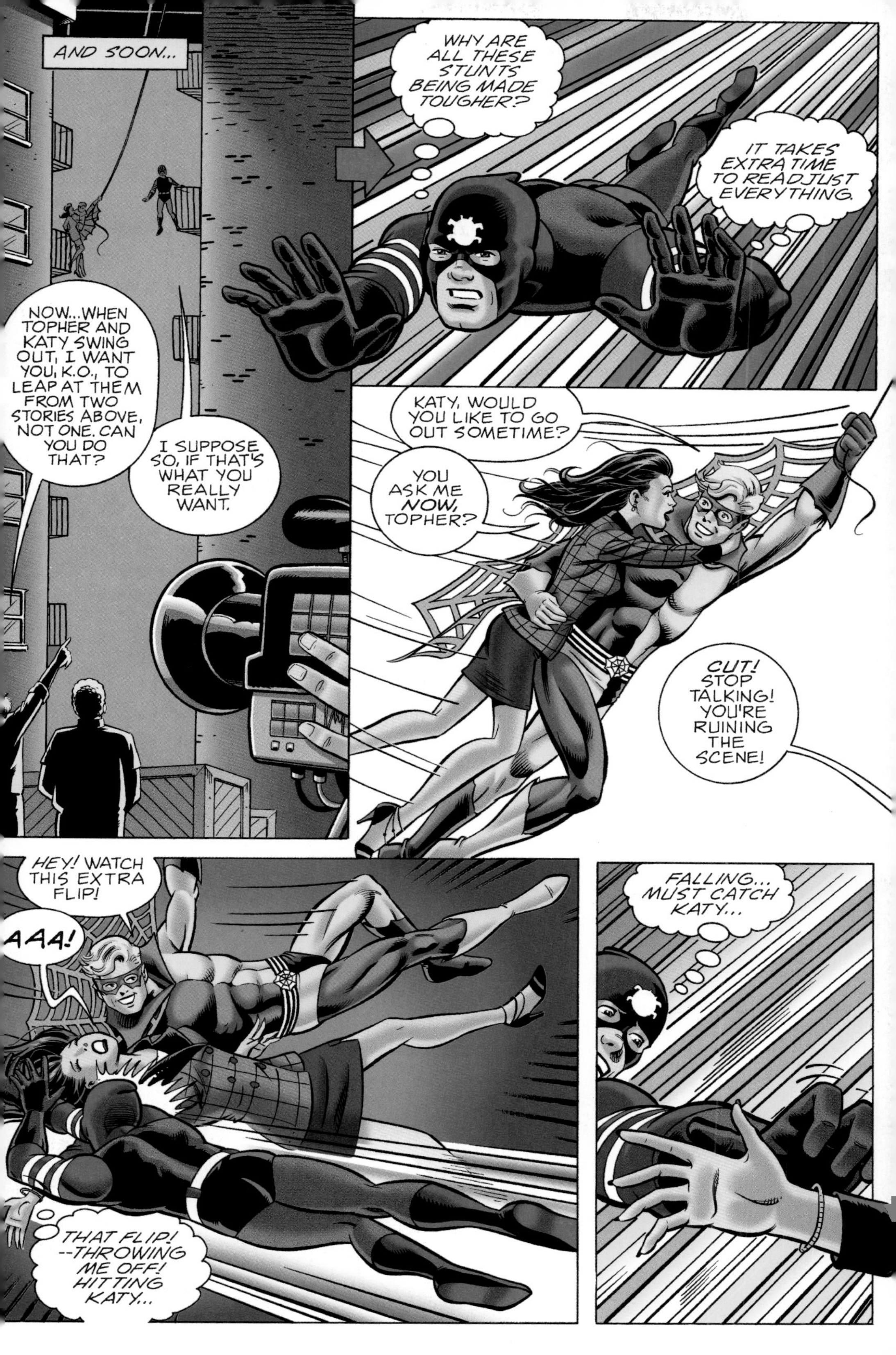
AND SOON...
NOW...WHEN TOPHER AND KATY SWING OUT, I WANT YOU, K.O., TO LEAP AT THEM FROM TWO STORIES ABOVE, NOT ONE. CAN YOU DO THAT?
I SUPPOSE SO, IF THAT'S WHAT YOU REALLY WANT.
WHY ARE ALL THESE STUNTS BEING MADE TOUGHER?
IT TAKES EXTRA TIME TO READJUST EVERYTHING.
KATY, WOULD YOU LIKE TO GO OUT SOMETIME?
YOU ASK ME *NOW,* TOPHER?
CUT! STOP TALKING! YOU'RE RUINING THE SCENE!
HEY! WATCH THIS EXTRA FLIP!
AAA!
THAT FLIP! --THROWING ME OFF! HITTING KATY...
FALLING... MUST CATCH KATY...

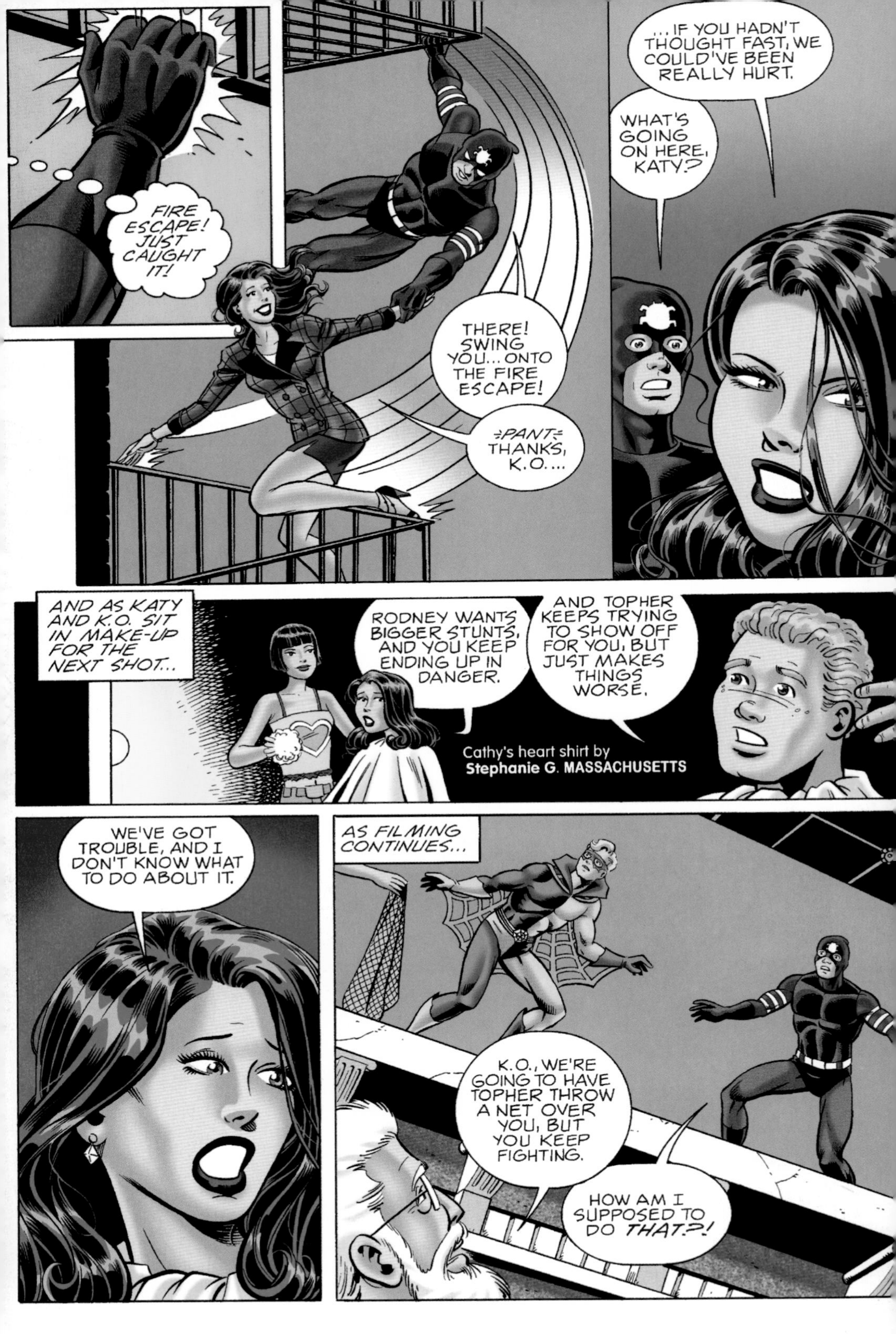

FIRE ESCAPE! JUST CAUGHT IT!
THERE! SWING YOU... ONTO THE FIRE ESCAPE!
=PANT= THANKS, K.O....
...IF YOU HADN'T THOUGHT FAST, WE COULD'VE BEEN REALLY HURT.
WHAT'S GOING ON HERE, KATY?
AND AS KATY AND K.O. SIT IN MAKE-UP FOR THE NEXT SHOT...
RODNEY WANTS BIGGER STUNTS, AND YOU KEEP ENDING UP IN DANGER.
AND TOPHER KEEPS TRYING TO SHOW OFF FOR YOU, BUT JUST MAKES THINGS WORSE.
Cathy's heart shirt by
Stephanie G. MASSACHUSETTS
WE'VE GOT TROUBLE, AND I DON'T KNOW WHAT TO DO ABOUT IT.
AS FILMING CONTINUES...
K.O., WE'RE GOING TO HAVE TOPHER THROW A NET OVER YOU, BUT YOU KEEP FIGHTING.
HOW AM I SUPPOSED TO DO THAT?!

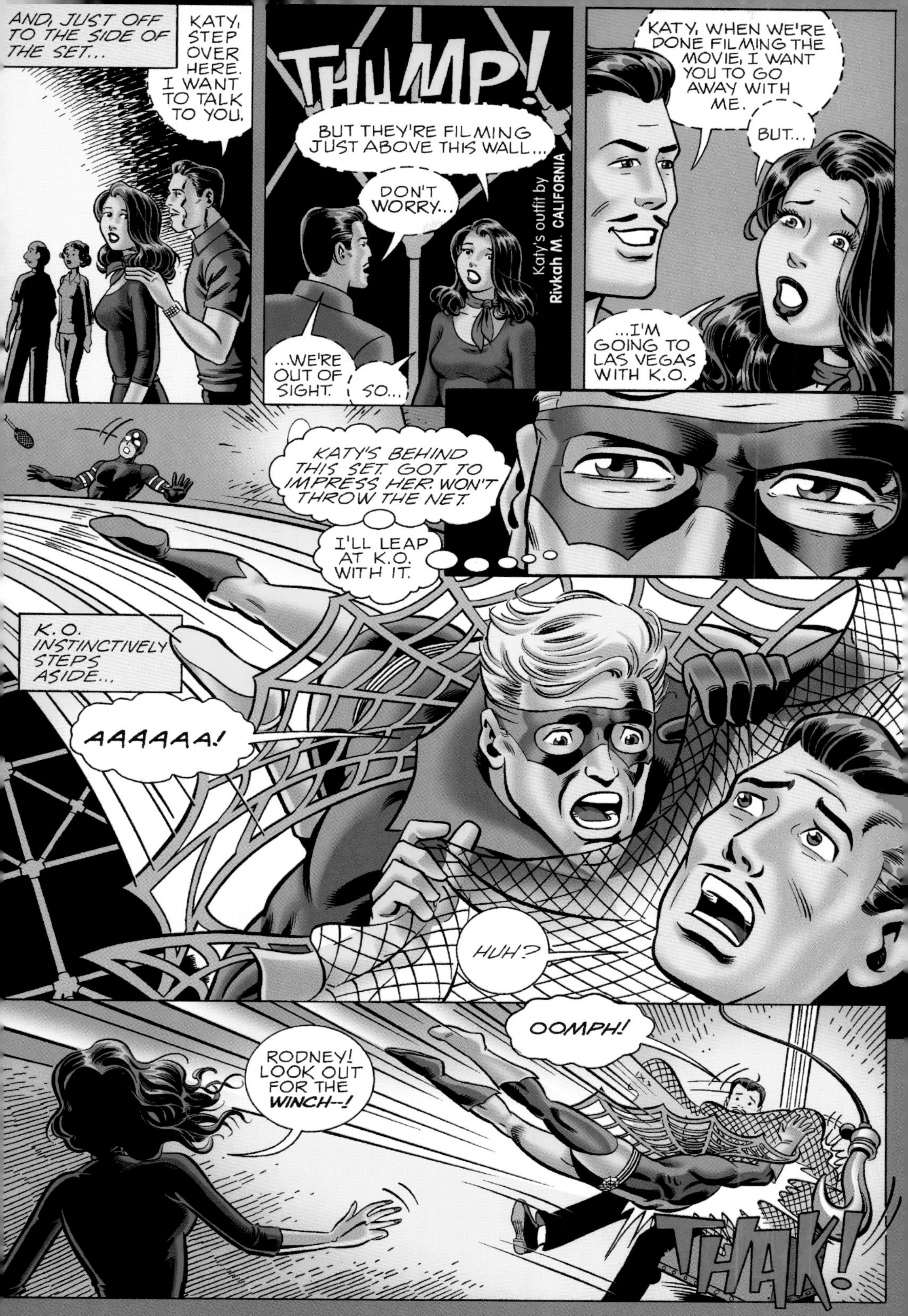
AND, JUST OFF TO THE SIDE OF THE SET...
KATY, STEP OVER HERE. I WANT TO TALK TO YOU.
THUMP!
BUT THEY'RE FILMING JUST ABOVE THIS WALL...
DON'T WORRY...
...WE'RE OUT OF SIGHT.
SO...
Katy's outfit by Rivkah M. CALIFORNIA
KATY, WHEN WE'RE DONE FILMING THE MOVIE, I WANT YOU TO GO AWAY WITH ME.
BUT...
...I'M GOING TO LAS VEGAS WITH K.O.
KATY'S BEHIND THIS SET. GOT TO IMPRESS HER. WON'T THROW THE NET.
I'LL LEAP AT K.O. WITH IT.
K.O. INSTINCTIVELY STEPS ASIDE...
AAAAAA!
HUH?
OOMPH!
RODNEY! LOOK OUT FOR THE WINCH--!
THAK!

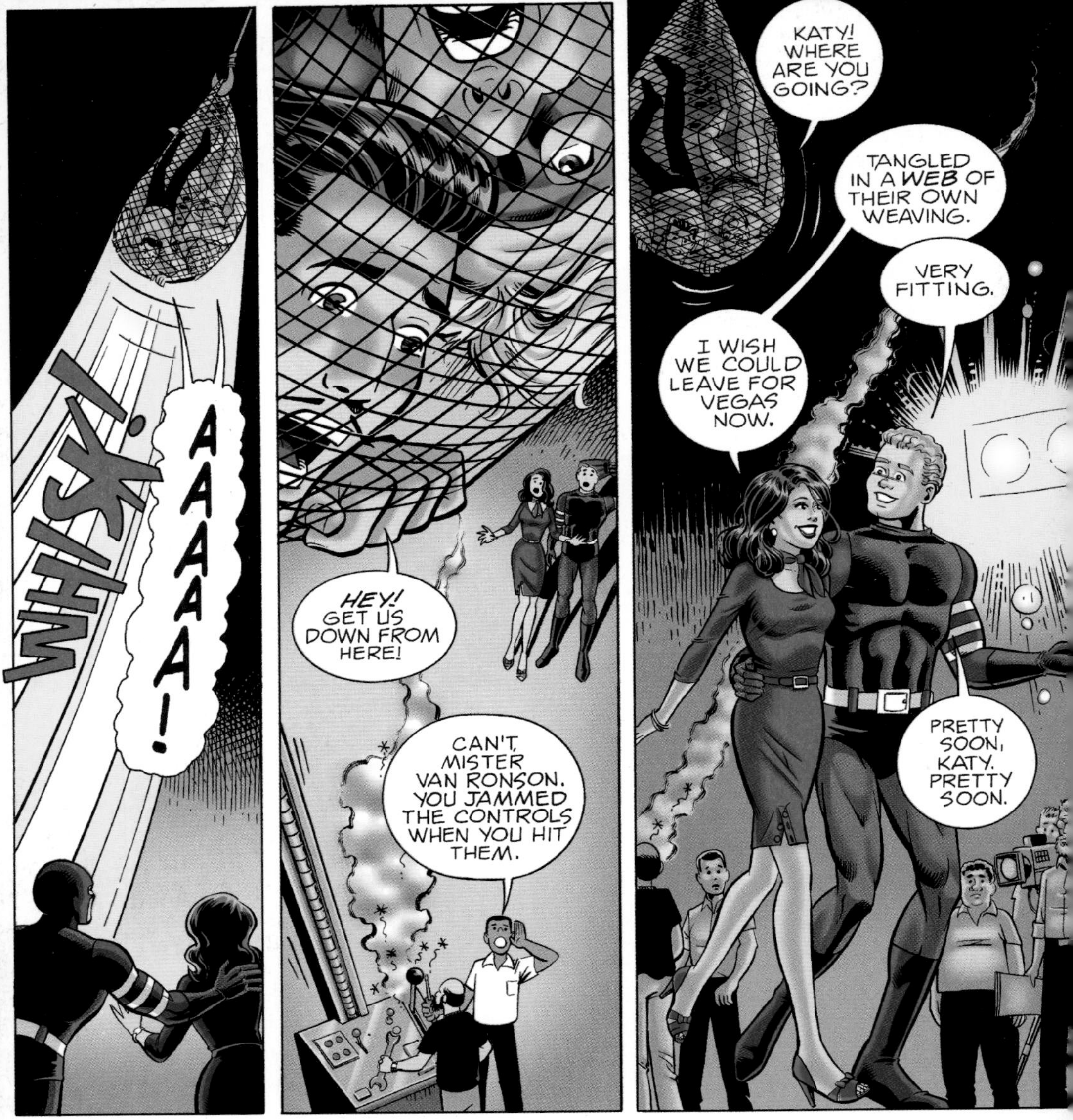
WHISH!
AAAAAA!
HEY! GET US DOWN FROM HERE!
CAN'T, MISTER VAN RONSON. YOU JAMMED THE CONTROLS WHEN YOU HIT THEM.
KATY! WHERE ARE YOU GOING?
TANGLED IN A WEB OF THEIR OWN WEAVING.
VERY FITTING.
I WISH WE COULD LEAVE FOR VEGAS NOW.
PRETTY SOON, KATY. PRETTY SOON.

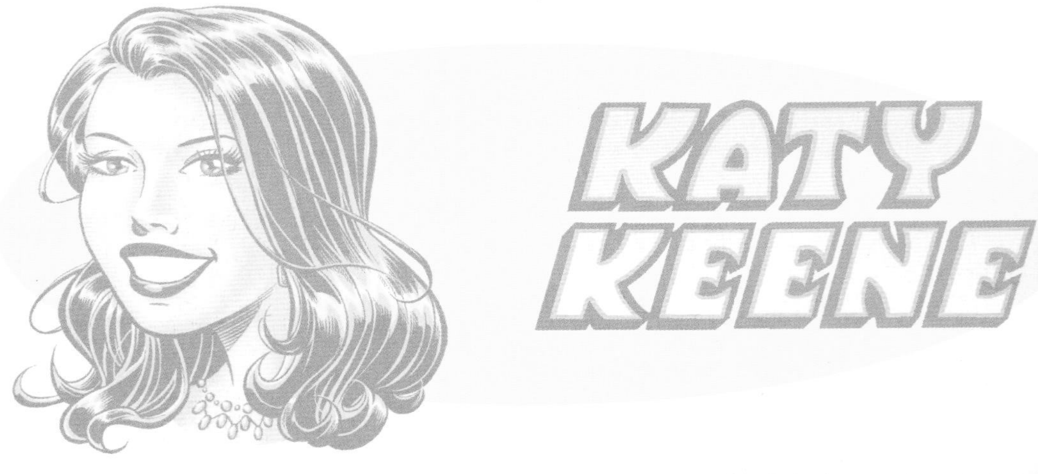
KATY KEENE

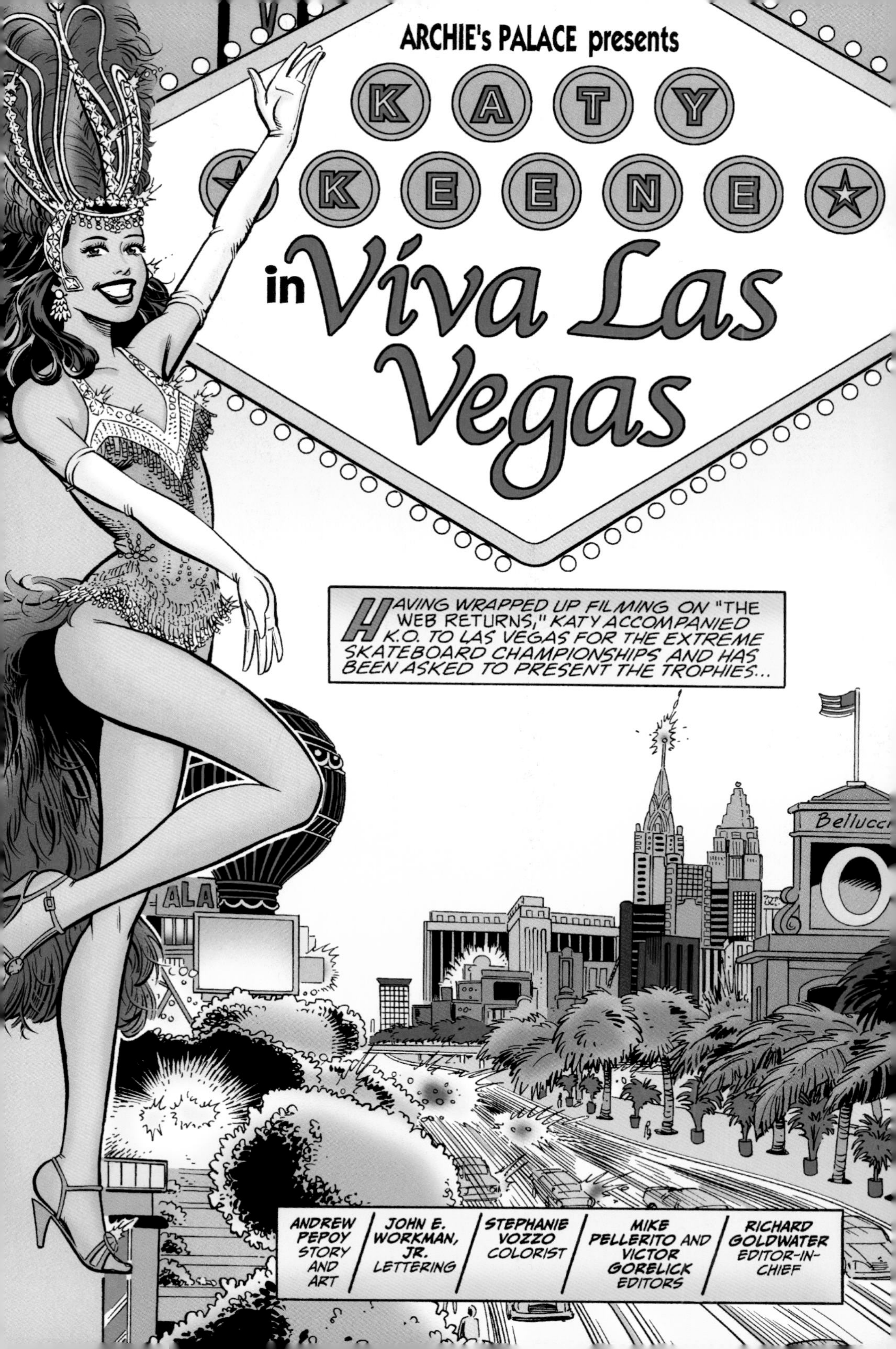

ARCHIE's PALACE presents
KATY ★ KEENE ★
in Viva Las Vegas
HAVING WRAPPED UP FILMING ON "THE WEB RETURNS," KATY ACCOMPANIED K.O. TO LAS VEGAS FOR THE EXTREME SKATEBOARD CHAMPIONSHIPS AND HAS BEEN ASKED TO PRESENT THE TROPHIES...
ALA
Belluc
ANDREW PEPOY STORY AND ART
JOHN E. WORKMAN, JR. LETTERING
STEPHANIE VOZZO COLORIST
MIKE PELLERITO AND VICTOR GORELICK EDITORS
RICHARD GOLDWATER EDITOR-IN-CHIEF

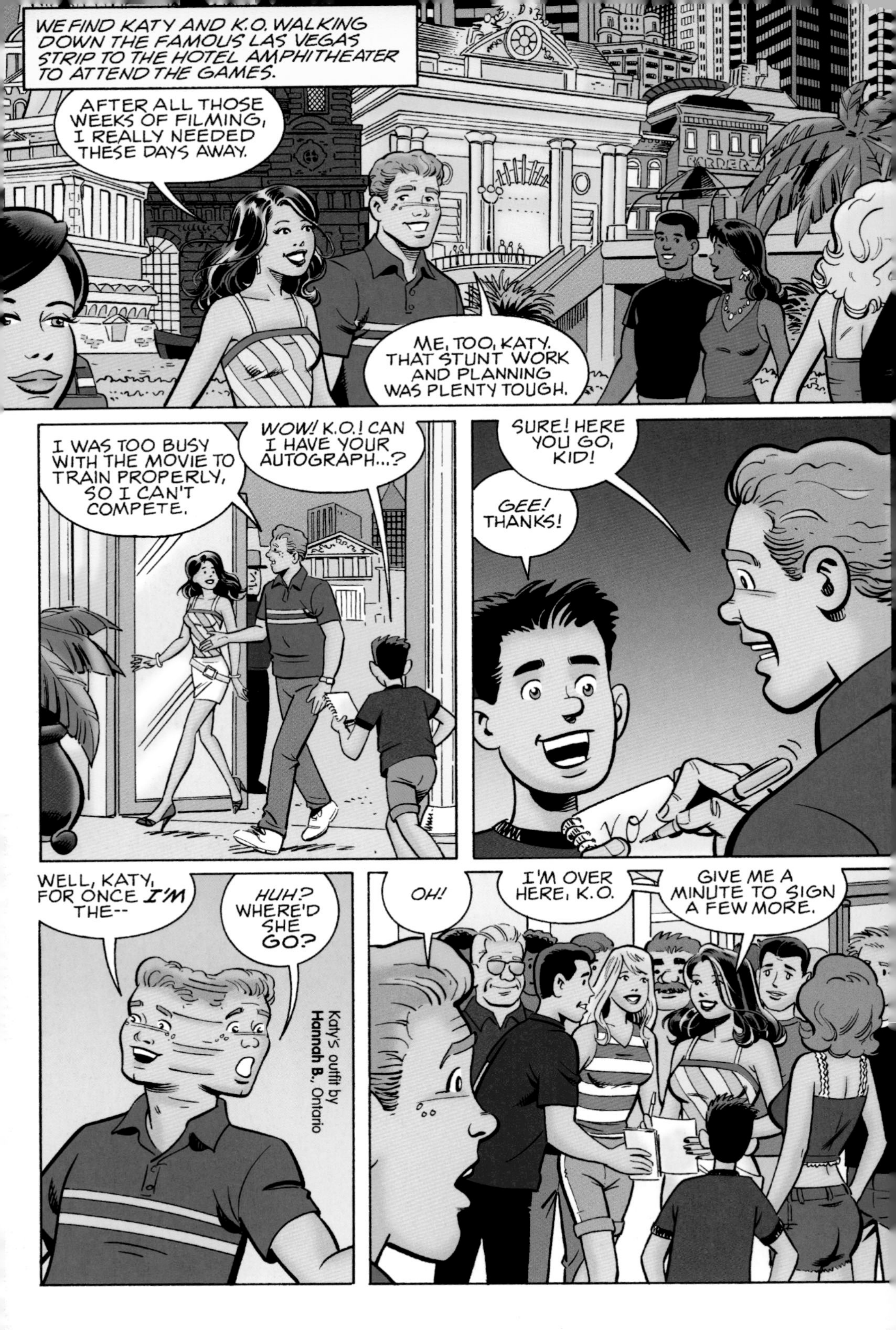
WE FIND KATY AND K.O. WALKING DOWN THE FAMOUS LAS VEGAS STRIP TO THE HOTEL AMPHITHEATER TO ATTEND THE GAMES.
AFTER ALL THOSE WEEKS OF FILMING, I REALLY NEEDED THESE DAYS AWAY.
ME, TOO, KATY. THAT STUNT WORK AND PLANNING WAS PLENTY TOUGH.
I WAS TOO BUSY WITH THE MOVIE TO TRAIN PROPERLY, SO I CAN'T COMPETE.
WOW! K.O.! CAN I HAVE YOUR AUTOGRAPH...?
SURE! HERE YOU GO, KID!
GEE! THANKS!
WELL, KATY, FOR ONCE I'M THE--
HUH? WHERE'D SHE GO?
Katy's outfit by Hannah B., Ontario
OH!
I'M OVER HERE, K.O.
GIVE ME A MINUTE TO SIGN A FEW MORE.

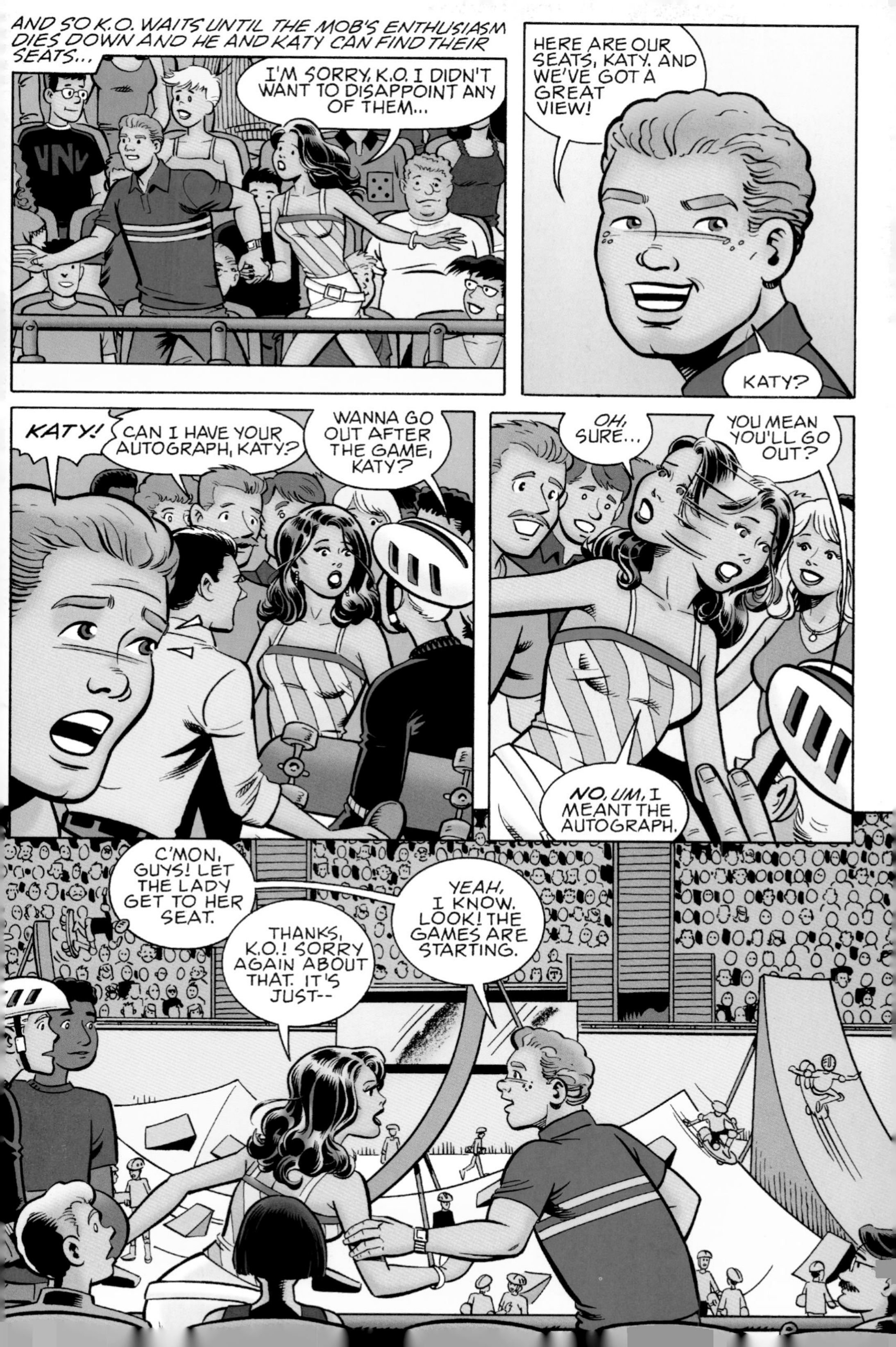
AND SO K.O. WAITS UNTIL THE MOB'S ENTHUSIASM DIES DOWN AND HE AND KATY CAN FIND THEIR SEATS...
I'M SORRY, K.O. I DIDN'T WANT TO DISAPPOINT ANY OF THEM...
HERE ARE OUR SEATS, KATY. AND WE'VE GOT A GREAT VIEW!
KATY?
KATY!
CAN I HAVE YOUR AUTOGRAPH, KATY?
WANNA GO OUT AFTER THE GAME, KATY?
OH, SURE...
YOU MEAN YOU'LL GO OUT?
NO, UM, I MEANT THE AUTOGRAPH.
C'MON, GUYS! LET THE LADY GET TO HER SEAT.
THANKS, K.O.! SORRY AGAIN ABOUT THAT. IT'S JUST--
YEAH, I KNOW. LOOK! THE GAMES ARE STARTING.

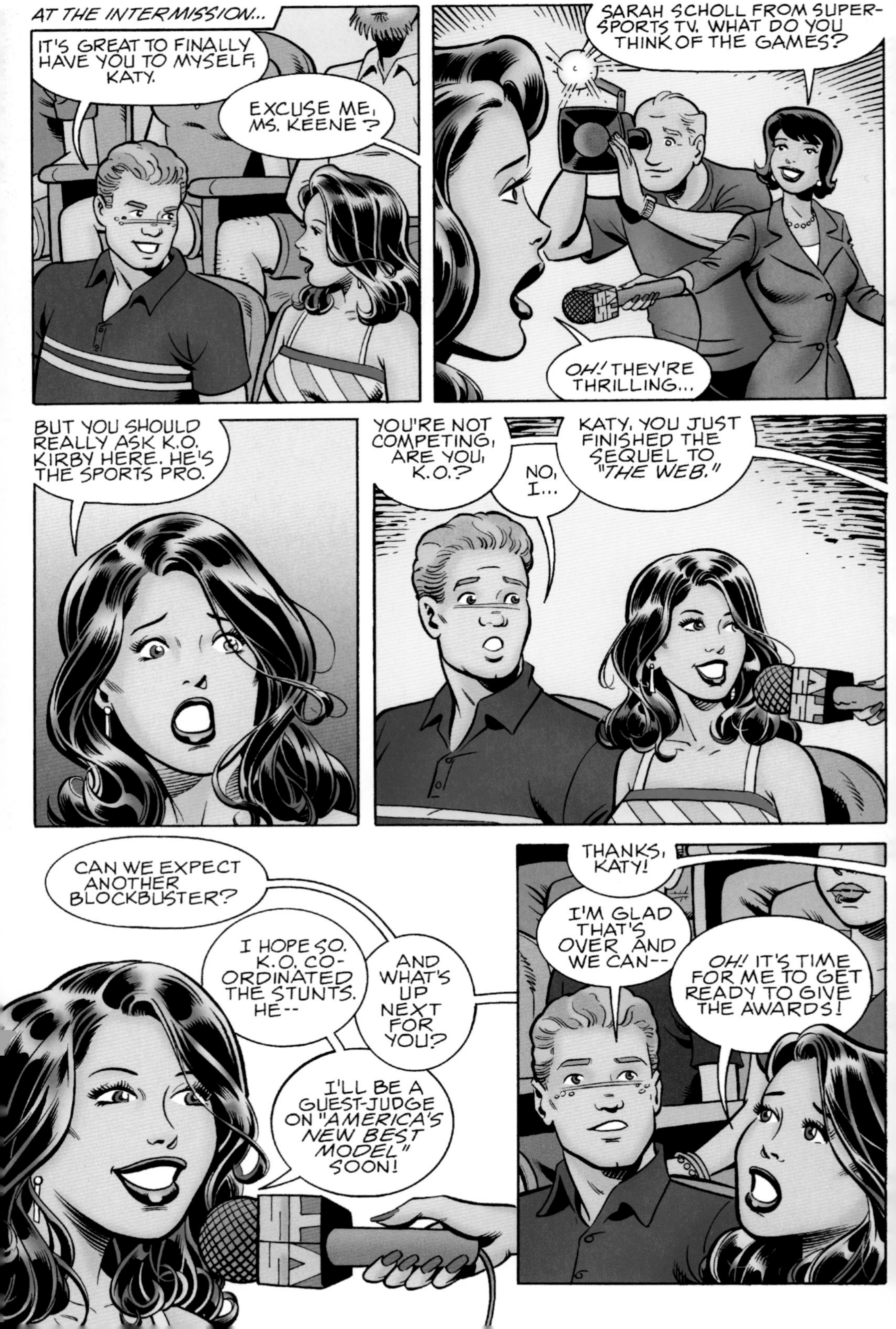
AT THE INTERMISSION...
IT'S GREAT TO FINALLY HAVE YOU TO MYSELF, KATY.
EXCUSE ME, MS. KEENE?
SARAH SCHOLL FROM SUPER-SPORTS TV. WHAT DO YOU THINK OF THE GAMES?
OH! THEY'RE THRILLING...
BUT YOU SHOULD REALLY ASK K.O. KIRBY HERE. HE'S THE SPORTS PRO.
YOU'RE NOT COMPETING, ARE YOU, K.O.?
NO, I...
KATY, YOU JUST FINISHED THE SEQUEL TO "THE WEB."
CAN WE EXPECT ANOTHER BLOCKBUSTER?
I HOPE SO. K.O. CO-ORDINATED THE STUNTS. HE--
AND WHAT'S UP NEXT FOR YOU?
I'LL BE A GUEST-JUDGE ON "AMERICA'S NEW BEST MODEL" SOON!
THANKS, KATY!
I'M GLAD THAT'S OVER AND WE CAN--
OH! IT'S TIME FOR ME TO GET READY TO GIVE THE AWARDS!

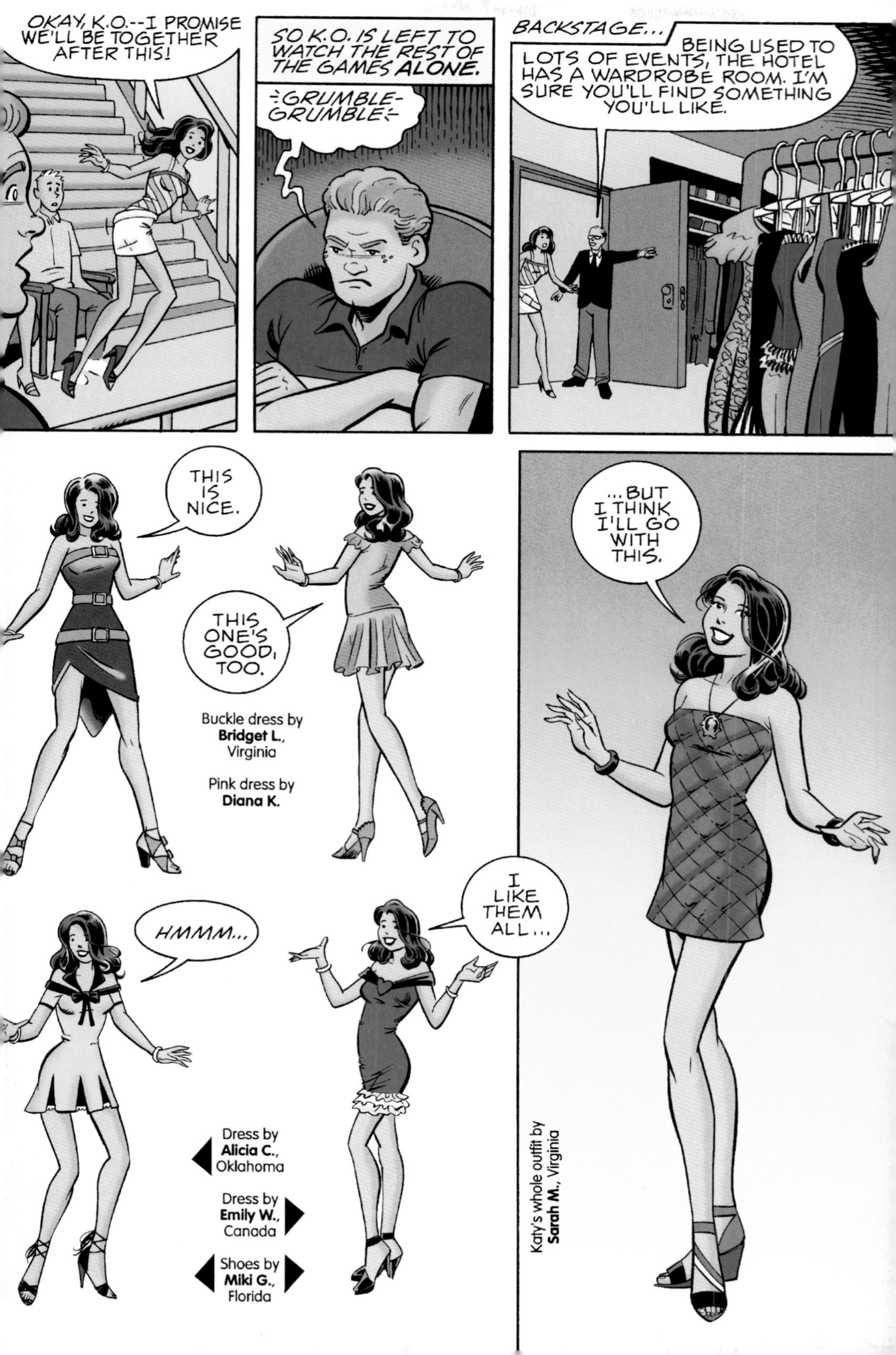
OKAY, K.O.--I PROMISE WE'LL BE TOGETHER AFTER THIS!
SO K.O. IS LEFT TO WATCH THE REST OF THE GAMES ALONE.
-GRUMBLE-GRUMBLE-
BACKSTAGE...
BEING USED TO LOTS OF EVENTS, THE HOTEL HAS A WARDROBE ROOM. I'M SURE YOU'LL FIND SOMETHING YOU'LL LIKE.
THIS IS NICE.
THIS ONE'S GOOD, TOO.
Buckle dress by Bridget L., Virginia
Pink dress by Diana K.
HMMM...
I LIKE THEM ALL...
Dress by Alicia C., Oklahoma
Dress by Emily W., Canada
Shoes by Miki G., Florida
...BUT I THINK I'LL GO WITH THIS.
Katy's whole outfit by Sarah M., Virginia

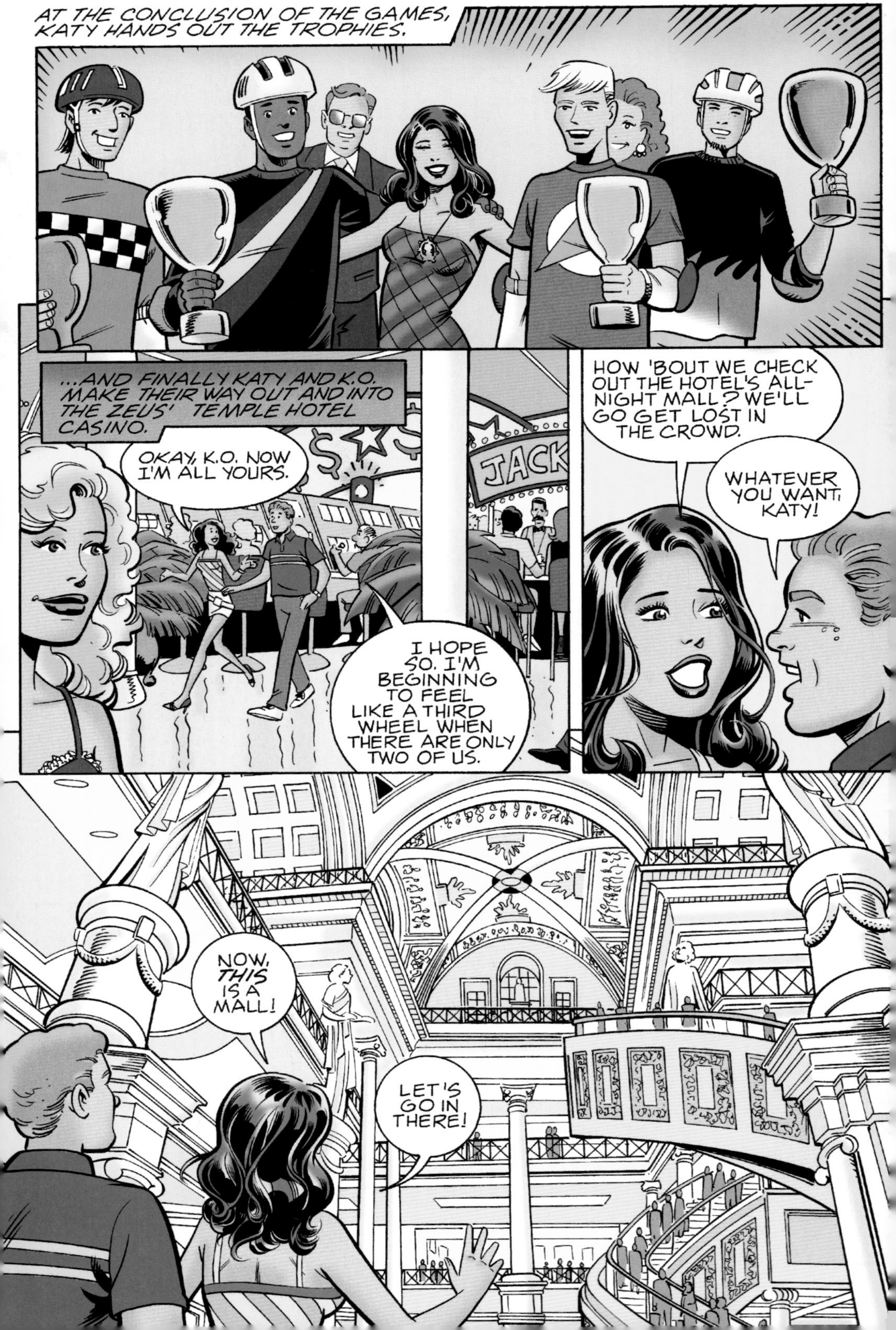
AT THE CONCLUSION OF THE GAMES, KATY HANDS OUT THE TROPHIES.
...AND FINALLY KATY AND K.O. MAKE THEIR WAY OUT AND INTO THE ZEUS' TEMPLE HOTEL CASINO.
OKAY, K.O. NOW I'M ALL YOURS.
I HOPE SO. I'M BEGINNING TO FEEL LIKE A THIRD WHEEL WHEN THERE ARE ONLY TWO OF US.
HOW 'BOUT WE CHECK OUT THE HOTEL'S ALL-NIGHT MALL? WE'LL GO GET LOST IN THE CROWD.
WHATEVER YOU WANT, KATY!
NOW, *THIS* IS A MALL!
LET'S GO IN THERE!

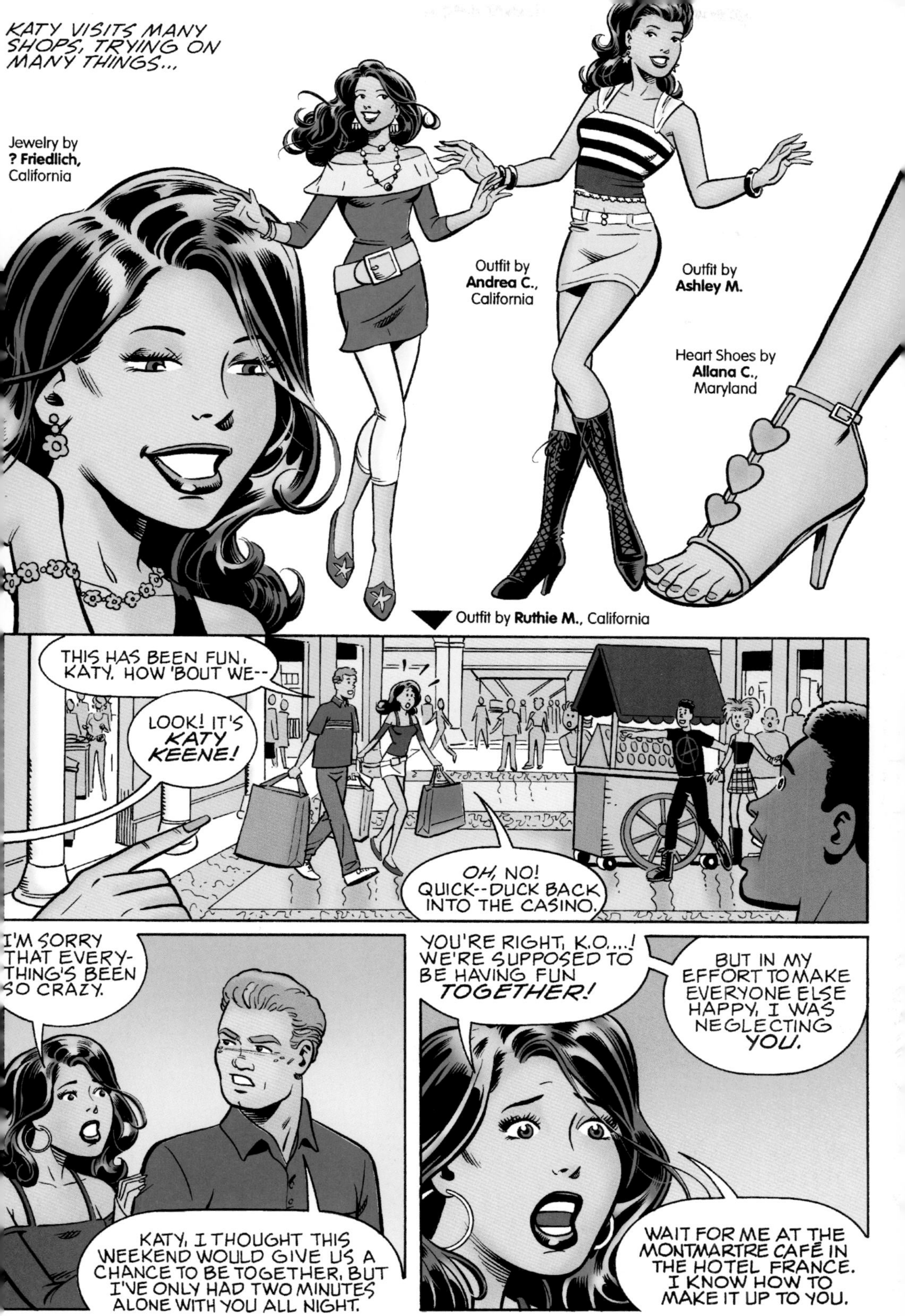
KATY VISITS MANY SHOPS, TRYING ON MANY THINGS...
Jewelry by **? Friedlich,** California
Outfit by **Andrea C.**, California
Outfit by **Ashley M.**
Heart Shoes by **Allana C.**, Maryland
Outfit by **Ruthie M.**, California
THIS HAS BEEN FUN, KATY. HOW 'BOUT WE--
LOOK! IT'S KATY KEENE!
OH, NO! QUICK--DUCK BACK INTO THE CASINO.
I'M SORRY THAT EVERYTHING'S BEEN SO CRAZY.
KATY, I THOUGHT THIS WEEKEND WOULD GIVE US A CHANCE TO BE TOGETHER, BUT I'VE ONLY HAD TWO MINUTES ALONE WITH YOU ALL NIGHT.
YOU'RE RIGHT, K.O....! WE'RE SUPPOSED TO BE HAVING FUN TOGETHER!
BUT IN MY EFFORT TO MAKE EVERYONE ELSE HAPPY, I WAS NEGLECTING YOU.
WAIT FOR ME AT THE MONTMARTRE CAFÉ IN THE HOTEL FRANCE. I KNOW HOW TO MAKE IT UP TO YOU.

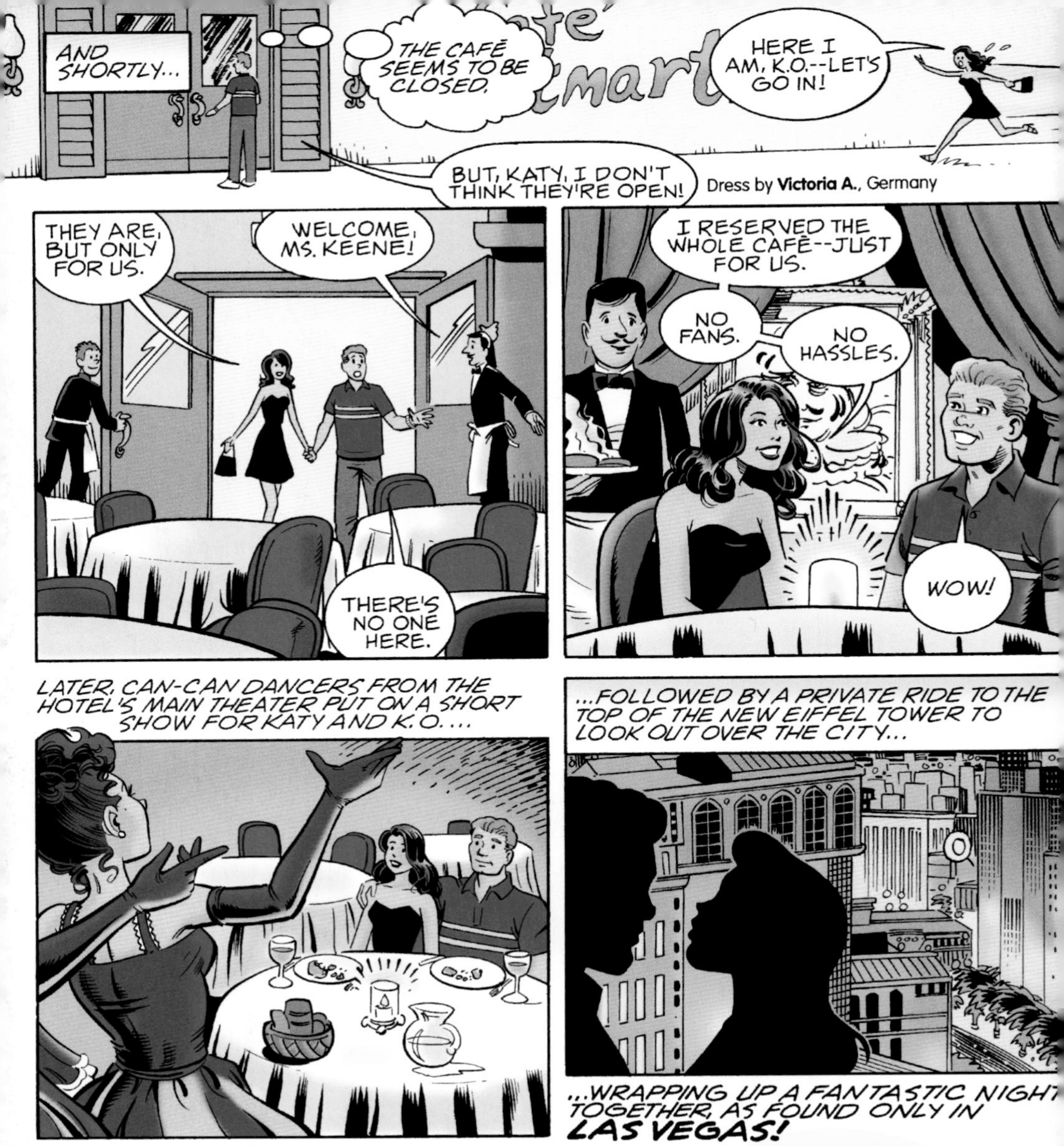
AND SHORTLY...
THE CAFÉ SEEMS TO BE CLOSED.
HERE I AM, K.O.--LET'S GO IN!
BUT, KATY, I DON'T THINK THEY'RE OPEN!
Dress by Victoria A., Germany
THEY ARE, BUT ONLY FOR US.
WELCOME, MS. KEENE!
THERE'S NO ONE HERE.
I RESERVED THE WHOLE CAFÉ--JUST FOR US.
NO FANS.
NO HASSLES.
WOW!
LATER, CAN-CAN DANCERS FROM THE HOTEL'S MAIN THEATER PUT ON A SHORT SHOW FOR KATY AND K.O....
...FOLLOWED BY A PRIVATE RIDE TO THE TOP OF THE NEW EIFFEL TOWER TO LOOK OUT OVER THE CITY...
...WRAPPING UP A FANTASTIC NIGHT TOGETHER, AS FOUND ONLY IN LAS VEGAS!

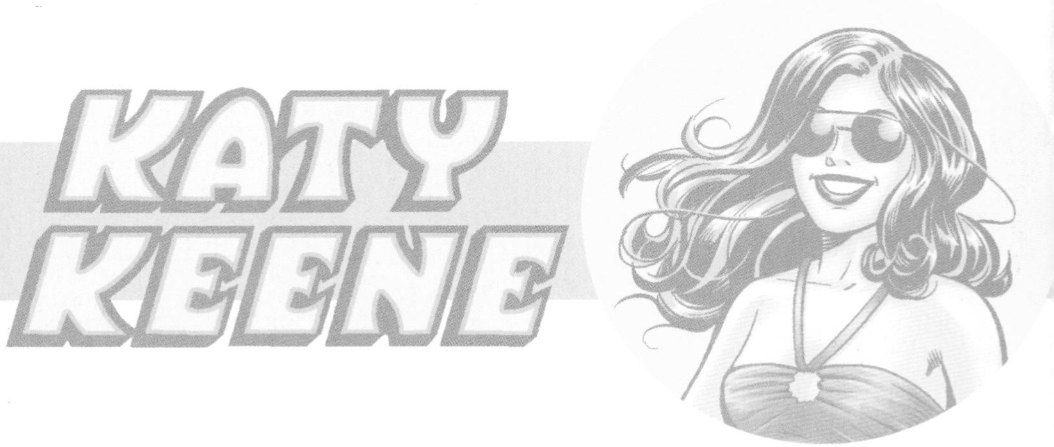
KATY KEENE

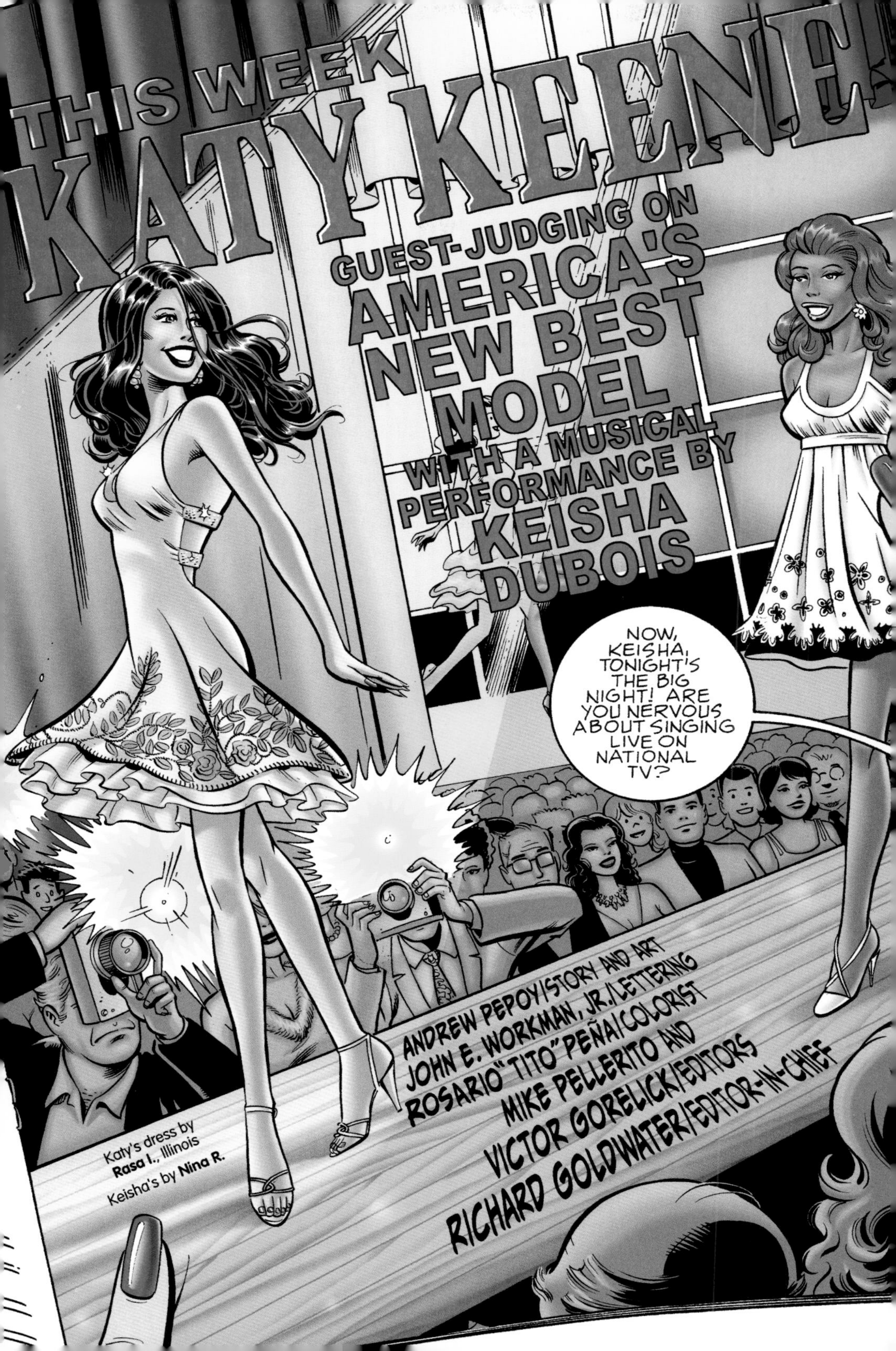
THIS WEEK
KATY KEENE
GUEST-JUDGING ON
AMERICA'S
NEW BEST
MODEL
WITH A MUSICAL
PERFORMANCE BY
KEISHA
DUBOIS
NOW, KEISHA, TONIGHT'S THE BIG NIGHT! ARE YOU NERVOUS ABOUT SINGING LIVE ON NATIONAL TV?
ANDREW PEPOY/STORY AND ART
JOHN E. WORKMAN, JR./LETTERING
ROSARIO "TITO" PEÑA/COLORIST
MIKE PELLERITO AND
VICTOR GORELICK/EDITORS
RICHARD GOLDWATER/EDITOR-IN-CHIEF
Katy's dress by
Rasa I., Illinois
Keisha's by Nina R.

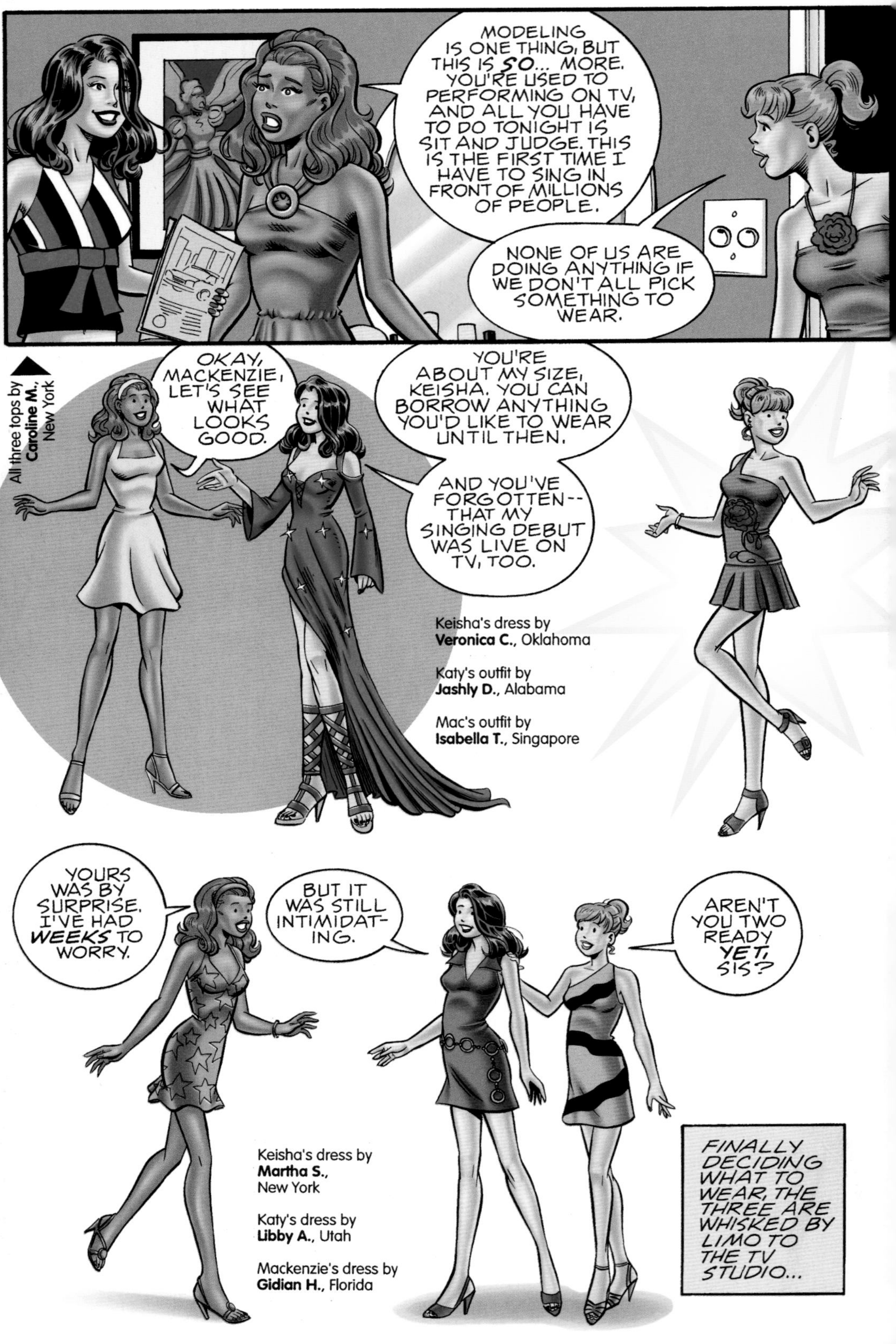
MODELING IS ONE THING, BUT THIS IS SO... MORE. YOU'RE USED TO PERFORMING ON TV, AND ALL YOU HAVE TO DO TONIGHT IS SIT AND JUDGE. THIS IS THE FIRST TIME I HAVE TO SING IN FRONT OF MILLIONS OF PEOPLE.
NONE OF US ARE DOING ANYTHING IF WE DON'T ALL PICK SOMETHING TO WEAR.
All three tops by Caroline M., New York
OKAY, MACKENZIE, LET'S SEE WHAT LOOKS GOOD.
YOU'RE ABOUT MY SIZE, KEISHA. YOU CAN BORROW ANYTHING YOU'D LIKE TO WEAR UNTIL THEN.
AND YOU'VE FORGOTTEN-- THAT MY SINGING DEBUT WAS LIVE ON TV, TOO.
Keisha's dress by Veronica C., Oklahoma
Katy's outfit by Jashly D., Alabama
Mac's outfit by Isabella T., Singapore
YOURS WAS BY SURPRISE. I'VE HAD WEEKS TO WORRY.
BUT IT WAS STILL INTIMIDAT-ING.
AREN'T YOU TWO READY YET, SIS?
Keisha's dress by Martha S., New York
Katy's dress by Libby A., Utah
Mackenzie's dress by Gidian H., Florida
FINALLY DECIDING WHAT TO WEAR, THE THREE ARE WHISKED BY LIMO TO THE TV STUDIO...

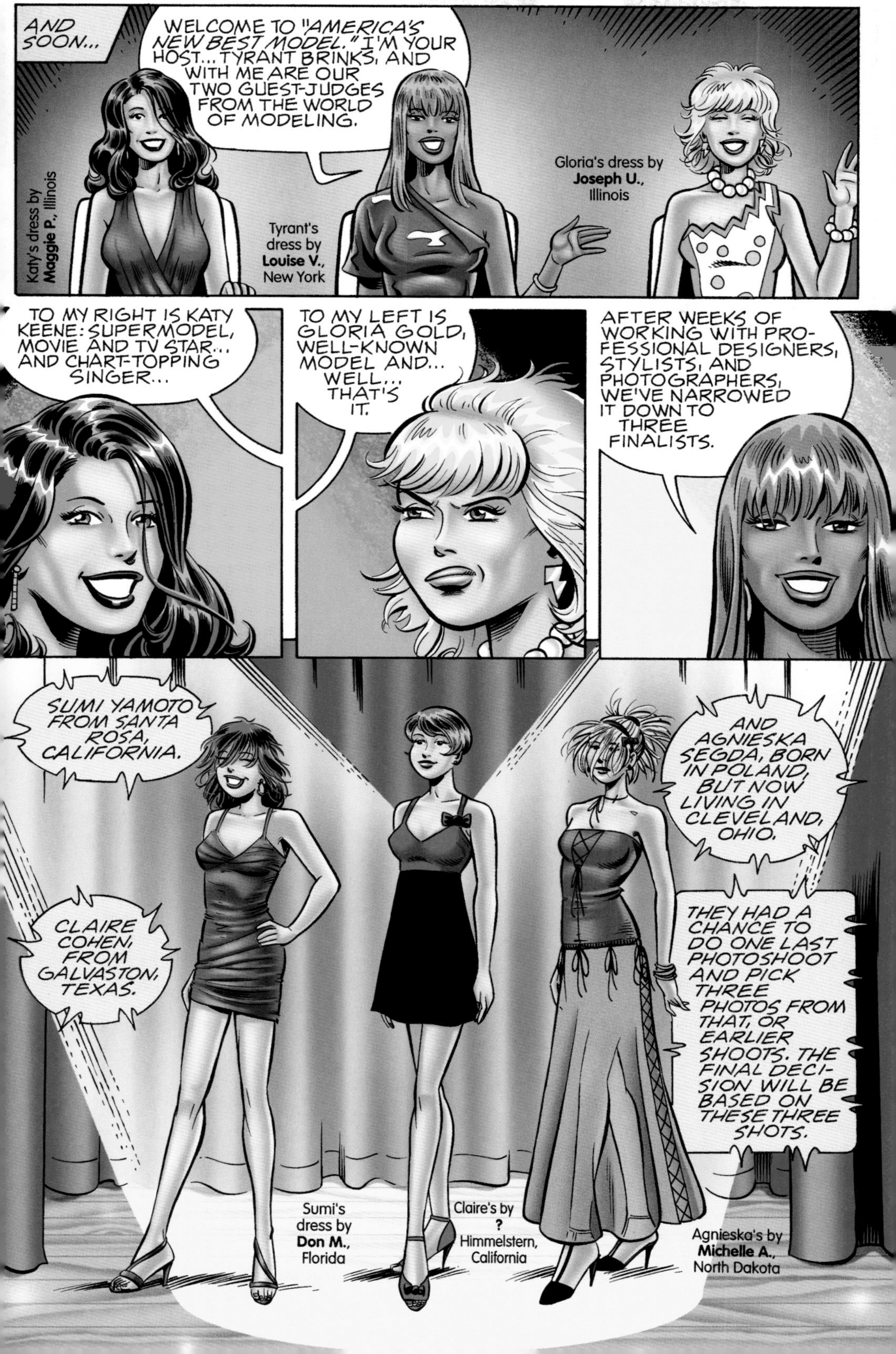
AND SOON...
WELCOME TO "AMERICA'S NEW BEST MODEL." I'M YOUR HOST... TYRANT BRINKS, AND WITH ME ARE OUR TWO GUEST-JUDGES FROM THE WORLD OF MODELING.
Katy's dress by Maggie P., Illinois
Tyrant's dress by Louise V., New York
Gloria's dress by Joseph U., Illinois
TO MY RIGHT IS KATY KEENE: SUPERMODEL, MOVIE AND TV STAR... AND CHART-TOPPING SINGER...
TO MY LEFT IS GLORIA GOLD, WELL-KNOWN MODEL AND... WELL... THAT'S IT.
AFTER WEEKS OF WORKING WITH PROFESSIONAL DESIGNERS, STYLISTS, AND PHOTOGRAPHERS, WE'VE NARROWED IT DOWN TO THREE FINALISTS.
SUMI YAMOTO FROM SANTA ROSA, CALIFORNIA.
CLAIRE COHEN, FROM GALVASTON, TEXAS.
AND AGNIESKA SEGDA, BORN IN POLAND, BUT NOW LIVING IN CLEVELAND, OHIO.
THEY HAD A CHANCE TO DO ONE LAST PHOTOSHOOT AND PICK THREE PHOTOS FROM THAT, OR EARLIER SHOOTS. THE FINAL DECISION WILL BE BASED ON THESE THREE SHOTS.
Sumi's dress by Don M., Florida
Claire's by ? Himmelstern, California
Agnieska's by Michelle A., North Dakota

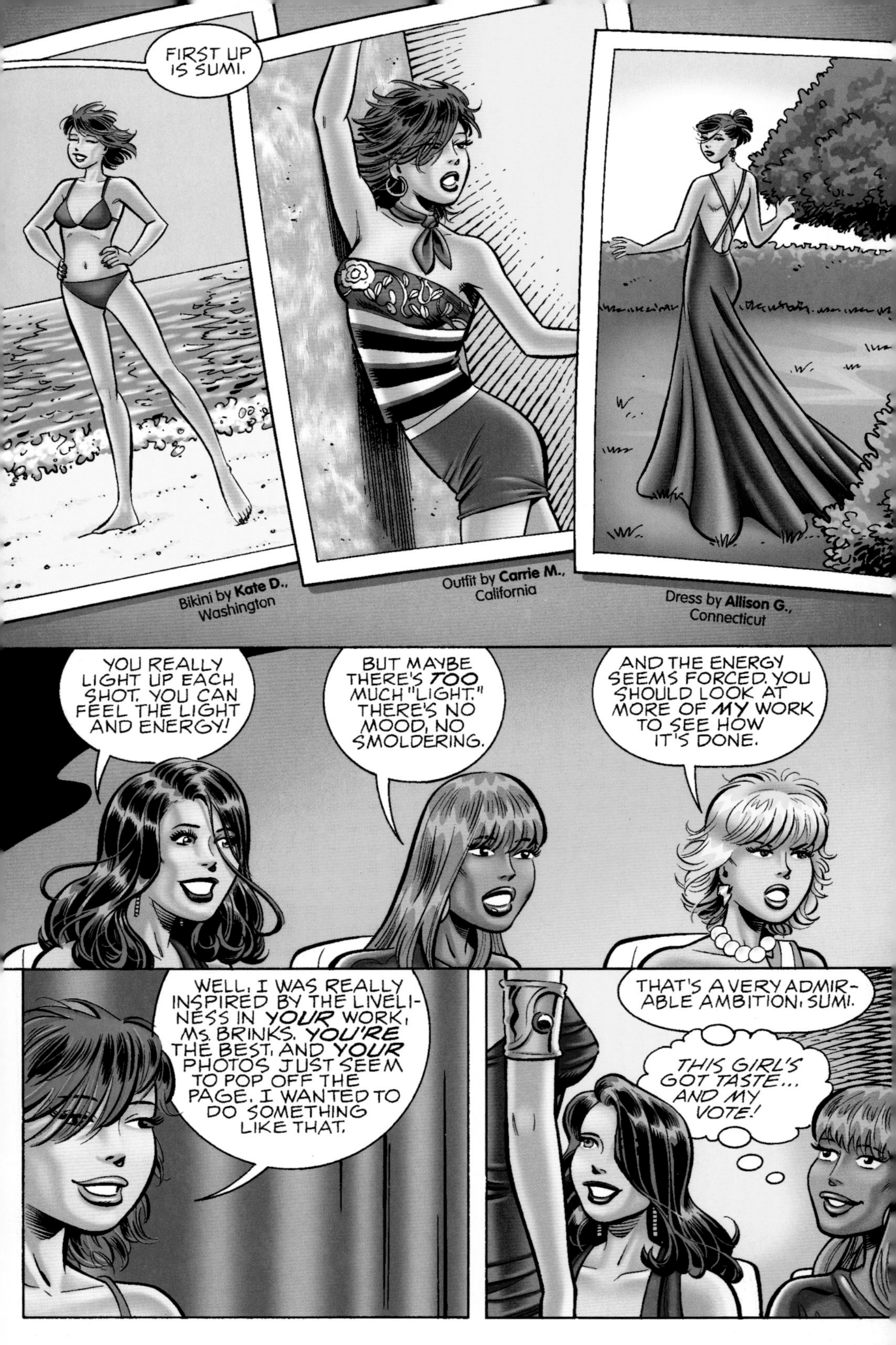
FIRST UP IS SUMI.
Bikini by Kate D., Washington
Outfit by Carrie M., California
Dress by Allison G., Connecticut
YOU REALLY LIGHT UP EACH SHOT. YOU CAN FEEL THE LIGHT AND ENERGY!
BUT MAYBE THERE'S TOO MUCH "LIGHT." THERE'S NO MOOD, NO SMOLDERING.
AND THE ENERGY SEEMS FORCED. YOU SHOULD LOOK AT MORE OF MY WORK TO SEE HOW IT'S DONE.
WELL, I WAS REALLY INSPIRED BY THE LIVELINESS IN YOUR WORK, Ms. BRINKS. YOU'RE THE BEST, AND YOUR PHOTOS JUST SEEM TO POP OFF THE PAGE. I WANTED TO DO SOMETHING LIKE THAT.
THAT'S A VERY ADMIRABLE AMBITION, SUMI.
THIS GIRL'S GOT TASTE... AND MY VOTE!

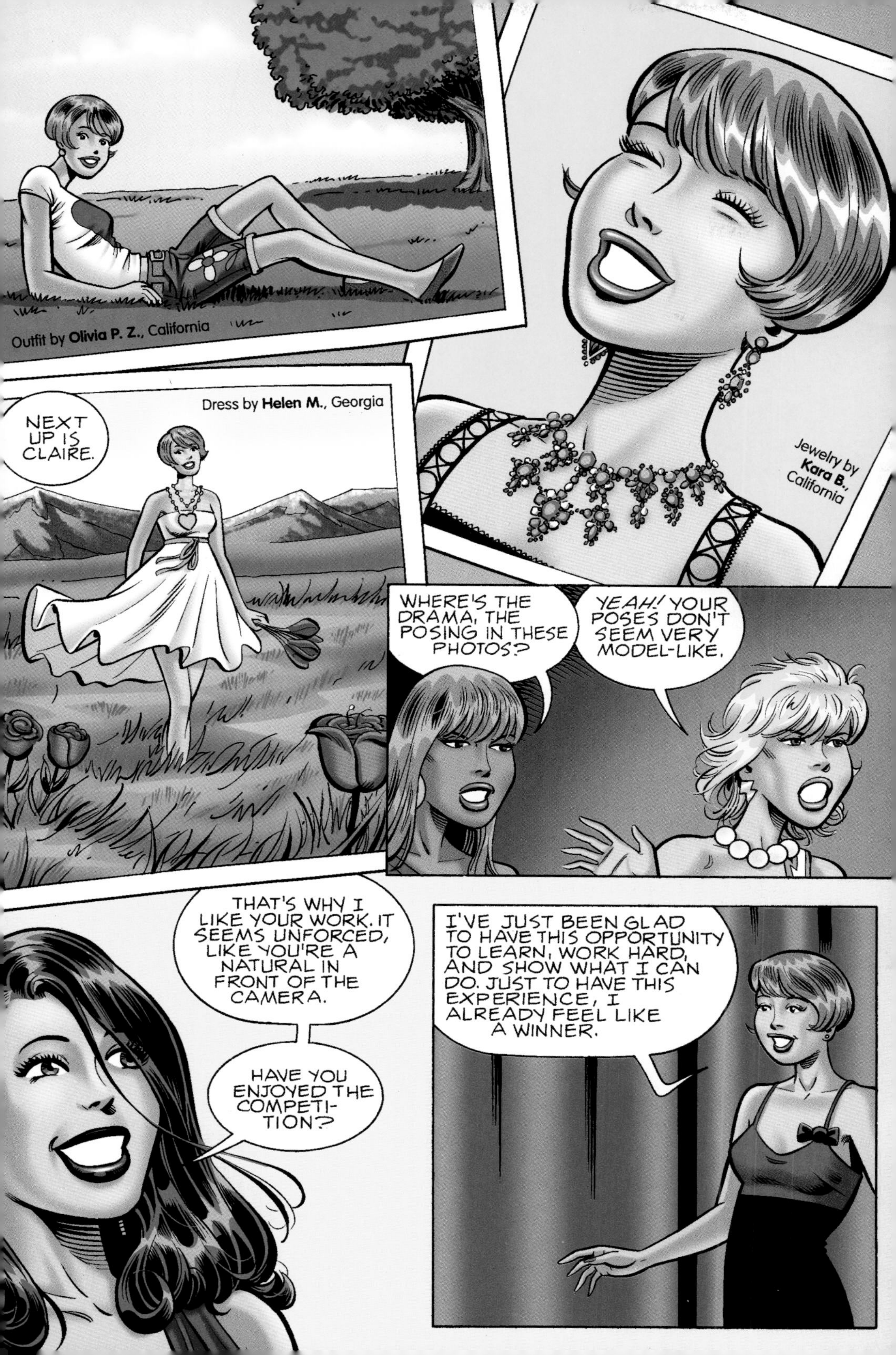
Outfit by Olivia P. Z., California
Jewelry by Kara B., California
NEXT UP IS CLAIRE.
Dress by Helen M., Georgia
WHERE'S THE DRAMA, THE POSING IN THESE PHOTOS?
YEAH! YOUR POSES DON'T SEEM VERY MODEL-LIKE.
THAT'S WHY I LIKE YOUR WORK. IT SEEMS UNFORCED, LIKE YOU'RE A NATURAL IN FRONT OF THE CAMERA.
HAVE YOU ENJOYED THE COMPETI-TION?
I'VE JUST BEEN GLAD TO HAVE THIS OPPORTUNITY TO LEARN, WORK HARD, AND SHOW WHAT I CAN DO. JUST TO HAVE THIS EXPERIENCE, I ALREADY FEEL LIKE A WINNER.

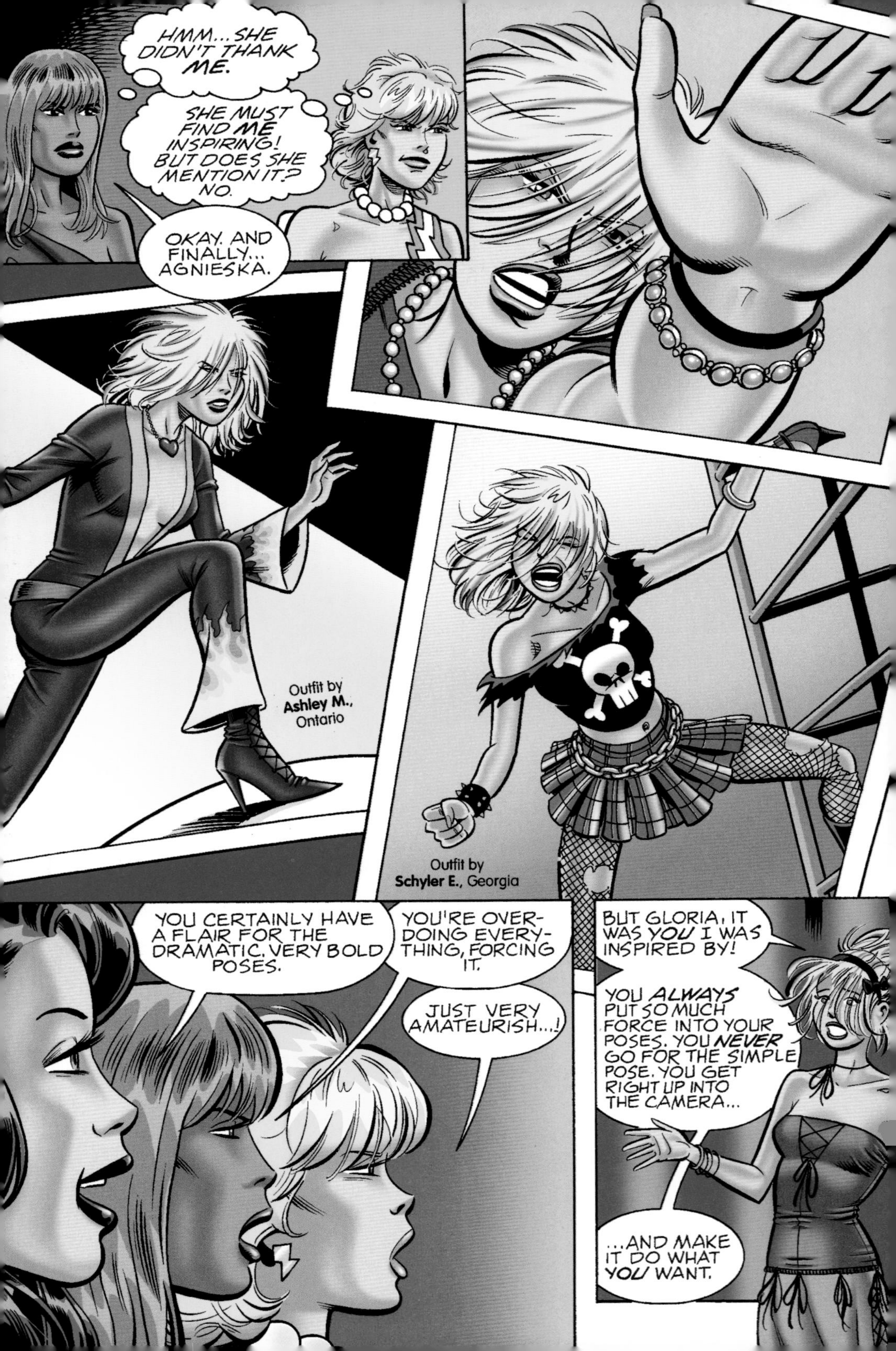
HMM... SHE DIDN'T THANK ME.
SHE MUST FIND ME INSPIRING! BUT DOES SHE MENTION IT? NO.
OKAY. AND FINALLY... AGNIESKA.
Outfit by Ashley M., Ontario
Outfit by Schyler E., Georgia
YOU CERTAINLY HAVE A FLAIR FOR THE DRAMATIC, VERY BOLD POSES.
YOU'RE OVER-DOING EVERY-THING, FORCING IT.
JUST VERY AMATEURISH...!
BUT GLORIA, IT WAS YOU I WAS INSPIRED BY!
YOU ALWAYS PUT SO MUCH FORCE INTO YOUR POSES. YOU NEVER GO FOR THE SIMPLE POSE. YOU GET RIGHT UP INTO THE CAMERA...
...AND MAKE IT DO WHAT YOU WANT.

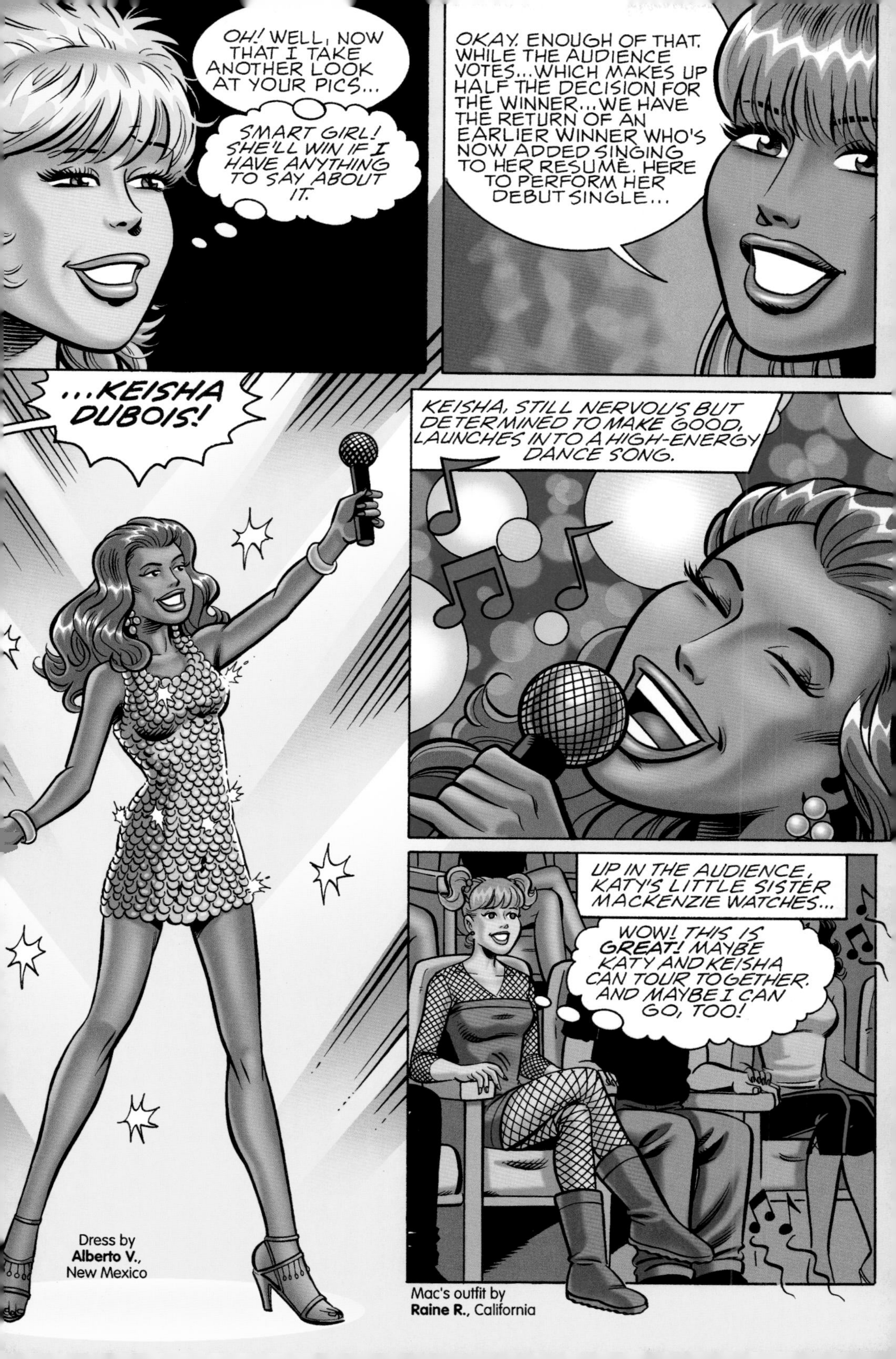
OH! WELL, NOW THAT I TAKE ANOTHER LOOK AT YOUR PICS...
SMART GIRL! SHE'LL WIN IF I HAVE ANYTHING TO SAY ABOUT IT.
OKAY. ENOUGH OF THAT. WHILE THE AUDIENCE VOTES...WHICH MAKES UP HALF THE DECISION FOR THE WINNER...WE HAVE THE RETURN OF AN EARLIER WINNER WHO'S NOW ADDED SINGING TO HER RESUMÈ. HERE TO PERFORM HER DEBUT SINGLE...
...KEISHA DUBOIS!
KEISHA, STILL NERVOUS BUT DETERMINED TO MAKE GOOD, LAUNCHES INTO A HIGH-ENERGY DANCE SONG.
UP IN THE AUDIENCE, KATY'S LITTLE SISTER MACKENZIE WATCHES...
WOW! THIS IS GREAT! MAYBE KATY AND KEISHA CAN TOUR TOGETHER. AND MAYBE I CAN GO, TOO!
Dress by **Alberto V.**, New Mexico
Mac's outfit by **Raine R.**, California

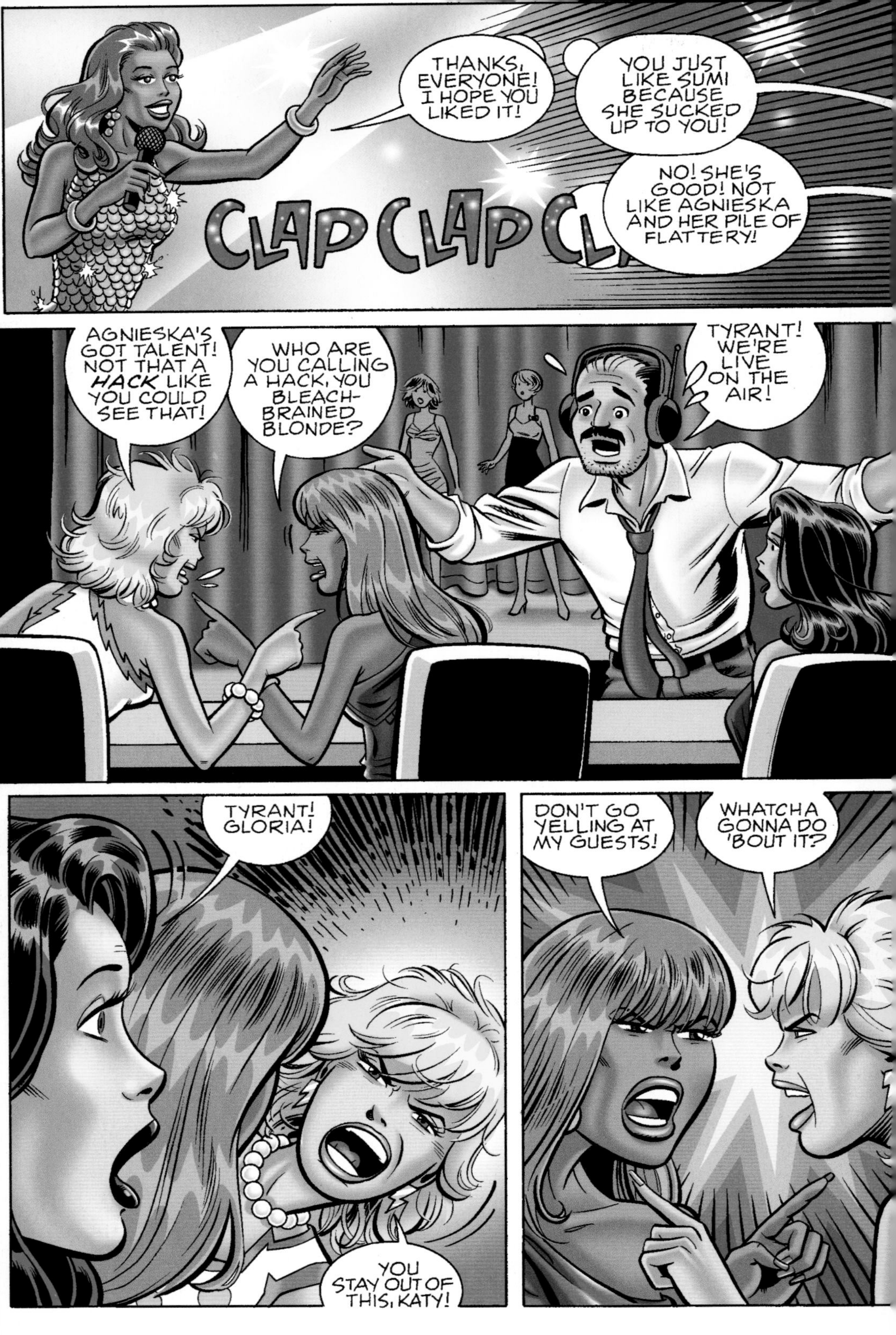
THANKS, EVERYONE! I HOPE YOU LIKED IT!
YOU JUST LIKE SUMI BECAUSE SHE SUCKED UP TO YOU!
NO! SHE'S GOOD! NOT LIKE AGNIESKA AND HER PILE OF FLATTERY!
CLAP CLAP CL
AGNIESKA'S GOT TALENT! NOT THAT A HACK LIKE YOU COULD SEE THAT!
WHO ARE YOU CALLING A HACK, YOU BLEACH-BRAINED BLONDE?
TYRANT! WE'RE LIVE ON THE AIR!
TYRANT! GLORIA!
YOU STAY OUT OF THIS, KATY!
DON'T GO YELLING AT MY GUESTS!
WHATCHA GONNA DO 'BOUT IT?

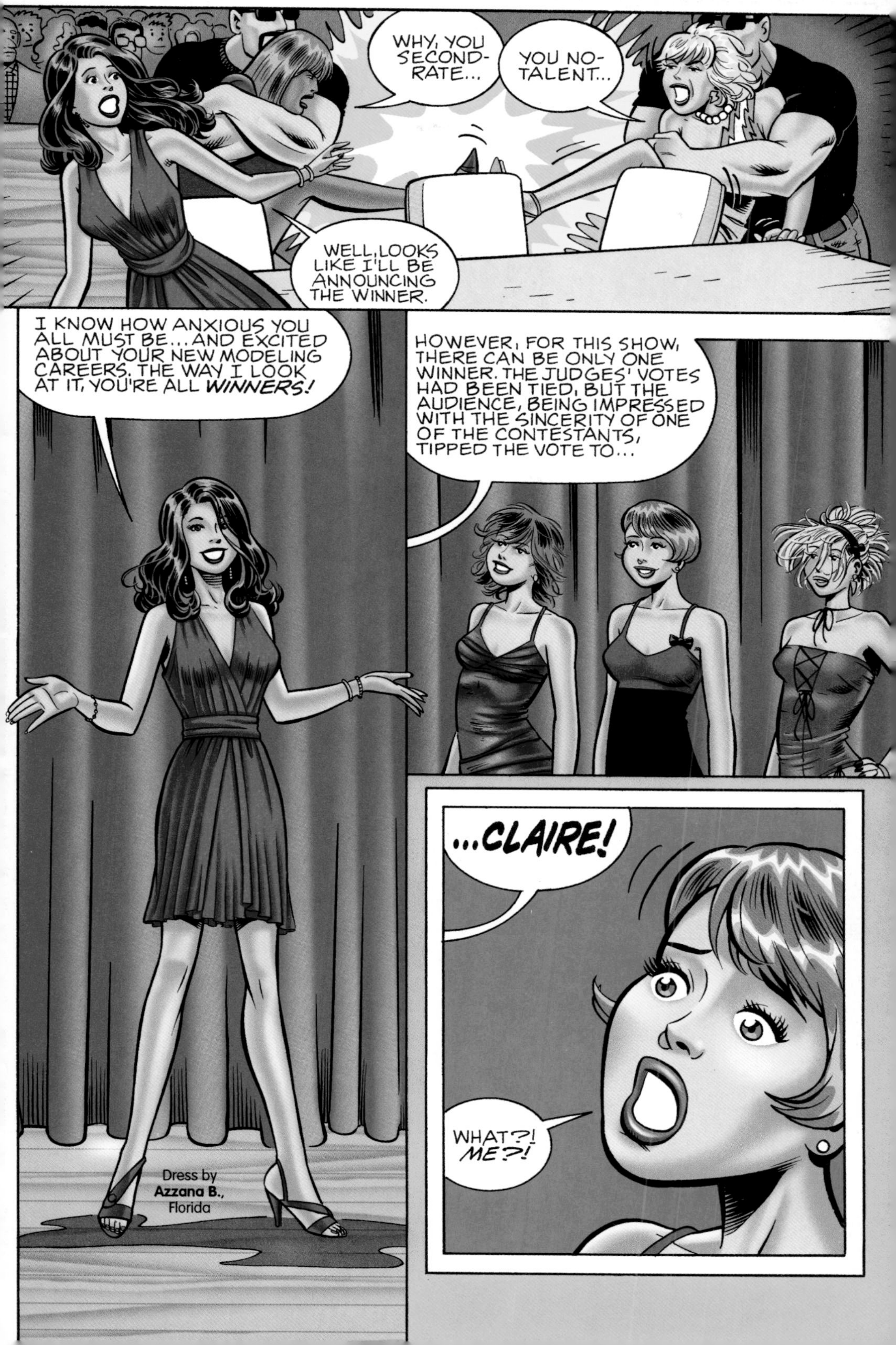
WHY, YOU SECOND-RATE...
YOU NO-TALENT...
WELL, LOOKS LIKE I'LL BE ANNOUNCING THE WINNER.
I KNOW HOW ANXIOUS YOU ALL MUST BE... AND EXCITED ABOUT YOUR NEW MODELING CAREERS. THE WAY I LOOK AT IT, YOU'RE ALL WINNERS!
Dress by Azzana B., Florida
HOWEVER, FOR THIS SHOW, THERE CAN BE ONLY ONE WINNER. THE JUDGES' VOTES HAD BEEN TIED, BUT THE AUDIENCE, BEING IMPRESSED WITH THE SINCERITY OF ONE OF THE CONTESTANTS, TIPPED THE VOTE TO...
...CLAIRE!
WHAT?! ME?!

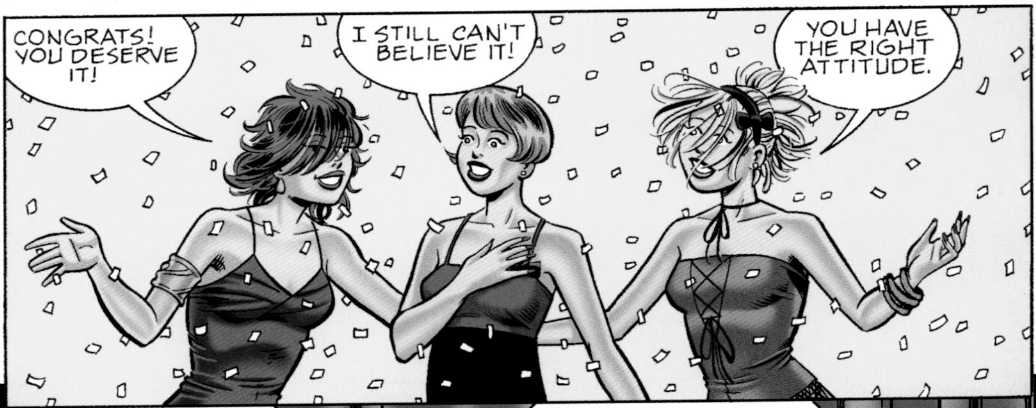
CONGRATS! YOU DESERVE IT!
I STILL CAN'T BELIEVE IT!
YOU HAVE THE RIGHT ATTITUDE.

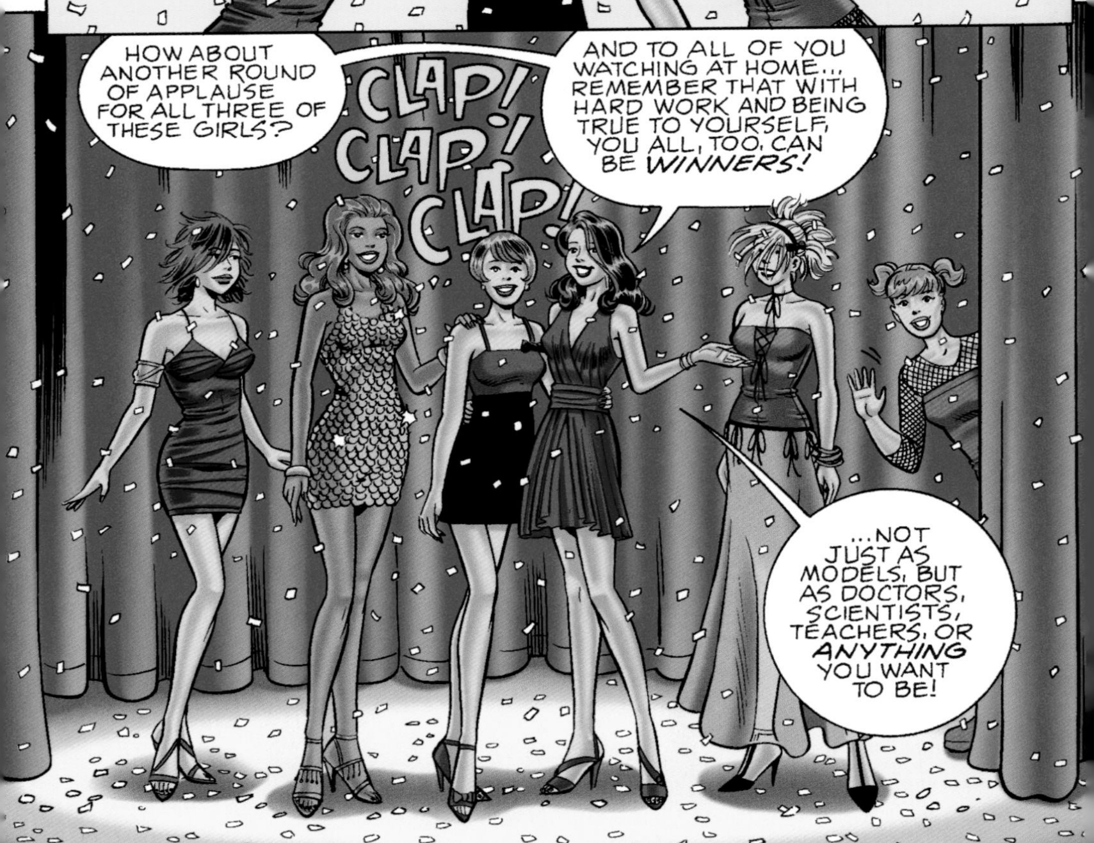
HOW ABOUT ANOTHER ROUND OF APPLAUSE FOR ALL THREE OF THESE GIRLS?
CLAP! CLAP! CLAP!
AND TO ALL OF YOU WATCHING AT HOME... REMEMBER THAT WITH HARD WORK AND BEING TRUE TO YOURSELF, YOU ALL, TOO, CAN BE WINNERS!
...NOT JUST AS MODELS, BUT AS DOCTORS, SCIENTISTS, TEACHERS, OR ANYTHING YOU WANT TO BE!

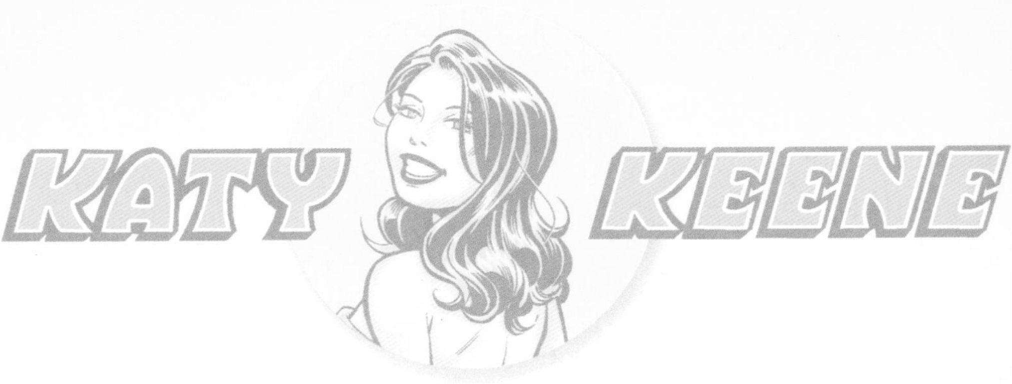
KATY KEENE

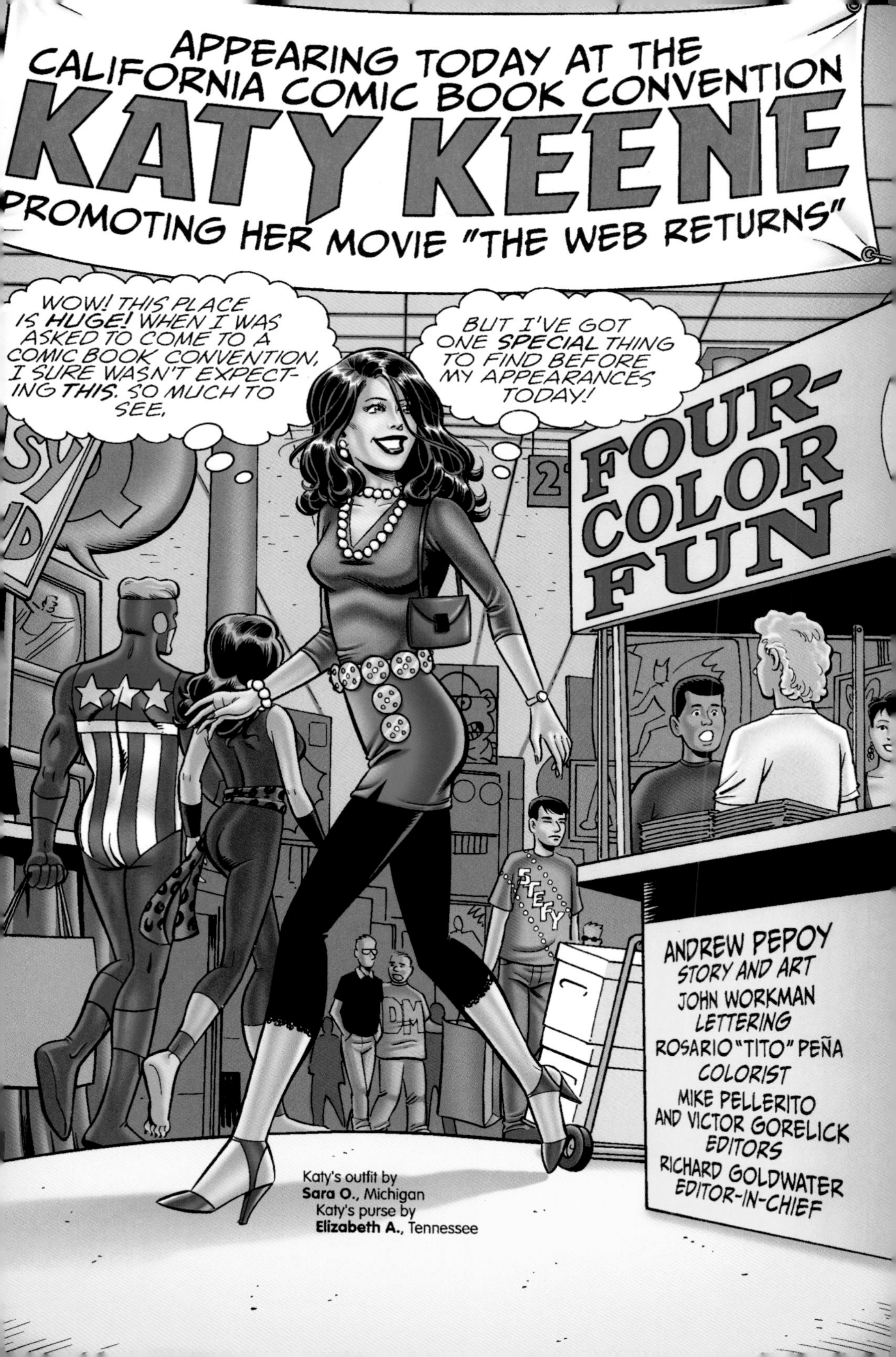
APPEARING TODAY AT THE CALIFORNIA COMIC BOOK CONVENTION
KATY KEENE
PROMOTING HER MOVIE "THE WEB RETURNS"
WOW! THIS PLACE IS HUGE! WHEN I WAS ASKED TO COME TO A COMIC BOOK CONVENTION, I SURE WASN'T EXPECTING THIS. SO MUCH TO SEE.
BUT I'VE GOT ONE SPECIAL THING TO FIND BEFORE MY APPEARANCES TODAY!
FOUR-COLOR FUN
STEFY
ANDREW PEPOY STORY AND ART
JOHN WORKMAN LETTERING
ROSARIO "TITO" PEÑA COLORIST
MIKE PELLERITO AND VICTOR GORELICK EDITORS
RICHARD GOLDWATER EDITOR-IN-CHIEF
Katy's outfit by Sara O., Michigan
Katy's purse by Elizabeth A., Tennessee

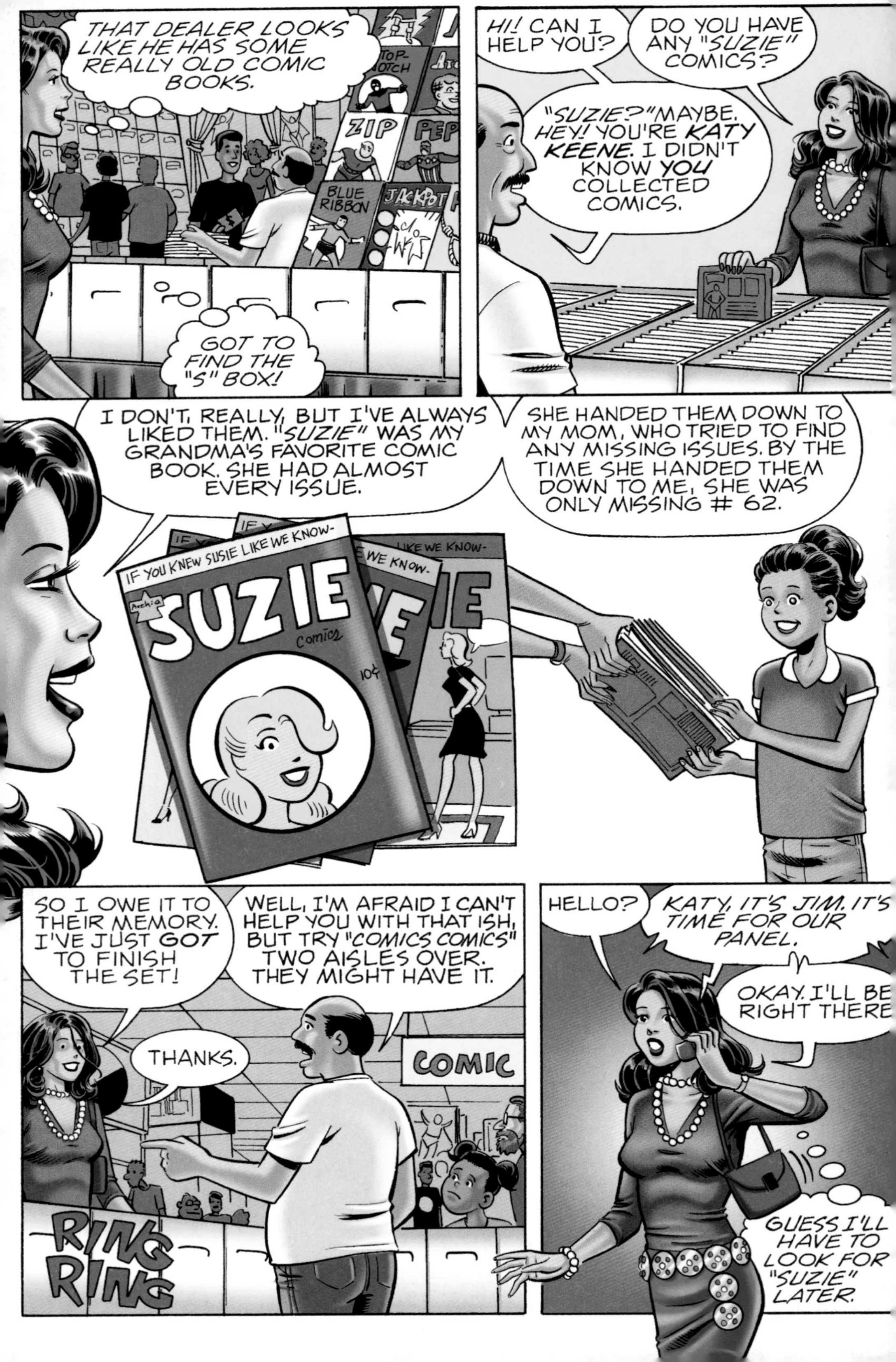
THAT DEALER LOOKS LIKE HE HAS SOME REALLY OLD COMIC BOOKS.
TOP-NOTCH
ZIP
PEP
BLUE RIBBON
JACKPOT
GOT TO FIND THE "S" BOX!
HI! CAN I HELP YOU?
DO YOU HAVE ANY "SUZIE" COMICS?
"SUZIE?" MAYBE. HEY! YOU'RE KATY KEENE. I DIDN'T KNOW YOU COLLECTED COMICS.
I DON'T, REALLY, BUT I'VE ALWAYS LIKED THEM. "SUZIE" WAS MY GRANDMA'S FAVORITE COMIC BOOK. SHE HAD ALMOST EVERY ISSUE.
SHE HANDED THEM DOWN TO MY MOM, WHO TRIED TO FIND ANY MISSING ISSUES. BY THE TIME SHE HANDED THEM DOWN TO ME, SHE WAS ONLY MISSING # 62.
IF YOU KNEW SUSIE LIKE WE KNOW-
SUZIE
Comics
10¢
SO I OWE IT TO THEIR MEMORY. I'VE JUST GOT TO FINISH THE SET!
WELL, I'M AFRAID I CAN'T HELP YOU WITH THAT ISH, BUT TRY "COMICS COMICS" TWO AISLES OVER. THEY MIGHT HAVE IT.
THANKS.
COMIC
RING RING
HELLO?
KATY, IT'S JIM. IT'S TIME FOR OUR PANEL.
OKAY. I'LL BE RIGHT THERE
GUESS I'LL HAVE TO LOOK FOR "SUZIE" LATER.

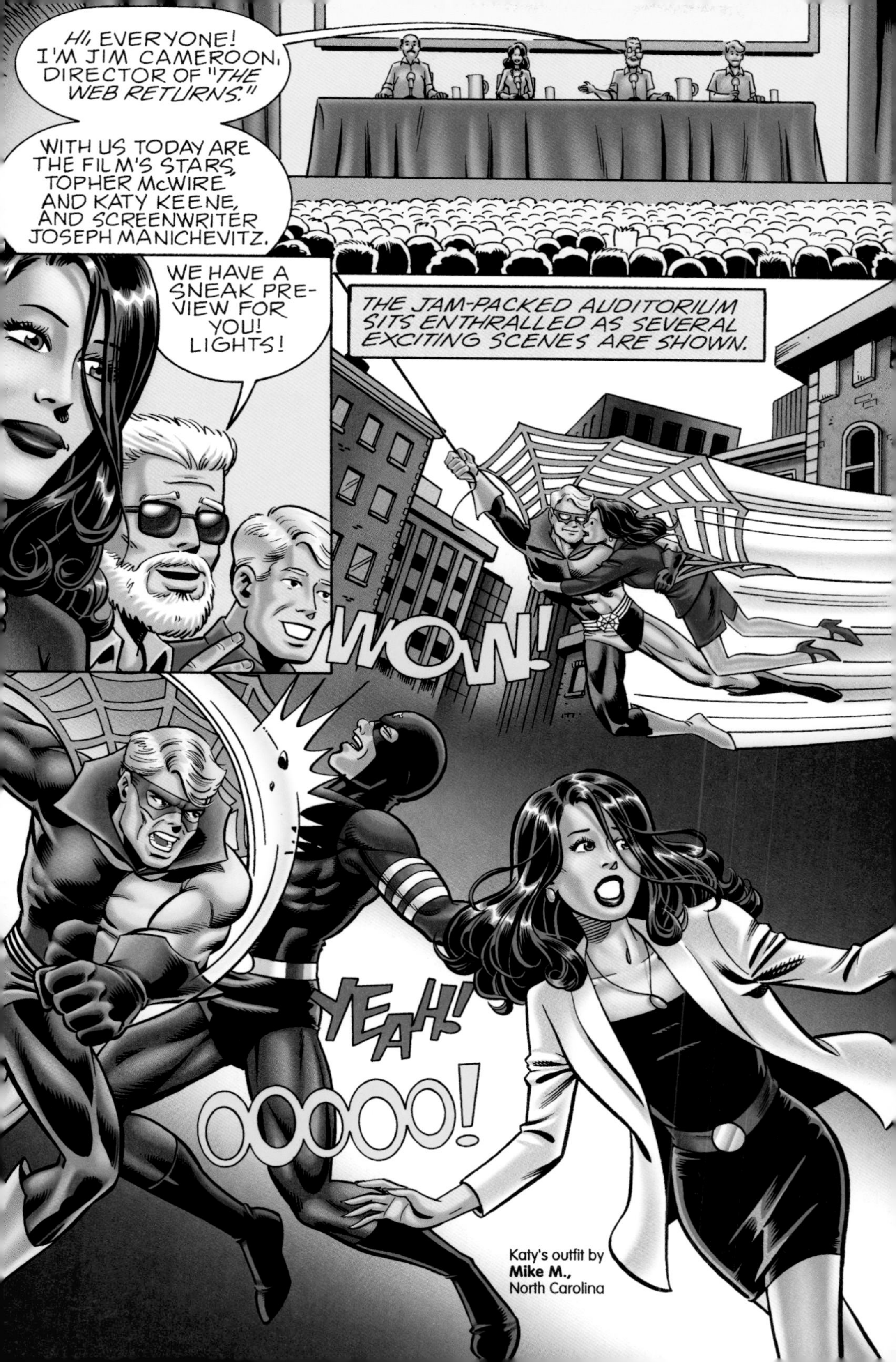
HI, EVERYONE! I'M JIM CAMEROON, DIRECTOR OF "THE WEB RETURNS."
WITH US TODAY ARE THE FILM'S STARS, TOPHER McWIRE AND KATY KEENE, AND SCREENWRITER JOSEPH MANICHEVITZ.
WE HAVE A SNEAK PRE-VIEW FOR YOU! LIGHTS!
THE JAM-PACKED AUDITORIUM SITS ENTHRALLED AS SEVERAL EXCITING SCENES ARE SHOWN.
WOW!
YEAH!
OOOOO!
Katy's outfit by
Mike M.,
North Carolina

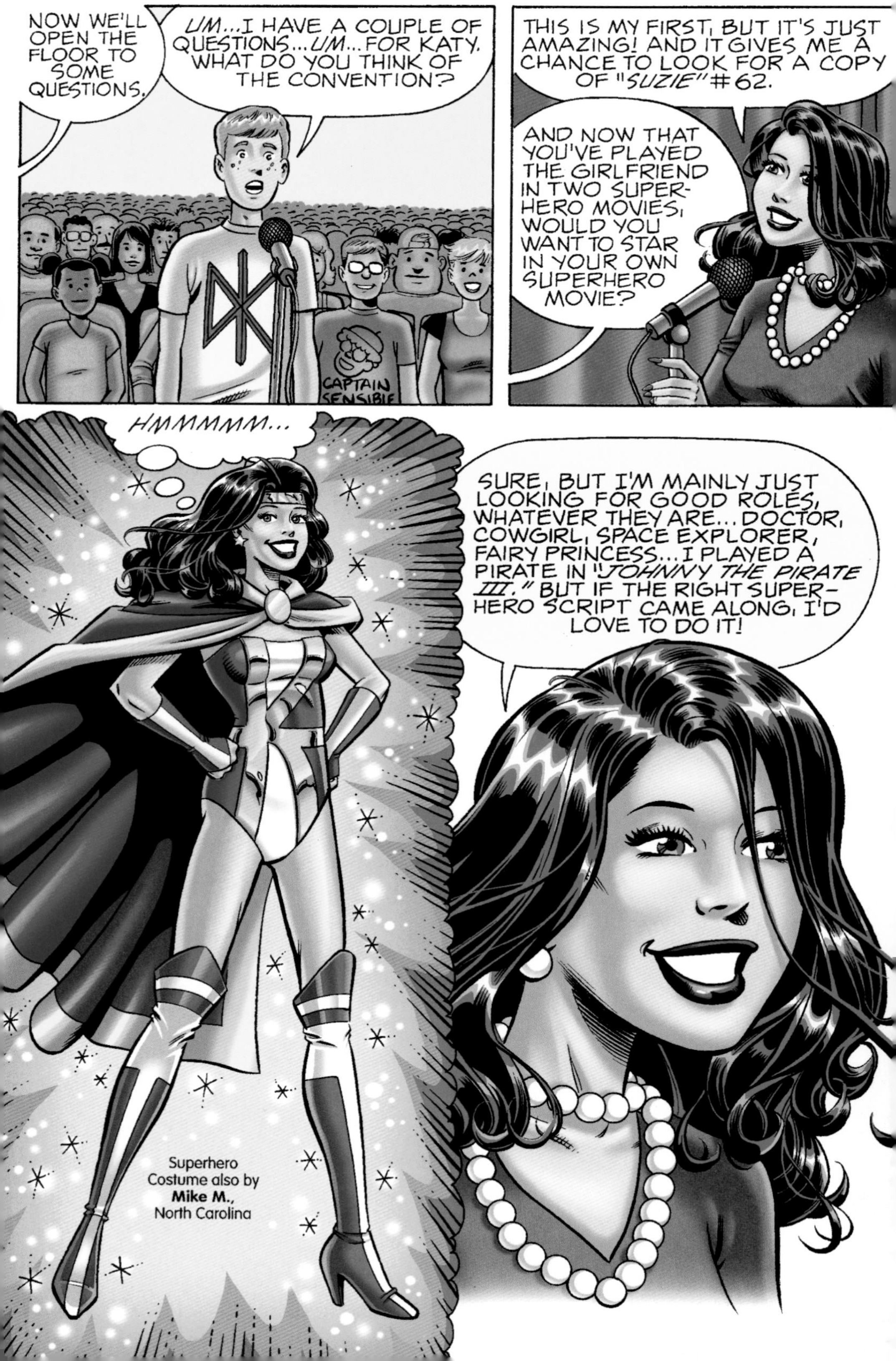
NOW WE'LL OPEN THE FLOOR TO SOME QUESTIONS.
UM...I HAVE A COUPLE OF QUESTIONS...UM...FOR KATY. WHAT DO YOU THINK OF THE CONVENTION?
CAPTAIN SENSIBLE
THIS IS MY FIRST, BUT IT'S JUST AMAZING! AND IT GIVES ME A CHANCE TO LOOK FOR A COPY OF "SUZIE" #62.
AND NOW THAT YOU'VE PLAYED THE GIRLFRIEND IN TWO SUPER-HERO MOVIES, WOULD YOU WANT TO STAR IN YOUR OWN SUPERHERO MOVIE?
HMMMMMM...
SURE, BUT I'M MAINLY JUST LOOKING FOR GOOD ROLES, WHATEVER THEY ARE... DOCTOR, COWGIRL, SPACE EXPLORER, FAIRY PRINCESS... I PLAYED A PIRATE IN "JOHNNY THE PIRATE III." BUT IF THE RIGHT SUPER-HERO SCRIPT CAME ALONG, I'D LOVE TO DO IT!
Superhero Costume also by **Mike M.**, North Carolina

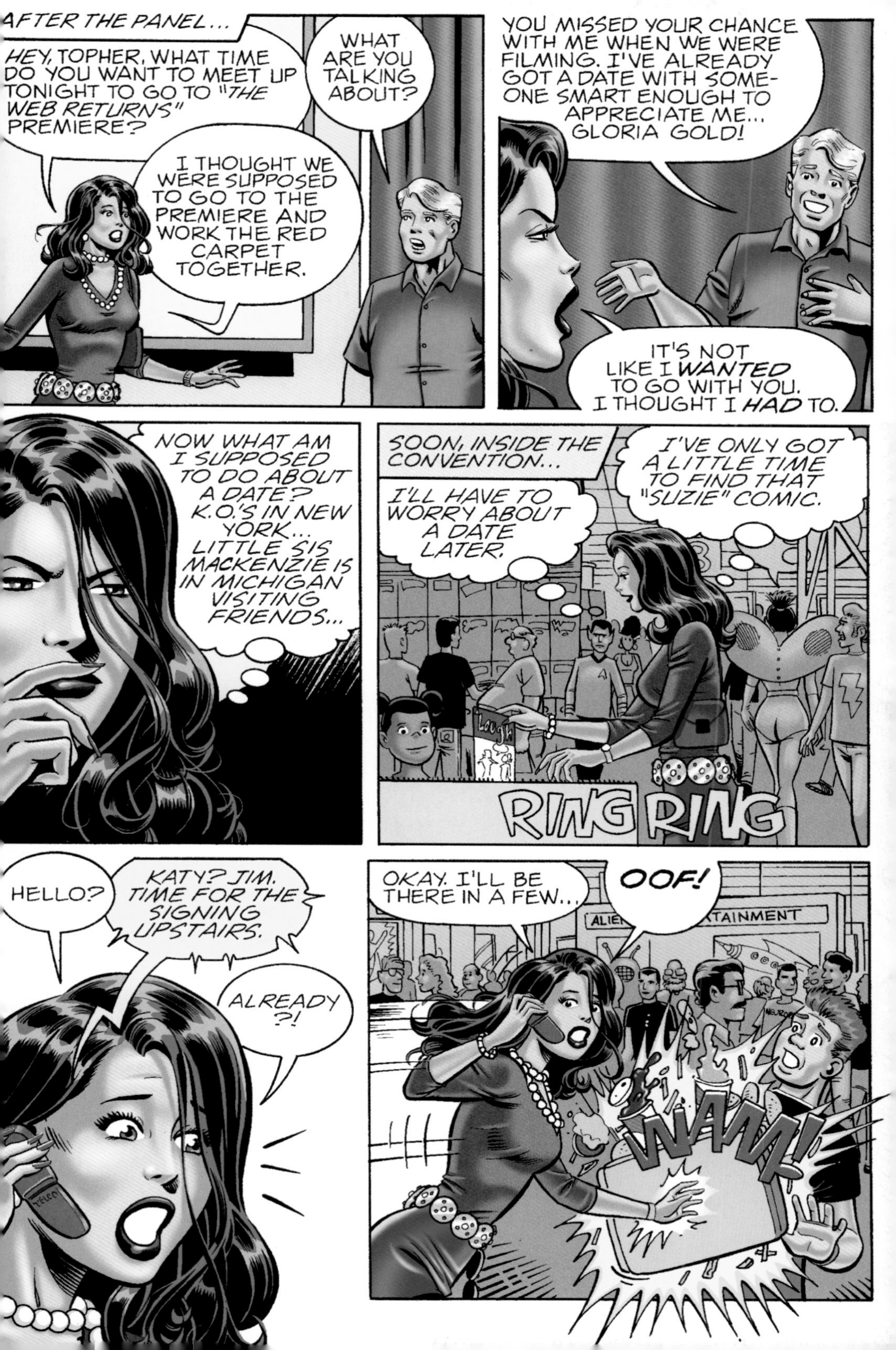
AFTER THE PANEL...
HEY, TOPHER, WHAT TIME DO YOU WANT TO MEET UP TONIGHT TO GO TO "THE WEB RETURNS" PREMIERE?
WHAT ARE YOU TALKING ABOUT?
I THOUGHT WE WERE SUPPOSED TO GO TO THE PREMIERE AND WORK THE RED CARPET TOGETHER.
YOU MISSED YOUR CHANCE WITH ME WHEN WE WERE FILMING. I'VE ALREADY GOT A DATE WITH SOMEONE SMART ENOUGH TO APPRECIATE ME... GLORIA GOLD!
IT'S NOT LIKE I WANTED TO GO WITH YOU. I THOUGHT I HAD TO.
NOW WHAT AM I SUPPOSED TO DO ABOUT A DATE? K.O.'S IN NEW YORK... LITTLE SIS MACKENZIE IS IN MICHIGAN VISITING FRIENDS...
SOON, INSIDE THE CONVENTION...
I'VE ONLY GOT A LITTLE TIME TO FIND THAT "SUZIE" COMIC.
I'LL HAVE TO WORRY ABOUT A DATE LATER.
RING RING
HELLO?
KATY? JIM. TIME FOR THE SIGNING UPSTAIRS.
ALREADY ?!
OKAY. I'LL BE THERE IN A FEW...
OOF!
WAM!

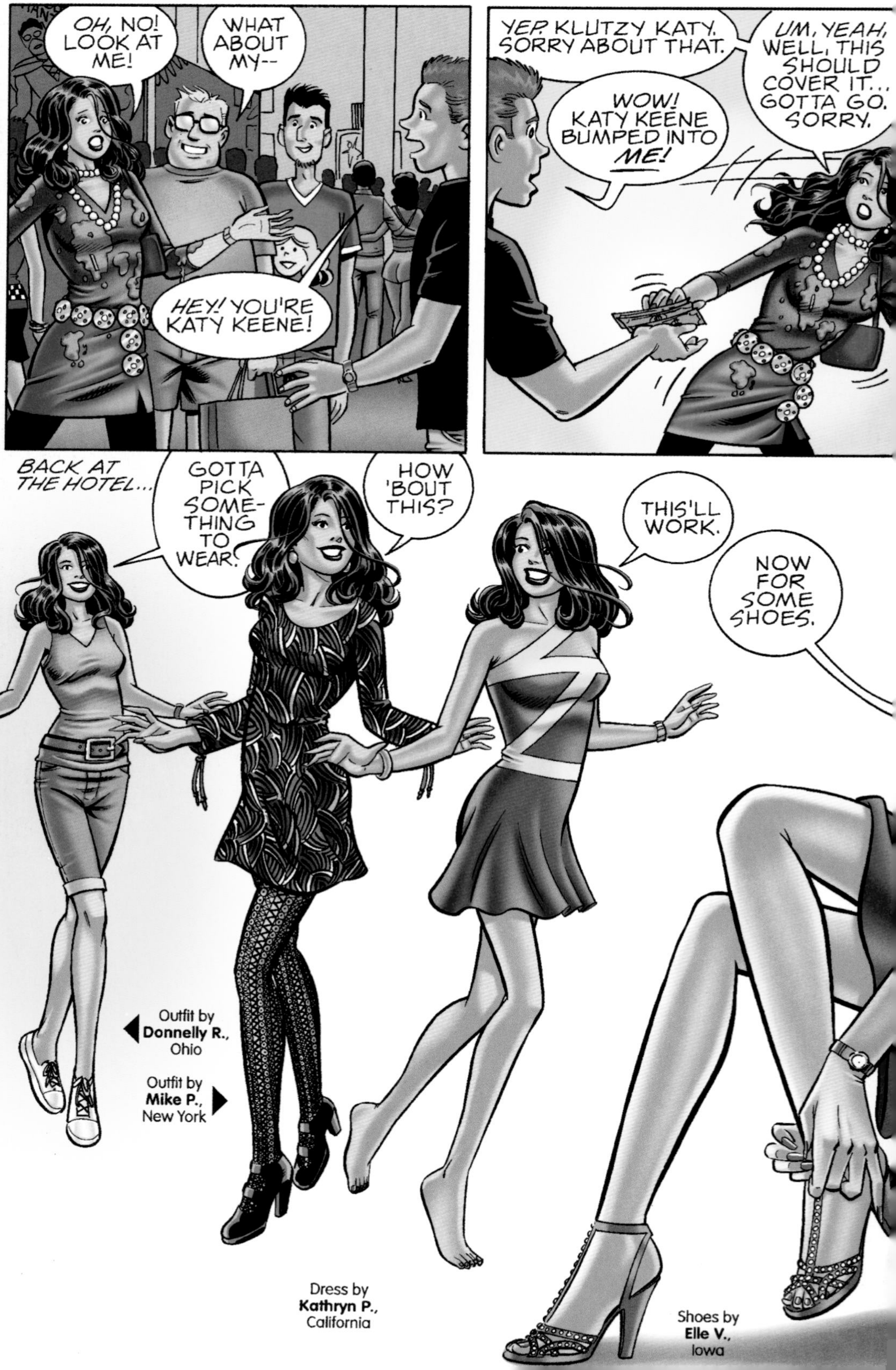
OH, NO! LOOK AT ME!
WHAT ABOUT MY--
HEY! YOU'RE KATY KEENE!
YEP. KLUTZY KATY. SORRY ABOUT THAT.
UM, YEAH, WELL, THIS SHOULD COVER IT... GOTTA GO. SORRY.
WOW! KATY KEENE BUMPED INTO ME!
BACK AT THE HOTEL...
GOTTA PICK SOMETHING TO WEAR!
HOW 'BOUT THIS?
THIS'LL WORK.
NOW FOR SOME SHOES.
Outfit by Donnelly R., Ohio
Outfit by Mike P., New York
Dress by Kathryn P., California
Shoes by Elle V., Iowa

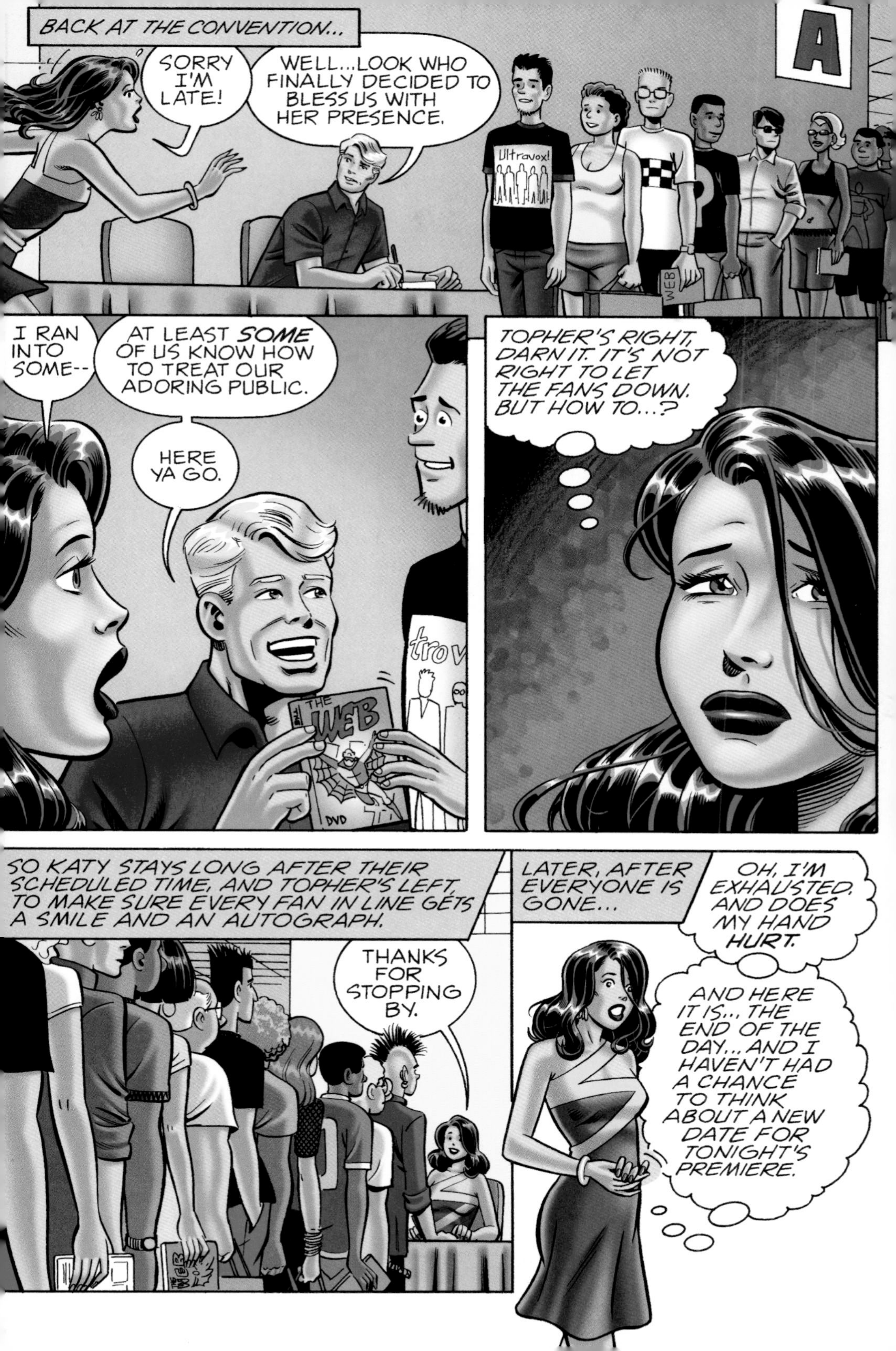
BACK AT THE CONVENTION...
SORRY I'M LATE!
WELL...LOOK WHO FINALLY DECIDED TO BLESS US WITH HER PRESENCE.
Ultravox!
A
WEB
I RAN INTO SOME--
AT LEAST SOME OF US KNOW HOW TO TREAT OUR ADORING PUBLIC.
HERE YA GO.
THE WEB
DVD
TOPHER'S RIGHT, DARN IT. IT'S NOT RIGHT TO LET THE FANS DOWN. BUT HOW TO...?
SO KATY STAYS LONG AFTER THEIR SCHEDULED TIME, AND TOPHER'S LEFT, TO MAKE SURE EVERY FAN IN LINE GETS A SMILE AND AN AUTOGRAPH.
THANKS FOR STOPPING BY.
LATER, AFTER EVERYONE IS GONE...
OH, I'M EXHAUSTED. AND DOES MY HAND HURT.
AND HERE IT IS... THE END OF THE DAY... AND I HAVEN'T HAD A CHANCE TO THINK ABOUT A NEW DATE FOR TONIGHT'S PREMIERE.

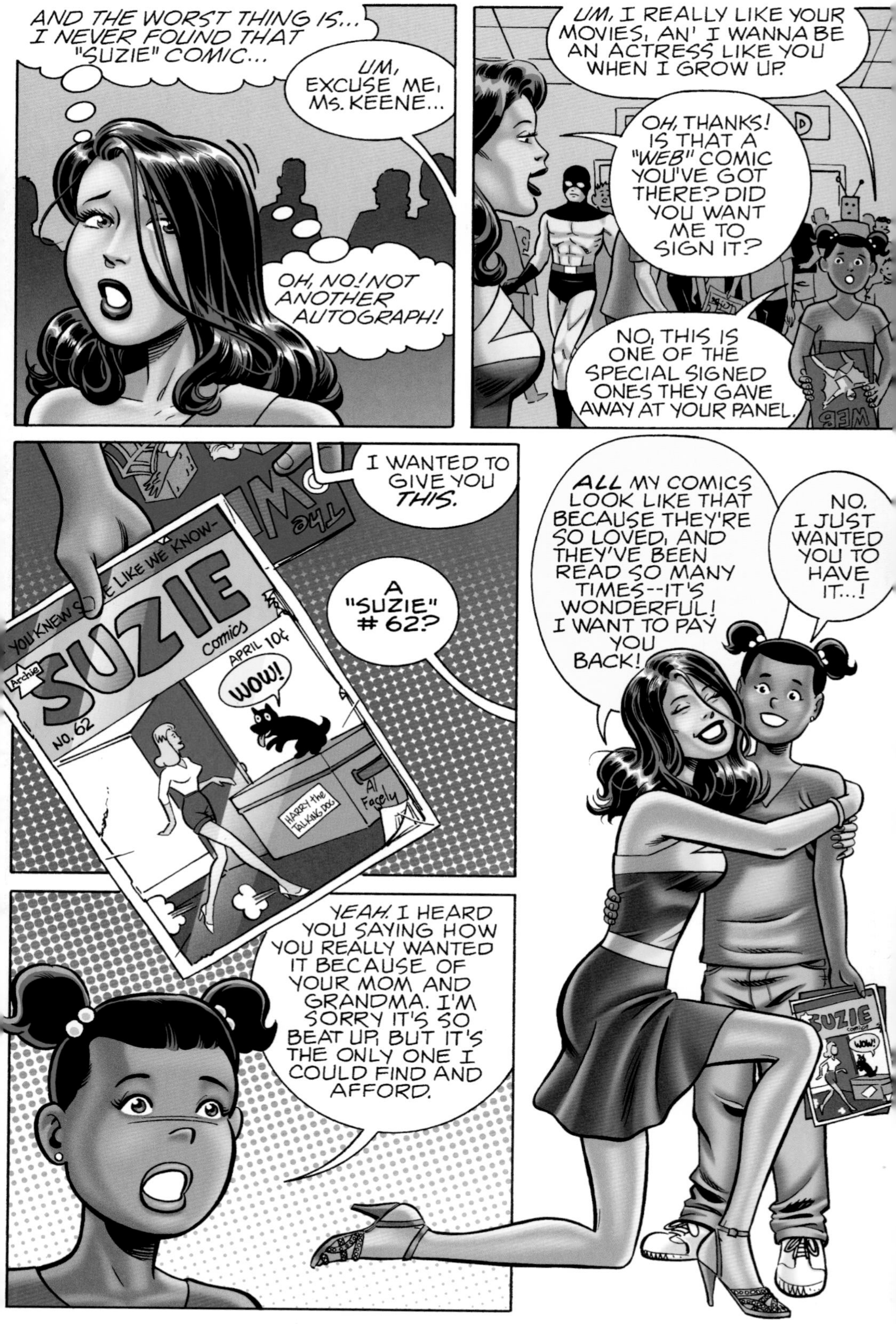
AND THE WORST THING IS... I NEVER FOUND THAT "SUZIE" COMIC...
UM, EXCUSE ME, MS. KEENE...
OH, NO! NOT ANOTHER AUTOGRAPH!
UM, I REALLY LIKE YOUR MOVIES, AN' I WANNA BE AN ACTRESS LIKE YOU WHEN I GROW UP.
OH, THANKS! IS THAT A "WEB" COMIC YOU'VE GOT THERE? DID YOU WANT ME TO SIGN IT?
NO, THIS IS ONE OF THE SPECIAL SIGNED ONES THEY GAVE AWAY AT YOUR PANEL.
WEB
I WANTED TO GIVE YOU THIS.
YOU KNEW S LIKE WE KNOW-
Archie
SUZIE
COMICS
APRIL 10¢
WOW!
NO. 62
HARRY the TALKING DOG
Al Fagaly
A "SUZIE" # 62?
YEAH. I HEARD YOU SAYING HOW YOU REALLY WANTED IT BECAUSE OF YOUR MOM AND GRANDMA. I'M SORRY IT'S SO BEAT UP, BUT IT'S THE ONLY ONE I COULD FIND AND AFFORD.
ALL MY COMICS LOOK LIKE THAT BECAUSE THEY'RE SO LOVED, AND THEY'VE BEEN READ SO MANY TIMES--IT'S WONDERFUL! I WANT TO PAY YOU BACK!
NO. I JUST WANTED YOU TO HAVE IT...!
SUZIE
WOW!

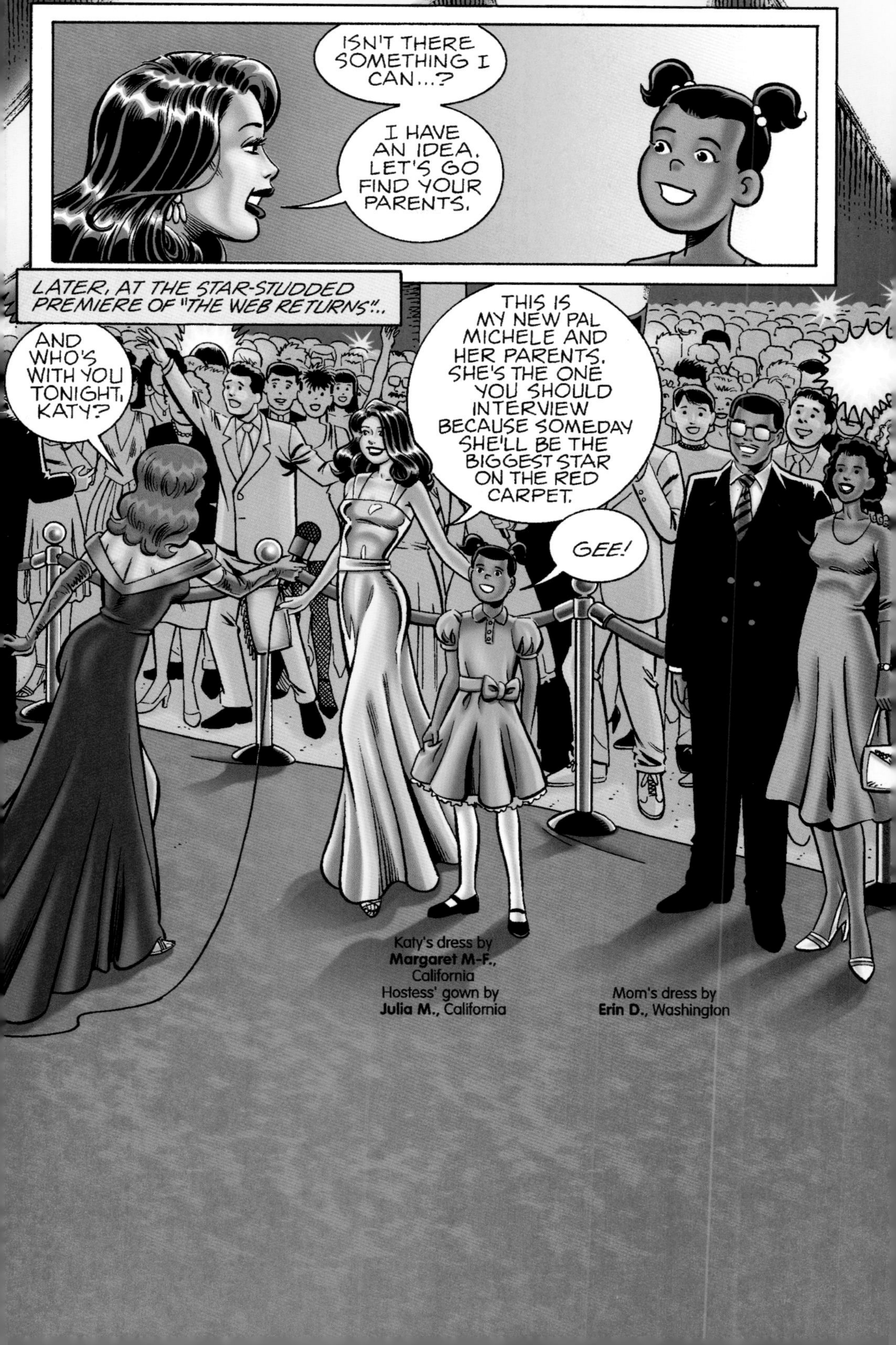
ISN'T THERE SOMETHING I CAN...?
I HAVE AN IDEA. LET'S GO FIND YOUR PARENTS.
LATER, AT THE STAR-STUDDED PREMIERE OF "THE WEB RETURNS"...
AND WHO'S WITH YOU TONIGHT, KATY?
THIS IS MY NEW PAL MICHELE AND HER PARENTS. SHE'S THE ONE YOU SHOULD INTERVIEW BECAUSE SOMEDAY SHE'LL BE THE BIGGEST STAR ON THE RED CARPET.
GEE!

Katy's dress by **Margaret M-F.**, California
Hostess' gown by **Julia M.**, California

Mom's dress by **Erin D.**, Washington

KATY KEENE®
Model Behavior

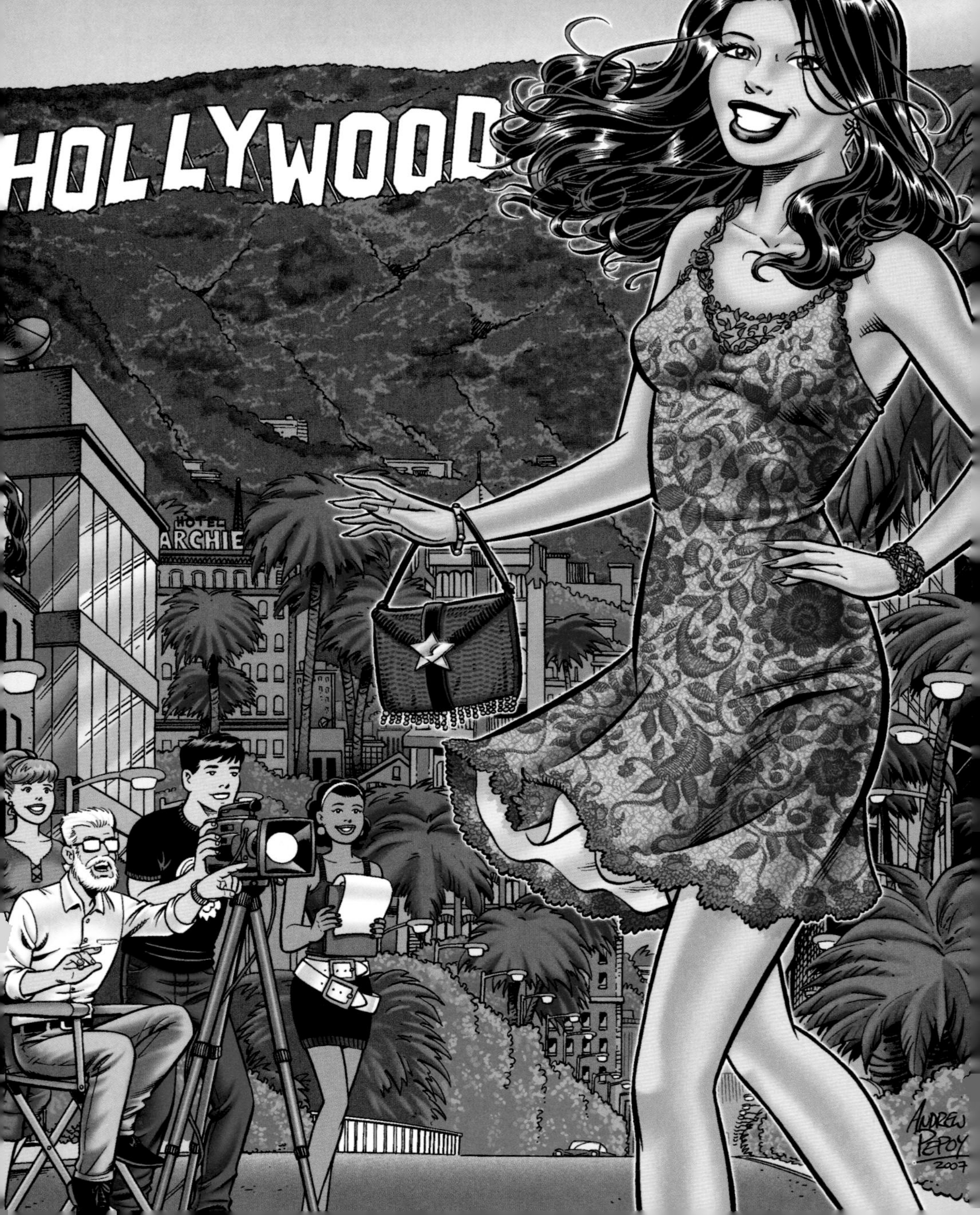
HOLLYWOOD
HOTEL
ARCHIE
ANDREW PEPOY 2007

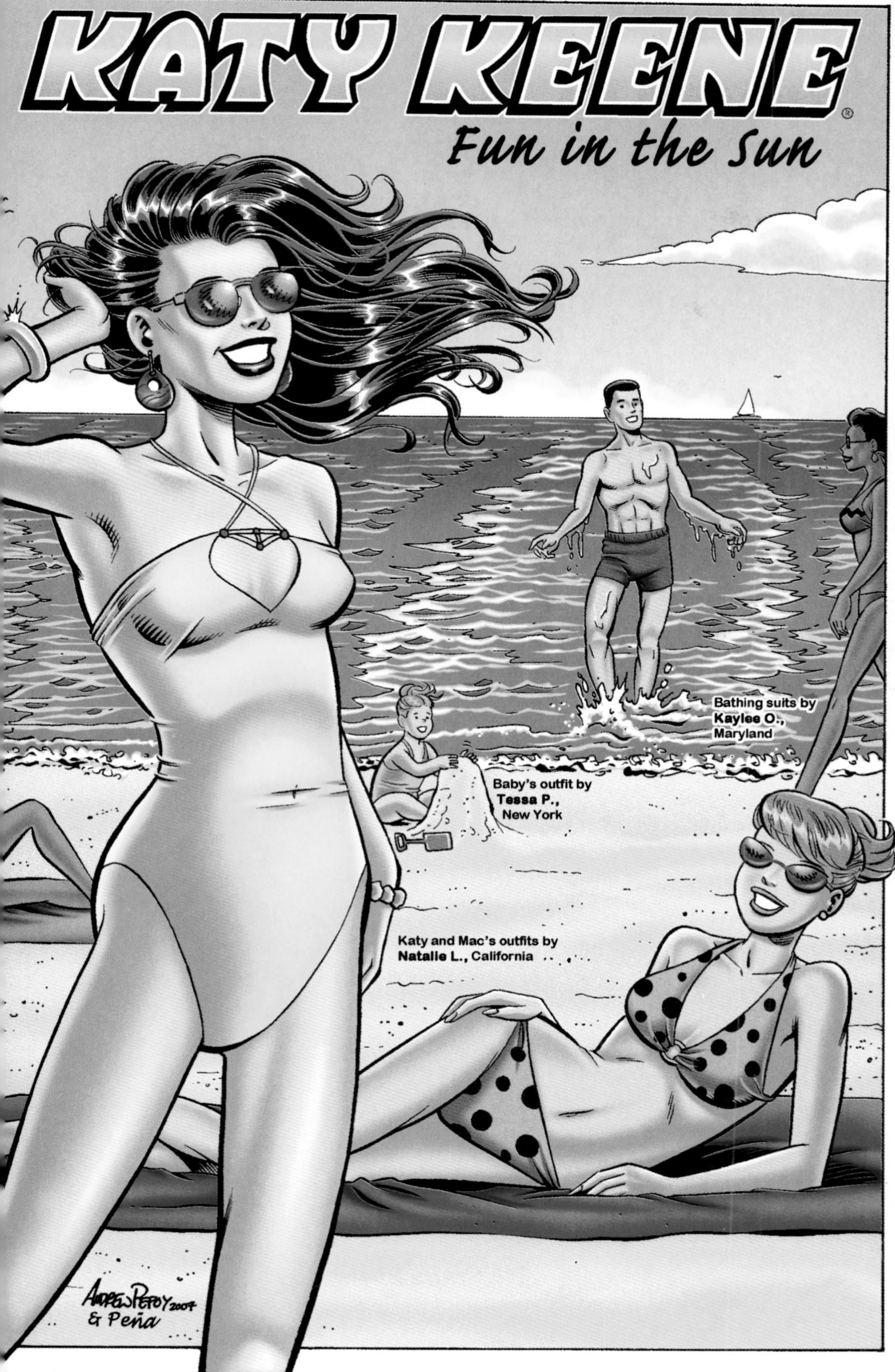
KATY KEENE®
Fun in the Sun
Bathing suits by Kaylee O., Maryland
Baby's outfit by Tessa P., New York
Katy and Mac's outfits by Natalie L., California
ANDREW PEPOY 2007 & Peña

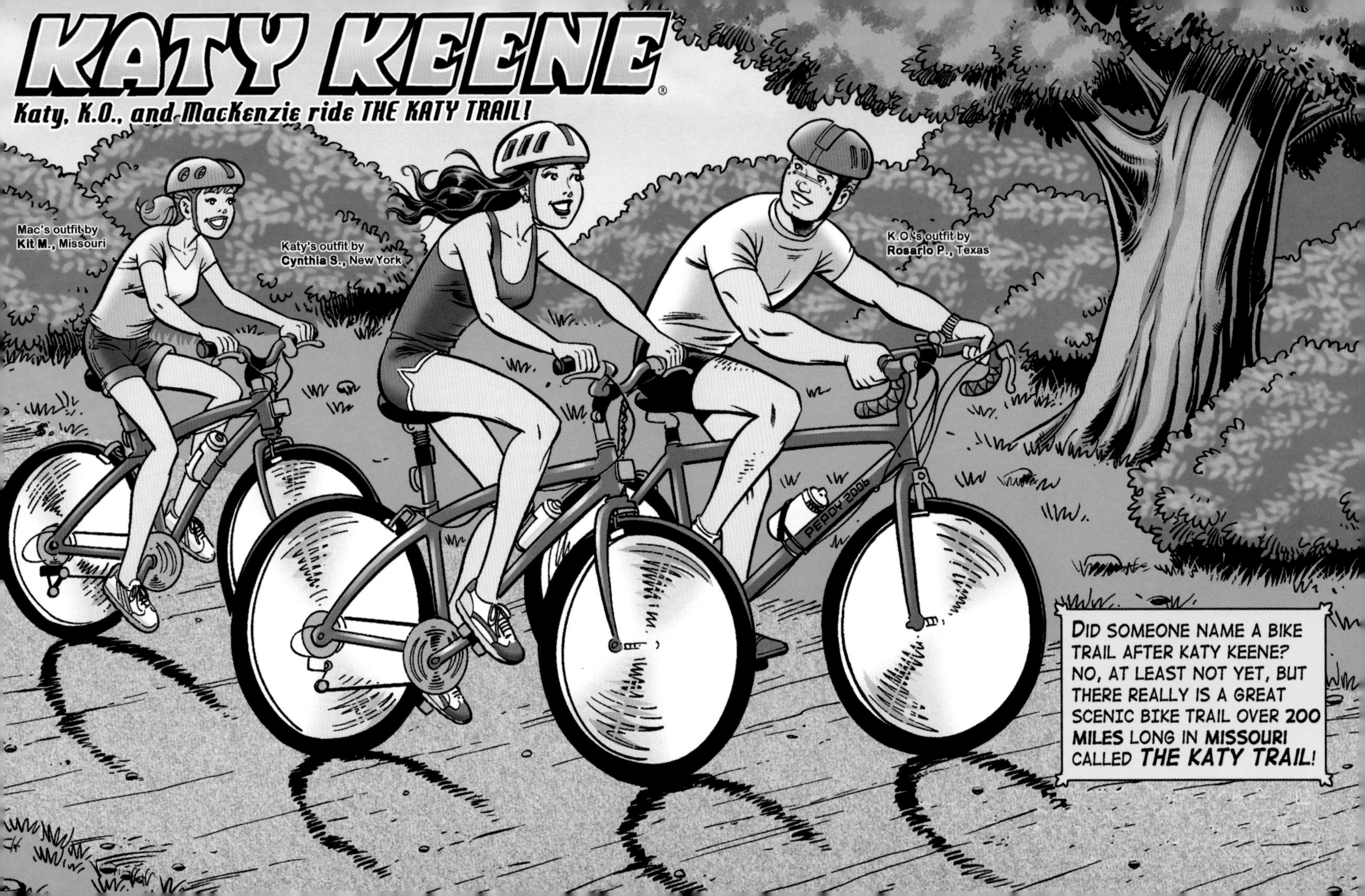
KATY KEENE®
Katy, K.O., and MacKenzie ride THE KATY TRAIL!
Mac's outfit by Kit M., Missouri
Katy's outfit by Cynthia S., New York
K.O.'s outfit by Rosario P., Texas
PEPOY 2006
DID SOMEONE NAME A BIKE TRAIL AFTER KATY KEENE? NO, AT LEAST NOT YET, BUT THERE REALLY IS A GREAT SCENIC BIKE TRAIL OVER 200 MILES LONG IN MISSOURI CALLED THE KATY TRAIL!

KATY KEENE

Paper Dolls

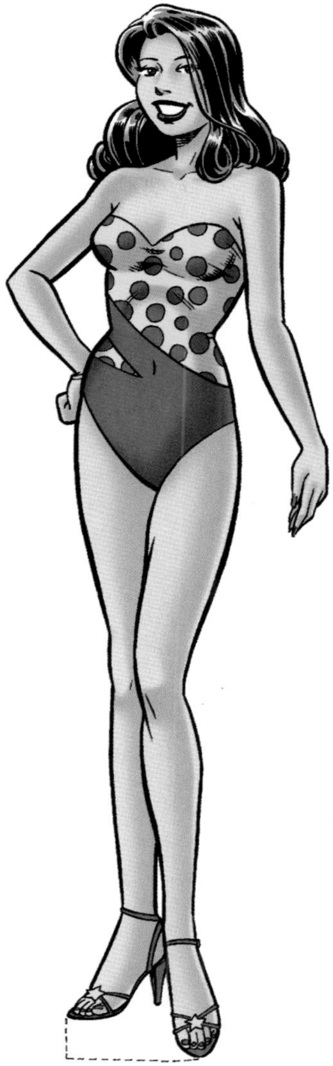

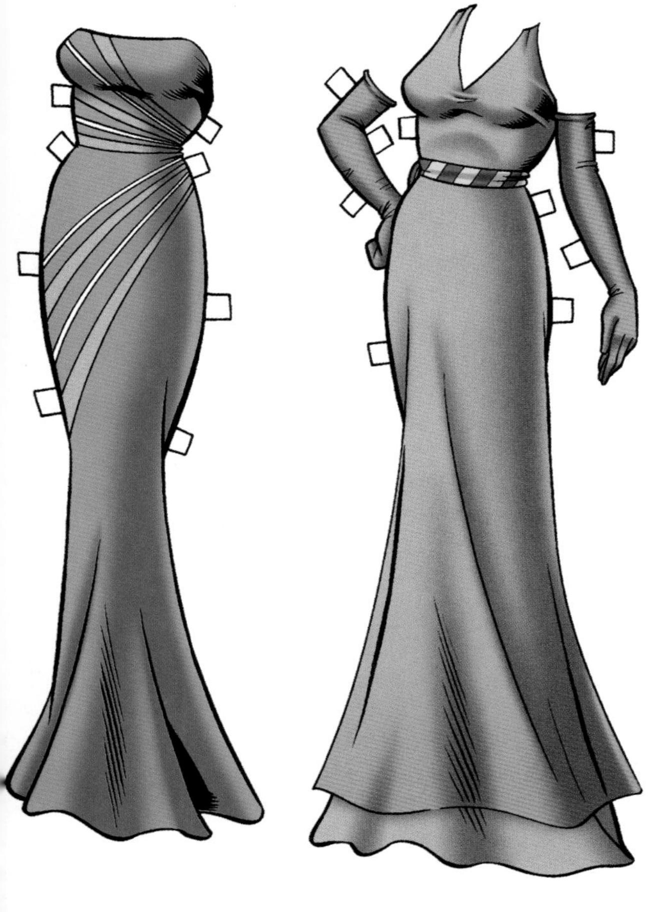

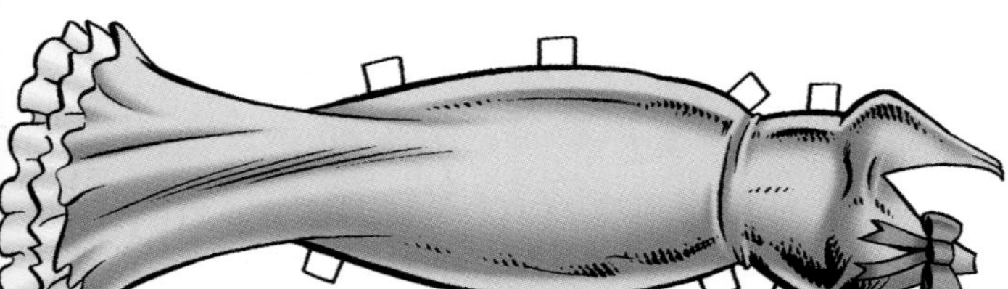

INSTRUCTIONS:
CUT OUT ALONG
OUTSIDE LINES
MAKING SURE
NOT TO CUT
OFF WHITE TABS

Katy Keene's Must Have Reading List

Romance Favorites

The Love Showdown
Sabrina The Magic Revisited
Betty & Veronica Bad Boy Trouble
Jughead The Matchmakers

Great for Laughs

Betty & Veronica Summer Fun
The Adventures of Little Archie Vol. 1
The Adventures of Little Archie Vol. 2
Archie's Classic Christmas Stories
Archie's Camp Tales
Archie Day By Day

Stories that Rock

The Archies Greatest Hits Vol. 1
Best of Josie and the Pussycats

(Two of Katy's favorite bands!)

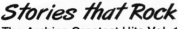

Look for More Great Reads at Archiecomics.com

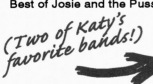